D0802546

ANTONIA'S CHOICE

Antonia's Choice

A Novel

NANCY RUE

Multnomah®Publishers *Sisters, Oregon*

This is a work of fiction. The characters, incidents, and dialogues are products of the author's imagination and are not to be construed as real. Any resemblance to actual events or persons, living or dead, is entirely coincidental.

ANTONIA'S CHOICE
published by Multnomah Publishers, Inc.

Published in association with the literary agency of Alive Communications, Inc., 7680 Goddard Street, Suite 200, Colorado Springs, CO 80920

© 2003 by Nancy Rue

International Standard Book Number: 1-59052-076-9

Cover image of woman by Jerome Tisne/Getty Images
Background cover images by Photonica and Corbis

Multnomah is a trademark of Multnomah Publishers, Inc., and is registered in the U.S. Patent and Trademark Office. The colophon is a trademark of Multnomah Publishers, Inc.

Printed in the United States of America

ALL RIGHTS RESERVED
No part of this publication may be reproduced, stored in a retrieval system, or transmitted, in any form or by any means—electronic, mechanical, photocopying, recording, or otherwise—without prior written permission.

For information:
MULTNOMAH PUBLISHERS, INC.
POST OFFICE BOX 1720
SISTERS, OREGON 97759

Library of Congress Cataloging-in-Publication Data:
Rue, Nancy.
    Antonia's choice : a novel / by Nancy Rue.
        p. cm.
    ISBN 1-59052-076-9 (pbk.)
    1. Bed and breakfast accommodations--Fiction. 2. Adult children of aging parents--Fiction. 3. Single women--Fiction. I. Title.
    PS3618.U35A84 2003
    813' .6--dc21   2003001337

03 04 05 06 07 08 09—10 9 8 7 6 5 4 3 2 1 0

For my family,
who have all chosen our children
and never counted the cost.

Acknowledgments

The people who have helped me in the writing of this book have done so out of great personal pain, and I deeply honor them. May God's infinite blessings be upon them.

Heather Carter

Tina, Carly, and Kalyn Rankin

Marijean Stewart

Michael Stewart

Robin Wolf

Tracy Lamb

Kristin Richardson

M. J. Lucas

Many thanks also to Bill Jensen, editorial vice president at Multnomah Publishers, for his ongoing faith in my work and his priceless input, and to Rod Morris, my editor, who has handled both the manuscript and my feelings with great compassion and kindness.

One

"ALL RIGHT," I CALLED OUT from the front door. "If we don't run to the car, we aren't going to get there. Ben, where are you?"

My son didn't show himself. Only his husky voice made its hoarse little way out from behind one of the living room columns.

"I'm not gonna run. I hate running."

"That doesn't surprise me," I said. "Tell me something you *don't* 'hate' this morning. *That* will surprise me."

"I hate—"

"Don't say 'hate,' Ben," Stephanie said. "I hate that."

My sister stopped rolling her suitcase across the foyer's fieldstone floor and lured Ben out from behind the column by the hand. Her dark eyes danced down at him. "What are you hating this morning, buddy?" she said. "Tell Aunt Stephanie all about it."

"Thank you, Steph," I said dryly. "You're so helpful."

"You're going to miss me and you know it," she said to me. Then she squatted down to meet the small, inquisitive face at eye level. "Come on, Ben. Dish, dude."

I didn't comment that it was no wonder Ben's vocabulary had gone completely down the tubes the last two weeks. Between Stephanie's twenty-seven-year-old slang and my mother's grand-motherly toddler-talk, it was amazing my usually precocious kinder-gartner could even put a complete sentence together now. But I just shooed both of them toward the front door. At least Stephanie had gotten the scowl off Ben's face. It was more than I could say for my own ability lately.

"Mama!" I called out over my shoulder. "Let's shake a leg."

It was a pointless request, of course. My classy mother never "shook" anything. It was customary for her to float, as she did now, down the steps into the foyer, one set of manicured nails resting lightly on the cherry stair rail while the other balanced a leather bag on her shoulder.

Every pristine white hair of her fashionable bob was in place, and English Toffee lipstick was drawn on without a hint of feathering into the tiny age wrinkles that fringed her lips. Silk sleeves fell down her arms in cascading folds. I knew she was aware that she was in danger of missing her plane, but the passing stranger would have thought she was making an entrance for a leisurely brunch.

And there I was, shoving my hair behind my ears, wearing wrinkles into my linen pants, and, at only 7:30 A.M., already wishing I'd worn flats instead of pumps.

"Mama," I said with forced patience, "we have to drop Ben off at school before I take you to the airport. You're going to need to step it up a little."

"I was just leaving you a little something upstairs," Mama said. She didn't "step it up" by so much as a millisecond.

"You didn't have to do that—"

"If I didn't there would be no end to the whining about your being the neglected middle child."

"I don't whine!" I said. I took the bag from her and headed for the door. "Thirty-seven-year-old women do not whine."

"Children always whine to their mothers, no matter how old they get."

I looked out at Ben, who was climbing into the Lexus under Stephanie's supervision. "Wonderful," I said.

For the moment, Ben was being cooperative, settling himself into the booster seat that had recently replaced his car seat and letting Stephanie help him buckle the belt. I knew the minute he saw me in the vicinity, he'd start wailing about something—anything.

I charged toward the trunk with my mother's bag, my head spinning once again into the day that lay ahead of me. I had to get Ben to school on time, or he wasn't going to get the perfect attendance award, and he'd be wailing about that longer than I could listen to him. According to the new regulations, Mama and Stephanie had to be at the airport two hours before their flight left, despite the fact that they were only flying from Nashville to Richmond. They'd probably stand in line at the security checkpoint longer than they'd be in the air. And then I had at least a ten-hour day at the office ahead of me, unless I brought files home to work on after Ben went to bed.

I slammed the trunk and looked at the back of Ben's dark head through the rear window. At the moment, he was rattling something off to Stephanie, his head bobbing, the crown hair I'd wet down so carefully—under protest—sticking straight up like a paintbrush.

It had taken two hours to get him to sleep the night before, and once he finally drifted off, he was awake two hours later in a wet bed. That happened at least five nights out of seven, so the chances of me actually getting any work done at home in the evenings were slim to none. But I was going to have to. If I continued to stay at the office until I was caught up, Ben would be home with Lindsay, the after-school babysitter, into the evening, which would lead to its own share of crying and carrying on once I came on the scene.

I slid into the front seat and started up the car. When I wasn't with Ben at home, he pitched fits. When I was with him, he pitched fits. The child pitched fits when he was asleep. I was ready to pitch one myself. Hence the plan I was going to present to Jeffrey Faustman this morning.

"I'm giving this posh neighborhood one last look," Steph said from the backseat as I pulled out of Belle Meade, "before I go back to my stinky little apartment."

"Stephanie Lynn," my mother said, "your apartment is darling." She looked at me pointedly. "You haven't seen it, have you?"

"No," I said, fighting the urge to remind my mother that she had asked me that at least fourteen times over the last two weeks.

"You aren't missing that much, Toni," Stephanie said. "Just think about my room at college, spread it over a living room, a kitchen, and a bedroom, and you've got my apartment."

"That bad, huh?" I said. I gave my little sister a grateful look in the rearview mirror. Fair or not, it was her job in the family to keep conversations from taking dead-end turns. She'd been working pretty hard at it during their stay. I suspected she'd go home to her "stinky little apartment" and collapse.

"Am I gonna be late?" Ben said.

"No," I said. "Do I ever get you there late?"

"Almost."

"Almost doesn't count."

"Other kids get there *way* early."

"So—you're here a *little* early." I swung into the tunnel of about-to-blossom dogwood trees that arched the driveway of Hillsboro Private School and snapped my seat belt open. "It's the best I can do, Pal."

Ben squirmed out of his booster seat, his face puckering as he eyed the front door. "I'm late," he said. "I can feel it."

"Did you give Aunt Stephanie and Nana a kiss?" I said. "You aren't going to see them for a while."

Ben's attention immediately shifted to his grandmother's face, and I groaned inwardly. His honey-brown eyes were narrowing into accusatory pinpoints.

"Why?" he said. "Why aren't I seeing them for a while?"

"We have to go home, buddy," Stephanie said.

"Why?"

"Because I have to go to work."

"No!"

"Ben, I have to take them to the airport," I said, pulling gently at his sleeve. "You'll see them again."

"When?"

"Soon," my mother said. She leaned over the backseat and tilted Ben's chin up with her fingers. "You remember what we talked about."

Ben nodded sullenly.

"You'll see us before you know it—and for a long time."

"But I don't want—"

"Let's go, Pal," I said.

I gave the sleeve another tug, which was obviously one tug too many. Ben snatched himself away from me, both elbows swinging.

"I don't wanna go to school! I hate school!"

"You do not," I said. "You love school. Kiss Aunt Stephanie good-bye. They have to go."

"No! I hate Aunt Stephanie!"

"Benjamin!" I said.

"Love you, too, buddy," Stephanie said.

Ben didn't appear to hear her as he struggled under my hands, which were dragging him onto the sidewalk. He wrenched himself away from me and stood, arms folded across his narrow little chest, gaze hard on the ground.

"You know you're going to be fine as soon as you get in there," I said. "So I don't see why we need to go through this every day. Here's your backpack."

I produced the Power Rangers pack, stuffed with lunch and crayons and an odd assortment of accessories Ben couldn't live without. He smacked it out of my hand and refolded his arms. It was all I could do to squat in front of him, rather than jerk him up by the arm and haul his little backside up to the front door.

"If I knew why all of a sudden you don't want to go to school anymore, I could help you," I said. "But since you can't tell me, all I can do is get you here." My eyes narrowed as I went for his little mental jugular. "But if you don't go inside, you aren't going to get the perfect attendance award, because you're going to be late."

The arms sprang away from his body like surprised springs, and he snatched the backpack.

"You made me late!" he shouted—for every Belle Meade mother in the parking lot to hear. "I hate you!"

I'd heard those three words countless times over the last several months, but I still felt as if I'd been shot every time they came out of his mouth. I even put my hand flat against my chest as I watched his lanky little figure tear up the sidewalk for the door. What had happened to the precious little preschool chunkiness—and the so-alive eyes—and the sweet, chirped-out words "I love you"?

As I climbed back into the Lexus, I hoped my mother and Stephanie hadn't heard Ben's parting shot, but the distress etched into Mama's face dashed that to the dust.

"He's just upset because we're leaving," Stephanie said even before I got the car into reverse.

"There's a lot more to it than that," Mama said. "And Toni, you know it."

I gritted my teeth, overbite and all. Somehow we had made it through two weeks without getting into this. There we were on our way to the airport, and she had to start in. We only had to get to I-40 and we'd practically be at the terminal. If I wanted to get a word in myself, I was going to have to cut right to the chase. "You're thinking that if Chris and I weren't separated, Ben wouldn't be acting this way."

Mama's eyes sprang open a little. "That's exactly what I'm saying. And I think it's worse because you've moved him five hundred miles from his father so he barely gets to see the man."

"Chris was just here the week before you came. They went to Disneyworld."

"It was a vacation," Mom said. "That doesn't constitute a relationship between a father and a son."

"It's something, though," Stephanie said. "I think Toni's doing the best she can—"

"Chris should've thought about his relationship with his son before he slept with another woman," I said. I'd already hit I-40. I had to move on.

"For heaven's sake, Antonia," my mother said. "Can't you forgive the man one transgression? It's not as if he was a drunk or into drugs—something he was refusing to change. Chris isn't going to make that mistake again."

I took my eyes off the Mercedes in front of me long enough to give her a look. "How could you possibly know that? *I* don't know it. I don't know that I can trust Chris now. He did it once—why wouldn't he do it again?"

"Because you would work on your marriage. But you won't even try. You refuse to go to counseling—"

"I don't believe in letting some third party who has no idea what I've been through tell me what to do."

I gunned the motor and slipped in front of a semi in the right lane. Maybe it was a good thing that most of the heavy traffic on I-40 was headed into Nashville while we headed out. This trip couldn't be fast enough at this point. As I checked to make sure the trucker I'd just cut off wasn't going to rear-end me, I caught

Stephanie's face in the rearview mirror.

She was sucking in her bottom lip, accentuating the Kerrington overbite. A tiny line had appeared between her wide eyes, and she was toying with one of the dark curls that fell over her shoulder.

Even as the angst built in her face, I still thought she was the prettiest of us three girls, inheriting our father's handsomeness in a way I could never hope to. It wasn't just the to-die-for hair, the willowy figure, the big eyes. It was the compassion that came out of every pore—and had me spilling my guts to her every time I got the chance. She knew, because I had told her, that there was more to my split with Chris than his affair. And she knew I didn't want to go there with Mama—who since our father's death five years ago had begun to deify marriage.

Besides, I didn't even want to go there with myself right now. My back was doing that thing it did every time I thought about Chris. It stiffened from the base of my spine to the back of my head, and my jaws tightened down as if Chris himself were in there with a ratchet set. I was going to be in pain any second if I didn't manipulate a subject change.

"Children need to be with their parents—both their parents," Mama said.

"Are you going to start comparing me to Bobbi?" I said. It was a pretty weak segue, but it was the best I could do on the spot.

"I never compare you girls to each other. But since you brought it up, Bobbi and Sid are both with their children, yes."

"And your point is?" I said. "Every time I've seen them over the last two years, they looked like a pretty miserable little group to me. Sid moping over in the corner. Bobbi with the two little ones hanging on her like baby monkeys with their noses running." I put up my hand. "No, make that Emil still breast feeding at age three and a half, and Techla hanging on Wyndham—who to me is more like a nanny than a teenage girl. Yeah, being together as a family is really working for them."

"You haven't seen them since you moved," Mama said. "What's that, two and a half months now?"

I didn't answer.

"They're actually doing better," Stephanie said. "I mean, at least it seemed like it Valentine's Day when I went over to take the kids their presents."

"They were in financial trouble over the past few years, you know that," Mama said. "Something like that can bring a family down. But the point is that they stayed together and toughed it out, and I think they're stronger for it."

I exchanged glances with Stephanie in the mirror. Her eye roll reflected my own disgust with Mama's always-predictable defense of Bobbi. Our older sister could rob a bank and Mama would find a way to make it a virtuous deed on Bobbi's part. *She's always been fragile,* Mama had said approximately a thousand times. *Her sensitivity is what makes her such a beautiful person.*

I loved my sister because…she was my sister. But in my view, Bobbi had always been a wimp. Her neediness was what made her such a pain to be around for more than thirty minutes. Besides, she didn't really need me when she'd had Mama fawning over her all her life.

I could feel my mother giving me a pointed look. "I think it helped that Bobbi is a stay-at-home mom."

"It might help Sid," I said, "but I don't think it helps Bobbi. Personally, I think it would do her good to get her focus off the kids and him for at least a couple of hours a day."

My mother chewed on that for a second before she said, "Bobbi's services as a babysitter certainly came in handy for you during those last months before you left Richmond."

"I didn't leave Ben there because I needed a babysitter," I said tightly. "Ben loves Emil. They're more like twins than Emil and Techla are. Ben was having a rough time, and I thought it was good for him to be with his cousin."

"No need to get defensive," Mama said. "I was just pointing out that—"

"So what's Sid doing now?" I said. I didn't really care what my brother-in-law did. He'd never been my favorite human being; he just came in handy at the moment.

"Something with computers," Mom said.

"I thought he lost his shirt in that dot-com thing he was involved in."

"This is different—he's doing something with websites, and it's obviously very successful."

"Ya think?" Stephanie said. "They just added a whole studio onto their house."

"That place was four thousand square feet to begin with."

Stephanie gave one of her signature snorts. "You don't exactly live in a shack yourself."

"My shack's rented," I said. "And I can only afford that because it belongs to a client."

"There's nothing wrong with the house you and Chris *own* in Richmond, either," Mama said. "I drive by it every now and then. Chris is keeping the lawn up."

I had never been so glad to see the Nashville terminal, or more grateful for the overzealous security people who blew their whistles if a driver left his car stopped at the curb for more than seven seconds.

"I would come in with you," I said, flipping the trunk release and whipping open my door, "but I really have to get to work."

"Not a problem," Stephanie said. She caught up with me at the trunk and planted a kiss on my cheek.

I felt a wave of longing. I really wanted her to stay.

My mother pulled me into her arms then, and I felt just as overwhelming a wave—of guilt. She really cared. I knew that. And I could be such a witch in the face of it.

Spine feeling like a piece of barbed wire, I hugged her back and whispered that I loved her. Mama's face looked pained as the guard blew insistently on his whistle and she pulled away.

"I love you, too," she said. "And I just want you to be happy. I know that if you would just—"

"Come on, Mama, before this poor man blows a gasket," Stephanie said. "Love you, Sis."

I blew them both a kiss and slid back into the front seat, cupping myself in leather. It was suddenly too quiet in the car. All the stuff Mama had just opened up about Chris and about Ben filled up the air space.

"I'm not going there," I said out loud. "Work. Think about work."

Not hard to do. I had the meeting with Jeffrey first thing that I needed to concentrate on.

As I waited behind a line of cars, I took a quick glance in the rearview mirror again to make sure I had the right look for the meeting. Aside from the tousled hair, the result of having done a whole day's work already, I was probably passable.

That sent a pang through me. Chris had always said that. I would come out of the bedroom after an hour in front of the mirror and he'd get that impish glimmer in his eyes and smile—his smile was so slow it was maddening—and he'd say, "You'll pass."

In his more amorous moments, of course, it had been different. The Louisiana drawl he'd tried so hard to hide since law school would ooze right on out into, "Baby, do you know how hard it was for me to keep my hands out of your hair this entire evening?"

"I'm so sure you were going to run your fingers through my hair while you were entertaining clients, Wells," I would tell him. "Give me a break."

"I'm serious, darlin'. I saw it all thick and blond and tucked behind your ears and I wanted to slide my fingers right in there."

"Get over yourself!"

"Look at your eyes, lookin' so brown, just a-twinklin' at me, telling me, 'Come here, boy.'"

"In your dreams."

"Let me just hug on that cute little ol' body—"

Uh-huh, I thought now. *Did you say the same things to that little paralegal you bedded down?*

I shook my head, tossing back my bangs. *Don't go there,* I told myself. *Do not EVEN go there.*

I went back to Jeffrey Faustman.

Whether or not my mother was right about the causes of Ben's behavior, it was obvious I was going to have to do something about it before he started slipping out at night with a can of spray paint. Not to mention the fact that Ben and I were miserable. It seemed like all we did was scream at each other. Chris and I hadn't even done that, which made me wonder why Ben had chosen that as his latest means of expressing himself.

During the two weeks my mother was there I had had to admit, begrudgingly, that she was correct about one thing: I wasn't spending enough time with Ben. An hour in the morning, trying to get cereal down his throat without tossing the whole bowl against the wall, and an hour and a half between the time I got home from work and the time he was supposed to be in bed really didn't cut it.

The night before, when I'd finally gotten Ben to sleep for the second time after the bed-wetting ordeal, I'd stayed up forming a plan, which by dawn sounded reasonable to me. Now I just had to convince Jeffrey.

The baggy-pants gardener was out in front of Faustman Financial Services putting in a flat of pansies when I pulled into the circular driveway. For a mad moment I wished I had his job, complete with the amount of derriere he was showing over the top of his rather pointless belt. To my knowledge he never had to take files home.

You know you love what you do, I told myself. *You'll get through this phase with Ben and then you can get refocused on the joys of handling other people's money. You can do this. You can do anything.*

I could feel myself setting my jaw, bringing my overbite into full view. As vain as I admittedly was about my appearance, I'd never wanted to have that fixed. I'd seen myself once when a TV camera had caught me cheering in the Orange Bowl, the year Florida was ranked number one, and I'd kind of liked the overbite. It gave me character. Chris always said so.

"Would you *stop!*" I said into the rearview. "What is with the Chris obsession today?"

I marched my little self up to the oak double doors and breezed into the foyer, where the brass umbrella stand and the leaf-perfect ficus plant greeted me. Regina Acklee looked up from the reception desk, blue eyes taking inventory.

"You on a mission this mornin', honey?" she said. She glanced at the grandfather clock that ticked solemnly across from her desk. "Jeffrey's gonna wish your mission was to get here on time."

"What am I, two minutes late?" I said.

"Ninety seconds." She gave me a toothy smile. "But who's counting?"

I set my briefcase down on the marble floor and sat on the edge of the chair at Reggie's desk. I could feel the bumps of the brocade through my pants.

"What kind of mood is he in?" I said.

Reggie glanced over both shoulders at the office, which was perfectly quiet except for the soft tinkle of Mozart. If anyone were blinking within a hundred feet, we would have heard it.

Reggie then leaned forward, fingernails tapping on the oak desktop. I couldn't resist a peek at what she had going today. One shade short of fire engine red, each with a slant of gold. The pinkie had a ring in it. I could never figure out how she typed with those talons.

"He's Mr. Business today," she said, barely moving her lips. "You know, all crisp—callin' me Miz Acklee and tellin' me to hold his calls."

"Oh."

Her eyes narrowed, revealing more of the makeup job that must take her two hours to apply with that kind of precision. I'd always been in awe of it.

"What kind of mission are you on, honey?"

Although I was an associate and Reggie was the receptionist, it had never bothered me that she called me "honey," "baby," "sugar," and assorted combinations thereof. I trusted her more than I did anyone else in the office, including my own assistant, who daily made it evident that it was my job she'd really rather have.

Reggie was watching me closely. "The way you're lookin'," she said, "this may not be the day to approach His Worshipfulness."

"I have to. I've got to spend more time with Ben, so I'm going to ask Jeffrey to let me work mornings here and afternoons at home. I can schedule all my appointments in the mornings, and if I have to do any evening meetings I can get a babysitter and do them after Ben goes to sleep. *If* he goes to sleep."

"Oh, honey, does he still have that screamin' thing goin' on?"

I nodded. "But I'm thinking that if I spend more time with him—maybe get him into some sports activities to burn up some of that energy—he'll start to settle down some. Don't they have soccer and baseball for kindergarten-age kids?"

"Are you kiddin', baby? Every child in Davidson County is on a soccer or T-ball team the minute he leaves the playpen."

"Then Ben's behind." I cocked my head at her. "And what's T-ball?"

"Oh, honey, you have got a lot to learn." She shook her head, wagging the strawberry-blond ponytail. She was the only nearly-forty-year-old woman I knew who could still get away with a ponytail at the office. And if Jeffrey had disapproved, he would have told her so long ago.

She was blinking at me now.

"What?" I said.

"I'm just thinkin'—and mind you, this is just my intuition—but I'm just thinkin' Jeffrey is *not* gonna go for that plan at *all*. Not the way he's acting this mornin'. First thing he did when he came in here was check to make sure everybody's desk was left neat last night."

"Why—so the cleaning crew would be impressed?" I said.

"All I'm sayin' is that if you could put it off till another day, you might have a better chance."

"I can't wait. Either Ben's going to pop a blood vessel or I'm going to haul off and smack him."

Reggie nodded, her very-round face soft. "I'm so sorry ya'll are goin' through this. I'm prayin' for you."

"Thanks," I said automatically.

Reggie was always reassuring me of her ongoing prayers, and I didn't have a problem with that. I'd been brought up with Sunday school and potluck suppers and mite boxes during Lent. But right now I just didn't see what good praying was going to do. Even God, I was sure, couldn't loosen Jeffrey up. That was going to be up to me.

I dropped off my briefcase and purse in my office, giving a list for the day to Ginny, my assistant, who greeted it with the usual poorly disguised lip curl. After stopping by the restroom for one last perusal in the mirror, I headed for Jeffrey's office. My pants were so wrinkled in the front they looked like an accordion, but otherwise I had the confident, professional look going on. It was all about attitude.

The oak door with its JEFFREY R. FAUSTMAN, JR. brass plate was closed when I got there. I knocked soundly and pushed it open. I hadn't called first and I didn't wait for an invitation to come in. Where I was headed, it was better not to give Faustman opportunities to say no to anything along the way.

Jeffrey's bald head, still bent over the desk as I stepped into his office, caught the carefully focused track lighting. I'd often wondered how he achieved the perfect shine on the completely hairless part of his head. It was as flawless as the thick fringe of auburn below it. I'd always meant to ask Reggie if she thought he waxed his cranium.

When he looked up, I caught the fleeting irritation behind his glasses, but as soon as he stood up it was gone. Jeffrey Faustman never lowered himself to emotion. With the clients he was cordial and showed an understated charm. Ours were the kind of clients who had been schmoozed over enough to be able to spot it the minute they crossed the threshold, and would turn on their heels to avoid it. With the staff, on Reggie's level, he was crisp and businesslike, bordering on abrupt, at times resorting to rude. With his associates, like myself, he was professional and polite, drawn into our personal concerns only on rare occasions. As I settled back into the Queen Anne chair in front of his desk, I was determined this wasn't going to be one of those occasions.

"Were we scheduled to meet this morning?" he said, glancing at his Day-Timer as he returned to his desk chair. He looked six-foot-three when he sat, or when he was standing over someone's desk, but he was barely six feet tall. I drew myself up as far as my own five-foot-four self would allow.

"No," I said. "But there's something I need to discuss with you before the day gets going."

"Mine is already going."

There were lifted eyebrows, which I ignored.

"I'm going to need to change my working arrangement. The details are outlined here."

I slid a file across his desk and leaned back against the silk brocade while he glanced over my plan. I had purposely not referred to it as a "proposal."

He closed the file and lined it up precisely on his desktop. "What's this about, Toni?" he said.

"It's about my needing to change my working hours."

"Why?"

"It's personal."

"I don't think I'm overstepping my boundaries by asking you for details."

He wasn't. I had to answer.

"My circumstances have changed," I said.

"Are you getting back together with your husband?"

"No!" I said, and then silently cursed myself. Bad move. Regroup. "No," I said, minus the exclamation point. "It's nothing like that. My son just needs more of my attention."

Jeffrey leaned back in his chair, formed a pistol with his two index fingers, and rubbed the tip of his nose with it. I'd only been in his firm for two and a half months, but I'd learned the first week that pistol-fingers meant he felt he had the upper hand.

I will not squirm, I told myself firmly. No more little outbursts. And no more information.

"I have very little experience with arrangements of this kind," he said, lowering the pistol only enough to uncover his mouth. "And what I have had has not been positive."

He stopped, obviously waiting for me to defend myself. I didn't.

"If I knew more about what you were up against…" he said.

No way. Nothing doing, I thought. *You are not going to make me vulnerable.*

"Am I prying?" he said.

"I think you're well enough acquainted with my work to know I will get the job done and done well, no matter what schedule I keep." I looked at the file and then at him and waited for an answer. If he said no, I told myself, then maybe I'd beg.

He pistoled his nose a few more times and, still leaning back like the Godfather, said, "Two weeks."

"Excuse me?" The words *I'm giving you two weeks' notice* whipped through my head.

"We'll give this arrangement two weeks and then review it. If you come up short, I'll expect you back in the office full-time."

I stood up and thanked him coolly—giving him a you-really-didn't-have-any-other-choice smile—and left his office. Then I closed the oak door behind me and sagged against it. *What would I have done if he hadn't said yes?* This was the most lucrative, upwardly mobile job in the entire Southeast for me, and I knew it.

But by the time Reggie came into my office fifteen minutes later, the satisfaction of a victory-over-Faustman had already taken over. I was looking up soccer programs on the Internet. Apparently Ben and I were in luck, because they were just starting to form teams for the spring season.

"How did it go, honey?" Reggie said, setting a cup of coffee on my desk. I was sure it had just the right amount of Sweet'N Low in it.

"Fine. I start my new hours tomorrow."

Reggie stared. "You are not serious."

"As a heart attack, girl. Was there ever any doubt?"

"Yes! I thought surely you were gonna come out of there cryin'."

"Nah. The Kerrington women don't cry. It's in our contract. Our father—may he rest in peace—made us sign it when we hit puberty."

"Now you're teasin' me," Reggie said.

I laughed, but it was almost true. We didn't actually sign on a line; it was more one of those unspoken family agreements that we all adhered to as if it were in the IRS manual. Daddy had definitely been the head of the household, at least as far as our behavior was concerned. All he'd had to do was look at Bobbi and she'd cry and run to Mama, who would attribute it all to Bobbi's "beautiful sensitivity." Stephanie didn't have to worry about it much because she'd never so much as bent a rule, much less broken one.

I, on the other hand, had tested them all and suffered the consequences—with no compensating psychological excuses provided by Mama. At one point in my early adolescence, I'd found myself in a room stripped of all my personal possessions, marking off each of my thirty days of confinement on a calendar. Interesting. I was the one who had turned out to be most like my father—calm, analytical, and in full control of my emotions.

Two

I DIDN'T TALK TO MY MOTHER until after Ben was asleep that night. It had been a long day getting myself organized for my new working arrangement, and Jeffrey's e-mail, which I received right after lunch, didn't make it feel any shorter.

Am still slightly less than optimistic about your new schedule, he wrote. *This may cause me to rethink some plans I had for your advancement. We'll see.*

"Jerk," I said out loud when I read it.

From the outer office, Ginny said, "Did you call me?"

I smothered a guffaw and told her no. I told myself that I was going to surprise Jeffrey Faustman with my productivity on the new schedule *and* get the advancement. This deal with Ben was only temporary—just until I could get him settled down. Time in itself, I thought, took care of a lot of issues. Not all issues, but this had to be one of them.

On my way home, I picked up a soccer ball to surprise Ben and, admittedly, to sneak him into a better mood. I'd signed him up for a soccer team on-line that afternoon, and had decided it might not be so bad. I'd been athletic in high school and college—okay, I'd been a cheerleader. Ben had some of my genes. And as for the job thing, I was too determined to make it work for it not to. What I did was, after all, who I was.

All was actually quiet on the home front when I slipped in through the front door and into the family room in the back part of the house. Ben was sprawled out on the Oriental rug right in front of the television, where the *Rugrats* had him entranced. He looked smaller than ever in two stories of cherry paneling and over-size burgundy leather chairs, with an impressive copy of Stuart Mill's portrait of George Washington surveying him from over the fireplace. Kevin Pollert, my client who owned the house and who was in Europe for two years, had a thing about his American heritage. The twelve-foot-high bookcases, complete with a sliding barrister ladder, always made me feel like I was sitting in the Library of Congress.

"Hey, Pal," I said to my son.

He rolled over and looked at me.

"Do I get a hug?" I said.

He shook his head.

"Do you want the surprise I brought you?"

Ben sat up slowly. "What is it?"

"Give me a hug and you'll find out."

He crawled to me and shinnied up my leg to put his arms briefly around my hips. They had all the enthusiasm of a pair of wet noodles.

"What's the surprise?" he said.

I reached into the shopping bag I'd parked next to the teakwood fern stand and produced the soccer ball.

"Cool!" he said.

"Cool" was encouraging. I tossed it to him. He missed and had to go scrambling to the marble hearth to retrieve it.

"I can't catch it," he said.

"Sure you can. They're going to teach you."

Ben took his hands off the ball as if I'd just announced he was holding a python.

"Who's 'they'?" he said.

"The people that coach your soccer team. You get to play soccer, Pal."

"I don't want to." His eyes began to cloud. There was a storm brewing, and I hadn't even gotten out of my panty hose yet.

"We'll talk about it later," I said. "You want pizza?"

"What kind?"

I sucked in air. "Whatever kind you want, Pal."

"Just cheese. No stuff on it."

"You got it," I said.

He inventoried my face for another fifteen seconds before he seemed satisfied that I would not try to finesse pepperoni or anchovies on there. Then he returned to the *Rugrats*. Angelica's tantrums were obviously preferable to anything I had to offer.

I moved on through the breakfast room to the kitchen, where I knew Lindsay would be happy to see me. She was the most cheerful human being I had ever encountered. I was sure I hadn't been that way as a seventeen-year-old. I wasn't that way now, for Pete's sake.

She was emptying the dishwasher, singing along with the Dixie Chicks on the radio and swaying her negligible hips. She was petite everywhere but her rather voluptuous chest, which she didn't necessarily downplay in a collection of snug shirts. Today's was pink. It had always seemed an injustice to me that any female actually had a figure like that when the rest of us could only dream.

When Lindsay saw me she snapped off the radio and then came at me with a hug. Her tanning-bed brown face lit up from smile to blue-shadowed eyes. I gave one of her blond tendrils a tug.

"How's it going, Lin?" I said. "Has Ben been good?"

"As long as I don't touch him," she said cheerfully. "He beat me in a game of Chutes and Ladders, and when I went to high-five him, he ran behind the chair." Lindsay dimpled. "I forgot how he is about that. Anyway, I hope it's okay that I just let him watch TV after that. It was the only thing I could think of."

"You did fine." I perched on one of the stools at the granite countertop and pressed my fingers against my temples. "Why don't you grab us each a Coke and we'll talk. I want diet."

"Is there something wrong, Mrs. Wells?" Lindsay said.

"Just stressed out over Ben." I watched her take two tumblers out of the cherry cabinet and move smoothly to the fridge for ice. It occurred to me that she was much more at home in a kitchen than I had ever been. And she'd probably make a better mother.

Lindsay set a Diet Coke, still spitting bubbles, in front of me and hiked herself up onto a stool.

"He's probably just going through some 'thing,'" she said. "My little brother did that."

"How old was he?" I said.

She looked sheepishly into her Coke. "Two."

"Right. And Ben's five."

"Going on six," Lindsay put in. "He always corrects me."

"Too old to be throwing tantrums, anyway. But I'm taking some action—and it kind of affects you, Lin."

"I'll do anything you want," she said.

"Stop. You're making this harder than it already is." I tilted my head at her. "I'm changing my working hours. I won't need you to come anymore."

"Oh." I think it was the first time I'd ever seen her approach anything close to sadness. But she recovered nicely and said, "Does that mean you get to be with Ben when he comes home?"

"It does."

"Then I'm happy."

I shook my head. "You are amazing. How do you manage to smile about absolutely everything?"

"It's a God-thing."

"Well, I gotta get me some of that." I reached out and put my hand over her very-tanned one. "I'm going to need a sitter some evenings. Can I call you?"

"Any nights but Wednesday and Sunday. I've got church."

"Excellent. This starts tomorrow, but I'm going to pay you for the rest of this week and next week, too."

"No! I couldn't take that!"

"You have to. It's business protocol. You get two weeks' notice or two weeks' pay. Don't ever let anybody get away with less."

"I'm not comfortable with this."

I grinned as I pulled my wallet from my purse. "Learn to live with it, girl, 'cause life is going to get a lot less comfortable as you get older. Trust me."

"I'll go say good-bye to Ben," she said.

As she headed for the family room, money in hand, I wandered down the short hallway between the powder room and the butler's pantry and across the foyer into the study. Stephanie's sheets were neatly folded at the end of the copper suede couch, which gave me a pang of sadness. She'd brightened up the ponderous feel of this dark red room with its overstuffed everything. In fact, she'd brightened up the whole house, and I missed her.

I went to the desk, intent on deciding how to set it up for

evening work, and noticed the flashing light on the answering machine.

"I'm leaving, Mrs. Wells," Lindsay said behind me.

"Do you know who the messages are from?" I said.

"I heard one of them when we first came in—I think it was your mother, only it didn't sound totally like her. I didn't hear what she was saying."

"Okay, I'll check it later." Much later. I gave Lindsay a hug, which she returned hard enough to crack a couple of my ribs.

"I'll miss you," she said.

"You won't have to miss me—I'll be calling you. And you can drop by anytime. We'd both love to see you."

"I don't know about Ben. He didn't even look at me when I said good bye."

"What did you expect? The *Rugrats* rule, remember?"

She nodded, but we both knew the *Rugrats* probably had nothing to do with it.

I avoided the family room and went back to the kitchen, where I kicked off my shoes and put a frozen pizza (just cheese) in the oven. Normally that would have been it, but tonight I could hear my mother's voice telling me that Ben needed fresh fruits and vegetables—that his diet was part of his problem—but, mind you, only *part*.

I pulled out a Granny Smith apple and some carrots and went to work. It wasn't something I did with a lot of prowess. In the almost seven years I'd been married, I'd been more about Chinese take-out and ready-to-nuke microwave dinners than anything homemade. My mother couldn't figure out how I'd turned out that way, seeing how Bobbi could crank out chicken Florentine with a baby on each hip. Stephanie always winked at me on the sly when that conversation came up. She and I were cut from the same dishtowel.

As I tossed the apple and carrots on the plate, something about the green and the orange that can't be reproduced in a crayon color took me right back to being six years old, sitting at the picnic table on the back patio in Virginia, swinging my bare feet and smiling back at the fruit and veggie face that smiled up at me.

"I can do that," I said half-aloud. "What does it take to make a face with produce?"

Just as Mama had always done, I formed a grin out of carrots and eyes out of apple wedges and rummaged in the cabinet for a raisin or two for nostrils. I grinned at it and carefully set it at Ben's place at the counter.

Mama had also "suggested"—she was always careful to suggest rather than actually tell me how to run my life—that Ben and I sit at the table for supper rather than park ourselves in front of the TV. "It's going to take a few nights for him to get used to it," she said. "But you two need some time to have conversations."

I couldn't quite bring myself to sit with Ben in the breakfast room where we'd shared our meals with Mama and Stephanie for two weeks. It was far too empty in there now, and the formal dining room that opened from the other end of the kitchen was completely out of the question. Between the columns and the chandelier, I was pretty certain Martha Stewart herself would feel cowed. Besides, pizza and a carrot face would get lost on a mahogany table that seated twelve.

The granite countertop was going to have to do, and while I waited for the timer to go off, I pulled out a couple of fringed place mats that looked like they could stand to be dry-cleaned and made an attempt to make the counter look festive. And then I couldn't put it off any longer.

"Ben—supper's ready!" I called out.

I tried to sound as cheerful as Lindsay, though to me I was something reminiscent of a waitress at the Waffle House, barking out an order for hash browns scattered-smothered-chunked-and-diced. Ben must have thought so, too.

"I wanna eat in here!" he called back, voice already teetering.

"We're eating in here tonight. I want to talk to you."

"I don't wanna talk."

"I do. Let's go, Pal! Chop-chop!"

"I don't want to chop-chop."

"That part's okay because I don't think I know what it means anyway. Come on, your pizza's getting cold."

He didn't answer. I heard the volume on the TV go up several notches. I went up several notches, too.

"Do you want me to start counting?" I said.

Still no answer.

Forget that, Toni, I told myself. *It never works anyway.* Lately I could get to fifteen and then drag him bodily to the desired destination and it still made no difference in his level of cooperation. If anything, he was even more defiant the next time.

I measured my steps to the family room, trying not to work myself into a lather. Ben was sitting straight up in front of the TV with his hands over his ears. It wasn't hard to figure out whether it was the *Power Rangers* or me he was trying to shut out.

I went to the television, snapped it off, and stood in front of it. Before he could let out the first wail, I squatted down to his level and said, "March, Pal. No arguments. We're eating in the kitchen. You can either get in there or I can carry you."

It was a cheap shot, I knew, but it worked. He scrambled up from the floor and threw himself out of the family room, through the breakfast room and up onto the stool. Anything to keep from being touched by me. That part was harder than the screaming and the back talk. It was almost as hard as the "I hate you's."

I shoveled a slice of pizza onto his other plate and put it in front of him. Then I dove into conversation before he had a chance to protest that there was too much cheese or not enough cheese or the wrong kind of cheese.

"Ben, what's up with you, Pal? Why are you mad at me?"

"'Cause you left me," he said.

"I know that much. We've had this conversation thirty million times."

"Not thirty million."

At least he looked at me then, though it was with a certain amount of disgust.

"Okay, twenty million," I said. "And you always say I left you at the babysitter. But Ben, I had to leave you. I *had* to go to work."

"I hate that you left me. That's all. I don't want to talk about it anymore."

The thunderheads were forming in his brown eyes already.

"Then let's talk about your soccer team," I said. "You want to go on the Web after supper and see the uniforms and stuff?"

"Uniforms?" The chance of thunderstorms lessened a few percentage points. "What color are they?"

"I can show you on the Web. Eat your pizza and your apples and stuff."

"You just tell me."

"Take two bites and I will."

Ben went for his plate and stopped. "Hey," he said. "It's a face."

"Yes, it is."

I held my breath and tried not to inspect him too closely as his little face decided what to do. Then slowly he began to smile.

He smiles just like Chris, I thought. *It takes him half an hour to get all the way to dimples.*

Except for his dark hair, also inherited from his father, Ben looked like me, right down to the small nose, the brown eyes, the inevitable overbite. But the smile was unmistakably Chris's, dawning on his face as slowly as a sunrise. It gave me an ache.

"Did Nana do that?" Ben said.

"No—I did it."

"No you didn't!"

"Yes I did! You little scoundrel. I know how to cut things up, too!"

"I hate when you cut things up! Don't cut things up!"

"Okay, fine! Ben, there's no reason to freak out about it. Just say you don't want—"

"I don't want it! I don't want it anymore!"

I could only stare at him. It wasn't just a tantrum that was being thrown here. My son was bordering on terror.

"Okay, Pal," I said. "I won't cut anything up ever if it scares you this much."

He was starting to shake, and I reached for him. He recoiled and threw himself off the bench, still screaming, and tore for the family room. He had the television on before I could get there, and he sat on the floor, knees pulled up to his chest, rocking back and forth. I watched him until he stopped shivering. He only ceased to scream because his voice was giving out.

"Are you all right, Ben?" I said.

"Yes. I wanna watch TV."

"You do that, Pal," I said—because I had no idea what else to say.

I sank into one of the chairs. My jaw was so tight my head was starting to pound, and I sat motionless to stop the sound of leather squeaking around me before I myself started screaming.

Man, I don't know if a soccer ball is going to cure whatever ails this child.

Within twenty minutes Ben was curled up on his side on the floor, breathing evenly. I waited until I was sure he was completely out before I picked him up and carried him toward the stairs.

The feel of his warm little body in my arms made me ache again. Ever since we had moved to Nashville, he had steadily grown more distant, until in the last few weeks, he'd backed away from my every touch as if my fingers were on fire. It hurt. And it surprised me that it hurt.

Unlike my sister Bobbi, who clung to her children every bit as desperately as they clung to her, I had never been naturally maternal. In fact, although I was thirty-one when I married Chris and was well into my career and had a healthy stock portfolio in place, we still hadn't planned to have children right away. When I discovered I was three months pregnant six months after our wedding, I slipped into *pre*-partum depression.

There were so many things Chris and I wanted to do. Buy a house that was more upscale than the one we had. Go to Europe (my dream) and Australia (Chris's). Probably most pressing of all, I wanted to start my own business before I became a mother. I couldn't see how that was going to happen with a baby.

Once I got past morning sickness, my vision changed. I *could* do it all, and I was going to. That was when the first bristling between Chris and me started. Until then, we were the perfect match. Both upwardly mobile, ambitious—yet fun. We belonged to a church we both liked and went most Sundays, and I was on the obligatory three committees. We never argued about money or pizza toppings or vacation destinations. We agreed on almost everything. Until I started making noises about starting my own financial firm anyway, as soon as Baby Wells was old enough to go to a sitter.

Chris only made a few well-aimed remarks during that period. I found out later that he thought once I cradled our child in my arms, I would opt for full-time motherhood. I did fall in love with Christopher Benjamin Wells III the minute I held his goopy form and looked into his indignant little face. I liked his attitude.

But he wasn't going to stop me from being all I could be. I tried to tell Chris that Ben would never be a happy child if his mother wasn't happy, and that his mother would never be happy staying at home. I was blown away the first time Chris said to me, "Mothers have no business going out to work when their kids are young."

My response? "Who are you and what have you done with my husband?" I had never had an inkling that Chris felt that way. He had always been supportive of my career, always seemed to like my drive and sophistication. We'd talked about our career goals more than we had anything else in our relationship—obviously more than we'd talked about child-rearing.

And so the battle had begun—me weaning Ben at six weeks and going straight back into the fray at the Richmond firm I worked for, and Chris taking every opportunity to try to wear me down. Each time Ben sneezed or had a bad night, Chris would attribute it to my working. When the neighbor's same-age baby crawled before Ben did, I got the blame. The child couldn't burp without my career goals being held up like Exhibit A. Never until then had I resented being married to an attorney.

Chris refused to help at all. Laundry could pile up to the ceiling, and he wouldn't lift a folding finger. We could completely run out of clean dishes, and he made no offer to even open the dishwasher. It infuriated me because we had always shared the chores that Merry Maids didn't tend to when they came twice a week. He was punishing me, which only served to make me more stubborn.

As I started up the steps now, I looked down at my sleeping son. It was going to be hard to put him into his bed, hard to let go of his warmth and pull away from the smell of little boy sweat and crayon wax. Chris had missed out on that. It wasn't just the housework that he eschewed; it was baby care as well. I could count on the fingers of one hand the number of times Chris had changed a diaper or popped open a jar of baby food. I thought at first that was part of my "punishment," until I realized that even if I had stayed at home, he would have been the same kind of father. It was a side of Chris I had never seen, and I was devastated by it when I did.

I shifted Ben's weight a little as I reached his room at the top of the steps, catty-corner from mine. His was the one room I had stripped of its Pollert decor and replaced with an assortment of Power Ranger posters and a set of Rugrats sheets. Even I knew that a portrait of John Quincy Adams was likely to give a small boy nightmares, although I had removed it and the rest of the room accessories as much to protect Kevin's investments as anything else. The array of Williamsburg teacups he'd had on the mantle wouldn't have fared well with the projectiles Ben hurled every time I asked him to brush his teeth or, worse, pick out a book for us to read together. Last night I had added a new touch—a waterproof pad under the sheets. As it was, I was already going to have to buy Pollert a new mattress.

I stood in the doorway, waiting for Ben to wake up, but he was still breathing deeply as I laid his thin little figure on the bed and covered him up. That last fit had worn him out.

It had worn me out, too, but I had to go downstairs and get back to work. As I headed for the staircase the phone rang, and I jumped like a startled squirrel. Silently threatening the caller with torture if Ben woke up, I made for my bedroom, dove across the rust satin comforter and snatched up the receiver from the Chippendale table beside the bed.

"Hello?" I whispered—with what I hoped was just the right amount of annoyance.

"Toni…honey?"

It was Mama. Or at least I thought it was Mama. Her voice was thick and slurred as if she'd been on a binge, and for a woman of her breeding, I knew that wasn't likely.

"Mama?" I said. "Are you all right?"

"No, I am *not* all right! How could I be all right?"

"I don't know. What's going on?"

"You didn't get my message?"

"No…what's—"

"I can't believe this has happened, Toni. I can't believe it!"

Her voice dissolved into sobs, and although I couldn't make out a word she was saying, she kept on, filling the phone line with hysteria.

"Mama!" I said. "Is Stephanie there?"

"Yes!"

"Put her on the phone."

I was already envisioning the house razed to the ground or one of Bobbi's kids in a coma as I heard the phone being transferred clumsily from one set of hands to another.

"Hi," Stephanie said. There was no emotion in her voice, which was just about as scary as Mama's carrying on, but it was at least intelligible.

"What in the Sam Hill is happening, Steph?" I said. "Has Mama gone off the deep end?"

"Just about."

"Well, what on earth?"

"Toni—just hear me out, okay? Don't lose it."

"What the heck is it!"

"Sid and Bobbi have been arrested."

"*What!*"

"We heard, like, the minute we got home—"

"Arrested for what? Is it tax problems? Were they in that deep?"

"No."

I could hear Stephanie breathing in tight breaths, as if she couldn't let the words go. My own body was starting to morph into slow motion, and I sat, cross-legged, on the bed and clung to the phone.

"Stephanie, just tell me what it is. What were the charges?"

"Trafficking in child pornography," she said.

Our silence then was so thick I could have wrapped my hands around it. Going into it was like forcing my words through a pillow.

"Child pornography?" I said. "You mean they were checking out pictures on the Internet? That kind of thing? *Bobbi?*"

"More than that," Stephanie said. "The police found a whole professional photography setup and darkroom in their studio. And files, hundreds of them, of little children—"

Her voice caught.

"*Their* children?" I said. "Their own children?"

"No. As far as the detective can tell—and she hasn't done a full inventory of all the pictures—there aren't any of Wyndham and the twins."

I found myself rocking back and forth. I got up and paced, jamming my hair behind my ears over and over.

"They arrested Bobbi, too?" I said. "Stephanie—there is no way Bobbi could've been involved in something like that. I know she can be a wimp with Sid, but good *grief!*"

"Wyndham says Bobbi was in on it."

"Wyndham?"

"She's the one who called the police. She told them both of her parents had a pornography shop, and she led them right to it."

I stopped pacing and squeezed my eyes shut. I was having a hard time imagining my fifteen-year-old niece marching into a police station with that kind of news. I could barely picture her asking an officer for directions. It had always been my opinion that Wyndham was pathologically shy and needed to get out of the nursery where Bobbi had her indentured as a full-time nanny.

There was a click and then Mama's voice on the extension phone, minus the sobs but still wobbling at the edge of panic.

"It's that fundamentalist church they let her go to!" she said.

"What are you talking about, Mama?" I said.

"Wyndham's been going to a church youth group with some friends," Stephanie said. "Evidently they were with her when she called the police."

"They've brainwashed her!" Mama cried.

"But they didn't plant pornographic pictures in the studio!" I wasn't sure I was making sense, but my mother was making even less than I was.

"Sid could have done this thing," Stephanie said. "We've always thought he was a sleazeball—he'd do anything for money. But not Bobbi. I know she didn't know a thing about it."

"Where are the kids?" I said.

"They're with Child Protective Services right now," Steph said. "We should have them in about an hour."

"And they will be with their mother by tomorrow morning!" Mama said. "We're getting a lawyer, and we're going to straighten this mess out."

"Call me the minute you know something," I said.

"Okay." Another sob caught in Stephanie's throat. "I wish you were here, Toni. This is so awful."

"Let's just take it one thing at a time. Mama, you hear that? Just try to get yourself calmed down so the children don't freak out. You have to be strong for them."

"I will—I will—because I know this is a horrible mistake. They'll never charge Bobbi with this."

"You keep hanging onto that. Call me tomorrow."

After I hung up, I discovered I was shaking. I had just fallen into *my* family role—bolster everybody up in a crisis. But I was far from bolstered myself.

Three

I DIDN'T SLEEP MUCH THAT NIGHT. All I could do was lie there and wonder for the five thousandth time in the past seventeen years, why Bobbi had ever married a—what had Stephanie called him?—"sleazeball" like Sid Vyne. And why we as a family had let her do it.

In our own defense, we really didn't think he was that much of a threat when Bobbi had started going out with him when she was twenty-two and out of college, working at a private preschool. She'd never dated much, certainly never seriously. It wasn't that she was unattractive or a complete drag to be with. I was always of the opinion, even when we were teenagers, that Mama had scared her away from men. The poor kid couldn't even handle her own father, so how was she supposed to deal with guys her own age? That was Mama's attitude. She was terrified that somebody was going to hurt Bobbi's delicate feelings and send her off into a nervous breakdown. At least that was the way I saw it. She sure didn't worry about *my* feelings. I was the tough one, she always told me. It didn't help my resentment of the kid gloves that were donned for Bobbi, when our mother put on boxing gloves for me.

I thrashed it over in my mind as I sighed and plumped the pillows and worked the Egyptian cotton sheets into a knot that night. When Sid came into the preschool to fix their computer one afternoon and asked Bobbi out, we all thought it would be another of those one-time dates Bobbi had had a handful of since college. None of us even paid much attention until after about the third date, when Bobbi started looking a little starry-eyed. By then it was too late. The charm Sid could secrete like sweat had entranced not only Bobbi but Mama. She was convinced that God had provided this man to continue to protect poor Bobbi the way she herself always had. Mama took us all to church and Sunday school a respectable number of times a year and then relegated God to a comfortable corner where she could bring Him out when He could serve some purpose for her. This was evidently one of those times, because she passed Bobbi on to Sid with none of the wailing and gnashing of teeth I'd expected.

I, however, did some gnashing, and so did my father. Although the two of us rarely saw eye to eye on anything, we were in agreement about Sid. I hated the way he ingratiated himself to my mother, bringing her flowers and complimenting her on her hairstyle, which looked exactly the same day after day. He was worse than Eddie Haskell on *Leave It to Beaver*. My father despised the way Sid agreed with absolutely everything he said. At first Daddy was amused that he could contradict himself in the course of a single conversation, and Sid would back him up on both points of view. After a while, he became contemptuous of Sid and maintained a permanent sneer whenever he was around.

But Bobbi didn't need my approval, or Daddy's. As long as she had Mama on her side she was safe. She must have thought she had Sid in her corner, too, and for the next seventeen years she tried to make us all believe that was the way it was. She never fooled me—not the way she grew increasingly introverted and ever more conjoined with her children. And now she wasn't fooling anybody.

The sleep I did get that night was riddled with dreams of Sid hoisting a huge camera—until he morphed into Jeffrey carrying the thing. As I was taking Ben to school the next morning, it struck me that one thing had already changed since that phone call: Jeffrey Faustman was no longer my biggest nightmare.

I tried to make conversation with Ben in the car, but it was hard to keep my mind on his responses, which as usual amounted to "no," "uh-uh," and "no way." And there were fewer of those than was customary. He was so quiet and still, it made me wonder.

"You didn't even wake up in the night," I said. "Did you sleep well?"

He shrugged. I steeled myself.

"Did you hear the phone ring?"

"No."

He stared listlessly out the car window for a few seconds and then turned to me, brow furrowed.

"Who was it?"

"Nana and Aunt Stephanie." I suddenly felt as if I were walking across a pond on slippery rocks.

"They comin' back?"

"No—I mean, not right away. They wanted to tell us that they got home safe."

"I want them to come back here. I don't want to go there."

We were pulling into the Hillsboro School driveway, and I parked so I could turn around and look at him full on.

"You mean Richmond?" I said. "You don't want to go to Richmond?"

"No," Ben said. He was storming up.

"We're not going back there anytime soon."

"Nana said we were! She said we were going back to Daddy's to stay forever. I don't want to! You'll leave me!"

"Whoa—whoa!" It was all I could do not to take him by his little shoulders. "Don't start throwing a fit, Ben. Nana is wrong. We aren't going back to Daddy until—well, I don't know. But it isn't soon. Besides, you have always gone to the babysitter. You used to love it—"

"I don't love it anymore! I hate it!"

"Okay, okay, look." I softened my voice. The terror was once again in his eyes. "No more babysitters for a while. I'm picking you up from school today. We're going home together. It's going to be just you and me."

He stared down into his lap, but I knew he wasn't seeing his miniature Dockers or the stain of a tear that had already splashed onto them. There was something both frightened and vacant in his eyes, and it chilled me right down to the tendons.

"I want things to be better for us, Ben," I said. "I'm trying to make them that way. But you've got to work with me here."

He lifted his head, only to lean it back against the seat. Then he smacked at the tears on his cheeks and went for the door handle.

"Am I gonna be late?" he said.

"No, Pal," I said. "You aren't late."

I watched him drag his backpack up to the front steps. He looked more like a little old man than a five-year-old boy, as if that backpack contained the weight of the world.

"You and me both, Pal," I whispered.

When Reggie was on her break that morning, she came into my office, steaming cup in hand with a tea bag tag hanging out of it. She closed the door behind her.

"Tea?" I said. "I was about ready for my fourth cup of coffee."

"You don't need caffeine right now, honey," she said as she planted the mug in front of me. "You need to drink that and tell me what's up with you."

"I'm just a little distracted." I pretended to read the tag.

"Distracted? Darlin', you are so far away from here I'm gonna need coordinates to find you. What is goin' on? Is it little Ben?"

"Partly." I abandoned the tea bag and put both hands on my forehead.

"Don't you try to tell me you just have a headache," Reggie said. "I've seen you swallow a handful of aspirin and keep goin' for five more hours. No little ol' migraine is gonna bring you down." She folded her arms, head wobbling from side to side. "I think you need to spill it, sugar."

I did need to spill it, before it ran over onto the floor. And there wasn't anybody right here and right now that I trusted more than Reggie.

I looked up. Her round face was wreathed with concern.

"You all right, honey?" she said.

I shook my head. And then I told her.

Throughout my monologue, her eyes continually widened. By the time I wound down, she could barely blink. She sagged back into my client chair, hands on her cheeks.

"I should've brought myself a cup of that, too," she said. "Oh, Toni—honey, I am so sorry. Are you 'bout heartbroken?"

"I'm madder than heck! How dare that scumbag drag my sister

down with him? She's not like me—I mean, Sid and the kids are her whole world. I hope she hasn't already had a nervous breakdown in my mother's living room."

"Then she's been released?"

"I'm sure she has. I've been expecting a call all morning."

Reggie turned to glare at my closed door, tapping her taupe-colored nails together. "You sure Ginny is getting all your messages to you? You know how she is."

"How she *was*. She had my coffee ready this morning. She actually *smiled* at me when I gave her a stack of files. Either I'm just completely out of it, or she's had a personality transplant."

"You know what it is." Reggie leaned into the desk. "She knows you've switched to part-time here in the office, and she thinks that's her perfect chance to slide right into your job." She cocked a finely lined eyebrow. "She took Jeffrey coffee this morning, too."

I could feel my eyes narrowing. "Just let her try."

"Yeah, but honey, that is not your biggest problem right now." Reggie got up and padded her way behind my chair and put her hands on either side of my neck, massaging with her fingers. "All right now, darlin'," she said. "This is a huge thing for you and your family. You're gonna need some support, and I'm right here."

"You're the only one who isn't going to write it up and put it in my personnel file." I reached up quickly and grabbed one of her hands. "That isn't all of it, of course. You know I value your friendship."

"Have ya'll found a church here yet?"

I shook my head. "I've been so busy getting settled—and with Ben acting up and all…"

"Huh," Reggie said.

"What huh?"

"I just don't think you can ever *be* completely settled till you have a church to go to. You wanna come with us Sunday, you and Ben?"

I didn't have a chance to answer. There was a light tap on the door, and Ginny poked her head of disheveled hair in. I knew she spent hours in front of the mirror every day getting that look, but I was convinced she did it with an eggbeater. Today it was stylishly lopsided, and she'd just done another color job. She was always on a search for the right shade for her tresses. She'd hit on a sort of mahogany hue this time. Given a darker shade of lipstick, she would have been a dead ringer for Grace Slick.

"Phone call for you, Toni," she said, smiling as if she were greeting a client with a hefty portfolio.

I exchanged glances with Reggie, who put her hand to her mouth.

"It's your little boy's school," Ginny said.

I could feel the mirth fading from my eyes as I snatched up my receiver. My jaw was already tightening.

"This is Toni Wells," I said.

"Hi, Miz Wells, this is Debbie Walker, the nurse at Hillsboro School. I have little Ben in my office, and he's running a temp. I think he needs to go home."

It was the first time they'd had to call me because Ben was ill. He was the only child I knew who had never had an antibiotic. He'd had a few colds and a case of the chicken pox in his five-year-old life, and that was it.

"I'll be right over," I said.

As I hung up, I realized that both Ginny and Reggie were still there, watching me. Reggie looked anxious. Ginny just looked nosey.

I left instructions for Ginny to notify Jeffrey and accepted a peck on the cheek from Reggie before I took off. I wondered as I drove through a misty rain if Ben was running a fever because he was sick or because he'd gotten so upset before I dropped him off. Of course, that happened every day, but he'd never become ill over it before. "Curse you, Sidney Vyne," I said to no one. "I already have enough on my plate without having to worry about your mess."

Ben was curled up on a cot in a tiny room at the back of the school office, his cheeks bright red and his eyes glassy. When I leaned over him, I caught a sweet smell on his breath.

"He's up to 102," Debbie Walker said at my elbow. "If you can't get it down with Children's Tylenol and a tepid bath, I'd call your pediatrician."

"I don't have one yet," I said. "I haven't even had a chance to call around."

Debbie pursed her lips. I turned back to Ben.

"How ya doin', Pal?" I said.

"I'm sick." His voice wavered.

"I know. I'm going to take you home and tuck you into your own bed. What do you want to eat?"

"I'm not hungry."

Debbie put a hand on one sizeable hip. "Don't force food on him. Just a lot of fluids."

"Uh-huh," I said. "Come on, Pal. Let's go."

I wanted to get out of there before Nurse Nightmare turned me in to the authorities for not knowing whether to starve a fever or feed it or whatever that folksy little saying was. Ben got to his feet and leaned precariously to the left like a sailboat ready to come about.

"I'll carry your backpack," I said.

"He's going to need a lot of hugs today, aren't you, Ben?" Debbie said—a little pointedly, I thought.

Fortunately, Ben was too sick to go into a fit about not wanting anybody within five feet of him. I wasn't going to test what would happen if I actually did touch him at this point. I just thanked the nurse and hurried him out.

He fell asleep on the way home in the car, and the minute I got him to the couch in the study, which was as far as he wanted to go, he was out like a light again. I was rummaging through the medicine cabinet in the downstairs powder room for some Children's Tylenol when the phone rang. I nearly broke my neck trying to get to it before it woke him up.

It was Mama. Her voice wasn't hysterical the way it had been the night before, but it was so tight it sounded thin, like a rubber band being stretched beyond its capacity.

"They told me at your office that you were home with Ben," she said. "How is he?"

"He has a fever and he's—"

"They won't release Bobbi."

I sagged against the counter. "You're not serious."

"Antonia, I would not be joking about something like this." The rubber band was about to snap.

"What's the deal?"

"Roberta has been arraigned on charges of 'child neglect and endangerment.'" Mama's voice broke. "Bobbi would never—"

"Whose children did she supposedly endanger?"

"Her own!"

"They think she actually knew about the studio?"

"They think she helped!"

"There is no way—what evidence do they have?"

"Pictures."

"I don't understand—"

"I just don't even want to say it!"

"Say *what?*"

"A picture of Techla, Toni. Naked. Posing."

We were quiet. I found myself squeezing the granite edge of the counter.

"Dear God," I said.

Mama went on, phrases coming to me in snatches. The twins missing their mother. Mama holding them most of the night. Emil sucking his thumb. Techla carrying the phone around, begging to be allowed to call Daddy and tell him she was sorry. I tried to grasp at something that made sense, and found nothing.

"I told her exactly how I felt about her lying about her mother," Mama was saying.

"Who?" I said.

"Wyndham. She shut herself up in the guest room, and I haven't seen her since."

The words came out as if she were ripping them from a page. I couldn't assemble them in my head. It was like trying to paste confetti together.

"All right, look," I said. "Have you talked to Bobbi's lawyer?"

"Yes."

"So what does he say? Has bail been set?"

"Toni, I don't *know!* It's all I can do to keep myself together for the twins. I didn't even know what questions to ask." She let out what could only be called a whimper. My classy, west-end-of-Richmond mother didn't make sounds like that.

"Do you want me to write up a list of questions to ask the attorney?" I said. "You know, better yet, you should talk to Chris." I was moving onto firmer ground, and I felt my voice going solid. "Do you want me to call him for you? I mean, it's not like we're at each other's throats—"

"I want you to come up here, Toni," Mama said. "I want you to pack Ben up and come back home and help us get through this. It's a family thing—I want you here."

I could feel my neck stiffening.

"Mama, I can't just drop everything and come up there to the rescue. I'll do all I can from this end, but—"

"That doesn't help me with these children!"

"Okay, so send Emil down here. He and Ben love each other…" I stopped, shocked by the sound of my own voice. Where on *earth* had *that* come from?

Wherever it had originated, it was going no further, because Mama snapped. Her voice went out of control, like the two broken ends of that rubber band.

"Send Emil down there," she said. "Break up the family even more—and make your sister feel like she *is* an unfit mother? What are you thinking?"

"Mama, that's all I can do right now. It's probably *more* than I can do. Now do you want me to call Chris or not?"

"No," Mama said flatly. "No, you just take care of yourself, Toni. That's what you do best." And she hung up.

I probably would have stood there pounding on the counter until my fist turned black and blue if Ben hadn't called out from the study. His voice, weak and wavy, cried, "Mommy! Make it stop! I don't want it—make it stop!"

By the time I got to the study, he was sitting up, the blanket wrapped around him, but I could tell he was still asleep. His eyes were glazed over, as if he were looking at a far different world than I was seeing, a world that was scaring him into deep, wrenching shudders.

I sat on the couch next to him and pulled him onto my lap. He pressed himself against me, murmuring "Make it stop" into my chest until the shaking finally faded into fitful tremors. I held him until he was still again.

And then I held him some more. I held him, and I ached.

Drop everything and go up there, I thought. *Can I do that? I can't do that.*

When the phone rang again, I considered not answering it. As it was, I carried Ben with me to the desk and stood there while the answering machine picked up. At the beep, it was Reggie's voice. I'd never been so happy to hear two "honey's" in the same sentence. With Ben still sleeping against my chest, I juggled the receiver to my ear.

"Reggie! Don't hang up!" I said.

"Wasn't plannin' on it. How's Ben?"

"Sick," I said. "I've never seen him this sick. I think he's hallucinating. You don't happen to have any Children's Tylenol, do you?"

She snickered. "A. J. and I usually use something a little stronger than that—but I can pick some up after work and bring it by."

Suddenly the thought of someone else in the house with me struck me as the best idea anybody had had all day.

"Come," I said. "But be forewarned—I need to talk. My mother called."

"How are things?"

"Worse. Can you stay for supper?"

"I sure can. A. J.'s drivin' tonight. And, honey, I'll bring it, okay? Don't you worry about cookin'."

I detected the smile in her voice. The thought of me at the stove was probably a little scary to Reggie. My jaw was softening already.

She arrived at five-thirty with a bag full of remedies the pharmacist had suggested—enough to medicate a small village of preschoolers—as well as a package of chicken breasts and all the fixings for hush puppies and corn bread. Ben was still asleep, and I finally tucked him back in on the couch when Reggie got there.

"Look how precious he is," Reggie said. "Sweet little ol' mouth."

I grunted. "It looks sweet now. Wait till he's feeling better."

But as she went off to take the groceries to the kitchen, I knelt down next to him and gingerly touched his hot cheek. Salty tears had left a trail, and I had the urge to kiss it away. I hadn't felt that kind of tenderness toward him since he'd started behaving as if I were the enemy—and that was even before Chris and I had split up.

Just a few weeks before, in fact. We'd tried to keep up a front for him and had swept even our controlled confrontations completely out of his earshot. It was one of the reasons I had let him spend some weekends at Bobbi's, so he wouldn't see us hashing things to rubble.

Something shifted in me then. Reggie found me still kneeling there, staring at Ben, when she came in with chewable tablets and a glass of apple juice.

"What's wrong, honey?" she whispered.

I held up a finger for her to wait and then roused Ben enough to get the pills and a few swallows of juice into him. He downed them placidly and curled back into a mewing little ball.

"I think you've been exaggerating about him," Reggie whispered. "Bless his heart."

I led her out into the foyer and leaned against a column, my eyes riveted to the ceiling, two stories up.

"Just what did your mama say, Toni?" she said.

I told her, each word as wooden and even as the teeth on the crown molding. Until I told her what had just occurred to me as I watched my son sleep. Then my voice got thick.

"Reggie," I said, "you don't think Ben saw any of those pictures in Sid's studio, do you? I mean, I did leave him there for whole weekends."

"Oh, honey, I don't think so. Wouldn't he have told you about something like that?"

I brought my eyes down to give her a look. "He won't even tell me what he did in kindergarten when I ask him."

"Somethin' that disturbing, though, it sure seems like he'd say *somethin'*."

"I don't know what to think." I tucked my hair behind my ears for probably the eightieth time that afternoon. "The problem is, I just don't know enough about this stuff to even know what we're dealing with." I patted my fist against my mouth. "Tell you what—while you're cooking supper, I'm going to get out my laptop and check this out on the 'Net."

"You're braver than I am," she said.

With the aromas of bacon grease and cornmeal wafting toward me, I set my laptop on the counter and made my way into the entrails of the Internet. What I found was in such sharp contrast to Reggie's humming and stirring and happy chopping, I wasn't sure it was real. I didn't see how it could be.

"Honey," Reggie said to me, "you're lookin' a little green there. What does it say?"

"You sure you want to hear?"

"I told you—I don't want you going through this alone."

"You might change your mind after this," I said, then read from the screen: "Trafficking in children and adolescents under the age of eighteen for sexual exploitation purposes is a global market, with links to arms and drug networks, as well as to legitimate businesses through money laundering."

"So your brother-in-law's in it for the money," Reggie said.

"Of course he is. It only makes sense—his dot-com venture went under—he's a computer fanatic—he's always had to have expensive cameras—" I grunted. "Actually, he had to have expensive everything. They have a wine cellar—there must be five hundred bottles of wine in there, and we're not talking the kind with the twist-off cap."

"Mercy."

"He had a sailboat—maybe he still does—a forty-foot thing he'd take to the islands with his buddies. And the vacations he and Bobbi and the kids took—I mean, who carts their children off to Club Med?"

"He does, I take it."

I nodded. "But I don't know, Reg. I always knew he was a jerk. I never wanted her to marry the slime bucket in the first place, but, I mean, could he possibly have sunk this low? Listen to this."

Reggie put a lid on the chicken and joined me at the snack bar.

"The Orchid Club," I said, referring to the screen. "That was sixteen guys who were into 'Lollies'—that's what they call the little girls they look at, short for Lolita."

"Oh, that is just tragic."

"They lived in all these different countries, but each of them had a video camera attached to their screens which enabled them together to watch a ten-year-old girl being—"

"Stop." Reggie sank onto the stool beside me. "Honey, you sure you want to read more? How much do you need to know?"

"I don't know." I backed out of the website and closed the cover to the laptop. "I don't know what I need. I just keep wondering how my sister could have this going on in her house and not know about it. She cleans the entire place every single day. You hardly ever see her without the vacuum cleaner and a can of Pledge."

"Yeah, but if he's the ogre you say he is, couldn't he just make that room off-limits?"

I considered that as I nibbled on my thumbnail. "I guess so. That has to be it. Bobbi is a milquetoast, but I have to believe she'd draw the line at this if she knew. You have never seen a total mother like her. Those kids are always dressed to the nines. She throws birthday parties with *themes*. She was appalled when I had Ben's last party at McDonald's." I tried to grin at Reggie. "She would definitely have Children's Tylenol on hand."

"Yeah, but honey, you aren't the mother who's in jail, now, are you?" Reggie got up to turn the chicken.

"You should see the scrapbooks she has for the kids," I went on. I wasn't normally a babbler, but I felt compelled to keep talking until something made sense. "Wyndham must have five or six of them just of her by now—all done with die cuts and theme pages."

"She's into themes."

"The pictures are exquisite. They never took their kids to Olan Mills, because Sid's photographs are so good."

Reggie turned from the stove as my eyes sought to meet hers.

"Some of the most beautiful pictures I have of Ben as a baby were taken by Sid," I said.

"And look what that pervert has turned his gift into," Reggie said. "Honey, don't you know he's going to burn in hell."

The thoughts I was spilling out suddenly stopped, as if they'd run into something they didn't want to see, much less express.

"You know what, Reg?" I said suddenly. "I don't really feel like eating."

Ben got restless after Reggie left, so I suggested I give him a bath, à la Nurse Nightmare's advice. He didn't have the energy to pitch a fit, but he shook his head so violently I gave up on the idea. I got more juice into him and another Tylenol. When he drifted off to sleep again, I put him in my bed and crawled in beside him in my pajamas, laptop on my knees. Despite Reggie's wariness, I needed to know more.

The money angle wasn't too difficult to read about. It felt good to get my blood boiling when I found out that a pornographer could make a CD that contained twenty thousand images of children and sell it for $25. With seven thousand twisted members in one group alone, all constantly hungry for new material, no wonder Sid had been able to build a new wing onto his house.

It also gave me a certain satisfaction to discover that Internet pornography was a federal crime, and that the FBI was probably involved in this case. I liked the idea of Sid surrounded by agents in black suits, all bellowing questions at him the way he bellowed at his own kids.

But Bobbi—Bobbi wouldn't last five minutes.

What disturbed me, as represented on the Internet trail I'd taken, was that in spite of how lucrative it could be, pornography on the Internet was not primarily based on the exchange of money.

Pornography is for the purpose of stimulating sexual fantasies, it said. I was about to explore more when Ben stirred beside me. I set the laptop on the bedside table and leaned over him.

"It's okay, Pal," I said. "You want some more juice?"

He was still again. Sure that he was asleep, I put my hand on his back to rub it. He came up in the bed as if I'd administered a shock treatment.

"Where am I?" he cried.

"You're in my bed. It's—"

"No! I don't want to be here! Don't touch me!"

I pulled my hand back.

"I'm not touching you, Pal. I thought you were asleep."

"Don't touch me when I'm sleeping! Don't!"

He scrunched his knees up to his chest and buried his face in them.

"Okay," I said. "No touching. Do you want to go in your own bed?"

He nodded into his knees and let me coax him out of the fetal position and across the hall to his bedroom. But the minute he was under the covers and I turned to go, he was sitting up again. His dark eyes pleaded at me.

"Don't go, Mommy," he said. "I'm scared."

At the point of exasperation, I knelt down beside his bed. "I just need to feel your forehead to see if you still have a fever. It'll just take a second."

He stiffened and sucked in his breath. I put my hand on his forehead. It was clammy. I was mystified as I pulled my hand away and got him to lie down again. I had been sure the fever was making his behavior even more bizarre, but this was something else.

"You promise you won't leave?" he said. "The whole night?"

"I'll be right here. I'm just going to go get my pillow and blanket so I can sleep on your floor."

"No! Take mine!"

He pulled a Rugrat-dotted pillow from under his head and started to yank off his comforter.

"No, Ben," I said. "I'm fine. You keep those."

He stayed up on one elbow watching me, until I curled up on the rug next to his bed. Slowly he sank back down onto the pillows. In the darkness, I could hear him whispering, "Make it stop. Please make it stop," until he fell asleep again.

Yes, I thought as I pulled his covers up around his chin. *Whatever it is, please make it stop.*

Four

WHEN I WOKE UP THE NEXT MORNING, Ben was leaning over where I still lay on the floor like a mangled coat hanger.

"What are you doing there?" His voice was still croaky from sleep, his face puffy and soft as a two-year-old's.

"You asked me to sleep here, Pal," I said.

"No, I didn't."

"Yeah, you did. I wouldn't have chosen this for a bed myself, trust me."

"No-o! I didn't make you sleep there!"

"You didn't 'make' me—you sort of begged me."

His head was going back and forth so fast, I was afraid he was going to slosh his brain.

"Never mind," I said. "How about some cream of wheat for breakfast?"

"I hate cream of wheat!"

Okay—so at least he was feeling better.

But he wasn't well enough to go to school, not with his temp still at 101, a fact I gleaned after much wrestling around with the thermometer. Only when I got him to stop screaming long enough to hear that I wanted to slip it under his tongue, not into his bottom, did he finally relent.

"I haven't done that since you were six months old," I said. "And even then I thought it was inhuman. Nana told me to stick it in your armpit—which, by the way, you thought was hilarious. You always were a ticklish little bugger."

He shook his head, lips still clamped on the thermometer. As soon as I got him set up with Tylenol, juice, and Johnny Bravo's latest episode, I called Jeffrey. He was, as always, in the office at 7:15, but he was less than pleased to hear from me.

"We agreed on *half* days at home," he said.

I closed my eyes to keep from getting defensive with him. I would rather have died, actually. "My child is sick—he's on the mend—and I will be in tomorrow," I said. "Meanwhile, I'll e-mail Ginny and see if there's anything I need to have immediately, and I'll work on it here."

"You'll be in for the files, then," he said. It wasn't a question.

"I'm sure Reggie will be glad to—"

"We can't spare Reggie."

I let silence fall. The man could send a courier and he knew it, but I wasn't going to be the one to suggest it, not even if my entire spinal cord turned to piano wire.

"Determine first if there's anything Ginny can't handle," he said finally. "We'll take it from there."

"I'm certain there will be several things," I said. "Consider the situation taken care of."

After he hung up, I let myself seethe. Interesting how when I'd first gone to work for Faustman Financial, I'd admired Jeffrey's steely, business-like approach. A month ago I would have found his insinuation that Ginny could do my job a rather clever ploy to get me high-tailing it straight into the office. Now he suddenly had the ability to stiffen my spine as fast as Chris could—and that was saying something.

I wondered as I made a pot of coffee strong enough to walk across the street by itself if Mama had gotten in touch with Chris. She hadn't sounded thrilled with the idea when I'd suggested it. Nothing was going to do except me coming up there. It was obvious, in fact, that she wasn't going to keep me posted on what was going on with Bobbi on her own. I knew how my mother operated. The punishing silence had begun.

I hiked myself up onto a stool at the snack bar and looked at the phone.

Bobbi's my sister, for Pete's sake. I can't just sit here and let her rot in jail.

I peeked in on Ben to make sure he was engrossed in *Johnny Bravo* and used the remote to turn up the volume a little. I held my breath, but he didn't seem to notice. Then I waited for the first drips of coffee to fall into the pot so I could fortify myself before I dialed.

Mama answered on the first ring, rasping out a hello like a cigarette alto.

"Mama?" I said. "Are you all right?"

"I've been up all night. I'm so glad you called."

At least I had one thing going for me. I eked a little more coffee out of the pot as it continued to drip.

"What's going on?" I said. "Is it Bobbi—is she with you?"

"No."

There was a weary silence.

"Did you ask the lawyer about bail?"

"There is no bail right now," Mama said.

I let my mug slam to the counter. "What do you mean no bail? They can't do that!"

"The government can apparently do anything it wants. I thought this was a free country—"

"The government?" I said. And then it dawned on me. "Oh—you're talking about the FBI."

I could almost hear her nodding. "I called Chris, like you said. He wasn't very encouraging." She said it as if the whole thing were Chris's fault. "He said that the government won't tell you what kind of case it really has. They can charge anybody—it's not like the district attorney."

"Well, yeah," I said. "Internet pornography is a federal crime."

"But it isn't Bobbi's crime!"

"I know, Mama," I said, even though I wasn't sure I knew anything at that point. "So you've been up all night worrying."

"No, I've been up all night with Wyndham."

"How's she doing?"

I could hear Mama muffling the phone with her hand. Her voice went even lower. "She's either the most stubborn child I've ever seen, or those fundamentalists have completely brainwashed her. She will not budge from this absurd story."

"Wyndham is being stubborn?" This was the girl who let her baby sister and brother slide pencils up her nose and teethe on her stereo equipment.

"If she would just tell the truth—tell them that she's lied about her mother—they would let Bobbi go and we could start to get back to some kind of normal life around here."

"You don't think she lied about Sid."

"No. They found that filthy stuff in *his* studio. But she didn't have to drag her mother down, too. It's all that obsession with Satan those fundamentalists have—"

"What kind of church is it that she's been going to?"

"Lutheran."

It was all I could do not to guffaw in her ear. "Mama, I don't think the Lutherans are fanatics. I know you think anybody less liturgical than the Episcopalians is a Bible-thumping weirdo, but come on—"

"Then you talk to her."

Ah. The hook. I went for the coffee pot again.

"Mama, I told you, I cannot come up there right now. My boss is on my back as it is—"

"I don't mean come up here. I want to send Wyndham down to you."

I put the coffee pot down. No amount of caffeine was going to carry me where this conversation was going.

"You said you wanted Emil," Mama said. "Him I can handle, and Techla, too. If you really want to help, you'll take Wyndham before I say or do something I'm going to regret."

"What are you going to do, slide bamboo shoots under her finger-nails?"

"I am not joking with you, Antonia. If you don't take her, I'm going to call Child Protective Services. I won't have a lying, deceitful child in my house."

"She's your granddaughter!"

"And Bobbi is my daughter."

I felt a chill. I had lived since the day I was born with the understanding that Bobbi could do no wrong in the eyes of the mother we shared, no matter how absurd her interpretation was. The time Bobbi was caught cheating on a test in fifth grade, Mama said Bobbi's fragile nature couldn't handle failure and she got her a private tutor. When in ninth grade Bobbi lied and said someone had stolen her jacket when in truth she'd left it in a movie theatre where she wasn't supposed to be, Mama said Bobbi was too sensitive to bear Daddy's punishments and took her to a psychiatrist. But this. This was over the edge, even for Bobbi-worshiping Mama. Wyndham was being expected to swallow far more than I ever had.

"Look, Mama," I said. "I know you don't think Bobbi can handle the consequences emotionally, but this isn't some high school prank—"

"Why should there *be* consequences, Antonia? She's innocent. It's Wyndham who's going to bear consequences if she doesn't—"

"Okay, what about Stephanie?" I said. "She and Wyndham have always been close, haven't they?" I was starting to pace the kitchen. "I mean, as close as Bobbi ever lets anybody get to her kids. Has Stephanie talked to her?"

"Yes."

Silence again.

"And?" I said.

"Wyndham refuses to change her story, and you know your sister. Stephanie won't push her like I've done."

But I am so not responsible for her! I thought. *I have more than I can handle right here with my own kid!*

I stopped pacing and, with the phone tucked in my neck, wrapped both hands around my coffee mug until they went white. Since when did I start using the phrase "more than I can handle"? That had never been in my vocabulary before.

"I suppose I'll just have to call CPS," Mama said.

"No. Make a plane reservation and let me know. I'll pick her up at the airport."

There was still another silence, this time a stunned one. Finally, my mother broke into it with a voice softened by tears.

"Thank you, honey," she said. "I didn't really want to send her off to a foster home. You know I didn't mean that."

I didn't counter that she *had* meant to manipulate me.

~∰◯

"I really didn't have a whole lot of choice," I told Reggie later when she called.

"Yes, you did. You could've let the state take her."

"There's no way I was going to do that! When you think about it, hasn't the poor kid been through enough? She's the one who blew the whistle on Sid, so she must have seen that stuff herself. She probably even saw her own little sister's picture. That would be enough to wig anybody out, much less a fifteen-year-old girl."

Reggie paused. "So it was just the younger girl who had her picture made by this idiot?"

"Yeah."

She let her thought rest in the air, where I could see it.

"Reg—you don't think he took pictures of Wyndham, too?"

"Why not?"

"But they didn't find any of her—at least, nobody's said anything."

"Just a thought. Honey, I don't mean to upset you more—"

"At the very least, Wyndham had to know about him photographing Techla. I mean, the child was never out of her sight. She was practically the surrogate mother."

"So maybe Wyndham's just mad at her mama because she *should* have known. Maybe that's why she's saying Bobbi was part of it, to get back at her for letting that animal get to his daughters."

"Do kids do that?" I said.

"Well…" Reggie's pause was uneasy.

"Go ahead," I said. "Look, I need all the information I can get right now. I'm probably going to have this child in my home tomorrow, and I haven't got a clue what to say to her."

"Well now, honey," she said slowly, "you know I'm not a mother myself, but I helped raise my mama's five, and I know how they can be."

"You're holding back on me. What are you trying to say?"

"I just wonder if Ben isn't acting up the way he is to get back at you for taking him away from his…home."

"You were going to say 'his daddy,' weren't you?"

"It's all the same, honey. Everything he knew got turned upside down and inside out, and I think he's fit to be tied at the both of you."

"He did act pretty much the same way with Chris when he was here as he does with me."

"Can you see what I'm sayin'?"

"Yeah."

"And you can see it without wantin' to slap me silly?"

"What?"

"I want to be able to be honest with you, sugar, without messin' up our friendship."

"I want honesty," I said. "I don't care what it is. If you see something that I don't, I want to know about it."

I had a visual of Reggie resting back in her desk chair, deflating like a tire. "I thought that's the way you'd be. Me, I'd be like to fall apart about now."

"I have to keep it together. I don't have any choice."

"There's a lot of that goin' on, isn't there?"

Ben took an early nap, and I was soon up to my armpits in the files Jeffrey sent over. A courier brought them, which made me smirk to myself. However, it was obvious the minute I dove into them that Jeffrey's choice of how many to send was part of a test to see if I really could handle the load.

I was well into handling it when Mama called to tell me that because of spring break traffic she couldn't get Wyndham a flight until Wednesday, almost a week away.

"Try not to torture her too much between now and then," I said.

"We're just walking around each other in silence right now," she said.

Which you do so very well, Mama, I thought. But I kept it to myself.

The next day, Ben was fine to go back to school. Not surprisingly, he was grumpy about that, and I tried to pump him up on the drive over with promises of things to come.

"We have our first soccer meeting this afternoon," I said. "You'll get to meet all the other kids that are going to be on your team."

He indicated that he wasn't sure he wanted to play soccer. That was at least an improvement on "I hate soccer!" so I ventured on.

"And your cousin is coming next week to stay with us for a while."

"What's a cousin?"

"You know, like Emil."

"Is Emil coming?"

I caught his face in the rearview mirror. It was lit up in a way I hadn't seen it in months. He actually looked like a five-year-old instead of an agitated little old man, and my heart sank.

"No, Pal, Emil's not coming. His sister's coming, though. You've played with her—"

I was sure he didn't hear the rest. He sent up a howl that lasted until I got him inside his classroom, where he immediately shut his mouth tight and ran to his cubbyhole to put away his backpack. Mrs. Robinette, his teacher, who looked to be about twelve, patted my arm.

"We all have our bad days, don't we?" she said.

I wasn't sure she was talking about me or Ben, but I nodded, and then I booked out of there. Maybe it would be good to get back to Faustman, where at least I knew what I was doing.

Over the next two days, I discovered that it was the *only* place. The soccer world was so foreign to me, I was surprised the other mothers spoke English. I was the only one not driving a mini-van or an SUV, and I was the last one to sign up for a day to bring snacks for practice. I wanted to wait and see what everybody else wrote down before I jotted in "a package of Oreos and a case of soda." I was glad I did, since everything on there sounded healthy and homemade and creative. Until then, I didn't know people actually made their own granola bars. One mother, a seamless woman with a large collection of diamonds on her left ring finger, seemed to sense my confusion and whispered that you could never lose with juice boxes and animal crackers. I wrote it in my Day-Timer.

Ben was shy with the other kids, but at least he didn't yell that he hated me while the coach was talking. The poor man was already at the beck and call of thirty women who seemed to have nothing else to do but guide their children on to stellar careers as the next Pelé.

The T-ball meeting the following day was merely for sign-ups, since teams wouldn't be formed until the end of May. There were more fathers there, and no talk of granola bars or juice in any kind of container. But I felt even more like a misfit than I had at soccer when they started talking about playing catch with our kids to develop their coordination and where to buy our own T-ball setup.

"What *is* T-ball anyway?" I whispered to the only other mother-alone that I saw there.

She stared at me almost in horror, as if I'd just asked to borrow her toothbrush, and said, "Honey—you are not serious, are you?"

I laughed as if I'd just successfully pulled her leg. When Chris called that night, it was the first thing I asked him.

"T-ball?" he said. "That's what they do with the little guys, to get them started in baseball."

"I know that much," I said. "But what does it look like?"

"It's a stand where you can set the ball and they can hit it, rather than you pitching it to them. I guess they can't hit a moving object yet at that age." Chris gave his signature "huh," which came out in a short, husky breath. "I figure if they can't hit a moving ball, they aren't ready for baseball."

"Well, too bad, because I've got Ben signed up. He starts in May—and he's playing soccer until then."

"What's this all about?" Chris said. "I thought you were too busy to get him into after-school activities."

"I just think he needs some outlets. You know how much energy he has."

"So, is that girl—what's her name, Lindsay—is she taking him?"

"No, I am. I'm working afternoons at home now so I can be available for Ben."

There was a long pause. I could picture Chris taking that all in, his brown-eyes-on-the-edge-of-green pondering some object on the coffee table as he processed information that had come as a surprise to him. His attorney self wouldn't let him reveal that he'd been caught off guard, of course. It was something he'd learned early in his career: any kind of agitation looked unnatural layered on top of the soft boyishness of his eyes and his smile, as if things negative didn't fit him. Juries, he said, didn't like to be jarred that way.

"I like the sound of that," he said now.

Like I was waiting for your approval, I thought. But I bit it back. I actually felt a little guilty about holding back the fact that Ben's behavior was getting worse.

"What I don't like," Chris went on, "is that I'm being left out of this equation."

Here it came. I closed my eyes and pretended I was talking to Jeffrey Faustman. "You can see him anytime you want to."

"Not when he's twelve hours away."

I dug my feet between the suede cushions on the study couch.

"Tell me something," I said. "If we were with you in Richmond and we had Ben in sports, would you make homemade granola bars?"

"What the heck does that have to do with soccer?"

"Everything, apparently. I didn't even know until my first soccer meeting that juice boxes are the drink of choice in the kindergarten set—did you?"

"Juice comes in boxes?"

"And would you catch balls while he hit them off the T?"

"You better believe it."

"Really. When? At 9 P.M., when you get home from the office? Or at 7 A.M. on Saturday before you go to the office?"

"I would find the time for my son."

"You'd pencil him in."

"Toni, come on—"

"I'm not trying to pick a fight with you, Chris. I'm just being realistic. I've always done it all since the day Ben was born, and I see no evidence that it would change if I came back to Richmond."

He stopped to ponder again. I took that time to congratulate myself. I could very easily have inserted the fact that although he had never had time to spend with Ben, he *had* carved out enough hours for a girlfriend. I tried never to lower myself to that tactic. Besides, he would only have countered with, "If you hadn't insisted on working, you would've had time for me and then I wouldn't have strayed." And then I would have been up all night with spinal pain all the way to my jaw. It was the one thing that had bruised me beyond reconciliation—the fact that Chris had never really said he was sorry about her.

"Okay," he said, "game point for you this time."

"Are we keeping score?"

Chris laughed his soft, husky chuckle. "You wouldn't have it any other way, little Miss Competition. I bet you can tell me without even looking it up what you've got in stock options versus what I've got."

"You betcha."

He chuckled again. "You're a piece of work, girl."

I had to grin. And *that* was why that bruise ached so deep in my soul.

"So," I said, "you want to talk to Ben?"

"Yeah—but listen. How's your mother doing? She was practically hysterical when I went over there the other night."

I had to do a double-take. "You went over there?"

"She called and asked for my help, so I went over. Anyway, I didn't do much to cheer her up."

"That's what I gathered. Is it really that bad?"

"It's worse. Toni, you know Bobbi could go to prison for a long time for this."

"If she had anything to do with it."

"Wyndham sure claims she did."

I sat up straighter on the couch. "Did you see her?"

"Yeah. Talked to her. Wasn't she always kind of wishy-washy?"

"Something like that. Why?"

"She's sure a hardnose right now. She told me she hoped they never let Bobbi out."

"Really." I pressed my temple with my free hand. "I guess I have my work cut out for me."

"What do you mean?"

"Wyndham's coming here to stay for a while—so my mother doesn't throw her to the wolves."

There was more pondering, and I didn't like the feel of it this time.

"Do you have a problem with that?" I said.

"I don't know. I just wonder if you have enough time for her."

The rest was so thickly implied I could almost see it.

"Let me go get Ben," I said.

With a little less than a week to get ready for Wyndham, I shifted into high gear. I decided to use the one bedroom upstairs that Ben and I weren't using, tucked down the hall that also led to the laundry room. It had its own bath, just as Ben's room did, which I was sure a teenage girl would die for. Beyond that, I was clueless.

I took one look at the heavy red drapes that fell into folds at the floor, and even I knew that wasn't adolescent material. I was surveying the probably overpriced artwork on the walls when I noticed a gift bag, spewing yellow tissue, on the dresser. The card peeking out of it read "Toni" in my mother's flawless penmanship.

For an eerie moment I thought she'd slipped into the house and was there even now—until I remembered that the day she went home she'd told me she had left "a little something" for me. Because just hours later our lives had been run over with a backhoe, I'd forgotten all about it. Since then no one had been in this room except the Merry Maids who, it appeared, had carefully lifted the little package and dusted under it.

I sank down on the satin comforter and opened the card. My mother's delicate Clinique scent was still on it.

Toni, she'd written inside, *I want only to see you happy. Perhaps this will remind you that the past was not all bad, and that happiness can be found again in what you once had. I love you—Mama.*

I was almost afraid to dig into the bag. The past wasn't a place I wanted to return to just then. But curiosity got the better of me and I gingerly pulled out the tissue paper in handfuls. In the bottom of the bag was a framed photo.

It was a picture of Ben and me and Chris, heads tossed about in various attitudes of gaiety, mouths wide open as if we'd reached the heights of joy. I was holding Ben on one hip, and Chris had his arm around my shoulders.

"When on earth was this taken?" I muttered to myself. "I don't ever remember us being *this* happy."

It took me several minutes to realize we must have been at a Memorial Day picnic, five months before I left Chris. We were in Bobbi's backyard—and Sid had taken the picture.

I dropped the thing on the bed and wiped my hands on the legs of my jeans. Laughing up at me were faces that had laughed with Sid—had looked at him, not knowing what he was capable of.

How could we not have seen that? I thought. *How could we not have known?*

I stared at it for a while, nausea rising up into my throat, before I picked it up with two fingers and dropped it, frame and all, into the wastebasket.

I returned abruptly to getting Wyndham's room teenager-ized. I went out that afternoon and bought a half-dozen teen magazines to get ideas, but after leafing through the first one I knew Kevin Pollert wasn't going to be in favor of my redecorating his guestroom with large neon stripes on the walls and assorted paraphernalia hanging from the ceiling.

I decided I would take Wyndham shopping after she arrived to pick out a new bedspread and some posters. Meanwhile, I packed the sterling silver and pewter knickknacks away, and then concentrated on Ben. I spent most of that weekend, when I wasn't catching up on work, prepping him for his first soccer practice on Monday.

I should have saved my breath.

Ben brooded all the way from the school to the soccer field Monday afternoon. He didn't start his actual screaming until I told him to go into the boys bathroom to change into play clothes. He didn't want to go in there by himself—but he wouldn't come into the girls side with me, either. A well-meaning father's offer to accompany him brought on an even louder torrent of shrieks. Finally, I told him he could practice in his school clothes, and I did manage to get his shoes changed.

As more and more kids arrived, bouncing up and down as if they couldn't keep their excitement inside their skins, Ben withdrew further into his, and my anxiety built.

"This is going to be a blast, Pal," I said to him about eighteen times.

He only looked at me suspiciously, and when Coach Gary blew his whistle and the kids flew at him like a flock of geese, Ben hunkered himself down on the bench and planted his feet two inches into the dirt.

"The coach is calling you," I said. "You don't want to miss out."

He might have bought that if I hadn't forgotten myself and given him an encouraging little push. He turned on me, teeth bared.

"You don't know what I want!" he said. "I don't wanna play soccer!"

"Hey, Benjamin!" Coach Gary called out cheerily. He had a bright red face and a thick neck and a gap-toothed grin that had every kid there charmed like the children of Hamlin Town—except mine.

"Just try it for today," I said. "If you don't like it—"

"I already hate it!"

"Miz Wells?"

Gary was at my elbow now. I looked up to see the team standing in a knot where he'd left them, gazing open-mouthed at Ben. I didn't look up into the bleachers, but I was sure the mothers had similar expressions on their faces.

I did look at Gary. He was still smiling, but his eyes drooped sympathetically at the corners.

"Why don't you just leave him with me?" he said. "I bet with you out of sight, he'll do just fine."

"No-ooo!"

It was the most terrified sound I had heard come out of my son yet. And to my bewilderment, he wrapped both arms around my leg and clung like a ball and chain.

"Don't leave me! Mommy—please—you always leave me. Don't leave me."

It would only be by the grace of God, I knew, if no one called CPS on *me*. I squatted down in front of Ben and peeled him from my leg so I could get him close enough to my face to restore some sense of privacy to our confrontation. We were completely on public display.

"I'll tell you what," I whispered to him. "If you'll go out there and learn to play soccer, I'll stay right here. I won't leave, not even for a minute."

He started to shake his head, but I put my finger to my lips. "Those are your only two choices, Pal. What's it gonna be?"

He didn't hesitate. "Don't leave," he said.

There was fire in his eyes as he trailed off behind Gary, but at least he was cooperating for the moment. There would be the devil to pay when we got home, but that was then. This was now.

Trying not to look as mortified as I felt, I climbed halfway up the bleachers and made it a point to sit next to one of the mothers, rather than isolate myself into a corner and endure their well-concealed whispers. Southern women, I had discovered, were professionals at dazzling someone with a smile and cutting her right down to her bone marrow the minute she looked away.

It wasn't until I was settled in sunglasses and a visor that I realized I was sitting beside the seamless woman with the diamonds I'd talked to at the meeting. She was holding the bejeweled hand out to me.

"Yancy Bancroft," she said.

I took her hand, careful not to impale myself, and said, "Toni Wells. It's Yancy, not Nancy?"

"Right. Family name."

"Nice. Very classy."

"Well, thank you," she said. "Aren't you sweet?"

Most things were in this part of the country. I smiled it off. That seemed to be all she needed to consider herself on an intimate basis with me.

"You know, my son went through something like what yours is going through right now, just about a year ago now."

"Oh?"

"He carried on so bad I wanted to keep a bag with me so I could pull it over my head—or his." She leaned in conspiratorially. "My mother had just passed on and I was in such a state. My daughter was fine, but Troy just absorbed it all, and I tell you, he was one handful."

"Oh!" I hoped soon for something I could actually respond to. I was running out of different inflections for the word *oh*.

Yancy's diamonds flashed in the sun. "You seem to be handling it a lot better than I did, but you know, just in case it gets to you, or he—what's his little name?"

His 'little' name? "Ben. His big name is Christopher Benjamin Wells III."

She looked puzzled for a second and then went on. "Just in case Ben doesn't get any better, you might want to call the psychologist we took Troy to. His name is Dr. Parkins, and let me tell you something, he is a miracle worker."

"Ah," I said.

"My name's on the roster. You just give me a call."

"I appreciate that."

Therapy. It had crossed my mind once or twice, but I'd quickly let it cross right back out. It wasn't something my family did—except in Bobbi's case. When Stephanie was a freshman in college and went to her R.A. about her homesickness, my mother nearly disowned her. Bobbi, however, had been treated to psychoanalysis as if it were an honor only to be bestowed on the first-born.

"So…do you have a church home?"

I looked abruptly at Yancy. "Excuse me?"

"Do y'all have a church home?"

I was only momentarily caught off balance. I had been asked that question by every third person I'd met since coming to Nashville, which wasn't surprising in light of the fact that there was a thousand-seat church on almost every corner of the city. Reggie had explained to me that I was now living on the buckle of the Bible Belt.

"No, not yet," I said.

Yancy looked at me as if to say, "Well, there's your trouble." Instead, she patted my knee and said, "Y'all are welcome to come with us this Sunday if you want to. It helps so much to have a church family when you're going through something like this."

I actually felt a little comforted. At least this woman wasn't muttering behind her hand to the rest of the soccer coffee klatch.

"Your number's on the roster," I said.

She gave my knee a squeeze. "You call me."

I didn't dismiss it from my mind. In fact, that evening while Ben was in the tub, I thought of it again.

It sure couldn't hurt to find a church, I thought. *We always had one growing up. Chris and I enjoyed ours—when we went.*

I tried to envision Ben and me going happily off to Sunday school and almost choked. One more forum for Ben to scream for all the world to hear that he hated me because I always left him.

Maybe, I decided, it would be good to get him used to the idea before I selected one of the corner Taj Mahals to take him to. That night as he climbed into bed—for once not screaming, because he was too exhausted—I said, "Let's say some prayers tonight, Pal."

His face immediately darkened.

"We have to pray to God, right?" he said.

I was startled. "Well, yeah. Who else?"

"I'm not praying to God." His voice rose dangerously. "You can't make me!"

"Why don't you want to pray to God?" I said.

"Because God doesn't care about little kids. And neither do you!"

He flopped himself over, buried his face in his pillow, and cried.

I couldn't have been any more mystified if he'd levitated himself right off the bed.

But that was nothing compared to my bewilderment on Wednesday when we met Wyndham at the airport. We had to wait outside the security checkpoint and watch for her to come down the concourse. I felt sorry for the girl, having to get off a plane in a strange town under these circumstances and having no one to immediately greet her and take her by the arm. When I did see her, struggling with a backpack that made her walk like the Hunchback of Notre Dame, it was all I could do not to run past the gate and go to her.

Even if I had been allowed to, I wouldn't have, because the moment I said, "Ben, there's your cousin—there's Wyndham!" he took one look at her and went as still as if he had been freeze-dried. Only his mouth moved as he cried out in utter terror, "No! I don't want her! Send her away!"

"Ben, do not—"

But I stopped. For my son had thrown himself to the floor and lay there in a fetal position. His screams filled the terminal.

Five

EVERYTHING BECAME IMMEDIATELY SURREAL.

My child at my feet, knotted and trembling.

My niece on the other side of the security gate, body dead still, face crumpling.

Strangers floating past with their stern, judgmental looks.

Security people and National Guardsmen coming to attention and tightening their lips.

I knew if I didn't do something soon I would melt to the floor like a watch in a Salvador Dali painting.

But what could I do? Wyndham obviously wasn't crossing that line with Ben in the state he was in—a soul-wrenching state. This wasn't defiance. It wasn't even a demonstration of resentment. It was abject fear, and it shuddered through me just as it did through my son.

That was the thing that forced me to lean over and pick him up. He remained in a twist of terror, still shivering, and pressed himself against me like a fist. I knew he had no idea where he was or who was holding him—or in fact that anyone was holding him. He had gone into some unseen world, and that was what frightened me the most.

With Ben in my arms, I motioned Wyndham over with my head. She lowered her own head and charged toward me, the back-pack bending her almost in half. When she got to me, I leaned into her for barely a second and then said, "Let's get down to baggage claim."

The next ten minutes was a succession of snapped-off phrases and bodily jerks and fragmented thoughts.

"I'm sorry, Wyndham—"

"No—"

Frantic head-whipping to locate the carousel.

"How many bags—"

"Over there. I brought too much."

"Sir, could you grab that—"

Hitching Ben onto one hip.

"Aunt Toni, I can get them."

Porter. We needed a porter.

Digging for a tip.

Ben clutching at my blouse.

I finally put two thought-fragments together long enough to decide that it would be best to leave Wyndham out front with the bags and take Ben to bring the car around. Walking away from her where she stood, vulnerably tall and painfully thin, I felt as if I were abandoning a puppy on the side of the road.

But if I didn't get Ben into a coherent state soon, I was sure he was going to slip away forever.

I'd left the Lexus on the top parking level, and I hurled Ben and me into the elevator to avoid the questioning eyes of the escalator traffic. As soon as the doors sighed together, I pulled Ben's chin up to look at me. He still didn't try to pull away, but his eyes were screwed shut.

"Ben," I said. "Look at me, Pal. I need you to look at me."

He released his face enough to squint. "Is she gone?" he said.

"You mean Wyndham?"

"No. Wyndy."

"Why are you afraid of her?" I said.

The doors came open and Ben stiffened in my arms. "I don't want her here," he said. "Make her go away."

"Okay, we have a problem then, Pal," I said.

I once again shifted him to the other hip. As white and fitful as he was staying, I wasn't going to chance putting him down.

"I can't make her go away," I said, "because her mom and dad are having trouble, and she needs a place to be."

Ben gave his head a violent shake. "They shouldn't leave kids when they're having trouble."

I could only stare at him. His brown eyes were wide and serious—and frightened. But even as I watched, they veiled themselves with sudden anger.

"Make her go away!" he said.

I shimmied my purse around to the front and pawed for my keys in its depths. There were as many jumbled thoughts in my head as there were items of junk in my pocketbook.

So is Wyndham yet another one of those people I "left him" with? Is that what this hysteria is about? It can't be about jealousy. The child claims to hate me. What—is he afraid she's going to hate me more than he does?

I was making no sense, even to myself. I finally wrapped my fingers around my wad of keys and shifted Ben to my other hip.

"Look, Pal," I said. "I'm not going to make her go away, but don't be thinking I'm going to pay more attention to her than I am to you. We're going to be a family for a while—"

"No! She's not my family!"

I clicked the door unlocked with the remote and managed to get it open with my now aching hand. Ben fell like a lead weight onto his booster seat, and I leaned in, my nose to his. My fear at the state he'd just emerged from and my anger at the one he was moving into were becoming a volatile mixture.

"Enough," I said. "Now, Wyndham is going to stay with us for a while and I am going to help her and I am going to help you and we are going to be fine. But you will *not* scream at her and tell her that you hate her, is that clear?"

He squeezed his eyes shut.

"Is that clear, Ben?"

"I hate you," he said.

Only the tears in his voice kept me from saying, *You know what? Sometimes I'm not that crazy about you either.*

I wouldn't have blamed Wyndham if she had fled from the curb before I got to her, but she was still there, and she seemed to have somehow pulled herself together. Her face, in fact, was a thinly hardened mask, like the shell of an M&M.

She and I struggled to get her two suitcases—each the size of a FedEx truck—into the trunk of the Lexus. My mother hadn't been kidding; she wanted this girl out of her house completely.

As I slammed the trunk, I could see Ben in the backseat. He had found the blanket I always kept on board, and had pulled it over himself, so that he resembled an Afghan woman in a *burka.* I let it go.

But I felt bad for Wyndham, who wasn't exactly everybody's best friend right now. I asked her about school and boys and what radio station she wanted to listen to, until I realized it was absolutely ridiculous. She was answering politely—that was always Wyndham—but the resistance was palpable. I was buttering burnt toast.

"Look, I know this is awkward for both of us," I said finally. "But I don't want to get into specifics right now." I nodded toward the backseat, where I was sure Ben was taking in my every nuance.

"Sure," Wyndham said. "I'm pretty tired anyway."

To my amazement—and my relief—she leaned back against the headrest and closed her eyes. In the blessed silence, with both of them shut up in their own little worlds, I had a chance to observe my niece in sidelong glances as I headed for the interstate.

She was much taller and thinner than she'd been the last time I'd seen her, which had only been December to April. Without the child-chubbiness in her cheeks, she looked strikingly like Stephanie.

Both my sisters had wavy dark hair. Bobbi always wore hers kid-friendly—ponytail poking through a hole in a ball cap, a braid trailing down her back at birthday parties, a scrunchie always at the ready on her wrist. Stephanie's was full and stunning, and Wyndham's was like hers, though with no apparent effort. Right now it was pulled up in a haphazard bun whose tendrils danced each time she cocked her head. It belied her obviously wretched inner state.

All three of us Kerrington girls had brown eyes, mine small and dark and intense, Stephanie's and Bobbi's large and soulful. Wyndham had inherited theirs, though from the few glimpses I'd gotten at her while I was juggling Ben and luggage and trunk lids, they were wary, cautious.

Why wouldn't they be? I thought. *I can hear Mama now telling her that Aunt Toni was going to rip her up one side and down the other.*

That would also account for her currently sucking in on the

overbite. Hers was understated, even more so than Stephanie's. She actually had a mouth like Sid's—full lips, a reluctant smile that had required coaxing even when she was a baby. As the first grandchild, she had endured a lot of that.

The thought of Baby Wyndham, wide-eyed and solemn in her infant seat, put a lump in my throat. How much of that innocence had been erased when she discovered her father's secret propensity for photographing little girls in the nude?

I hadn't spent much time thinking about what had actually occurred—how she had found out Sid was a pervert. While she seemed to doze in the seat next to me, my mind sought out every possible scenario.

Did she slip into the studio one day when nobody was home? Pick the lock? Sneak around, sweating, scared to death that Sid was going to come in and find her, but riveted to the horror she was finding?

Or did she know about it for months? Overhear conversations? Happen on it in an e-mail? Pick up the extension phone on an incriminating conversation?

There was one possibility that I didn't want to go to—except that it niggled at me. Was Reggie right? Had Sid taken nude photos of her, his still-forming adolescent daughter?

I glanced at her again. Was she closing her eyes against humiliation she couldn't bear?

I looked down at my hands, which had formed a death grip on the steering wheel, and thought, *Sid, you heinous beast.*

When we got home, Ben refused to take the blanket off. In the interest of any dignity Wyndham might have left, I scooped him up, burka and all, and deposited him in the family room. By the time I got back to the door from the garage, Wyndham already had her entire compliment of luggage in the kitchen, and she was sitting, toes turned inward, on one of the suitcases. I recognized it as the jumbo bag Mama had taken on her European tour.

"Wyndy, girl, we do have chairs," I said. "Why don't you pick a stool and I'll fix you something to eat. You must be starving."

"I'm not that hungry," she said, though she did trade the suitcase for the stool on the end.

"We can take your stuff upstairs after I get you fed. I mean, unless you want to go up right now and get settled. You're probably tired, huh? Isn't it amazing how just sitting on a plane for hours can wear you out?"

"I guess."

Her eyes went to the counter, probably to keep me from seeing that she was rolling them. I was babbling, I knew. I felt like an idiot and sat down beside her.

"Look, Wyndy—"

"Aunt Toni—" She looked up, her face wearing the M&M mask again. "Could you not call me that, please?"

"O-kay," I said slowly. "I'm sorry. I didn't mean to horn in on something special between you and the twins."

"Just call me Wyndham."

Her voice was sharp, her face hard. But in the next five seconds, both flipped through changes as if she were being remotely controlled.

"I don't mean to be rude," she said. "It's probably stupid—you can call me whatever you want."

"No, Wyndham it is. I know how I feel when somebody calls me Antonia. Your grandmother is the biggest offender—"

"Could we please not talk about her either?" Wyndham was by now boring a hole in the granite with her eyes. "I know I'm being rude."

"You aren't being rude." I resituated myself on the barstool so I could face her. "But let's talk about a couple of things we *can't* avoid, okay?"

I could feel her hardening again.

"I'm not going to yell at you," I said. "I'm not Nana—trust me."

She at least trusted me with a glance slanted in my direction.

"I just want to hear your side of the story. We're going to be together for a while." I looked at the pile of luggage and grinned. "*Quite* a while, from the looks of things, and I don't think we should waste our energy sidestepping the obvious. There's an elephant in the room and we can't ignore it."

I let a silence fall. Wyndham visibly squirmed, until she

apparently figured out I wasn't going to say anything else unless she responded.

"I just have to know one thing, then," she said. "I mean—if it's all right."

Note to self: Do something about this child's confidence level before she frustrates me right into a bottle of Valium!

"Go for it," I said. "I can already tell you it's all right."

Even at that, she played with her fingers and wiggled her foot until I thought I would scream.

"I just have to know if you believe me," she said finally.

"I'll tell you what I *don't* believe. I don't believe that you're making this whole thing up. Obviously, there are some real gaps in what I've been told, though. I want to hear what you have to say."

Wyndham nodded slowly. She, too, sat taller in the chair and straightened her shoulders and tilted up her chin. The words *Assume the position* came to mind.

Then she said, "I knew for a while what my father was doing and I went to my mom and she said I was lying and so I got some proof so she would believe me because I didn't want him hurting any more little kids. That's when I found out she was in on it, too, and then I didn't know what to do—so I went to my friends at church and they made me go to the pastor and he helped me go to the police."

She sagged, and some of the starch went out of her face. I waited for her to catch her breath and go on, but she looked at me and nodded, as if the state had rested.

"Okay," I said. "How did you know what your father was doing?"

Abruptly, Wyndham turned her face away. "You don't believe me."

"It isn't that. I'm just trying to clarify for myself."

She shook her head. The tendrils bounced playfully, once again belying the burden that lay beneath them. "I just think my word should be good enough. And they found all that stuff in the studio."

"You're absolutely right," I said. "But what about your mother? How did you find out that she was involved?"

I could see her neck turning to steel. In that respect, the poor kid took after me. I knew it would be only a matter of minutes before she'd be clenching her jaw and I would get nothing out of her.

"Let's do this, then," I said. "Look me in the eye and tell me that you know your mother was in on this thing with your dad. If you can do that, I won't press you for details."

She nodded immediately, but I didn't pat myself on the back. I wasn't going to pry any more out of her tonight, and I knew it. Those shoulders were locking up tight for the duration. I was also praying that my intuitive powers were sharp enough to detect any deception in her eyes.

Interesting. I hadn't even thought of praying until now.

Wyndham, meanwhile, swiveled around on the stool, clenched her thighs with her hands, and leaned so close to me, I could see the tiny blood vessels burning in her eyes.

"Aunt Toni," she said, "I am telling you the truth. My mother knew, and she let it happen."

I could only sit there and hold her gaze, watching a film of tears form. This wasn't the breathless string of words I'd heard earlier. Nor was it the bitter accusation of a resentful child. There was pain in this, real pain.

"I know you're telling the truth, Wyndham," I said. "I'll stand behind you."

She flung herself at me, and as I put my arms around her, I could feel her holding back the sobs.

"You can cry if you want to," I said. "Heaven knows you have plenty to cry about."

But she pulled away, shaking her head and smearing off the tears with the tips of her fingers. I noticed that her nails were bitten down to the quick, and her cuticles were raw.

"I'm going to go up and put my stuff away, if that's all right," she said. She was at once lighter, leaping for her luggage and hoisting the backpack over her shoulder.

"You don't want to eat?" I said.

"Maybe later, okay?"

"Sure."

Once I had her and everything she owned safely up in her room, I went down to the family room to deal with Ben. My heart went to my throat when I couldn't find him.

"Ben?" I said. "Ben—don't mess with me, Pal, this isn't funny. Where are you?"

He poked his head out from the cherry armoire. I had visions of smashed CD cases under his feet.

"Get out of there. What are you doing?" I said.

"Hiding. From her."

I knelt down on the floor and extricated him from the cabinet. Fortunately, there were no damages in his wake.

"What is the deal?" I said. "Wyndham's not the boogeyman, for Pete's sake. Why don't you like her? Aside from the fact that I left you at her house."

Ben tried to make a dive for the armoire again, but I shut the door firmly. He pressed his face against it, refusing to look at me.

"She seems to like *you* just fine," I said. "She didn't pull a blanket over her head."

"I hate you," Ben said, matter of fact. "You left me with her."

I rocked back on my heels. "She babysat for you when I left you at Aunt Bobbi's."

He put his hands over his ears. A low rumble began in his throat.

"Okay, look," I said, while I could still be heard, "I won't leave you with her while she's here, I promise. She's not the babysitter now. She's just your cousin."

"Emil's my cousin," Ben said.

But he wasn't screaming, and he was peering at me through spread fingers, which were now over his eyes.

"Is she gonna sleep here?" he said.

"Uh, ya think? Yes, she's going to sleep here."

"Not in my room!"

"No, silly. She has her own room."

"Where?"

"In that one room upstairs that we don't use."

He whirled on me as if he'd just caught me trying to sneak a syringe into his hind parts. "That's next to mine!"

"Sort of."

"No, it is! I don't want her there!"

"Well, I'm sorry, but this isn't the Marriott, okay? It's the only room we have open, and I want you to stop this."

But stop he did not. The screaming, the spitting, the purpled face went on until 9 P.M. In the midst of it, I gave Wyndham a heated-up Marie Callendar's potpie to take up to her room and gave up on getting any food into Ben after I forced him to take a couple of hunks out of a hot dog and he promptly upchucked them onto the kitchen floor.

When I ordered him upstairs to take a bath, he stiffened up so hard I carried him up like a board and put him into his bed, still covered with soccer practice dirt. I offered to sleep on his floor. He didn't want me there. I threatened to leave and go to my own room. He didn't want that either. All attempts were met with such horrific screaming and body slamming, I was sure the neighbors thought WWF was in training right there in sedate Bell Meade.

Finally, I did the only thing I could think of. I slapped him in the face with the palm of my hand.

It stung us both, I knew, from the shock in his eyes. I wanted to grab him and press him to me and cry into his hair, but he jerked himself to the far side of his bed like an antagonized snake. And then he cried.

I sat on the floor outside his bedroom door until he gave out, around 10:30. By then I had dug the heels of my hands so far into my eyes I was surprised they were still in their sockets when I got up to check on Wyndham.

Mama's house probably did seem like the Marriott compared to this, I thought. Maybe I had made a huge mistake bringing her here.

"Wyndham," I whispered at her closed door.

There was no way she could be asleep after all that, but she didn't answer. I pushed gently on the door handle, but it didn't turn. It was jarring to feel a locked door in my house, and yet somehow I didn't blame her.

I guess you have to shut out as much ugliness as you can, Wyndham. I'm about ready to do the same thing myself.

~*~

But there was no shutting out the next several days.

Ben refused to be in the same room with Wyndham, much less the same car. Once I enrolled her in school, I had to coordinate their drop-off and pick-up times and my own arrival and departure from work until I felt like an uptown bus. The kitchen turned into a short-order café, and the upstairs bedroom doors a scene from a Marx Brothers comedy.

I would have refused to put up with it, except that Ben took to holding his breath until he passed out or simply wetting his pants whenever Wyndham was in the room. I kept them apart as much for Wyndham's sake as for Ben's, because I could see how it wrenched her every time he threw a fit at the very sound of her voice.

But I could also see that it didn't altogether surprise her, and that was what made me change my mind about pressing her for details. It wasn't about her mother this time—it was about why my son recoiled at the sight of her. I was becoming frightened by what was starting to niggle its way into my thoughts. *What if Ben saw Sid taking pictures of Techla and even of Wyndham herself? What if that was one trauma too many, piled on top of Chris's and my separation and our moving away from Virginia?*

I had to be reassured that I was wrong.

But to get that information out of Wyndham was going to require the perfect time and place. Oddly enough, it was Yancy Bancroft who provided the time.

At soccer practice on Wednesday, her little boy, Troy, was handing out invitations to his birthday party, and Ben received one. I held my breath when he opened it. He had yet to make a friend at school, and I wasn't sure his don't-touch-me-attitude didn't extend to kids his own age. But he gave Troy a slow smile and then came running to show me. It gave me a lump in my throat.

"Use that couple of hours for yourself," Yancy whispered to me when Ben had scampered off.

"You don't want me to stay with him?" I tried to laugh, though I knew it came off as a weary grunt. "You don't know what you may be getting yourself into."

"I told you, I've been there," she said. "And besides, honey, you look like you could use a nice massage or something, bless your heart."

"I look that bad, huh?"

"No, you're the type that will look sensational in her casket. But I know the signs of strain. I used to see them in my own mirror every day." She gave my knee a squeeze, as I'd discovered she was wont to do. "Don't forget about our Dr. Parkins—or my invitation to church."

"I know," I said. "You're on the roster."

But my mind was going to neither psychologists nor pastors. I was already trying to figure out the right venue for my talk with Wyndham.

I felt somewhat guilty, blindsiding her the way I was going to do, but I had to find out something about Ben, or I *was* going to be calling Dr. What's–his–name—for myself. I did want to set up something special for Wyndham, however, because I'd spent precious little time with her in the week she'd been with us. I was usually cattle-prodding Ben into the bathtub while she was having supper, and by the time I got him to sleep, she was already locked in her room. The longest conversation I'd had with her was the night I was washing out Ben's urine-soaked pajamas at 2 A.M. and she got up to make sure everything was okay.

"Just an accident," I said.

She nodded knowingly at the pj's swimming in the sink. "I've done this a few times."

"The twins are bed-wetters?"

"Just Emil. Most of the time she got up with him, but I did sometimes."

"She?"

"Yeah, you know, her."

"Your mother?"

Wyndham winced. "Do I have to say she's my mother? If I have to talk about her, can't I just call her Bobbi?"

I dried my hands slowly on a towel, gathering my once-again-scattered brain parts.

"You're really angry with her, aren't you?"

"Yes," she said. Then she went back to bed.

Yeah, I thought, *I have really got to do something soon.*

Reggie suggested the Union Station Hotel.

She was in my office, collating a new package I'd designed for my clients, which Jeffrey had begrudgingly approved. Ginny would normally have been doing the compiling, but she was currently in a closed-door meeting with Jeffrey.

"You're not worried about what they might be talking about in there, honey?" Reggie said, tapping her lips with a peach-hued nail.

I grunted. "No. That woman can't hold a candle to me and I know it. What I *don't* know is how I'm going to handle this with Wyndham. You sure the going-to-tea thing is my best option?"

"Well, honey, after you told me what she's like, I think it's perfect."

"Tell me again what I told you."

I knew perfectly well, but I was having more and more trouble keeping my thoughts together when it came to the home situation. They were constantly strewn in my head like pieces of confetti.

"You said she isn't the kind of teenager who paints her bedroom black and beats her head against the wall while she listens to Papa Roach."

"I know I didn't say Papa Roach. I don't even know who that is."

"It's one of those angry rock groups." She gave me a sly grin. "Honey, you're gonna have to get hip if you're gonna be raisin' a teenager."

"How did *you* know about them?"

"That child that lives next door has his music blarin' day and night. I watched MTV till I saw the guys."

"What the heck did you do that for?"

"I like to know who I'm prayin' for—and honey, that boy needs some serious prayer."

This wasn't helping my case of confetti head.

"Anyway, honey," she went on, "you said Wyndham doesn't fit

the profile you drew from all those teen magazines."

"That's for sure. She's conservative right down to her underwear. There wasn't a thong to be found in the laundry I sent out."

Reggie shook her ponytail. "I don't see how anybody wears those things anyway. I'd feel like I had a permanent wedgie going on."

"What's really atypical is that she's all about the fact that I have my cotton blouses done up at the cleaners. I told her she could add hers to the pile and she showed more enthusiasm over that than anything I've tried to do for her since she's been here."

"That's an easy one." Reggie straightened a stack of papers with a hearty smack on the table. "She wants to be like you."

"No way. Poor kid."

"Well, she sure doesn't want to be like her mama, now, does she?"

Reggie and I exchanged looks. I shivered.

"Okay, so—the tea thing…" I said.

"Four o'clock Saturday. The woman that took the reservation said there would be china teapots and damask napkins and sterlin' silver spoons. I'm thinkin' pure class—probably D.A.R. and Junior Leaguers all over the place." Reggie leaned across the stack of packets and squeezed my hand. "Darlin'—you are a brilliant woman. You can do this. And besides, I got you covered in prayer."

I actually said a little prayer myself when Wyndham and I walked into the Union Station Hotel on Saturday. She lit up, eyes like birthday candle flames, when she saw everything Reggie had promised. I felt a pang of guilt and let her savor the salmon croquettes and the cucumber sandwiches before I broached the subject of Ben.

As we chatted first about the choice of teas and her well-understated passion for Jane Austen, I noticed that she had painted her nubby fingernails for the occasion, in a shade pretty close to mine. *Reggie was right again,* I thought.

I decided to abandon my planned lame attempt to work it into the conversation and just go for it. She deserved at least that much respect.

"I have to ask you something," I said.

"Not about Bobbi."

"No, I made a promise to you. This is about Ben."

She drew her linen napkin across her lips, and her eyes, searching my face, became guarded.

"It really is about him, not you," I said. "You and I have been walking around Ben's behavior like it's that elephant on the living room floor I was talking about, and I just think we need to address it."

"He hates me and you want me to go because I make him act like a little gorilla."

I couldn't contain the laugh that burst out of me. "A gorilla?"

"I didn't mean to be rude."

"No—I love it! That's exactly what he acts like! It really is that bad, isn't it?"

She was still watching me warily.

"I don't want you to go," I said. "He's been like this for a long time, since right before we left Virginia. It isn't you."

Wyndham nodded stiffly.

"However, it's intensified since you came. He seems very frightened of you, which I can't understand. You are the sweetest, nicest—"

"I'm not! Aunt Toni, I'm so not!"

She clapped the napkin over her mouth, eyes darting in all directions. I forced myself not to glance around to see how many Daughters of the American Revolution were bolting for the door.

"Okay," I said. "Let's don't go there. If you can tell me why Ben's so terrified of you, do, and I'll drop it."

She dove on that. "I can't help you. I wish I could but I can't."

"All right," I said cheerily, "then let's order dessert. That cherry torte is calling my name."

I don't do "cheerily" very effectively, especially when I've just blown it. The pall of dishonesty was on our little tea party, in spite of my best efforts to dispel it. Wyndham didn't say much after that, until we were on the way back to the house, where I would drop her off before backtracking to pick up Ben.

"Aunt Toni?" she said. "There's something I need to do."

Make a total disclosure, I hope! was my first thought.

"Tell me what you need," I said.

"I need to go to church."

"Oh. Well—okay."

"See, ever since I started going to church in Richmond with Michelle—she's my friend—everything has started changing. I mean, it's better, you know."

"Uh-huh."

"My youth group—they're the ones I trusted when I couldn't hold it in anymore about my parents. And they went with me when I told the pastor and when I went to the police. There were like three people holding my hands when I went in to make my statement." A shadow crossed her face. "She wouldn't let them be with me when I had to talk to the FBI."

"Which 'she' are we referring to this time?" I said.

"Your mother."

I bit back a laugh. We were finally getting somewhere, so I didn't think this was the time to chortle in her face.

"So go on," I said.

"The only bad thing about coming here was that I had to leave all of them. But Reverend Michaels, he told me that no matter where I was there would always be other people on their Christian journeys who would help me." Her voice was getting thick. "I really need that."

"Then we'll make it happen. Lord knows, I've had plenty of offers." I went through my mental file—Reggie, Yancy—and found the perfect one. "You know what, Wyndham? I think it's time you met my friend Lindsay."

I called Lindsay before I left to pick up Ben. She was so tickled to hear from me, I could almost feel her giving me one of those rib-breaking hugs through the phone.

"My niece is here from Richmond," I said. "She's fifteen and she's had a rough time and she wants to go to church. I wondered—"

"Put her on!" Lindsay said. "Let me talk to her!"

Wyndham took the phone rather gingerly and gave a tentative hello. I left to fetch Ben.

He greeted me in the Bancrofts' well-stocked playroom, looking quietly satisfied with his booty—a bagful of "Army guys," a miniature soccer ball he'd won playing "Pin the Ball on the Goal," and a half-eaten piece of cake wrapped in a napkin.

Yancy was calmly orchestrating everyone's departure. It dawned on me that this was the first time I'd seen her without sunglasses and a visor. Her eyes bulged slightly, as if she had some kind of thyroid condition, and her cut-short hair was a nondescript color. Reggie would have been all over it with a make-over, but the serenity with which Yancy watched little boys smear their frosting fingers on her woodwork was a look I knew I could never achieve. Her eyebrows gave a happy lift when she saw me.

"Was he okay?" I whispered to her.

"Perfect. He and Troy are like old buddies now." She gave the playroom a flourish with the diamond hand. "It's Disneyland over here—you should let Ben come and play."

"I would love to, but I never know how he's going to—"

"Been there, done that," she whispered back. "Now go home and enjoy him while he's still in a good mood."

I was liking this woman more all the time.

Ben did stay in his mellow state all the way home, carefully scrutinizing each plastic figure he drew out of the bag. I watched him sadly in the rearview mirror.

This is the way he used to be all the time, I thought. *He never tore around screaming like a banshee.*

That wasn't just a figment of a wishful imagination. Ben had always been a quiet, thought-filled little boy, even as a baby. He was so much more like Chris than me that way. He had preferred puzzles and Legos and massive dirt cities in the sandbox to climbing trees and leaping over tall buildings with a single bound any day. One rainy afternoon when he was four I suggested he play Superman or something. He and Chris had both looked at me like I was nuts—Ben from the fort he was constructing out of Tupperware, Chris from over the top of *The Wall Street Journal.* In fact, the only mischief Ben had ever really gotten into was things like dismantling the clock radio and using all the baking potatoes for astronauts in his toilet-paper-roll space station.

That, I thought, looking once again into the rearview, *that is my little boy back there.*

But that child disappeared when we pulled into the garage and Ben said, "Is she still here?"

"Yes," I said.

"Where is she?"

I turned to face him. His little dark brows were furrowed, and a tiny line had appeared between his eyes.

"You want me to go check it out, Pal?" I said.

He nodded.

"I will. But sooner or later we're going to have to work this out with Wyndham, okay?"

"Not okay," he said.

I let it drop and went in the house. Wyndham had vacated the kitchen, and so had the phone. I followed the sound of her voice up to her room, where the door was uncharacteristically wide open, and she was sitting up in the middle of the bed, phone in hand, eyes alive.

Okay, who are you and what have you done with my niece? I thought.

She waved to me and put her hand over the mouthpiece. "Lindsay wants me to come over tonight. If that's not okay…"

"It's fine!" I said. "As long as you aren't going to get drunk and chase boys."

Her eyes went round.

"I'm kidding. Of course you can go."

It put Ben back into some semblance of normalcy—whatever that was anymore—when he watched Lindsay pull away an hour later with Wyndham in her front seat. He actually sat at the counter with me and ate half a bowl of macaroni and cheese before something I said sent him skittering back to the television set.

He was already asleep on the couch—the little party animal—at 8 P.M. when Wyndham called and asked if she could spend the night at Lindsay's and go to church with her in the morning. I could hear other young voices in the background.

"Is Lindsay throwing you a welcome bash or something?" I wouldn't have been surprised. That was Lindsay's MO.

"We're having pizza," Wyndham said. "These guys are so nice here."

"Guys?"

"Guys—like boys *and* girls."

"Oh."

"They're being so great to me. Reverend Michaels was right—I just feel so much better already. Not that you aren't wonderful, Aunt Toni—"

"Hey, whatever it takes. Have a good time."

Lindsay's party went on all of the next day and into the evening. There was a series of phone calls, keeping me updated on the hamburgers Lindsay's father was cooking in the backyard for lunch, the youth group meeting at four, the worship service at six. I had Ben in bed, reassured that Wyndham was not in the building, when she came home—she and Lindsay and a young man in his early thirties with square shoulders and a square head and square wire-rimmed glasses.

"Aunt Toni," Wyndham said, "this is Hale—he's the youth pastor."

Only then did I see that her eyes were red and puffy, as if she'd spent most of the weekend blowout sobbing.

"Nice to meet you," I said in Hale's general direction. "Wyndham, what's wrong?"

Wyndham looked from Hale to Lindsay as if they were in charge of the lifeboats. Hale nodded at her. Lindsay squeezed her hand.

"I have something to tell you, Aunt Toni," Wyndham said. "And they're going to help me."

"Why do you need help?"

"Because," she said, "you aren't going to like it."

Six

WE STOOD THERE IN THE FOYER for a full fifteen seconds, the chandelier's light hitting the fieldstone floor in glaring pools. It was as if we were all in a scene where no one knew the next line.

I didn't even know the characters. Hal, or whatever his name was, I'd never seen before, and here he was about to become privy to some intimate detail of my life. And Lindsay was a kid, somebody who'd watched my child and emptied my dishwasher. That was all I knew about her.

The most distant stranger of all was Wyndham herself. The M&M shell, the cowed shoulders, the eyes directed toward the floor were all gone. She looked washed-down to her bare essentials, and yet she had assumed the position. The shoulders were squared. She was ready to talk.

Suddenly, I just wasn't sure I was. The foreboding was so thick I could have hacked at it with a machete.

"Okay...so...do you want to sit down?" I said.

"Can we go in the kitchen?" Wyndham said. She looked at Lindsay. "That's where me and Aunt Toni always talk."

We always talk? I thought as I led the way down the hall. *That's news to me.*

But she had apparently talked to *these* people, and they'd given her whatever it was she needed to now spill something to me. I was already too wired to sit down at the snack bar, so I leaned against the food prep counter and faced Wyndham and Mr. Youth Pastor on their stools. Lindsay busied herself making coffee and preparing an array of Oreos that no one touched.

"Miz Wells," Hal-or-whoever said. He gave my last name four syllables. "I think it's only fair to you to tell you how this all came about."

"That'd be nice," I said. Maybe that would chase off some of the thoughts I was having, like *Why did you have to drag all these people into it, Wyndham? Why couldn't you just tell me in the first place?*

"I connected with Lindsay and all the kids at the church, like, right away," Wyndham said. "I knew they were what Reverend Michaels said—they were God people."

"Lutheran?" I said—for no apparent reason.

"We're nondenominational," Lindsay put in.

I didn't ask if the guy with the square glasses did strange things with snakes or anything. I just nodded for Wyndham to go on.

"I don't know how it happened exactly. It was just a God-thing. We were all in this circle praying last night—it was so cool—I didn't think anybody but my youth group in Richmond did that—anyway, I just started crying and everybody was, like, right there, and I just started talking." Wyndham's eyes were filling up even as she spoke. "I told them there was something I needed to tell you. And they heard it and then they called Hale."

And then Hale, Hale, the gang was all there, I thought. I was grasping none of this. I wanted her to get on with it.

"That's where I came on the scene," Hale said, drawing out every word like he was pulling it out of himself with a string. "They're real good about not handling heavy issues on their own. That can get real dangerous—"

"Okay, so what heavy issue are we talking about?" I said.

Wyndham stared down at her hands. Hale and the gang notwithstanding, she was struggling again. I leaned across the counter and put my hands on top of hers.

"I don't care what it is, Wyndham," I said. "I'm not going to blame you or yell at you or whatever else it is that you're so afraid of. Just tell me. I obviously need to know or you wouldn't have brought in the intervention team!"

She looked at me tearfully. "When Ben stayed with us last fall—three times—Sid took pictures of him. Naked."

I went numb.

The one piece of confetti that had swirled time and again in my head—the one piece I had refused to pick up and try to piece together with the others—had just blown into my face. But I felt nothing—nothing except the world suddenly becoming a different place around me.

"He took pictures of little boys, too?" I knew I sounded as if I had just been told there was no Tooth Fairy, but I didn't care how naive I was coming off.

"Oh, yeah," Wyndham said. "Emil, Ben, lots of other little boys."

"Oh, dear God," I said.

"Amen to that," Hale said.

No one else spoke. I had no idea where Hale and Lindsay were. I could only see Wyndham, sobbing in front of me. It was clear there was more inside her, wanting to rush out now that the floodgates had been opened.

"What else?" I said.

"Every time Sid took pictures of him, he told Ben he would come after him—with a knife—and cut him—if he ever told anybody."

"Sid said that to my son?"

Wyndham nodded miserably. I found myself leaning toward her until our noses almost touched.

"Wyndham," I said, "you have to tell me, because this is my child we're talking about. Do you know all this for a fact?"

"Yes."

"How do you know it?"

She floundered again, looking at Hale as if only he could save her.

"You're doing great," he said.

Wyndham grabbed for his hand and clung to it. I waited in agony.

"I know it's a fact." Her voice was barely audible. "I know it is, because when he was done photographing Ben, he would call me and I had to take Ben away. I heard him say that stuff to Ben—and then he would say, 'Make him shut up.'"

"What do you mean, 'make him shut up'?" I said.

"Ben was screaming so hard—just like he does now—maybe even worse."

"And did you make him shut up?" My voice was accusatory. I couldn't help it. My fingers had a homicidal grip on the countertop.

Wyndham shook her head. "I didn't want to be part of it. I just took him to…her."

"To Bobbi."

She nodded. She was so racked with sobs, words were now obviously impossible.

There *were* no words to explain what I had just heard. That my son had been violated by his uncle with a camera. That he had been threatened. That my own sister had known—and done nothing.

"Please don't be mad at me for not telling you before," Wyndham said. She was wringing Hale's hand.

"I'm not mad at you. You're not to blame for this. Why would you be afraid of me?"

She couldn't answer.

"Because you thought I wouldn't believe you?"

"No!"

"Then why—"

"Because Sid said he would kill me! He said he would drown me in the bathtub the next time—"

"The next time?"

"Don't make me say it, please! Tell her, Hale. I can't!"

I looked helplessly at Hale. He was a man in pain.

"The next time he took pictures of her. Nude," he said.

My gaze shifted to Wyndham. She was covering her face with both hands, her shoulders drawn together in shame.

I rounded the counter and swung her chair to face me. I tore her hands down and took hold of her chin.

"Now you listen to me," I said. "Not one single part of this is your fault. You are not to blame—and you have nothing to be ashamed of. There will be none of that here."

"But men are looking at those pictures on the Internet! They're seeing me naked."

"I know—and we're going to get them, every last one of them. I'm going to get on the phone with Uncle Chris tonight—"

"I don't think he'll believe me!"

"You leave that to me. We'll make sure no one ever sees those pictures again. We'll make sure they all go down."

"I just want Sid to go down," she said.

She leaned back against Lindsay, who was suddenly behind her, rubbing her shoulders. I had forgotten she was even in the room.

I had, in fact, forgotten everything except what had just unfolded in front of me. I left Wyndham in Lindsay's hands and paced, fingers on my temples.

"Miz Wells," Hale said. "You know anything you need for what you have ahead of you, we're here for you."

I gave an automatic nod in his direction. And then I stopped. Nothing could be on autopilot anymore. There were no learned responses for any of this. No one had taught me how to react when I found out my son was the victim of pornography—at the hands of his own family.

I studied Hale, who was quietly watching me, his fingers, square like the rest of him, folded on the counter. The eyes behind the wire-rimmed glasses were as saddened as if this had happened to one of his own.

"Okay," I said to him. "Is that a genuine offer? Because I don't have time at this point to follow up on something that's not the real thing." I glanced at Wyndham, who was now deep in conversation with Lindsay, and I lowered my voice. "I am so at a loss right now."

Hale nodded and got up to cross the kitchen. He leaned one hand near the top of the refrigerator and talked with the other one. As bulky and square as he was, his gestures were gentle. I found myself wanting to cry.

"We have resources we can connect you with," he said. "We can take care of things around here while you deal with whatever you have to deal with. We can certainly pray with you."

"But I don't even belong to your church."

"You think that makes a difference to God?"

"It might," I said. "I haven't been to church in so long…"

"This isn't some kind of club where you have to keep your dues up."

Hale smiled at me. The poor thing had a face that looked

vaguely like the front of a Mack truck—and yet it was so kind. I didn't like the fact that I felt so vulnerable there with him, back slouched against the refrigerator door, lost and grasping and—ungelled. But there was no condescension in the look he gave me. It was as if he thought I knew where I needed to go, and he was willing to help me get there. He did know about teenagers. Ben was one thing—he was my own child. Wyndham, though, was something else altogether.

"I need to know what to do for her," I said. "You don't pose naked at fifteen and get over it just because you've spilled your guts. I know that much."

"Yes, ma'am—there are some issues. Big ones." He shook his head, ponytail brushing his shoulder. "I'm not a psychiatrist. I'm just trained to spot problems and get kids where they need to be."

"Are we talking therapy?" I said.

He gave the girls a nervous glance. "Why don't you call me tomorrow? You've had to absorb a lot tonight."

I nodded as he fished a card out of his pocket and handed it to me.

"I'm sorry about your little boy, Miz Wells," he said. "I'm real sorry about that."

I couldn't even say thank you. I suddenly wanted all of them—Hale, Lindsay, Wyndham—to go away.

"Lindsay," Hale said, "let's you and me head out. It's gettin' late."

"Can we pray before you go?" Wyndham said.

Hale looked at me, eyebrows raised.

"Of course," I said.

Somehow I got myself into our bedraggled little circle and let Wyndham cling to my hand on one side and Hale put his paw in mine on the other. I had no idea what Hale drawled out to God. I only knew his voice made my throat ache with held-back tears.

When they left, Lindsay making Wyndham promise to let her pick her up for school in the morning, Wyndham suddenly deflated like a bicycle tire. She said she wanted to go straight to bed.

"You going to be all right sleeping alone?" I said.

"I'll be fine," she said. "I always lock my door so he can't get me."

I made a conscious choice not to put my hand over my mouth in horror. It surprised me that anything else could shock me now.

"Good night, hon," I said as she squeezed me tightly. She had obviously been taking hugging lessons from Lindsay.

"Thank you for not being mad at me, Aunt Toni. Because if you didn't want me, I don't know where else I would go."

I sat at the bottom of the steps for a while after she went upstairs, the brass chandelier and the Maxfield Parish Limited Edition print and the brocade drapes all hanging heavily around me like relics of some time that no longer mattered. With them hung the loneliness—the suffocating sense that I was suddenly a stranger in the same place I used to control.

I have nowhere to go either, Wyndham, I thought. *We're adrift here—you and me. And Ben.*

Ben.

It shuddered through me—the thought that I hadn't even been upstairs, hadn't gone to him since I'd found out.

I don't want to see him, I thought. *Why don't I want to see him?*

The answer was clear and cruel.

Because now you know what you've been avoiding all along—and now you have to remember every time you look at him.

I got up, went up to the master bathroom, and threw up. Then I went to my son.

Only his paintbrush cowlick was sticking out above the covers when I tiptoed to his bed. The rest of him was burrowed in like a frightened animal in hiding. I sank to my knees on the floor.

"Oh, Pal," I whispered. "I am so sorry. I am so, so sorry."

He didn't stir, and I was glad. If he woke up and felt somebody in the room, he would scream in terror—sure it was Sid come to "get him." Or Wyndham, there to take him to Bobbi.

I grabbed a handful of my own hair and squeezed. "Dear God," I said. "No wonder he's so terrified of her. Dear God."

I rocked on my knees and said it—*Dear God*—over and over, until I fell asleep with my head on my arms on the side of Ben's bed. I woke up with a start when the first weak light cracked through the blinds, and I scurried away before Ben could open his eyes and find me there.

I understand now, Ben, I wanted to tell him. *And it's laying right here in my chest.*

I understood something else, too. There was no way I could make Ben live night after night in this house with Wyndham unless we had some kind of intervention. Hale came to mind. I went downstairs in search of his card, which I'd left on the counter, and only by sheer willpower refrained from calling him that minute. It was, after all, 5 A.M.

I went through all the motions of getting ready for work, though I couldn't imagine concentrating on some Nashville music baron's stock portfolio. I waited until Lindsay picked up Wyndham, as promised, before I got Ben out of bed. Wyndham seemed better, more hopeful, as she kissed me on the cheek and went out in her freshly starched shirt and her newly painted fingernails. The pain in my chest went so deep, I could barely breathe.

But if getting all of that held-back horror out made that kind of difference in Wyndham, I was optimistic that it would work for Ben, too. It was already somewhat easier to tolerate his croaky little, "I hate getting up! I hate going to school!" because I knew where it came from. Still, it went through me like a broadsword.

He went straight for the TV when he was dressed, but I steered him firmly to the breakfast nook where I had Mickey Mouse–shaped toaster waffles, swimming in butter and syrup, ready for his dining pleasure. I didn't give him a chance to express his hatred for those.

"I want to talk to you while you have breakfast, Pal," I said.

I sat across from him at the table, and he blinked his wide brown eyes at me.

"Don't you gotta get ready?" he said.

"I'm ready."

"No—don't you gotta get stuff in your office and get stuff in your bedroom and call that Reggie lady? Don't you gotta do all that?"

It was my turn to blink. "Do I usually do all that?"

He nodded. Then he stabbed Mickey Mouse in the left ear with his fork. "But don't talk. I hate talking."

"I know. And I know why." My heart was pounding so hard, I could feel it in my throat.

His brow puckered. "You don't know."

"I do know. I know what happened to you at Aunt Bobbi's."

Almost without hesitation, the plate flew across the table, and Mickey landed with a smack to the floor. Ben planted both hands over his ears and went straight to screams. I pulled his hands down and held them tight, shouting over him.

"It's all right, Ben! Uncle Sid is in jail! He can't hurt you!"

Ben squeezed his eyes shut and shook his head in that way I was always sure was going to cause brain damage. But I kept shouting.

"Listen to me! Wyndham isn't going to hurt you either. She's sorry about all of that. She didn't want to have anything to do with it."

I stopped. It was pointless to go on. Ben had slipped into a frantic state, clutching at the place mat and screaming into another dimension.

"All right—all right—I'll stop," I said. "No more talk. I promise. No more talk."

He stopped screaming, but the instant I let go of his hands, he ripped himself away from the table and ran out of the room as if Sid were indeed on his heels. I got up and scooped the waffle into the trashcan and leaned my forehead against the refrigerator door.

At that point, I only knew one thing. I knew unequivocally that there is no guilt like the guilt of a mother who has watched her child disintegrate before her eyes, and hasn't faced up to what was happening.

Work was out of the question. The bluebloods could rest in Ginny's hands for another day. I didn't even care that she was the one who answered the phone when I called to say I wouldn't be in. As soon as I hung up on her smug good-bye, I called Hale Isaksen and made an appointment. Then I tugged Ben out of the armoire and took him to school, and for once he seemed eager to escape from me—and into the classroom where no one would ask him to remember.

Hale's office was in the west wing of the two-block complex that made up Green Hills Community Church. A rolling lawn as manicured as a golf course and banks of blazing pink azaleas against every wall made the campus look polished and perfect—not at all the kind of place where the people inside would know anything about exploited children.

A receptionist in an Evan-Picone suit directed me down a hall whose walls were alive with pictures crayoned by kids. After the first few happily lopsided drawings of "Mommy Daddy and Me," I couldn't look at them anymore. Still, they taunted me as I hurried past—"We're normal. Your kid's not. Nah-nah-nah-nah-nah-nah…" By the time I got to Hale's office, the pounding I gave the door must have sounded as if I were about to make an arrest.

Hale looked unruffled, though, as he let me in and gave me the four-syllable greeting and offered me coffee. I declined. I'd already thrown up again that morning, and I didn't want to take any chances with the off-white Berber at my feet.

While Hale poured himself a cup, I scanned the walls. He had all ages covered. There was a poster of everything from Veggie Tales to the Newsboys, which I assumed was a Christian rock group. I didn't see anything about Papa Roach.

I did see several framed diplomas, though I could only read the two closest to me. Our pony-tailed pastor had a master's degree in psychology from Duke University and a master's of divinity from Fuller Theological Seminary. The landscaping notwithstanding, maybe I had come to the right place after all.

"You want to lead the way?" Hale said to me. He didn't sit behind his desk—which was cluttered with enough gadgets to fill the toy aisle at Wal-Mart—but settled into the overstuffed armchair identical to the one I was sitting in. Both were snuggled up cozily to the corner window. If I hadn't had such a critical agenda, I might have asked him how he rated the corner office.

"First of all," I said, "I want to thank you for getting Wyndham to open up to me. That was a quantum leap last night—I doubt she ever would have disclosed all of that to me if it weren't for you."

I could see protest in his eyes, but I didn't have time for false modesty and pushed past it.

"But it's a mixed blessing. Now that I know, I understand my son's reaction to Wyndham—and a lot of his behavior the past several months. At the same time, I now see that I can't possibly keep the two of them in the same house unless I can make him—Ben—understand that nothing is going to hurt him—or her—anymore." I glanced up at the master's degree certificate on the wall. "I think maybe you can help us with that."

Hale pulled his square hand across his mouth, and his eyes looked uneasy. The degree wasn't kicking in.

"I was thinking of some kind of intervention," I said. "Ben isn't going to listen to me. I tried that this morning. I'm the one who left him there—at my sister's house. For all he knows, I'm in cahoots with her."

"You're probably right there," Hale said. "But Miz Wells, I don't think an explanation from me is going to solve this."

"Ben's a smart kid. I think coming from the right source—"

"It isn't Ben I'm thinking about—I mean, not directly. Was he behaving this way before Wyndham came to stay with you?"

"To a degree. She's definitely exacerbated the situation, though."

"So it probably isn't going to get any better as long as she's there—and neither is she."

"I plan to get her into therapy." *Plan* was perhaps too strong a word. I could say it was definitely one of the hundreds of things that had whipped through my head in the last twelve hours.

"Can I just tell you what I think from what I've seen in Wyndham already?" Hale said. "Then maybe we can make more headway here."

"Sure," I said, though I could feel my back stiffening.

"Wyndham made a big step over the weekend," he said. "Huge. She now knows she has your support, and that'll go a long way in her healing process. But she has even bigger issues, issues neither you nor I am equipped to deal with, I'm sure. There's the shame—you saw her last night—and it doesn't matter that she didn't go out on her own and sell herself on the street, she still thinks it's her fault. The world revolves around kids that age. They think everything is about them."

He looked at me, eyebrows raised as if waiting for a signal that I could handle more.

"Go on," I said.

"And then there's the guilt. She didn't fight her father or turn her mother in sooner or run out of the house with little Ben in her arms and go straight to the police. Threats or no threats, we all think we should be heroes and we can't stand ourselves when we're not."

"I hear that."

"Plus she's angry."

I shifted in the chair. "I don't see evidence of that. Ben has a nonexistent fuse, but she—"

Hale was patting his chest. "She keeps it all in here, and I think it's raging. Between that and the self-loathing, she's just a time-bomb tickin' away."

"Where do you see that?" I said.

"She's not taking care of herself, for one thing. Does she eat? Sleep?"

"Not much. But she paints her fingernails and wants me to send out her blouses to be starched."

I caught myself looking at my own nails, at the ends of my professionally laundered sleeves.

"My guess is that she hates herself so much, she's trying to be somebody else," Hale said.

"But don't you just do that kind of thing when you're fifteen? I tried to be Dorothy Hamill."

"That by itself wouldn't be a danger sign, if it weren't combined with other things. Have you noticed the cuts on her legs?"

"What cuts on her legs?" I grimaced. "I obviously haven't."

"The kids were all dangling their legs in the pool at Lindsay's the other night, so she had her jeans rolled up. One of the girls asked her if she'd cut herself shaving, and she said she did." Hale's eyebrows went up again. "If she did, she was shaving with a buzz saw."

"Where are you going with this?"

"Self-mutilation." He said it gently, as if the words themselves might cut me. "Kids will do that when they're so depressed they want to see if they can feel anything. Or it's one of the things they'll do when they hate themselves. It could be both with Wyndham."

"If that's what she's doing."

"Right."

"You don't think you can address that with her? She obviously has a lot of respect for you already, and the church approach seems to work for her. She asked me if she could go to church here." I tried a smile. "Seems like the perfect combination to me, if you're willing."

"I'm not willing to get into something I can't handle."

The weight of his voice surprised me. It was as somber as the air that seemed to sink down on us as he leaned toward me, his fore-arms on his knees, his square hands marking his words.

"I think she's severely depressed," Hale said, "and I think she could become suicidal. I'm sure we don't know the half of what's happened to that girl, and when she finds out she has to face it all, she's going to want to run the other way."

"You think she'll try to kill herself? Even knowing she has my support now?"

Hale's eyes locked onto mine. "Can you give her support any time of the day or night for the next year at the least—and take care of what your own child has to face? Is there that much of you to go around?"

The programmed response was, of course, *Yes! I can do that— and become president of Faustman Financial and rescue every retiree taken to the cleaners by the bull market with one arm in a sling.*

But it hit me again that all previous bets were off. None of them had involved the kind of senseless, twisted issues that lay before me now.

"I don't know," I said finally. "Because I don't know what's going to be involved. But my guess is no."

The air grew more oppressive. I wanted to get out of there, and I even reached for my purse, which I had managed to kick all the way into the corner under the chair. I turned upside down to retrieve it, and when I came up, face throbbing, Hale was already halfway up.

"Why don't you sit down for just another minute?" he said.

I barely perched on the edge of the seat, and then only to make sure half my belongings hadn't rolled out onto the Berber. I was feeling less put-together by the second.

"Look, I don't want to waste your time," I said. "You've put things in perspective for me and I appreciate that, but since you can't really help me further—"

"I didn't say that," Hale said. "I just said I couldn't be her therapist. But I know some people who probably can."

I pulled my head up from my gaping purse. "Are you talking about a support group—something like that?"

"No. I'm talking about a residential facility where Wyndham will get twenty-four-hour care and intensive therapy and continuous spiritual direction."

He thrust them upon his fingers—each one a requirement I couldn't blink at. I sat staring at his hand, all denial seeping away.

"You think she needs a psychiatric hospital," I said.

"This is a treatment facility serving only adolescent girls. They specialize in treating victims of abuse. It's not drug rehab or a correctional unit. It's a healing place."

"Where is it?"

"Ridgetop—about twenty miles north of here. It's faith-based—all competent, certified doctors and psychologists." Hale hesitated. "Now, it's pricey, but some insurance companies do cover limited stays. Never long enough, but—"

"Don't worry about the money," I said. "That can be taken care of." I grunted to myself. We'd finally entered an area where I felt competent, and I was brushing it off. "You think they can help Wyndham?"

"I think it's worth looking into. I can call and see if they have space, then we can take it from there." He paused. "That is, if you want my help. I'm not trying to push myself in here."

"You're not pushing. I appreciate it—at least until I get my bearings. This is a little out of my comfort zone."

Hale shook his head. "This is out of everybody's comfort zone, Miz Wells."

"Call me Toni," I said.

Though at the moment, I wasn't sure that was who I was at all.

$\mathcal{S}even$

HALE CALLED TRINITY HOUSE while I was still sitting in his office trying to make some kind of sense out of the images of my niece carving her initials into her legs and my son screaming in her arms as he was hauled away from my leering brother-in-law and my sister smiling above it all while she blithely pasted birthday party photos into a scrapbook. I had to press both hands against my jaw to get it unclenched. If I'd thought it through any further, my teeth would have ground to powder. As it was, the muscles in my face were throbbing.

"You okay?"

I looked up to see Hale watching me, one palm pressed over the phone receiver.

"What did you find out?" I said.

"They have a bed available. If she's approved, they can admit her a week from today."

MTV-like visions of juggling Wyndham's and Ben's comings and goings for seven more days flashed through my already-crowded brain, but I nodded. I didn't have a whole lot of choices.

While Hale scribbled things on a notepad and murmured uh-huhs into the phone, I tried to manufacture some.

I could send Wyndham back to Richmond, where my mother would promptly pack her off to foster care unless I could convince her that Wyndham's condition more than proved that she was telling the truth. Mama was Wyndham's grandmother—that had to count for something, no matter how obsessed she was with her precious Bobbi.

But then what? Mama was no better equipped to handle Wyndham at home than I was. She already had Techla and Emil, who, it suddenly occurred to me, were probably in dire need of some professional care themselves.

There was no way around it. We either had to put Wyndham in a residential facility here or in Richmond. Or some kind of state-operated—

I nixed that before it even had a chance to take shape in my thoughts. I'd once had a client whose brother was in the state psychiatric hospital in Virginia. The stories he told me had made a slow death by strangulation sound preferable.

Hale hung up the phone and came out from behind the desk to join me in the catty-cornered chairs. I'd gone down so many mental bunny trails by then, I felt as if he'd been absent for hours.

"So far so good," he said. "The woman I talked to—" he consulted the pad—"Betty Stires—says that just from what I've told her, Wyndham will probably be a good fit. She's having a packet delivered here which I can get to you tonight so you can start the paperwork."

"What kind of paperwork are we talking about?" I felt myself let go a little. Paperwork was something I knew how to do.

"They'll need Wyndham's medical records, plus whatever information the police in Richmond will give us, and your proof of guardianship—"

"I don't have guardianship. I don't know who does at this point. Wyndham was just here for a visit." I shook my head, bangs flopping down onto my eyebrows. "Never mind. I'll get all of that taken care of. What else?"

"We'll know more when we get the packet," Hale said. "Why don't you see what you can do with that much, and then if you want we'll get together tonight and take it from there. I can also help you break all of this to Wyndham, if—"

He paused, ponytail swinging slightly to the side as he tilted his head.

"Yes, I still want your help," I said. "I'm clueless about this kind of thing."

"Who isn't? None of us thinks somebody we love is going to be abused. Why would you prepare yourself for something you never think is going to happen?"

"She hasn't exactly been abused."

Hale's eyes went still behind the square-rimmed glasses. "I don't know what else I would call it."

"I think of abuse as hitting."

"It's using any kind of power to make someone do something they don't want to do and shouldn't have to do. The results are the same whether you belt somebody across the mouth or scream into their face—or take their picture naked. It all ends up in shame."

I felt as if *I* had just been belted in the mouth. Hale's eyes softened.

"I'm sorry—I get a little hot about this."

"So pornography is considered abuse," I said.

"It's considered sexual abuse." Hale looked down at his square hands, as if to give me the privacy to react. "By taking pictures of them, this man molested every child he photographed."

He didn't add the rest. He didn't have to. It was there in the silence: *Including your child, Toni. Even yours.*

I spent much of the afternoon trying to get the ball rolling on guardianship. I was glad to have that to do to keep my mind from returning to what Hale hadn't said. When my thoughts did sneak back to it, I just kept reassuring myself: *Once I get Wyndham settled at Trinity House, I can focus on Ben. Now that I know what's wrong, I can work this out. One thing at a time.*

Logic and organization—I only had those few tools in my bag. Maybe, I thought, I ought to try to emulate Hale somehow, too. I'd known the man less than twenty-four hours and I already wanted to be like him when I grew up. He was, so far, the sanest person on this whole scene.

Determining Wyndham's current guardianship meant a phone call to my mother, and I went at it with less of a sense that I was going into battle than I'd felt lately when dialing her number. Firm but gentle, soothing, that was the Hale-way. Coax a change of heart out of Mama so she would ease up on Wyndham—and on me. If she wanted this to be a matter for the whole family, then that was exactly what I was making it.

Mama answered the phone halfway through the first ring, voice raspy. She sounded as if she'd just polished off half a carton of Camels.

"Mama?" I said.

"Toni."

"You sound terrible. What's wrong?"

"What *isn't* wrong?"

"Still no word on bail?"

"No word on anything. Unless you're calling to give me some good news."

"I have news," I said slowly. "I don't know how good it is, but it definitely sheds some light on things."

"What kind of light? Are you talking about Wyndham?"

"I am. Just hear me out, now." I tried to make my voice softer. "She told me last night that she was photographed by Sid, too, Mama, just like Techla. I know they haven't found any pictures of her, but—"

"Yes, they have. Last night."

By now I would have thought I'd be getting used to the sensation of being slammed in the chest with a heavy object, but each time it was more painful than the previous slam—as if it were hitting the same sore spot that hadn't had a chance to toughen up.

"They found photos of all three children on the Internet," Mama said. "They brought them over here for me to identify them. I had to look at my own grandchildren—"

Mama's voice teetered out of control, careening into the walls of her living room and taking her sanity out of my reach.

"Mama!" I said over her. "Try to get a grip. You can't lose it now!" So much for sounding like Hale. "You have to tell me something—listen to me!"

"What—what more can I tell you, Toni? The world has already fallen about as hard as it's going to fall."

"Did they find any pictures of Ben?"

"Ben? Your Ben?"

"Wyndham told me that Sid took pictures of him, too. She said that he always gave Ben to her to take to Bobbi when he was done.

Bobbi knew about it, Mama, and that is part of what's driving Wyndham out of her mind. Now, I need your help. I have to get Wyndham into a residential facility and to do that I need to establish guardianship."

"I'll tell you who has guardianship of that girl." The voice that scraped my eardrums was not my mother's. "The devil owns her now. That's the only way she would turn on her own mother like this."

"Mama, come *on!* Since when did you start believing in the devil?" I shook my head, hand pressed to my left temple. "Okay—look—forget that. Let's just get down to cases here. I'm trying to get some help for Wyndham so I can—"

"You take that girl's side and you are as good as dead to me, Antonia. Those fundamentalists can have the both of you."

"What are you *talking* about? I'm trying to get some help for *your* grand—"

She heard none of it. I was talking to a dial tone.

Head reeling, I punched out Reggie's number.

"Good morning, Faustman Financial. This is Regina. How may I help you?"

"You can tell me whether you believe in the devil," I said.

"Toni, honey?"

"Are you a fundamentalist, Reggie?"

"What on *earth?*"

"Never mind. Reg, I need the name of a good lawyer."

"You need somebody to help you get yourself committed, sugar?"

I took a breath, quite possibly the first real one I'd drawn all day.

"No. You are not going to believe what's happening."

"Try me."

"You sitting down?"

She was by the time I finished telling her everything that had gone down since Wyndham's return from her weekend with Hale et al. I could picture her sunken back into the leather chair, nails gripping the arms, face wreathed with concern. I could hear it in the exclamations she was punching out, and it was moving me toward tears. I choked them down into my chest with everything else I was packing in there, waiting to be slammed yet again.

"I'll get on my little church hot line and see if I can find you a lawyer," Reggie said. "Don't move. I'll call you right back."

But I had to move. I couldn't sit there and let the thoughts take over. Who knew how long it was going to take for Reggie to work her magic? I could be nuts by the time she called back.

The only other thing I could do—the thing I *had* to do—was call Chris. He had a right to know what had happened to his son. I gripped the receiver. I just had to phrase it right or the whole conversation was going to turn into another ploy to bring me back to Richmond.

So why not go back? I thought. Wouldn't this whole thing be a lot easier with a lawyer husband—okay, estranged husband—on hand to work out all these kinks? Wouldn't he be sure Sid—and Bobbi— got what was coming to them?

I let go of the phone and pressed my hands into my face. Bobbi. Dear God.

It was odd for me—thinking *Dear God*—but who else would know why on earth my sister, my flesh and blood, had let this happen to her children? To *my* child?

My chest took another hit, this time from my own thoughts. "Dear God," I whispered. "Please don't let me kill her. Please, just don't give me a chance to kill my sister."

The phone rang, jangling through my chest cavity and jerking my jaws into locked position. I picked up the receiver and said a tight, "Hello?"

"Her name is Faith Anne Newlin," Reggie said. "My hot line says she's the best family law attorney in Nashville. Tammi Trice's sister-in-law used her—she worked miracles in that nasty mess of hers. You got a pencil, honey?"

I grabbed one. My chest stopped throbbing.

"There's one thing I don't understand," Reggie said when I'd written the lawyer's number down. "Well, there are a lot of things, but for openers, why in the world won't your mama believe this child when there is proof all over the place? I mean, how could the woman *not* have known what was going on in her own house?

Especially as tight as she had that umbilical cord still tied to those children?"

"You don't know my mother," I said. "She could've caught Bobbi standing in the middle of that studio with the camera in her hand, pointed right at Wyndham's naked behind, and she'd come up with some excuse."

"I do *not* understand that."

"Who does understand irrational behavior? Mama *can't* admit Bobbi has done something wrong, because that would mean she has to let go of an illusion that has kept her going for years."

"That your sister is perfect?"

"That *she* is. She couldn't prove it by the way I turned out, and she sure couldn't prove it by her choice of my father as a husband, so that left Bobbi." I gave a sniff. "The fact is, Stephanie is more perfect than the rest of the bunch put together, but by the time she was born Mama had used up all her worship on Bobbi. Poor Steph has been trying to get Mama's approval practically since the day she was born."

"So whose approval were you gunnin' for?" Reggie said.

I had to think about that for a second. "Daddy's, I guess. And after he died, it was people like Jeffrey Faustman."

I could almost hear Reggie shuddering. "Honey, ya'll give new meanin' to the term *dysfunctional.*"

"Tell me about it. I need to call that lawyer before the lunacy gets passed down any further."

Faith Anne Newlin sounded like she was about fifteen on the phone, though Reggie swore that Tammi What's-Her-Name's sister-in-law said she'd been in practice for at least five years. But I liked her no-nonsense approach when I talked to her. I needed somebody business-like and crisp to get me pulled back together.

"I can probably have this wrapped up by tomorrow morning," Ms. Newlin told me. "I'll call you first thing and have you come over and sign the papers. Where can I reach you?"

I had to pause. I didn't even know where I was at that moment, much less where I was going to be the next day. But things had to be better by tomorrow, just having gotten this far. I gave her my number at work.

Then I called Reggie back.

"What's the weather like there?" I said.

"Partly cloudy and mild until somebody mentions your name. Then Jeffrey's barometer hits rock bottom. I'm trying to batten down the hatches a little."

"Do what you can," I said. "But don't give anybody any details."

"Unh-uh."

"Listen, Reg, let me ask you something. You know the Green Hills Community Church? It's down on—"

"I know it. "

"Are they fundamentalist—I mean, are we talking prudes who would overreact in a situation like this?"

"Honey, I don't use labels like that," Reggie said. "They're Christians, and they have an excellent reputation for dealin' with real issues. If you want to debate the end times, go somewhere else. But if you have somebody in trouble, that's the place to go." Reggie paused. "Any particular reason you're askin' me this, honey?"

"No *rational* reason, no. I'm just trying to sort through everything and throw out what's only going to confuse me more. This whole thing makes little enough sense as it is."

I could hear the leather squeaking as Reggie readjusted in the chair. "I'm not following you," she said.

"My mother thinks the fundamentalists have gotten to Wyndham and now she's possessed by the devil and that's why she's turned her mother in."

Reggie spat out a laugh. "That just doesn't make sense *at* all. That woman is *tragic*. Honey, if the fundamentalists thought Wyndham was possessed, they'd be trying to drive the devil *out* of her! Lordy, Toni, they're Christians, too!"

"Okay. I'm just trying to get my head straight."

"Then look someplace else besides your Mama. Bless her heart, the icing has slipped off that woman's cupcakes."

"I know."

"And you can't be worryin' about her now. You got Wyndham and Ben to take care of."

"I know."

"So what's your next step?"

"I have to break the news to Wyndham," I said quickly, before Reggie could break in and tell me what my next step was. "She isn't going to be happy about it. She said last night that if I didn't want her, she didn't know where she would go."

"Bless her heart."

"But I do have a place for her to go—what else can I do? I'm just going to have to convince her that this is the best thing."

"When's that going to happen?"

"Tonight. Hale Isaksen's coming over—that's the youth pastor."

"I know about him. Everybody in town knows about him. God has definitely sent you to the right place."

I didn't ask her why God would give me any kind of directions at all, seeing how I'd barely given Him the time of day lately. I wasn't in the mood for a theological discussion.

"And where's Ben going to be durin' this little get-together?" Reggie said.

"Ugh." I put a hand in the small of my back and started pacing the kitchen. "He has soccer practice today, which means he'll be worn out, so with any luck I can get him into bed by…" I blew air out between my lips. "Nine or ten o'clock, give or take a couple of screaming fits."

"You think he'd go to McDonald's and an early movie with me?"

"Oh, Reg, you don't have to do that."

"I know it. I want to."

"I'd feel like I was completely taking advantage of you."

"Now you listen to me, girl." Reggie was undoubtedly sitting straight up in the chair, tweezed eyebrows arched up to her hairline. "You have got one mess on your hands and there is no way you're going to be able to get through this by yourself. You better cling to every friend God's giving you who's willin' to get some of it on 'em. Now—do you think Ben would be comfortable going out with me for a while tonight or not?"

I laughed—a now-unfamiliar sound inside my head. "Does he have a choice?"

"No, I don't think he does," Reggie said. "Bless his heart."

It was the first miracle I had ever experienced—the fact that Ben went meekly off with Reggie at 5:30 that night. It might have been the lime-green Volkswagen Beetle Reggie drove up in that intrigued him, complete with a large stuffed frog poking its giant bulging eyes out of the sunroof. Or perhaps it was the tiny Power Puff Girls decals on her fingernails. Or it may have been that he would have done just about anything to get out of the house after I told him Wyndham was coming home soon. Reggie whispered to me that it was just one of God's little miracles. One look at the grin on Ben's face as he climbed into her front seat, and I believed her. It did stab me, knowing that he didn't smile at me that way. But now that I knew why, I was going to fix it. I just needed to get Wyndham handled first.

Hale arrived shortly thereafter, and we had a chance to look through the Trinity House packet at the kitchen snack bar over coffee before Lindsay pulled up with Wyndham. From the photographs, it appeared to be a surprisingly un-Tennessee-like place, with Spanish mission–style stucco buildings and saltillo tiles on the floors and a spare, monastic-looking chapel off in a clearing, sans azalea bushes. It had none of the gracious Southern charm of the Green Hills Church. In fact, it reminded me of a convent.

"Have you ever been to this place?" I said.

"Many times," Hale said. "I've even made some day-long retreats there."

"*You* have? What were you retreating from?" I put my hand up before he could answer. "That is so none of my business. I'm sorry—I'm losing it here."

Hale chuckled. Even his laugh had a square, solid sound that made me want to lean on it.

"It's okay," he said. "Mostly I was retreating from myself—and of course that's exactly who I found when I went there."

"Yourself."

"They have some amazing people at Trinity. The residential part of it is for abused girls, but the rest is open to anyone who is seeking…whatever they're seeking."

"It would have to have something to do with God, I assume."

Hale gave a square shrug. "I don't know what else would be worth seeking."

I went back to the pamphlet, which I'd pushed aside in order to peruse the more official looking materials. A moment later I heard myself whistle.

"You found the price," Hale said.

"Three thousand a month."

"That includes room, board, intensive counseling—"

"How 'bout membership in the country club?" I ran my finger down the bulleted list of benefits Wyndham was going to receive for my money. I noticed, oddly, that the nail on my index finger was now short and ragged. I didn't remember chewing it off.

I knew I could swing the cost for a while. I'd spent part of the afternoon looking at my financial statement, figuring out which assets to liquidate. Fortunately there were plenty that were in my name alone. I didn't know how Chris was going to react to all this. I still hadn't called him.

"How long do you think it'll take?" I said. "Until she's—what—cured? Rehabilitated? What do you say?"

"Healed, I think, is the word. I don't know. It probably depends on how hard she works—how hard she lets God work. And how much support she has."

I grunted. "She has me. Period. My mother has written her off—both of us, actually. Something about us being possessed by the devil."

"I wouldn't doubt that the devil has everything to do with this situation." Hale got up to pour himself another cup of coffee and looked back at me over his shoulder as he crossed the kitchen. "But I don't see the devil in you. Wyndham could do a lot worse than having you on her side."

"What else am I supposed to do? Right now, she doesn't have anybody else."

"You could elect not to help her."

"Right. And I'd never sleep at night. I may not go to church, but I do have a conscience."

"Conscience. God." He sat down again, squinting against the steam rising from the mug. "In this case, I think it's the same thing."

"Then it's a freebie," I said. "If God's in this, it isn't because I thought about asking Him."

I expected something like, "It's never too late to start," or "Why not ask Him now?" I got neither. Hale just sat there looking square, like a rock. It kept me from fleeing when I heard Lindsay's car pull into the driveway.

"You get this thing started," I said to him. "I have no idea where to even begin, so I'm going to follow your lead."

"You okay?" he said.

Whether I was or not, Wyndham rushed in through the door from the garage, looking a little less starched and primped than she had that morning. Both of us seemed to have wilted as the day had gone on. But when she saw Hale and me there, her face lifted visibly, and at first I thought her eyes were shiny. As she came closer to hug me, though, I saw that they were actually glassy, feverish. The smile, the flush, it was all forced, as if she thought it ought to be there and she needed to make it so.

"Hungry?" I said.

She shook her head, the mop of dark curls jiggling nervously from the ponytail atop her head. "Lindsay and I had fries with some of the girls." She glanced at me warily. "I hope that's okay?"

"Of course. You don't see a seven-course meal here waiting for you, do you?"

Her eyes grew more nervous. "You want me to fix you something? As long as I'm staying here, I can cook. Earn my keep or something."

My heart took another hit. I looked helplessly at Hale.

"Who did you go out with?" he said.

As Wyndham headed for the refrigerator she listed several names that Hale seemed, from his nods, to recognize.

"You want me to fix you a salad, Aunt Toni?" she said.

I shook my head and pointed to one of the snack bar stools. Glancing from one of us to the other, she climbed up on it, next to

Hale. I was across from her, pressing sweat marks into the granite with my palms.

"They're all great girls," she said to Hale, still using an obligatory cheery voice. "I love it here. I thought no group could be like my group up in Richmond, but these kids are so cool. I'm so glad I'm here."

Stop, I thought. *Hale, do something. Make her stop before I start hating myself more than I already do.*

Hale, however, seemed bent on dragging the same line of conversation into next week.

"What did ya'll talk about?" he said.

"Just girl stuff." She rolled her eyes elaborately. "It feels so good to talk about something besides you know—the yucky stuff that's been going on with me. I feel normal again."

I looked at Hale, but he was still studying Wyndham. "Did you talk about shaving your legs?" he said. "You girls always seem to wind up talking about shaving your legs."

The flush disappeared from Wyndham's face. Her eyes darted to her calves, and she pulled both of them, clad in black Lycra, up another notch on the stool so that she could wrap her arms around them.

"We didn't talk about that," she said.

"Do we need to?" Hale said. "You were showing some pretty bad gashes at the pool yesterday."

"I just have to be more careful."

I could feel my eyebrows twisting. If there was one thing I had learned from my five years of being a mother, it was how to tell when a kid is lying. Hale obviously knew it, too, because he was going right for the jugular. "You sure we don't need to talk about it?" Hale's voice, if possible, was getting softer even as it grew firmer. I personally was ready to confess every sin I'd ever committed right there on the spot. He touched Wyndham's sleeve lightly. "I'm not one to ask a lady if I can look at her legs. But how about that arm?"

Wyndham's chin came up slowly from her knees, her eyes riveted to his.

What is he doing? I thought.

"You want to show us your arms?" he said. "We're not going to do anything to you, Wyndham, we just want to help you—your Aunt Toni and me."

"I *was* doing—some stuff," she said in a voice I could barely hear. "I stopped, though. Now that I'm here with Aunt Toni and everybody, I'm not depressed anymore. I'm gonna be okay now."

I'm completely lost, I wanted to say. *Somebody tell me what's going on.*

"Let's have a look, huh?" Hale nodded toward her arm. "You're with people who care about you. You need to show us what's going on."

Something shifted in Wyndham, something visceral. Moving mechanically, as if she herself were no longer in her body, she unbuttoned the cuff on her white blouse and slowly rolled up the sleeve. I gasped out loud.

There was a three-inch cross cut into Wyndham's forearm. It looked raw and angry, puffed red at the edges of the wound with no sign of a scab. It was a recent injury, done that morning at the very earliest.

"Wyndham," I said. "Honey—oh."

"Don't be mad at me, Aunt Toni! It's the last time—I promise. I don't need to do it anymore. I can stop now, because you want me here. You still want me here after I told you about Ben!"

"But didn't you do that just today, Wyndham?" Hale said.

I wanted him to stop. The look on Wyndham's face was so agonized, I didn't want him pushing her anymore. But she nodded.

"It's the last time, though!" Her mouth drew up, her eyes closed. It was a contortion born of pain. "I just wanted to see if I could feel—and I can! I can now! So I can stop!" She turned to me with her eyes still squeezed shut. "Aunt Toni, please—"

I reached across the counter and put my hand on the arm that was still covered by a sleeve. She winced. Her eyes locked into mine.

Dear God, I thought. *She IS mutilating herself.*

"You've been through a horrible thing," Hale said, as if from some other dimension. "It has taken a terrible toll on you, and you're going to need some help being healed. You can't just stop."

"But I'm away from *him* now."

"And that's a start. But all that he did to you isn't going to disappear overnight."

"But God can do miracles! He's already done one—he's brought me here!"

Her eyes searched my face, rummaged through it for a rescue, as if I myself were God.

"Your Aunt Toni can't heal you," Hale said. "She'll be there for you, but she can't do it. God's going to need some time to work in you."

Wyndham paused, her face marble-still as if she were dumping out one set of responses to replace them with another. When she spoke, her voice was lower, steadier, but even that was forced. "I'll go to counseling then," she said. "I'll do whatever you want—just let me stay here."

So let her stay here. Let her just go to counseling. She's dying right now, for heaven's sake.

"I'll work hard, I swear," Wyndham was saying.

She was starting to cry, hard, dry sobs without tears. Even as Hale opened his mouth I put up my hand to him and leaned toward her.

"Honey, I know you're going to work hard, and I'm arranging for the very best people to work with you. They're at a place called Trinity House."

"It's here?" The hope in her eyes broke my heart.

"Near here," I said. "I'll be able to visit you as often as they'll let me."

I watched as the realization dawned on her, and the fear gathered on her face.

"You're sending me away?"

"No—don't put it like that! I'm getting you the best help money can buy. And I'm going to be there for you. Hale says this place is wonderful."

But Wyndham was shaking her head. "Why can't I just stay here and go to therapy? Why can't I be with Lindsay and the kids from church? That's all I need. Them and God and you."

I looked at Hale.

Your turn, my eyes said to him. *I can't go there.*

"Your Aunt Toni and the kids at church aren't therapists, Wyndham," he said. "You need trained people around you twenty-four hours a day."

"Why?"

Hale ran his fingers over the cross engraved into her arm. Wyndham pulled herself away, wrapping both arms around her torso and rocking back and forth.

"I'm sorry," she said. "I'm sorry. I know I'm just a huge burden to everybody."

"Wyndham, stop!" I said. "You are not a burden. I'm doing this for you because I love you. I want to get you through this."

"But you're saying I'm too much for you to handle."

"She *is* 'handling' you," Hale said. "The best way there is."

"I try not to be any trouble—"

"Wyndham."

She looked up at Hale, the muscles in her neck so tight I was sure her throat would snap.

"Your Aunt Toni has to think about Ben."

Wyndham's eyes snapped to me, so wild they were almost without expression. "You *are* mad at me about him, aren't you? I should never have told you!"

"No, Wyndham. This isn't your fault!"

"Then why am I the one who's being punished?"

It was a question I couldn't answer. I let all the lame responses I could think of die on my lips and shook my head.

"I'm sorry," I said.

Wyndham stared at me for a full thirty seconds before the fight drained out of her. Then she sat looking dully at the handle of Hale's coffee mug.

"When do I leave?"

"In about a week," I said. "That gives us time to get you ready. We can buy you some—"

"I'm ready now. You should just send me now."

"There are things we have to do."

Wyndham stood up. "Can I just go to bed? I'm really tired."

I looked at Hale for a cue, but he had his eyes closed.

"Sure," I said. "We can talk more tomorrow."

She shrugged and left.

A visible pall descended over the kitchen.

"Gee," I said to Hale. "That went well."

Hale folded his arms across his chest. "I don't think we could have expected much more."

"I just feel like I'm letting her down."

"She thinks you are—but don't let her take you with her. You're doing the right thing. She's going to get all of her confidence about this from you in the next week."

"Where is mine supposed to come from?" I said. "Right now I have about this much." I held my thumb and index finger a quarter-inch apart.

"God. At least, that's where I get mine." He raised an arm to reveal a dark spot the size of a dinner plate in the armpit of his T-shirt. "I was sweating bullets the whole time."

"Then I hope He tells me this is the right thing to do." I got up, paced toward the coffee pot, turned my back on it. "I'm having second thoughts. Did you see the way she looked when she walked out of here? I might as well have been sending her to Auschwitz as far as she was concerned."

The words hung in the air between us just long enough for both of us to register them. I was already headed for the doorway when Hale said, "Maybe you'd better go check on her."

He was behind me as I took the steps two at a time and banged on Wyndham's door.

"Wyndham, let me in," I said.

There was no answer. The knob didn't budge when I tried to turn it. Without a word I stepped out of the way, and Hale shoved his square self against the door. In a vignette frozen by horror realized, Hale and I stood in the doorway, and Wyndham looked up at us, bald guilt in her eyes, the razor poised over her wrist.

There was no longer any doubt in my mind.

Eight

WYNDHAM CRIED HERSELF TO SLEEP in my arms. Thankfully she was out of it before Reggie returned with Ben, who was asleep in *her* arms. By the time Reg got Ben tucked into his bed, Hale and I were finishing our debate in the hallway over whether to call the hospital and try to have Wyndham admitted, or deal with the situation ourselves.

"I'm afraid if I put her in Vanderbilt or something, she'll think I'm ready to wash my hands of her," I said. "She already feels rejected enough."

"If you're going to keep her here, it's going to mean a twenty-four-hour suicide watch until you can get her into Trinity," Hale said. "You can't do it all. I can do some but even at that—"

"Look, I can't ask you to do any more," I said. "You're not even related to her. Heck, most of the people who *are* related to her won't even help her."

"She's a sister. If you decide you want to try to keep her here until next week, I'll see if I can set up a schedule with some folks I know—and I'll put a call in over at Trinity and see if Betty Stires can place her sooner."

"I guess I can swing that, too."

Hale looked at me closely. "What do you mean, 'swing it'?"

"Pay people to watch her."

"No, these will be volunteers."

"I don't even know them!"

"It's what we do. We're a Christian community."

"But I don't belong to it—although I guess I could make a donation to the church. I'd have to. I couldn't sleep if I didn't."

That's about the point where Reggie joined us. "You never sleep anyway, honey," she said.

"For tonight, I'll take the first shift and you go in and try to rest some," Hale said to me. "I mean, if you're comfortable with me bein' here."

"Comfortable? Try to leave and I'll take your arm off."

Hale grinned, mouth square. "You sure keep your sense of humor, don't you?"

"What was humorous about that?"

"You have a sleepin' bag, honey?" Reggie said. "I'll bunk in there with the little Angel Boy, and that way you can get some decent sleep before you take over for Hale."

"Angel Boy? You're talking about *my* son?"

"Yes, bless his heart."

Even with all the bases covered, I slept very little. When I did drift off, I awoke with my jaws clenched so tightly my teeth were aching. I finally gave up around midnight and joined Hale in Wyndham's room. He was perched in the window seat, looking decidedly out of place among the satin envelope-pillows. I sat on the Oriental rug at his feet and leaned against the bed, digging my toes into the deep pile. Wyndham's sleep-breathing was audible behind me.

"I haven't thanked you for handling telling her," I said. "I would have really screwed it up."

I could see Hale's eyebrows lifting. "And I didn't? She came up here to slit her wrists!" He shook his head. "I think I was too hard on her."

"I don't know. If it had been me, I'd still be sitting down there beating around the bush. Besides—" I glanced up at Wyndham's sleeping form and lowered my voice. "She's sicker than I thought. I think this was going to happen sooner or later. You just got us there sooner."

"I hate it for her," he said. "The fact that we caught her is a God-thing, I think."

We sat in silence for a few minutes, listening to Wyndham breathe. I wondered how she could sleep with all that was doing battle inside her. It could only be an escape for her. I wished I could make one that easily.

"The only reason I haven't picked a church here is because I don't have the time to be on committees and all that," I said.

Hale looked at me curiously. "Neither does God, I suspect."

"I believe in God, though."

"You wouldn't be doing this for Wyndham if you didn't."

"You keep saying that, but don't give me too much credit. I'm not consciously asking God to show me what to do."

"You're doing what you're doing out of love."

"Am I? I feel like I'm sending Wyndham away so I don't have to deal with her."

"But you will have to deal with her—or she won't get better."

"And I can't deal with her here, or my son won't get better. As soon as she's gone, I can start working on him."

"Sounds like love to me," Hale said. "There's a lady at Trinity you might want to look up when you go over there. Her name's Dominica Marquez."

"Can she help me with Wyndham, you think?"

Hale nodded, slowly. "Yeah. I think you'll be surprised what she can do."

"I don't know if I can handle any more surprises."

Hale and I took turns sleeping during the night. Wyndham woke up only once, long enough to murmur that she was sorry she was doing this to me. That did nothing to assuage the guilt I was already feeling.

Reggie took over for me while Hale went off to gather the troops for the rest of the day and I got Ben to school. My son was in an unusually good mood—at least he didn't overturn his Fruit Loops or scream that he hated me before we got into the car.

"Did you have fun last night?" I asked him as we headed for Hillsboro.

"I like that Reggie lady," he said.

"She's pretty cool, huh?"

"She wasn't taking care of me."

I glanced in the rearview mirror. "What do you mean she wasn't taking care of you?"

"She said she wasn't taking care of me, she was just being my friend, so that was okay." He scowled. "I told her I don't like people taking care of me."

"*I* take care of you."

"No, you give me to other people to take care of me. I don't like that."

A switch went on in my head. "You mean like Aunt Bobbi?" I said.

Immediately, both hands went over his ears. "I don't want to talk about it!" His voice rose dangerously.

"Okay, Pal. Subject's closed. Done. Over."

He kept his hands plastered to the sides of his head, but he didn't say any more.

I waited until I'd gotten him out of the car in front of the school before I bent down and said to him, "I just want you to know that Wyndham is going to be moving out of our house in just a few days—after the weekend."

Ben's eyes narrowed. "How many wake-ups is that?"

I counted. "Six."

"No, that's too many."

"She isn't going to hurt you, Pal."

He wasn't buying it. He hitched his backpack up and turned and ran for the building. I just stood there, eyes burning.

"Dear God," I whispered. This time I added, "Tell me what in the Sam Hill to do."

When I got home, Reggie was gone and Hale was back. Wyndham was still asleep, and Hale was on the phone, adding a name to a list of four he'd already scrawled on a piece of my notepaper, engraved in gold letters, FROM THE DESK OF ANTONIA WELLS. When he hung up, he gave me a grin.

"You're set until eleven-thirty tonight, and then I'll be back. Oh—and Betty Stires says the sooner you can get the paperwork to her the faster she can expedite Wyndham's admission. Until then, I'll keep you staffed so Wyndham has somebody with her all the time."

"I owe you—in a major way," I said.

He waved me off with one of his big, squared-off hands. "You'll be okay until ten this morning? Sherry Gibbons will be here then."

"I can deal with Wyndham during the day."

"Don't you have to go to work?"

"Oh." I pressed my fingers to my eyelids, which were stinging from being open for too long at a stretch. "Yeah, I guess I do. If I still have a job."

"Reggie says you're pretty indispensable over there."

"Yeah." It was odd how, for a fleeting moment, that seemed utterly unimportant.

When Sherry Gibbons arrived, I made sure Wyndham looked okay with her and then went down to the study to call Jeffrey. Even as I was dialing his number, I knew I should have been calling Chris. But I still couldn't do it.

Get yourself totally together first, I told myself. *That's the only way to talk to Chris.*

So Jeffrey it was right now, and I knew I was going to have to take charge of the conversation. I was pretty sure even God didn't expect me to handle Jeffrey Faustman "with love."

"Good morning, stranger," Jeffrey said. His voice was cool. "Mind telling me what's going on?"

Actually I would mind, I thought. *I so do not want you in my personal business—especially* this *personal business.*

"I can't tell you how sorry I am that these unavoidable circumstances have arisen," I said.

"What unavoidable circumstances?"

"But I have everything under control now. In fact, I'll be in around one o'clock. Anything I should know about before then, in case I need to get my thoughts together?"

"I don't think so." The temperature had gone down several degrees. "Ginny seems to be doing very well, keeping things in order in your office."

You jerk, I thought. But I said, "She's a gem," though I didn't add that she was somewhere in the zircon category. "I'll let her know I'll be coming in."

"No need. I'll tell her. I'm having lunch with her shortly."

"How lovely." *I hope you both get acid reflux.*

But as I hung up, I couldn't hold onto a wish for heartburn, at least not for Jeffrey. After all, he was trying to run a business, and I wasn't exactly forthcoming with information to explain my mysterious absences. Ginny was another story, the little opportunist.

But even harboring hope for indigestion for her wasn't as delicious as it had been two weeks ago. If only Ginny's licking her chops over my job was all I had to worry about.

I was in a suit and panty hose by twelve-thirty and welcoming the next shift on the Wyndham watch at 12:50, a pudgy little woman named Bunny who walked like a rugby player. I figured she could handle Wyndham, and I actually had my foot out the door when Hale called.

"Betty Stires says that if you can get the guardianship papers faxed to her by 5 P.M. today, you can bring Wyndham on Thursday. How perfect is that?"

"You must have some kind of pull out there."

"You want to go see Trinity tomorrow?" he said. "I'll drive you if you want. It might not be a bad idea for you to visit the place before you take Wyndham there."

"You're probably right. She might feel less like I was dumping her off if I actually bothered to go check it out. What time?"

We set it up for one o'clock, and then I hurried off to Faustman. I got there before Jeffrey and Ginny were back from lunch, and it looked like Ginny did have everything in order. I was glancing over the neatly fanned files on my desk with the typed pink phone messages clipped to each one when Reggie came in. She'd been away from her desk when I passed through the reception area, but she must have smelled me in the building because she was carrying a cup of chicken-and-dumpling soup, which she tucked into my hand.

"I know you haven't eaten all day," she said. She groaned as she sank into one of my client chairs and put a hand to her forehead. Her nails were magenta today, and the Power Puff Girls were gone. "Honey, you have got one hard floor. My backside is killin' me. Tonight I'm bringin' a cot."

I looked up from the dumplings. "Tonight?"

"Somebody's got to watch little Angel Boy while you watch Wyndham, and so far I'm his favorite—or didn't he tell you?"

Reggie's eyes were dancing. I couldn't help grinning at her.

"You and Hale. You're the only reason I still find it possible to smile at this point."

"Honey, I think you're amazing." She cocked an eyebrow at me. "Maybe a little too amazing."

"What does that mean?"

"Means I'm waiting for you to start running around tearin' your hair out. That's what I'd be doin'."

I set the half-empty mug on the desk. "I had my little breakdown Sunday night. What good would it do to keep that up? Besides, it's coming together. Wyndham's getting into Trinity Thursday. Once she's gone I can convince Ben that all the bad guys are now locked up, and we can get on with our lives."

The phone rang, and Reggie reached for it, but I shook my head and picked it up myself.

"Speaking of getting on with my life," I said, hand over the mouthpiece. I uncovered it and put on my professional voice. "This is Toni Wells."

"Oh," said a male voice on the other end. "It is?"

"Ye-es," I said, patiently. "May I help you?"

"Well, I don't know. Your assistant told me you had left town for the rest of the week and wouldn't be able to get back to me."

"I'm sorry. My assistant must have gotten some mistaken information. Who am I speaking to?"

"This is Charles R. Marshall."

He said it as if the initial alone should have brought me to attention, but the name meant nothing to me. I flipped through the files on the desk but there was no "Charles R. Marshall" typed on a tab. I scribbled the name on a pad and shoved it toward Reggie, but she shook her head and hurried out. I whipped the chair toward my computer and typed in his name. Through it all, he remained silent on the line.

"You still with me, Mr. Marshall?" I said.

"Yes, but I'm beginning to wonder why. You were recommended to me by one of your clients who thinks you hung the financial moon, but so far I'm not impressed."

How would you not be impressed? I wanted to say to him. *We've only been on the phone for twenty seconds!*

"Have we let you down in some way, Mr. Marshall?" I was coming up with no *Marshall, Charles R.* on the screen. Reggie returned, a blank look on her face.

"Nothing in my files," she whispered. "Let me check another place."

She hurried out again. Charles R. Marshall cleared his throat gruffly.

"Do you normally not return phone calls?" he said.

My brain was so fried, I couldn't untangle that sentence enough to know whether to say yes or no.

"Have I not returned a call from you, sir?" I said.

"Try five of them. And don't tell me you didn't get the messages because your assistant assured me she put them right into your hand. She was actually rather appalled that you left town without getting back to me, and she said if I called today she could probably help me herself."

I bet she did, I thought.

"There's obviously a problem in our communication system here, Mr. Marshall," I said smoothly. "I'm going to have to remedy that, but in the meantime, please accept my apology. What can I do for you?"

"I don't know now. You haven't exactly instilled confidence in me."

"Then it sounds like we need to meet face-to-face so I can fix that. Would you like to come in to the office? What's convenient for you?"

I yanked open my bag and pawed for my Day-Timer.

"Tomorrow afternoon," he said. "Three o'clock."

I was still groping around in the depths of my bag but I wasn't coming up with my date book. "Tomorrow at three," I said, pretending to check my schedule. "Perfect."

"And your office is where in the building?"

"I'll be waiting for you at the reception desk."

· That seemed to settle his neck hairs down a little. He agreed, gruffly, and hung up. I turned my bag upside down on my desk and was tearing through every item of its contents for the Day-Timer when Reggie blew in, waving something printed off the Internet.

"I looked in Jeffrey's 'To Pursue' file," she said. "Charles R. Marshall—entrepreneur—independent music videos. There's a note here, says, 'Court him.'" She wrinkled her nose. "Jeffrey wants to date this man?"

"No, that means Jeffrey planned to hunt him down and do whatever it took to get his business—wine him and dine him and all that."

"I know. It's just the thought of Jeffrey courting *anybody* makes me want to lose my lunch. Speaking of lunch—did you finish that soup, honey?"

"Oh, man!" I'd found my Day-Timer.

"What? Did you spill it?"

"No, I told Marshall I'd meet him at three tomorrow and I'm going to Trinity with Hale at one." I reached for the phone, and then I sat back.

"What?" Reggie said.

"It isn't going to look good if I reschedule. He already thinks I'm a flake." I glared toward Ginny's empty office. "Two bits she was setting this up so she could take care of the client herself. She never gave me any of his phone messages."

"You oughta tell Jeffrey."

"Right, and get a lecture on how if I had *been* here that wouldn't have happened. I'll just be back by three o'clock, that's all. I'm only going to look the place over. If I leave there by two-thirty I'll be back in plenty of time. I'll ask Yancy Bancroft to take Ben to soccer. Just don't let Ginny get ahold of Charles R. Marshall if he gets here before I do."

"You sure you don't just want to call him and make it three-thirty?"

I shook my head. "I already feel like Sid and Bobbi are running my personal life. I've got to try to keep them out of my job."

I leaned back in the chair and closed my eyes, which felt like they were being marinated in hot sauce.

"You got any Visine or anything?" I said.

"What you need is a good night's sleep."

"Soon. After Thursday, this is all going to be almost over."

Nine

I GOT ON THE PHONE TO Faith Anne Newlin to make sure she could have the guardianship papers ready to fax to Trinity House by five. She was still upbeat in that adolescent way she had, but there was something guarded about her voice when she said, "I'm almost positive I can make that happen. I'm waiting for one more phone call."

"From who?" I said. "I thought this was a slam dunk."

"From your mother." Faith Anne seemed to be measuring her words by the teaspoonful. "She wanted to try to talk to Roberta before she gave the final okay."

"Doesn't my mother have guardianship at this point?"

"She does, but she seemed bent on consulting the biological mother before she signed it away. I wouldn't worry about it," Faith Anne added hurriedly. "The FBI isn't allowing anyone access to your sister until she's a little more cooperative."

"Unbelievable," I said. "No, I believe it. There's very little I *wouldn't* believe at this point."

Faith Anne purred sympathetically and promised to call me the minute Mama got back to her. I told her Mama was lucky it wasn't me she was going to be talking to.

When I hung up I reached for the printout on Charles R. Marshall, but the words only screamed out Mama's name, in vain, as it were. I'd given Reggie what I thought was a plausible explanation for Mama's attachment to Bobbi, but I wasn't satisfied with it. My mother might be disillusioned, but she wasn't a complete idiot by any means. She'd always been sharp enough to catch me at every sly trick I'd tried to get by with as a kid.

But that was where I always got hung up. Bobbi had been just as determined to have her own way as I was, she just didn't have to sneak because Mama explained it all away. Mama had even stood up

130

to Daddy on her behalf, which was something none of us did, not even me.

I let the Marshall papers drop to the desktop and leaned back in my leather chair. If I could just close my eyes for a few minutes, I might be able to concentrate.

It wasn't Charles R. Marshall's voice that formed in my head, though. It was Daddy's, barking at Mama in the hallway outside my bedroom door where Mama had dragged him after he'd exploded outside Bobbi's and sent the girl into hysterics. I was thirteen. Bobbi was fifteen.

"I am *not* going to let this slide, Eileen," he said, loud enough to be heard over Bobbi's sobs.

"Let what slide?"

Mama was talking through gritted teeth, the way she talked to me in clothing stores when I was arguing for tighter jeans. A Southern lady did not yell at her children. Nor did she talk back to her husband, a fact that sent me scurrying to my door so I could press my ear against it. I didn't want to miss a word, especially if Bobbi was finally going to get what was coming to her. I was clueless as to what she'd actually done, but as far as I was concerned, she deserved punishment just to make up for all the times she'd gotten off scot-free.

"There is no excuse this time!" Daddy shouted. "No psychiatrist, no physician, no blaming it on Toni's influence."

I grinned into my doorknob.

"All right, then, I'll speak to her," Mama said, teeth still clenched.

"No! *I* will speak to her. I'll do more than speak. I'm going to slap some sense into her."

"Do you want to drive her straight into a mental institution?"

"If they'll set her straight, yes! I've had it with her crying and her simpering and her running behind your skirts. I've had it since she was a baby. Now I'm going to do something about it!"

"No," Mama said.

No? I thought. *Did you just tell him no?*

It was all I could do not to open the door at least a crack so I could catch this action. It promised to be something to see.

"You have never shown her the love she's entitled to," Mama said. "You have always pushed her away."

"God's teeth!" Daddy roared.

I remembered him thundering down the stairs and slamming out the front door. Mama didn't go after him. She headed straight for Bobbi's room. I sagged back to my bed, disappointed. I'd really hoped for once that Daddy *would* take off his belt.

"Oh, sorry."

It was a new voice in the milieu, and it took my eyes springing open before I realized it was Ginny, standing in my doorway.

"I'll come back later," she said. "I didn't know you were taking a nap."

"I wasn't taking a nap." I picked up the printout. "I was contemplating how I am going to make amends with Charles R. Marshall tomorrow."

Ginny's already Gothic-white face paled. "Maybe I could—" she started to say.

But I waved her off. "I've got it handled," I said.

She didn't move, as if she were expecting a tirade that would burn her skin. But I just didn't have the energy. Besides, the phone rang. Ginny dove for it, but I put my hand over the receiver and motioned for her to leave.

"Close the door behind you," I said.

I waited to hear her pad across the carpet to her desk, but there wasn't a sound. Ten to one she was listening at the door. You did that when you were desperate for information.

It was Faith Anne on the line. She cut right to the chase: Mama had signed the papers.

"She just had to wag me around some first," I said.

"It's a pretty hard wag," Faith Anne said. "She's only giving you temporary guardianship. Six weeks, or until Roberta is released. She says she can't 'betray' her daughter any more than that."

"Excuse me while I throw up," I said. "Fax those babies to Trinity. I want my niece as far away from those psychos as I can get her."

~∰◔

Ridgetop was only about twenty miles from Nashville, and gave
Hale and me a drive full of rolling hills and gracious plantation
houses and fruit trees in early bloom. Mid-April was showing off for
us, Hale told me.

Actually, I only noticed after he mentioned it. I was noticing
very little that didn't directly relate to my family craziness. But when
he pointed it out, I did see that the cherry trees were bending over
with clumps of blossoms, and that every self-respecting garden was
alive with tulips, waving yellow and purple flower-hands as we drove
past in his Jeep Wrangler. The plastic windows rattled in the April
breeze.

"Sorry about the noise," he shouted to me.

"What?" I shouted back, and then I shook my head. "Don't
worry about it. This car fits you."

Hale grinned. "No frills—and you can always hear it coming."

"And square," I said. "I mean, you know, not like '*a* square'—
just very much 'there.'"

"Nah, you were right the first time. I *am* a square. But don't tell
the kids. They've somehow come up with this idea that I'm cool."

"Wyndham's convinced. She thinks you walk on water."

"Nuh-unh."

"She asked me again this morning why *you* couldn't just counsel
her."

The ponytail swayed back and forth across his shoulders. "I
haven't got 24/7 to devote to her for the next however long."

"My mother's giving me six weeks. You really think she's going to
need more than that?"

He shot me a look. "Look what we've got going right now—
somebody at her elbow 24/7. And does she look like she's ready to
snap out of it anytime soon?"

I shook my head grimly. I'd taken my shift from midnight to 4
A.M., and during most of that Wyndham had been crying in dry
sobs and telling me she hated herself. The grade of sandpaper lining
my eyelids was getting coarser.

"I'm not going to drop her, though," Hale said. "How fast she gets healed is going to depend on how much support she gets. I'll be over there to see her at least once a week."

"Where did you come from, anyway?" I said.

Not long after that, he pulled the Jeep abruptly onto a dirt road which led through a tunnel of trees and over a hill just sprouting its first wildflowers like an adolescent chin. Over the other side was a stone arch, and swinging from it was a simple sign that read Trinity House.

The buildings that came into view as we passed under the arch didn't look much different from the pictures in the brochure, but the starkness I'd seen there didn't exist "in the flesh." Even before I unzipped the window, I could sense a welcoming quiet a camera couldn't capture.

Hale turned off the ignition and leaned back until the seat creaked. "I think they should've called it Tranquility Base. That's what comes to me every time I come here."

I suspected from the sudden smoothness in his face that he came here more often than he had let on.

It was the equivalent of a two-city-block walk from the parking lot to the main building's entrance, which Hale said was done by design to preserve the peacefulness. It gave me a chance to notice what I'd picked up on in the photos, that though the grounds were beautiful, they were only landscaped in the most general sense. Belle Meade's manicured flower beds and meticulously trimmed holly hedges were missing, and in their place were sycamore trees with solitary swings hanging from their branches and benches ringing their trunks. A stand of birch trees with ferns about their feet was left to its own natural, bushy beauty, and ivy ran wild up the sides of the stone building. Kevin Pollert's gardener would be reaching for his Valium if he saw this. It didn't look unkempt, merely untamed. There was probably something symbolic in that, but I didn't try to figure it out. What I did need to figure out was why my palms were sweating.

I wiped them furtively on the back of my skirt while Hale introduced us to the elfin receptionist, who offered us coffee before she went off to find Betty Stires. I passed up the caffeine and watched Hale dump three packets of sugar into his cup.

"You aren't a health freak, are you?" I said as he plowed a spoon through it.

"Nope. Too bad they don't have any half-and-half."

"This is making me nauseous. What is wrong with me? You'd think I was the one who was about to be locked up in here."

Hale stopped stirring to look at me. "Is that the way you feel— like you're locking Wyndham up?"

"Aren't I? I mean, I'm not exactly giving her a choice."

"Yeah, but I think it's more like you're setting her free."

I shrugged. "I wish I felt that way."

The sound of heels clicking on Mexican tile diverted us both to the receptionist returning with a tall woman in turquoise raw silk. I was reassured that this was nothing like a state psychiatric hospital. No wonder it cost $100 a day.

"I'm Betty Stires," the woman said, graciously extending her hand to me. Her fingers were warm around mine, and she didn't respond to the fact that my palms were once again oozing sweat. Very blue eyes crinkled shut as she smiled. "You're Toni Wells, I assume. Welcome to Trinity House."

I was glad she turned at once to Hale, because I couldn't think of a thing to say. What was *wrong* with me? I didn't freak out like this normally.

But, of course, nothing about this was normal. I was checking out a residential mental health facility for my niece who was suicidal because my sister had allowed her to be photographed nude by her father—

"Why don't I start by showing you around," Betty was saying as I jerked myself back to her. "That way we can talk as we go."

I was grateful. I couldn't imagine trying to sit in a chair and focus without fidgeting myself into a froth. I was also glad that Hale already knew her and could keep the conversation going, though I was fast coming to the conclusion that Hale could carry on a dialogue with a gas pump. I needed a few minutes to repackage all this unexpected emotional stuff that was suddenly showing up.

Pearl-and-turquoise earrings bobbing gracefully from her lobes, Betty led us at a fast clip through the main building, which consisted of a number of airy rooms with large windows, any one of which looked more inviting than the living room at Kevin Pollert's. His decorator would probably have shuddered, too, right along with the gardener, and written the decor off as dismally minimalist. At least the clean lines and uncluttered tabletops didn't add to my rattled mental state. Betty explained that Wyndham would attend her group therapy sessions there, and that her individual tutoring would take place there as well. Her schooling, she told us, would be secondary to her healing. Education she could catch up on; her mental and emotional state had to be dealt with right away.

We left the main building, Hale and Betty still chattering and me nodding my head as if I were actually following what they were saying, and crossed to what looked like a cloister. A two-story U-shaped building created a courtyard bordered by covered walkways. Vines sheltered the court, some of them already bearing thick bunches of wisteria blossoms that hung like grapes over the benches and ponds. Tufts of wild strawberries worked their way up between the stones.

"This is the residential section," Betty was saying. "The living quarters are on the second floor, and the common areas and healing rooms are on the first. Wyndham will, of course, have a great deal of individual therapy in the healing rooms—our staff-to-patient ratio is excellent. Most of the rooms are in use right now, but I can give you a peek at one, and then we'll stick our heads into Wyndham's room."

"Did you get the fax from my attorney yesterday?" I said.

"Yes." Betty's smile was patient. "We can look at all of that back in my office."

"Relax," Hale whispered to me as Betty led the way under the arched walkway to our right. "Wyndham's in, or she wouldn't be doing all this."

"I *am* relaxed," I lied.

I could feel my heart beating up into my throat. I swiped my hands across the back of my skirt again and straightened my shoulders.

Don't be an idiot, I told myself. *This woman's going to think you're the one she's booking.*

After looking in on a low-ceilinged meeting room that opened out onto a stone patio and a gentle slope of Japanese cherry trees, we went up a set of wide stone steps to an inner hallway where the polished oak floor was crisscrossed with light from beneath the doors of the rooms on either side of it.

Betty opened one near the end, overlooking the courtyard below. Just as the brochure had shown, it was small and white and had a rounded window through which sunlight poured as if on demand. It seemed less cell-like than in the picture as I stood there, imagining Wyndham moving in with her starched blouses and her nail polish. My heartbeat was up around my neck. It was a far cry from the room she was sleeping in right now, and it bore no resemblance to the room Bobbi had decorated for her.

She was going to hate me.

"Any questions yet?"

I looked at Betty, who appeared to have been watching me for a good minute. I could feel my face going hot.

"You okay, Toni?" Hale said.

"Who is under these circumstances?" Betty said. "Why don't we go down to my office and look over that paperwork?"

I breathed. That I could do.

This time, Betty fell into step beside me, leaving Hale to make his way behind us.

"I want to reassure you that we won't just leave her in that room by herself the first night," she said. "Down here we have our newcomers' room where she'll sleep for probably the first three or four nights, or until we feel like she's relatively comfortable."

She pushed open a door and nodded for me to peek in. There were two beds there, each equipped with a down comforter about five inches thick and a pile of pillows. Between them was a padded rocking chair.

"There will be someone observing her all night," Betty whispered, as if Wyndham were at that moment ensconced in down. I felt a little better, though not much.

On our way back to the main building, Betty stayed at my elbow, pointing out the dining area, the movie room, which rivaled any home theatre I'd been privy to, and the wing that housed the healing rooms.

"I'll have Wyndham's therapist look in on us before you go," Betty said. "I know you'll want to meet her." She turned and winked at Hale. "I think you'll like my choice."

"Dominica?" Hale said.

"Yes."

"Thanks be to God. You rock, Betty."

Betty looked at me, face blank. "I rock. First time I've ever been told that."

I felt myself relax by a degree. Betty was professional, but she was warm, she didn't gush, she seemed real. Normal. I wanted normal.

Guardianship papers weren't my usual gig, but I felt somewhat more centered shuffling them around back in Betty's office than I had hearing about the facility's expertise in sexual abuse and post-traumatic stress disorder. I zinged through the Trinity House contract as well and didn't hesitate to sign it.

As soon as I was finished, I capped my pen and reached for my bag.

There was a tap on the door, and a head poked in. Clear gray eyes in a face the color of café au lait scanned the room and settled their gaze at once on me. I couldn't pull my own eyes away, and so I sat blinking and feeling transparent.

"Dominica—come in," Betty said. She swept a hand toward me. "This is Toni Wells, Wyndham Kerrington's aunt. Toni, Dominica Marquez."

There was no rustling of silk as the rounded woman left the doorway and came toward me, hand outstretched. She was wearing a white muslin top that came down over the knees of a pair of chinos, and she moved with her neck straight and her head high, as if she were five-ten rather than the barely-five-foot she was stretched to. The outfit, the bearing, the shiny waves of short, dark hair brushed elegantly back from her face gave her a regal look, something along the lines of *The Little King* comic strip. I would have been amused if she hadn't held my gaze the way she did. She left me little choice—if I didn't continue to maintain eye contact, I was going to be moved to curtsy.

"Toni, I've been anxious to meet you," she said, though it struck me that Dominica Marquez was probably seldom anxious about anything.

She looked at Hale with a grin but said to Betty, "Is there time for us to talk?"

"We're finished here," Betty said. "She's all yours."

"Why don't you come with me?" Dominica said, turning those eyes back to mine.

Hale got up, but Dominica gave him a pat on the chest, which was approximately as high as she could reach.

"Not you, bud," she said.

"Hale's going to be involved," I said.

"Yeah, but I already know more about him than I actually want to." Dominica wrinkled her nose at him, and he grinned.

He looked more square than ever next to her roundness, but not nearly as big as he had before she came in. There was a power about her that I found…intimidating. It made me bristle.

I made a point of glancing at my watch several times as I followed her back to the cloister-building and into a cool, dark hallway. It was already 1:45. Visions of Charles R. Marshall pacing in front of Reggie's desk came to mind.

"I really need to leave by 2:15," I said as she unlocked the door to a corner room.

"Sure. Come on in."

She swung open the door and leaned against it as I passed her to go inside. The room was bathed in light and dotted with floor cushions that appeared to have come from various points on the globe.

"Pull up a pillow," she said, closing the door behind me.

I glanced back at it and wondered crazily if it locked from the outside.

Then I smacked myself mentally and dropped onto the first cushion I came to—a red affair reminiscent of the Ming dynasty—and tried to look nonchalant as I crossed and recrossed my legs in an effort to keep my thighs inside my skirt. A run popped out on one knee and made its way up toward my hemline.

"Dang it," I muttered.

Dominica sat on a cushion directly across from me. "That's why I never wear panty hose. Course, in my line of work, I don't have to. What do you do, Toni?"

I was more than happy to fill her in, just so she would know my clumsiness was not an indication of my overall ineptness at life. She nodded appreciatively, but I didn't think she was impressed. She turned at once to a file folder on a low, black-lacquered table near her elbow.

"I've been looking over Betty's notes on Wyndham," she said. "I'll be doing some assessment of her, spend several sessions getting to know her before we really begin our journey, but I wanted to give you an idea of what our approach will be. Then you can ask any questions you have."

"Good." I tried to arrange myself a little more professionally on the pillow. The run crept up my thigh.

"Here's the deal," she said. "We're all about God here. The real-ness of God and a personal connection with God will be a part of everything that happens in this room."

She stopped and looked at me, the gray eyes expectant, as if I might possibly stand up and leave. I wasn't sure I would ever be able to stand up. My legs were already falling asleep in the position I was sitting in.

"I figured that," I said. "This *is* a Christian facility—and any-thing church-related is the only thing that seems to be keeping Wyndham from going off the deep end at this point. It was a church youth group that gave her the guts to go to the police to begin with."

"We can thank God for that," Dominica said. "But this isn't one big youth rally here. This is going to be work—the hardest kind of work."

"I figured that, too," I said.

She went on as if I hadn't answered. "Let me clarify what that means. Our belief is that the Father's idea of Wyndham, before she was born, was who He intended for her to be. God doesn't create garbage."

I thought of Sid and stifled a grunt.

"The minute she hit oxygen, like all of us, the coping with a world that has basically gone to the dogs started. She did whatever she had to do to get by, the result being a rather false self. We all have one." Dominica tapped the folder with a set of stout brown fingers. "In her case, there was more than the usual amount of coping going on. Incest tends to make a child more false than real. Like most of us, she hates her own phoniness, but she hates it so much she wants to kill it."

I couldn't keep myself from pulling back, and I knew I was blinking my eyes as if someone had just thrown dirt in them. Could this woman be any more blunt?

"Until she realizes God loves her and wants her to know Him by knowing Jesus Christ," Dominica went on, "and until she has a genuine shift and knows that that's the way she's going to realize and be who God created her to be, she's going to continue to think she wants to die. The self-hatred, the shame, the guilt—it's all too much for her. But she can be healed, because we've got all the time in the world to help her get to know a compassionate Christ. In the meantime, it will be the job of everyone here to keep her from taking her own life. My part will be to get her to her true self, her soul, where Christ is waiting for her. Otherwise, we've just kept her alive, ignoring the fact that she still feels sinful and helpless and worthless and can't ever express the rage that's tearing her apart inside. She could leave here and go on to be easy prey to every abusive man who comes along—or she could become a prostitute, promiscuous at the least. I have to lead her into Christ's arms so that she can learn that those things aren't who she is. God's child is who she is. It's going to scare her spitless, and she's going to have to believe that God is in every minute of it or she won't make it."

Again she stopped and looked at me, this time almost accusingly.

What? I wanted to shout at her. Instead I said evenly, "I have no problem with that."

"That's not enough."

"Excuse me?" I knew I was gaping at her, and I hoped she found me as rude as I found her.

Dominica leaned toward me, both hands on the floor between

the legs that were now stretched out into a V. "It isn't enough for you to merely acquiesce. You have to either be in the trenches with us, or I'm going to ask you not to have contact with her for a while."

"What do you want me to do? I'm not going to come in here shouting 'Praise the Lord' every ten seconds, if that's what you mean by being in the trenches."

"No, that's not what I mean." There was a trace of a Hispanic accent when she spoke in clipped terms the way she was now, almost as if she were snapping at me.

"Then what *do* you mean?" I snapped back.

"You won't hear 'praise the Lord' coming out of me every other word, either. Nothing wrong with it—I just reverence God differently." She leaned in a little further, so that I could see the two fine lines that furrowed into her forehead just between her eyebrows. "I'm talking about you *knowing*, right in here—" she pushed her fist against her chest—"that God can turn this whole thing around, and He will if she'll have the faith and do the work He's asking her to do. You have to know it—not just believe it, not just say it—you have to know it like you know your own name. And you have to be living your own life like that. If you want, I can work with you, too."

"Me?"

"No extra charge."

Her eyes were twinkling. I knew mine weren't. I would rather have been duking it out with Jeffrey Faustman at that point than dealing with her insinuations.

"I've got my faith under control," I said, voice stiff. "And I have my son to deal with, too, for a while, anyway."

It was Dominica's turn to blink. "Your son?" She picked up the file and glanced through it.

"He was photographed by Wyndham's father, as well. That's something you need to know, because Wyndham was involved. I know she has a lot of guilt about it."

To my surprise, Dominica's eyes softened as she looked at me again. "I'm sorry. You've got a double whammy coming at you. Who's your boy's therapist?"

"He doesn't have one."

"Why not?"

The eyes were immediately snapping again.

"Because as soon as I get Wyndham out of the house and convince him that he never has to see Sid again, I think he's—"

"Toni, what do you think happened when this sociopathic piece of slime took your son's picture?" She was so close to me now, I could feel the warmth of her breath on my face.

The back of my neck was bristling so hard by this time, I put my hand up to it. "I try not to go there. I haven't seen the pictures."

"I'm talking about in here," Dominica said, tapping her forehead. "In his little mind, and in his little soul. He was molested, Toni, and probably in more ways than one. There's no way around it."

"I don't know that Sid ever touched him. He was doing it for the money."

"There are a thousand ways to make a buck that are a whole lot easier than what he was into. No porno 'artist' just does it for the money. He does it because he's a screwed-up, twisted individual."

"I don't know that he ever touched Ben," I said again. I was wrestling myself up onto my knees.

"He didn't have to for it to be considered molestation. But chances are, he did touch him—I'm sorry, the odds are against Ben on this one. Either way, he's been bruised, right down to his core. You can't fix that by yourself."

By now I was on my feet. I froze there, staring down at her. She was no longer accusing me, nor was she examining my spiritual records. The eyes that held mine as she stood to face me were two round pools of concern.

"Your brother-in-law isn't a businessman, Toni." Her voice was husky and thick. "He's a child molester, and your child is one of his victims. He's going to need help. A lot of help."

Ten

SOMEHOW I GOT OUT OF Dominica's healing room. I don't even remember saying good-bye, and I doubt that I did. I think her last words to me were, "Get your son into therapy as soon as you can," but I couldn't swear to it in a court of law. Every part of me was numb, my brain most of all.

I later recalled her saying, "You and your family may never fully recover unless you all have the opportunity to discuss the effects of what happened with a qualified professional, preferably a Christian. Be there for your boy—don't make him go through this alone."

But at the time, I moved out of there in a state something like that of a leg that has fallen asleep. Even the words that moaned in my head did so tonelessly: *He was molested. Ben was molested. It isn't just a matter of semantics. My son—my baby—was molested.*

Hale was having another cup of coffee in the lobby. I didn't even speak to him; I just pointed toward the parking lot. I was vaguely aware of him touching my elbow—probably because I was about to miss the doorway—and guiding me silently to the Jeep. By the time we got there, the numbness was beginning to wear off, and the pins and needles of reality were stinging me everywhere.

"I'm not going to ask if you're okay," Hale said as he started the ignition. "I can see you're not. Is there anything I can do?"

"Not unless you can erase the last ten minutes," I said.

"Dominica a little hard on you?"

"Why didn't anybody tell me straight out that Ben was probably *physically* molested by that snake? Why didn't *you* tell me?"

Hale didn't take his eyes off the windshield, but I could see them sagging at the corners.

"Just drive this thing straight to Richmond," I said. "He touched my child, and I'm going to hurt him. I'll rip off his—!"

I held out a claw toward Hale, who didn't look.

"I'm so sorry," he said.

"Not half as sorry as he's going to be when I get ahold of him. I'm getting a flight up there tonight."

"You're serious." Hale's square fingers were gripping the steering wheel like steel bands.

"You going to try and stop me?"

"Me and the FBI. Ben and Wyndham don't need you in jail, too."

"Then what do you expect me to do?" I could hear my voice rising in pitch, in volume, in hysteria. I actually clawed at my throat.

"Do what you're already doing," Hale said.

"But now I know—"

"What do you know that you didn't know before?"

"That chances are my little boy was *touched* by that freak. This could scar him for life. He's already done a complete transformation from the child I was raising."

"You didn't put that together before?"

"I don't know anything about this stuff! Why would I put that together?"

Hale took his eyes off the windshield long enough to give me a penetrating look. "Because you didn't want to," he said.

It took me a second to spit out a reply. "Are you saying I was in denial?"

"Of course you were."

"What is this—Slap Toni in the Face Day?"

"You're ready. Look at you—you're about to start chewing my upholstery. You're ready to know it all and you're ready to fight. You don't want us pussyfooting around you."

I swore. Only later did I wonder if Hale had been offended. He didn't show it at the time. He just said, "You want to pull in somewhere—get some lunch and talk?"

"I couldn't eat if you shoved it down my throat," I said.

"Something to drink?"

I looked at my watch and swore again. It was 2:45. "I've got to get to the office," I said. "I have a client coming in."

"Right now? You think you're up for that?"

"No! The only thing I'm up for is tearing out Sidney Vyne's lar-
ynx with my teeth—just for starters."

I caught Hale glancing anxiously at my hands, which were shaking in my lap. I brought them up to my jaws and pressed against
the throbbing. I wasn't going to have any tooth enamel left at this
rate.

"Can you call Reggie and cancel your appointment?" Hale said.

"The guy's probably on his way there by now. Can you just drop
me at the office? Reggie'll take me home later…or I'll grab a cab."

"I can wait for you—"

"No! I can cope, okay? I'm not falling apart!"

"I know you aren't—but it's okay if you do."

"Oh, uh-huh. And then who's going to deal with all this? Take
the Broadway Exit—it's over in Westend."

Hale stopped trying to console me and merely followed the
directions I barked out at him. Once again, I doubt whether I said
good-bye to him, although I do recall his saying, "I'm praying,
Toni. Believe me, I'm praying." I had the door swinging open
before he brought the Jeep to a halt in front of Faustman, and I was
inside the building, I'm sure, before he could even get it into first
gear.

I was already talking as I charged into the reception area.
"Reggie, see if you can get me a flight out of here tonight—to
Richmond."

"Richmond?"

"That—that *thing* touched my child, and I am going to go up
there and rip him a new—"

"Toni—honey, let me work on that flight for you while you
attend to Mr.—"

I followed her eyes behind me. A guy of about thirty with a thick
neck and a magenta face stood with his arms folded across his chest
like a high school dean of boys.

"Charles R. Marshall," Reggie said faintly.

There was no need to tell me that, really. The man was alternating
between glaring at me and pointedly looking at his watch. The grandfather clock behind him was just finishing its third chime. I sucked in

about a liter of air. If I could just get out one civil sentence...

"I'm sorry, Mr. Marshall," I said. "Something has come up. When can we reschedule our meeting?"

"We can't," he said.

I pressed my fingers to my temples, and I could feel myself wincing. "What?" I said.

"It's either right now, or I take my business someplace else."

"Then do it. Go someplace else. I really don't have the time."

I waited for him to stomp out the door. I needed for him to, before he morphed into Sid Vyne before my eyes and I went after the poor man with my fingernails.

But he only narrowed his eyes at me, his face growing redder and his neck growing thicker.

"Excuse me?" he said.

"I said—"

"I heard what you said—and your boss is going to hear what you said!" He turned to Reggie, who was uncharacteristically silent behind me. "Get your manager out here."

"Mr. Faustman is in a meeting—"

"Get him out here or I'm gonna bust his door down! I'm not gonna stand here and be treated like—"

"So don't stand there!" I said. "Take your business someplace else—go!"

"Not before I register a complaint."

"Oh, for heaven's sake, grow *up!* You think you have problems, my friend? Then take them to somebody who gives a hang, okay, because I *so* do not. I just found out my five-year-old son has very probably been molested by my own brother-in-law—*after* being pornographically photographed by that same sick, twisted animal—and I'm looking at a lawsuit, therapy, and a child who may never be the same. So I do *not* have time for you or your whining or your bloated ego. So take it—"

"Mr. Marshall," said a voice behind me. "Jeffrey Faustman. How are you, sir?"

Jeffrey skirted me smoothly, his hand extended to Charles R., who did not extend his in return.

"I'm a little upset at the moment," Marshall said, shoulders shifting.

"I can certainly understand that, sir. It looks as if we have a situation here that has nothing to do with you. Unfortunately, you've borne the brunt of it. Would you like to step into my office and we'll see if we can't take care of you?"

Marshall barely looked at him. He was still drilling his beady little eyes into me, reminding me more of a boar by the second. I was breathing hard and drilling back, ready to go after him again if he or Jeffrey gave me the slightest provocation. I felt Reggie's hand on my arm, but I shook it away.

"I want an apology first," Marshall said.

"I'm sure Ms. Wells will be forthcoming with one." Jeffrey's voice was as thick as peanut butter.

"So let's hear it," Marshall said to me. "I'm a busy man. I don't have time to be jerked around."

"Then go someplace where they'll put up with you," I said.

I yanked myself away from Reggie's second attempt to restrain me and stormed past both men and into my outer office. Ginny was poised inside the door, and she jumped back like a startled cat as I threw it open and crossed to my own office, where I slammed the door so hard that my MBA diploma fell off the wall and landed on the carpet with a thud. I kicked it across the room and stood staring at the shards of glass that dropped in slow motion from the frame.

I don't know how long I stood there, or when Ginny inched the door open and said, "Mr. Faustman would like to see you in his office."

"Get out," I said.

"I'm just telling you—"

"And I'm just telling *you. Get out.*"

It could only have been a few moments later when Reggie came in. I realized then I still had my purse over my shoulder and my jacket on, which was fine, because I was on the way out.

"Did you get me a flight?" I said.

"I did not."

"Fine. I'll get one myself."

I started for the door but she didn't budge from in front of it. Though her face was pale, even under the makeup, the eyes weren't moving and neither was the body.

"What do you think you're going to do up in Richmond, honey?" she said.

"I can't let him get away with this!" My voice cracked, taken over finally by tears. "I have to let him know he's not going to get away with this!"

"You can do that. But first you have to take care of Ben. Where is he?"

"He's at soccer practice. What time is it?"

"Almost four."

"I have to go get him."

"In this condition, honey? Have you looked at yourself in the mirror?"

"I don't care what I look like!"

"Ben will when he sees you lookin' like the Boston Strangler. One glance at you and that poor little angel's liable to have a breakdown. He can't see you like this."

I shook my head. I could feel my face crumpling.

"What am I going to do, Reggie?"

"You're going to make arrangements for Ben, and then we're going over to your house and we're gonna sort this out. Who's with Wyndham?"

"Bunny—I think." I smacked at the tears on my face and drew back with fingertips soaked in mascara. "She can't see me like this, either."

"And the last person you want to see is Jeffrey, so let's get out of here and we'll figure it out on the way. You got your cell phone?"

I nodded as I followed her out of the office. "I can call Yancy from the car."

"Mr. Faustman is waiting for you," Ginny said as I passed her.

I stopped, despite Reggie's pressure on my arm. "Why don't you go in there and take my place this time, too?" I said to Ginny. "Since you do it so well."

Her contempt was palpable. I couldn't have cared less.

Yancy agreed to keep Ben for the evening. She said he and Troy were becoming like Siamese twins so she would have had a hard time separating them anyway.

"You all right?" she said, just before I hung up.

"I don't know what I am. What was that child psychologist's name again?"

"Parkins," she said. "Dr. Michael Parkins. Let me give you the number."

Reggie and I decided to go on to my house after all. She pointed out that as big as it was, we could still talk and never be heard by Wyndham. "Two people could live in that place for weeks and never see each other," she said.

"That's the way it is with Ben and me," I said. My hands went up to my face again. "I have been so hard on him, Reggie. And I've neglected him. What was I thinking? Why didn't I get this? Why didn't I figure it out? I'm such an idiot."

"Let's go back to you being mad at Sid," she said. "I think that was a little healthier."

"Chris."

"You can be mad at him, too."

"No—I have to call him. We have to do something about Ben before he completely goes off the deep end."

"Or before *you* do." Reggie stopped at a red light and looked at me. "I've never seen you like that."

"I've never felt like that. I wanted to kill Sid—with my bare hands. I still do."

"You want some help?" Reggie gave me a sad smile, and then she shook her head. The ponytail lurched as we moved through the intersection. "We've got to focus on Ben. And you. Now, when we get there, I'm going to fix you something and you are going to eat it. While I'm doing that, you do what you have to do to get yourself calmed down enough to face Ben when he comes home. And Wyndham."

"Yes, ma'am," I said.

As soon as she was busy in the kitchen and I had checked in on

Wyndham and Bunny—who was sitting by the door like Rin Tin Tin while Wyndham dozed—I shut myself up in the study and paced until I could breathe without hyperventilating. If I didn't have it all together before I dialed, I wasn't going to be able to deal with him.

Chris was, miraculously, in his office when I called, and even more amazingly, he had a minute to talk.

"You don't have some important client about to walk in?" I said.

"What's the deal, Toni?" he said. "Since when does one of our conversations take more than five minutes?"

"Since right now."

There was a silence. When he spoke, his voice had lost its edge. "What's going on?"

"I didn't call you before because I didn't know—okay, look—Wyndham has disclosed some things. It's about Ben."

"What about Ben?"

He was already showing signs of unraveling and I hadn't even said anything yet. I was careful as I laid it all out for him, including Wyndham's suicide attempt, Trinity House, and what Dominica had told me.

There was another silence.

"Chris?" I said. "You okay? I know it's a lot to swallow at once."

"And I'm only swallowing about half of it." His voice was dead even.

"What are you saying?"

"I think it's patently ridiculous to think that Sid would risk taking pictures of our kid."

I stopped padding up and down in the study and pressed my hand to my forehead. "*What?*" I said. "What about this *isn't* ridiculous? They found pictures of his *own* children, for Pete's sake!"

"That's exactly my point. They have evidence that he photographed them. Has anybody given you any hard proof about Ben? Has the FBI recovered photographs of him?"

His voice sounded dry, as if he were questioning a hostile witness on the stand.

"You think Wyndham is making this up?" I said.

"The girl is freaked out—you said yourself she's suicidal, which I can understand. I don't think she knows what she's saying."

"Why on earth would she put this on me? It means me sending her away from here, and she doesn't want that!"

"What she wants is a connection with you so you won't abandon her, too."

"That's absurd," I said. "If she doesn't know what she's saying, then how could she figure out something that sophisticated? Good grief, Chris, stop being an attorney for seven seconds. She's a victim, not the defendant."

"Look, I'm just not in a rush to believe that Ben was involved in this, whether it was just pictures or whatever else it is this shrink told you happened to him."

You're in worse denial than I am, I thought. I felt myself sinking. I'd been prepared for him to blow up. I hadn't expected him to blow me off. I wanted to smack him, but I wasn't sure whether it was out of anger or the need to wake him up.

"I know you don't want to believe it," I said, with all the control I could muster. "I didn't either at first. But we can't afford to be in denial, not if we're going to help Ben." I groped back through my memory of my meeting with Dominica. "We can't let him go through this alone."

"What kind of help are you talking about?"

"He needs professional help, or this could really mess him up. He's already—"

"He's not messed up."

"Chris, for crying out loud! He screams over nothing, he's afraid of the dark, he wets his bed, he doesn't want me out of his sight and when I'm there he hates the sight *of* me."

"He's behaving that way because he isn't with both of his parents in his own home."

"He wasn't with both of his parents when he *was* in his own home. You were never there—*I* was never there." I closed my eyes. As hard as it was to stop, I couldn't go down this path, not right now. "It isn't about that. He's responding to abuse. He was molested, Chris."

"You don't know that."

"If he was photographed by Sidney, he was molested, whether he touched him or not—and there's a good chance he did. This doesn't make you want to rip Sid's scalp off? *And* Bobbi's?"

"Let's say he did…touch Ben."

I took a long, controlled breath. "Okay."

"How much can that affect him? He's five years old. He'll forget about it in six months."

"You're not listening to me! He needs us to help him!"

"Then let's help him. You and me. You come up here, and we'll sit down with him and we'll talk about it."

"You don't think I've tried that?" I was talking between clenched teeth. "We don't know how to help him, Chris."

"Why not? We're his parents. Let's handle this thing within the family. We can protect him."

"Oh, yeah. Let's circle up the wagons—now that the damage is already done!"

"If he was photographed and if he was touched, whatever, he's too young to know what that means. He just needs time, and he needs us—together."

"How dare you?" I said.

"What?"

"How dare you use this to try to manipulate me!"

"You think that's what I'm doing?"

"If I came up there with Ben, would you agree to let him see a therapist? Would you work with the person? Would you take your turn making sure he gets there? Would you cut down your work hours so you could spend time with him when he needs you?"

"You're making it sound like this is suddenly going to run our lives."

"It's already running mine. And unless you're willing to do this *with* me, I'm staying right here—where I have some support."

He let only a crack of silence split the conversation.

"If you're going to go ahead and get professional therapy for Ben, why do you need my approval?" he said.

"I don't need your 'approval.' I just wanted you to know. I

thought you'd want him to have the best help possible."

"How much is this going to cost?"

"I don't know. Insurance will cover some of it, I'm sure. Does it matter?"

"No, of course it doesn't matter. You're making it sound like I'm some kind of cold fish. Just the fact that you're so worked up has got to be affecting him."

"I did not do this to him, Chris. And if you want to hear me get worked up, say something like that to me again."

"All right—all right—look, just do what you have to do, but don't make a bigger thing out of it than it really is."

"How much bigger does it have to get?"

I was close to tears, and I wasn't doing much to hide them. I didn't care what Chris thought.

"You crying?" His voice went soft. "Toni Wells doesn't cry."

"She does now. She also screams obscenities at clients, so watch it."

"This woman—this shrink—"

"Dominica. She's a Christian therapist."

"She's got you thinking the worst. Why don't we just see what the psychologist says about Ben before you jump to any more conclusions? I'd like a second opinion."

"If I can get a meeting with him in the next few days, is that too short notice for you to get down here?"

Another silence—a longer one.

"You think I need to be there?" he said.

I didn't answer him.

"Let's do this," he said. "You see what he has to say and then we'll decide if I really need to make a trip to Nashville. Fair enough?"

I waited for another surge of rage to come up and rip a string of profanities out of my mouth, but it didn't materialize. Instead, I sat there, stunned, because what I heard in my husband's voice was fear—pure fear.

When we hung up, I looked up Dr. Parkins's number and dialed it.

Eleven

MY TALK WITH DR. MICHAEL PARKINS was brief. After I told him about Ben's situation, he said we needed to talk right away and would tomorrow afternoon be too soon? Was he kidding? I was ready to go over to his office right then.

But I still asked Reggie to check into his background for me, find out if he had a specialization in sexual abuse and post-traumatic stress syndrome, which she said she'd do first thing in the morning. Then I steeled myself for going into the office and facing Jeffrey.

It wasn't what I wanted to do, but once I got somewhat calmed down—which I had to for Wyndham and Ben—I realized that no matter how much of a jerk Charles R. Marshall was, I'd still been irrational with him. I did have to face the music on that, and find out if I still had a job. At the rate I was hiring therapists, I was going to need the money.

The next morning, once I'd promised to have lunch with Wyndham and had dropped Ben off at school—with the promise that I personally would pick him up for soccer—I made my way reluctantly into the office and went straight to Jeffrey. Ginny was just coming out his door when I got there, hair now a raven black, pulled up tightly into a bun. Was it my imagination or was she going for a more professional look? Oddly, I was more amused than threatened.

"Do you have a minute?" I said to Jeffrey from the doorway. Light glinting off of his bald head, Jeffrey nodded to a chair. I shut the door soundlessly behind me and all but tiptoed into place.

"I want to apologize for my outburst yesterday," I said. "Did you lose Mr. Marshall's account?"

Jeffrey shook his head, the pistol-fingers rubbing the end of his nose

"I would be happy to write him a letter," I said. "Unless you think that would make things worse."

"The man is not a stone wall, Toni, and neither am I. Why didn't you tell me what you and your son were going through?"

It took me a minute to remember that I had spewed the news about Ben's molestation in Marshall's face with Jeffrey right there on the scene. I was sure the people back in the mailroom had heard it. It was probably all over Westend by this time.

"Do you think I'm an ogre?" Jeffrey said.

"No, of course not. I just try to keep my business and personal lives separate."

"But you haven't been able to pull that off, have you?"

I bit back a retort and merely looked at him.

"You aren't here half the time you need to be, and when you are here, you aren't really here, not completely. Ginny has had to take up your slack—"

"Which I'm sure she is more than happy to do. Look, Jeffrey, could we just cut to the chase? If you're letting me go and replacing me with Ginny, please just say it."

Jeffrey's eyebrows lifted in surprise. "That's a little blunt."

"It's honest. I don't think either one of us has time to beat around the bush."

"All right." Jeffrey leaned forward, hands folded neatly on the desk. "I suggest you take the rest of the week off and get your life in order. Then come back Monday, ready to go back to full-time here at the office."

I expected a rush of relief. All I felt was panic. I could barely get done what I had to with Ben and Wyndham on half-time. Full-time was out of the question. But how was I going to maintain without the salary I was making? There were more stocks I could sell, an IRA I could get into, but how long was that going to last—especially if Chris was going to keep his head in the sand and not help pay for Ben's therapy?

"You have to think about it?" Jeffrey actually looked insulted.

"No—sorry," I said. "I'm just...trying to sort."

"That's why I'm giving you the rest of the week off. Get your head clear, get your life back on track, come back ready to do what I know you can do."

He smiled, though no mirth reached his eyes. I didn't smile back, nor did I say what I wanted to. But I thought it, bitterly, as I left his office. *Thanks for the generosity, Jeffrey—but I think it's going to take longer than a weekend to get my life back on track. If I ever do.*

Ginny had some papers I needed to sign ready for me when I stopped by my office. I didn't give her any instructions. I barely gave her the time of day.

"Will I see you Monday?" she said as I was leaving.

There were a number of things I wanted to say to her, not the least of which was, *You're really enjoying all of this, aren't you?* But suddenly I just didn't have the steam. All I could tell her was the truth.

"I don't know. I guess you'll see me if you see me."

I then went to Reggie's office where she was just getting off the phone. She lowered her voice as I scooted a chair close to her desk.

"Dr. Michael Parkins checks out great," she half-whispered. "Not only is treatment for sexual abuse and PTSD his specialty, but he teaches workshops all over the country for *other* child therapists, *and* he has a book coming out at the end of this year."

"Great," I said. "At last—a lucky break."

Reggie gnawed at her lip, chewing away a strip of Luscious Rose lipstick that matched her nails.

"What?" I said.

"Well, honey, I don't want to sound—oh, whatever, I don't care how I sound. If you're gonna be doin' this the Christian way, you can't be chalkin' this stuff up to luck."

"I don't get it."

"You're putting Wyndham in a Christian facility, you're taking Ben to a Christian therapist. You don't think maybe God has a little bit to do with all this? You don't think this is Jesus' healing at work?"

"This psychologist is a Christian?"

"Is that some kinda big surprise?"

"Not when I think about it. Yancy's the one who recommended him to me, so it makes sense."

"The point is, a man who knows the Lord is the very best person to be working with Angel Boy, now don't you think?"

"Yeah—especially since I'm not sure I know Him. I never even thought about it that way, to tell you the truth. I guess I'm completely disconnected."

Reggie waved me off with her hand. "Get on outa here, honey. You don't feel connected? You've got Hale—Dominique—"

"Dominica."

"Yancy, me, the whole Trinity House, for heaven's sake. Sounds like you're pretty well networked to me." Reggie leaned in conspiratorially. "You think that's an accident?"

"Maybe not. But it's like I keep telling Hale, I'm not consciously asking God for all this stuff."

"It's not all about you, sugar. The rest of us are askin' our little heads off."

"And I appreciate it. I really do." I shrugged. "What the heck—it's working."

"You just keep jumpin' into what God's givin' you and you're gonna be fine, darlin'."

"I never heard that in church."

Reggie sniffed. "I guess you just went to the wrong church."

"I probably just wasn't listening."

"Then maybe you better start."

I had lunch with Wyndham at the house that day—a rather chilly affair over chicken salad and croissants from Provence, what I considered to be the only decent place to get bread in Tennessee. She didn't appear to be impressed. She was polite but removed, and I didn't seriously blame her. I felt like Benedict Arnold by the time I got ready to leave her with Bunny so I could go see Dr. Parkins.

"I'm sending you to Trinity House because I love you and I want you to have a happy life," I said to her back as she went up the stairs. I was standing at the bottom, car keys in hand.

She stopped midway to the top and turned to me. "Why does everybody think I need to be shipped off to be fixed before I can be happy? You're just like her."

"Bobbi-her or my mother-her?"

"Bobbi. I told her once that I wanted to kill myself, and you know what she did?"

I shook my head.

"She sent me to the school counselor."

I fumbled so as not to drop my keys. "You told your counselor you were suicidal and she didn't—"

"I didn't tell her. I got in there and I couldn't say anything." Wyndham's voice broke. "All I wanted was for my mother to care about me for ten seconds."

"But I'm not like her!" I said. "I'm not sending you off for some-body else to fix you. I'm going to be involved. You're going to see me once, maybe twice a week, and we can talk every day. I'm going to give you everything I can."

Wyndham gave an unconvincing nod and went on upstairs, where Bunny was waiting. I was once again riddled with doubt.

But I had to focus on Ben, which wasn't hard to do once I reached Dr. Parkins's office in the 100 Oaks section of Nashville. His office was in a renovated house, vintage 1935, with a white picket fence and a backyard full of playground equipment. I read the sign out front twice to make sure I hadn't pulled up at a preschool. The play yard at Hillsboro didn't look this inviting.

The waiting room, which at the moment was empty of people, was a colorful collection of beanbag chairs and toy boxes and mobiles hanging from the ceiling. I was about to drop into a bright orange bag, at the suggestion of the young woman who looked more like a coach at the YMCA than a receptionist, when an inner door opened and a man of about forty stepped out. Although I was clenching my jaws in abject parental fear, I could feel myself break into a grin at the sight of him.

"Michael Parkins," he said, sticking out a freckled hand to me. "The kids call me Doc Opie."

The reason for that was obvious. 'Doc Opie' had almost neon, carrot-colored hair arranged in short spikes on top of his head. There wasn't a visible inch of him that wasn't covered in freckles, and his ears stuck out from both sides of his head, making him look for all the world like Yoda of *Star Wars* fame. The grin and the effervescent blue eyes, however, completed the true picture—he was a dead ringer for Opie from *Andy of Mayberry.*

"What should *I* call you?" I said.

"You can call me anything you want. Just don't call me late for dinner."

There was a thud from the direction of YMCA-Girl's desk. She was giving Doc Opie a rim shot.

"What should I call *you?*" Doc Opie said.

"Oh, I'm sorry. I'm Toni Wells. I'm Ben's mom."

"Come on in—"

"Before you go," YMCA Girl said, "make him promise not to tell you any more corny jokes."

Doc Opie pretended to look hurt. "The kids think I'm hilarious."

"Just don't laugh," she said to me. "It only encourages him."

Doc Opie's office looked less like a psychologist's digs than a corner of F.A.O. Schwartz. It was the kid version of Dominica's healing room, complete with child-sized furniture, cushions on the floor, baskets of stuffed animals, and a table supplied with big sheets of paper and buckets of colored markers. I had the sudden urge to doodle. I was fidgeting like I was on a blind date.

"I do have some adult chairs," he said, motioning to a pair of bowl-shaped papasan chairs like the ones I'd seen at Pier 1 Imports. "Why don't we sit over there?"

I lowered myself carefully into the bowl of a chair, first removing a large stuffed toy turtle which I then held in my lap because it seemed a shame to put it on the floor and because Doc Opie made no offer to take it off my hands.

Doc Opie flopped into his chair and crossed his legs at the ankles. His deck shoes swung just above the floor like a little boy's. He was, in fact, more boyish even than Chris. Everything about him was casual—the yellow sport shirt, the khaki Dockers, the irresistible grin—yet it was genuine rather than studied. I had known guys at the country club who worked very hard to get that look.

But I wasn't put off by his youthful air. I felt, in fact, rather secure clutching a stuffed turtle and sitting in a large bowl. At least, as secure as I was likely to feel under the circumstances.

"Do I need to give you any more background or whatever?" I said.

"Sure," he said. "Why don't you go over again what you told me on the phone yesterday and we can flesh that out a little bit." He had a Southern accent that spoke of growing up out in the country and later learning correct grammar. It made me want to say *y'all* next to some obscure word like *diaphanous*.

I told him as much as I knew, ending with Dominica's advice to me. At that point, Doc Opie was nodding his head solemnly, all traces of merriment gone from his eyes.

"She's absolutely right," he said. "Ben needs professional help. It doesn't have to come from me. If you decide after we talk that you don't want to bring him here, that's fine, but take him somewhere." He smiled faintly. "This isn't like the car salesman telling you that you need a new vehicle, and have I got a deal for you."

"*Do* you have a deal for us? I mean—you know, can you help Ben?"

"It's very possible that I can. I'm not going to give you any guarantees, and don't ever believe a psychologist who tells you he can. A lot depends on whether Ben and I can develop a relationship—and whether you and his father and I can work together."

"His father is a whole nother story." I filled him in on Chris, finishing up with, "He thinks Ben's behavior is because of our separation. Could that possibly be?"

Doc Opie wobbled his head from side to side. "Did your separation happen after the abuse, as far as you know?"

I nodded.

"Sometimes a sexually abused child will appear to be functioning normally until another major life stressor brings the effects of the abuse to the surface. He might have reacted to your separation without the abuse, but probably not with this intensity. Again, I'll need to see him to determine that. Tell you what—let me tell you what I do know and then you can discuss it with your husband. And then if you want me to meet Ben, I can assess him and we'll take it from there."

"Please—tell me what you know," I said. "I want information. I feel like I'm trying to function in a fog."

"Most parents of abused kids say that. Let me see if I can clear some things up."

Over the next forty-five minutes, Doc Opie told me that if we decided to put Ben in his care, we would need to commit to about six weeks' worth of biweekly sessions and then reassess whether we wanted to continue with him. He asked me to keep in mind that backsliding and regression and hostility on Ben's part might all be part of his healing.

"Nothing I'm not used to at this point," I said dryly.

The first stages of therapy, he told me, would involve Ben in remembering, not denying, the abusive incidents; fully recognizing, not minimizing, the effects of the abuse; and realizing that the abuser is responsible for the abuse but that he—Ben—was going to have to find ways to cope with it.

"I will, of course, give him the tools to do that," he said.

That was about the time I took a pad and pen out of my purse and asked if I could take notes. I used the turtle for a desk.

My job, Doc explained, would be to help Ben endure the emotional upheavals that were going to be part of his healing. I—and Chris—would be the ones to reassure him over and over that his pain would pass.

"That's going to be tricky," I said. "My son pretty much hates me right now."

"I haven't seen him in action," he said. "But I've never known a five-year-old that actually hated his mother. He's mad as heck at you—and you yourself know that the more you love somebody, the madder you can get at him."

"Yeah, I hear that."

"I can help with that part. We'll address that early on—that this wasn't your fault and that you're here to help him. I've never had one yet that didn't come around if the parents were patient and would work at it."

"Work I can manage," I said. "Patience—I don't know."

He rubbed one of his Yoda-ears. "You have somebody you can

work with? I mean, about your own issues?"

I didn't answer, and he didn't pursue it.

"Ben will warm up to you again naturally," he said, "though probably slowly, once we erase the tapes that are now playing in his mind. At least, that's my guess at this point. I'll know more after I talk to him."

"What tapes?"

"The thoughts that won't stop. Ever have those?"

I could feel my eyebrows going up. "Ya think?"

"Ben's are telling him that the world is a dangerous place, that people can't be trusted, that he deserved what he got, that he's a bad person."

"He's five!"

"That's the tragedy of it, isn't it? And it's the molest that does that. Even one incident can twist a child's whole view of the world. And it sounds like this might have happened more than once and fairly close together, which means he never had a chance to stabilize in between."

I couldn't look at him as I nodded. "Sometimes he wakes up screaming 'Make it stop!' Is that what he's trying to stop? All that evil stuff in his head?"

"Could be."

"Why didn't I know that? I'm his mother, for Pete's sake!"

"One of the things I encourage you to deal with in your own work is any guilt you're feeling."

"I left him there—on several occasions—for entire weekends. Of course I feel guilty. Why didn't I know better than to let him anywhere near Sid Vyne?"

"That's what I mean. You'll need to find a way to work that out, which is why I suggest having a therapist of your own."

"You don't do big kids, huh?" I said.

He grinned at me. "We're all kids, aren't we? Listen, guilt's really natural for you right now, but ask your therapist to help you get a handle on it, because your job with Ben is about now, not about what's already happened."

"You need to spell that out for me," I said.

For the first time, Doc Opie leaned forward in his chair so that his feet touched the floor. "You're going to need to provide him with an environment that *he* feels is physically, psychologically, and emotionally safe." He ticked each one off on a freckled finger and gave me a long look. "Don't play up what's already happened. Quietly deal with the subject of the molest if he brings it up, but focus more on making his world a safe place for him to be."

"I thought it was already safe," I said.

"Look." Doc Opie's eyes softened. They were the kindest eyes. "Even the most psychologically healthy individuals from stable families will develop symptoms of post-traumatic stress disorder after something like this. Even if you were a perfect parent, which nobody is, you couldn't have prevented Ben from suffering the aftereffects of sexual abuse. He's reexperiencing the trauma over and over, then he's forcing his emotions to go numb so he won't have to feel them, then he's back to reliving what's happened to him. That's the reason for the sleep disturbances and the hypervigilance and the anger and the fears. Not you."

I blinked against threatening tears. "So how do I set up this safe-house thing?"

"We're going to let Ben tell us what he needs. You won't be in on the sessions, and I won't tell you everything that goes on in here, but I'll tell you what you need to know in order to meet his needs at home. We're going to be a team—you, me, his father, and anybody else who's significant in his life."

"How long is it going to be before he starts getting better? I feel like I'm dealing with an emotionally disturbed child."

Doc Opie sat back. "I don't want you to freak when I tell you this, but the process of healing can be painfully slow."

"How slow?"

"Therapy for sexual abuse survivors usually requires at least a year."

"Wow."

We were quiet for a minute.

"Can I ask if this is going to be a problem for you financially?" he said.

"It'll be fine. Whatever it takes."

The words seemed to be coming out of someone else's mouth. With each new sentence out of Doc Opie's mouth, Ben's situation sounded more grave. I was more than on the verge of tears.

"How on earth are you going to do this?" I said. "I can't even get him to talk to me about it—about anything. I'm afraid he's too far gone already."

"If he's anything like his mother, he's a pretty tough little character. We'll play it out of him."

"Play it out of him?"

"Play therapy. Pretend games, stuffed animals, blocks, drawing pictures, playing with clay." He rubbed his hands together and grinned. "It's the best part. We have fun in here. And listen—the earlier the abuse takes place in a person's life, the more severe its impact. *But* the long-term negative consequences do not have to happen. He doesn't have to be permanently damaged. When there's positive intervention and support, we can turn this around and he can overcome all this and live a normal, happy life. You believe in God, Toni?"

"Yeah—yeah, I do."

"Then you won't mind my talking to Ben about God."

"No."

"About Jesus?"

"Not at all. I'm afraid I haven't done it much."

He grinned again. "After I get done with him, you will. Our Lord's part of the team."

I started to close the pad, but Opie put a hand up to stop me.

"One more thing," he said. "Tell your husband that if he's going to help Ben, he's going to have to shed any denial he might have. He's going to have to be willing to suffer painful feelings right along with him." He shrugged. "The up side is, there's healing in it for each of you, too."

I shook my head. "I just want Ben to get better. When can you see him?"

"How about Friday?"

I didn't tell Ben that night that he was going to be seeing a psychologist. I had to prepare myself for the next day's trip to Trinity House with Wyndham, and I was quickly figuring out that I could only focus on one trauma at a time.

Wyndham, I'm sure, didn't think I was focusing on anything but getting rid of her as we drove up to Ridgetop the next day, no matter what I said.

"I don't think you're crazy or anything," I told her when I couldn't stand the silence any longer. "You're going to get a lot of rest here, which you need after all you've been through."

No answer.

"Think of it this way," I went on. "At least you'll only have to take care of you. No little brother and sister hanging on you, getting into your stuff."

"I miss them!" she said, and burst into tears.

She cried into her hands the rest of the way, and when we pulled into the parking lot, she pulled her head up and sobbed in the direction of the building.

"Aunt Toni, please," she said, "don't make me stay here."

"It's not forever. Just until you get healed. It's like being in traction with a broken leg, you know. Once you're on your feet again, you're out of here."

"And then what? Where do I go then?"

I'm sure my clumsy mental fumbling for an answer was smeared all over my face.

Wyndham nodded. "I knew it. You don't know, do you?"

"Let's not worry about that now. You're going to be taken care of, that's all you need to know. I'm not going to abandon you."

She didn't say a word, but the look she gave me fairly screamed, *You already are.*

Betty Stires was there to meet us, and she appeared to be pulling out all the stops to make Wyndham feel comfortable. Once they'd chatted—with Betty doing most of the chatting—she took her to meet Dominica while the elfin girl at the reception desk and I went through Wyndham's suitcases, pulling out anything that she might be able to use to hurt herself.

"Shoelaces?" I said as Elf Girl—Katie—denuded Wyndham's Nikes.

"Yes, ma'am. We've had girls try to hang themselves with a string of them tied together."

I put my hand over my mouth.

"I'm sorry," Katie said. "I didn't mean to upset you."

But I shook my head. "Too late. I've been upset for weeks now."

She nodded sympathetically and put Wyndham's disposable razor in the taboo pile.

"She's going to get pretty hairy," I said.

"We supply electric shavers." She held up a nail file. "And we give manicures. She'll feel very pampered."

Or very controlled, I thought. Once again I was a tangle of doubt.

By the time Betty and Wyndham returned, with Dominica marching behind them, I was in knots. I could hardly swallow when Betty said to Wyndham, "Why don't you say good-bye to your Aunt Toni now, and I'll take you up to see your room?"

I put my arms around my niece, but she didn't hug me back. She stood, stiff and unyielding, as I whispered in her ear, "I love you. It's going to be okay."

She didn't answer, but turned away and looked at Betty. "Okay," she said. "Let's go."

There was no backward look, no last-minute change of heart about the hug. She just followed Betty obediently to the door and disappeared through it.

"How ya doin'?" somebody said.

It was, of course, Dominica. I'd forgotten about her completely.

"That was the hardest thing I ever did," I said.

"I know. But I bet it was the most *important* thing you've done so far."

I was still staring at the now-closed door. "Do you really think so?"

"I wouldn't be here if I didn't. Hey, you want to take a walk?"

I didn't know what else I was going to do with myself, how I was going to be alone with the guilt, so I nodded.

Dominica led me out the front door and down a side path which led away from the building and down a hill. Within minutes, Trinity House was out of sight, and we were making our way through a field of poppies and daffodils that looked as if it had arisen from the April page of a calendar. I ran my fingers listlessly across the tops of some tall Queen Anne's lace.

"I hope I can explain something to you," Dominica said.

"I hope you can, too," I said, "because right now I am so confused."

"I'd wonder about you if you weren't. What I want to say is that I know I was hard on you the other day when you were here."

"Don't worry about it."

"You seemed very removed. I wanted to make sure you knew just what Wyndham—and you—are up against. I won't be dealing with her that way. She's going to receive a lot of God-love." I could feel her looking at me. "I'm not seeing that distancing in you today. You're really hurting."

"Ya think?" My voice was bitter, and I immediately regretted it. "I'm sorry. Yeah, I'm hurting, and I don't usually hurt. When something comes up, I look at it, I deal with it, I move on. This is…this is just bizarre."

"Most people say it's surreal." Dominica plucked a wild daisy and proceeded to pull off its petals and toss them to the breeze. "You know, you *are* dealing with this, and you *are* moving on. You took a huge step today. It's just not going to happen overnight."

"That's what Doc Opie told me."

Dominica let out a laugh, a fountain-bubbling kind of sound that surprised me. "Your son's seeing Doc Opie?"

"You know him?"

"Yes, I know him—we've worked together. He's the best. The *best.*"

She was smiling at me, her even white teeth gleaming against the brown lips.

"I misread you," she said. "You're a lot more real than I gave you credit for being."

"Is that a compliment?"

"Best thing I could say to somebody. A lot of times it's grief that forces people to become who they really are—if they're willing to trust God enough to experience it."

"Is that what this is—grief?"

"Yup."

I grunted. "I think I'd rather skip it."

"You can't, not if you want to get healthy and you want your kids to get healthy. Hey, Jesus grieved, and if it's good enough for Him, it's good enough for us."

"Wonderful." I sighed, a long, deep breath that filled me up and at once deflated me.

"It's like there's been a death," Dominica said. "In a way there has been—your kid's lost his innocence. That's a huge loss."

"I hate this."

"Nobody likes it, but there it is. We have to work through it."

"I don't know if I *can* get through it." I pressed my hands against my jaws. "Can I just tell you that I feel absolutely overwhelmed?"

"You can tell me anything you want. In fact, why don't you come in and see me next week—see if maybe God and I can help you with some of this?"

I shook my head before I even thought about it. "Thanks, but if I take on one more bill, I'm going to have to get a second job, and I can't even handle the one I have." I grunted again. "I never thought I'd hear myself saying that. I can handle anything. Right."

"What bill? I come with the package—you're already paying for me. I do the family's therapy, too." She held her hand out, palm down, and wiggled it back and forth. "Granted, I usually counsel the parents on how to get along with the girl that's in here, but I still feel fine about giving you individual help. If you aren't handling this, you sure can't help Wyndham, and she's going to need you." She gave me a sly look. "Do it for Wyndham. You're feeling guilty, so give her this. Make you feel better."

"You are bad!" I said.

"I do whatever I have to. I like to see people get healed."

"I'll think about it."

"I can't ask for more than that." She gave a mischievous glance upward. "At least, not from you."

I actually didn't think about it that much over the next twenty-four hours because I had to focus again on Ben. I was beginning to feel like a ping-pong ball, bouncing back and forth between concerns for him and worries about Wyndham. But now that she was safely tucked away at Trinity House, I could stay on Ben's side of the table, at least for a while.

I picked him up for soccer practice that afternoon, and I was surprised that he didn't whine about going. In fact, he was obviously anxious to get there.

"Am I gonna be late?" he said from the back seat. "Coach Gary doesn't like us to be late."

"You're going to be *way* early. No sweat."

"Did you bring my right shoes?"

"They're in your bag."

"What about my knee pads?"

"Check."

"My socks?"

"Check."

"Am I gonna get there in time to put them on? Should I put them on now?"

"Pal, you can put them on anytime you want to." I was almost in tears as I tossed the bag over the seat to him. It seemed like I wanted to cry no matter what happened, good or bad. There was a permanent lump in my throat.

That's probably why when I sat down in the bleachers next to Yancy Bancroft and she said, "How you doin', hon?" I burst into tears.

"Well, bless your heart," she said, rubbing my back. She let me cry for a minute before she said, "Do you see your sweet babyness down there on the field? Isn't he just the cutest little ol' thing?"

I looked up to see Ben slamming the side of his foot into a soccer ball and sending it sailing crookedly across the field.

"Coach Gary says he kicks that thing like he's trying to put it out of its misery," Yancy said.

I cried harder.

"Honey," she whispered to me, "what are you doing for lunch tomorrow?"

"I don't know—probably nothing," I said. "I can't eat."

"Let's do something about that. Let me take you to a little place that just opened over on Music Row. We'll get us a back booth and talk. Let me pick you up at 11:00."

I nodded and through my tears watched my son smack his foot into the ball again. If he was thinking what I was thinking, that was Sidney Vyne's head he was kicking.

Oh, how I wished it were.

Twelve

LA BELLE MEUNIERE WAS A STUNNING AFFAIR on Nashville's Music Row—a street so named because it was literally a string of recording studios and offices dedicated to the propagation of music, largely country-western.

Yancy and I had to take our sunglasses off the minute we walked in the door because the lighting was dim and the walls were paneled in mahogany, giving it the same ambience as Keith Pollert's family room. The tables were marble-topped, the seats Italian leather; the servers glided across the polished wood floor balancing trays laden with gourmet entrees that smelled of lemon butter and capers.

"This isn't your typical meat-and-three," Yancy murmured to me as we waited for the as-yet-absent hostess to appear and seat us.

She was referring to the Southern lunchroom tradition of giving diners a list of meats on a chalkboard to select from, along with an assortment of vegetables from which to choose three. "Vegetables" usually included macaroni and cheese, applesauce, mashed potatoes drowning in gravy, and the ever-popular fried okra.

This food looked and smelled so divine, my mouth was watering. I almost literally hadn't had a bite to eat in days.

"I think I'm actually hungry," I said to Yancy.

"That was my plan. I just hope you don't lose your appetite before we get seated."

We both looked around for the hostess, but there was no one forthcoming, and a small crowd was forming in the vestibule behind us.

"Didn't you say they just opened?" I said. "They probably just don't have their act together yet."

"So sorry, madames!" A muscular man with a professional smile and eyes that made him appear overworked, if not harassed, greeted us with a stack of leather-bound menus under an arm that bulged beneath his Brooks Brothers sleeve.

"Are you in the weeds today?" I said.

He gave me another smile, this one more spontaneous. "You have worked as a waitress?" His French accent smoothed English into a piece of satin.

"Every summer in college," I said. "You can't beat it for the money if you make good tips."

"You must tell my hostess that. She quit this morning." He dazzled us with yet another smile as he led us to a table as if he were strolling onto a football field. "But no worries—we will make certain madames have a superb *dejeuner* or it is on the house."

"You're on," Yancy said. She sank into leather opposite me in a booth and smiled into my face over the menu until Frenchy disappeared. "Did you see him flirting with you? Cute little ol' French thing."

"Oh, nuh-uh."

"Either that or he wanted to hire you."

I gave a grunt as I perused the menu. "I may be looking for a new job soon. Mine is just too much right now, but I tell you, I can't really afford to quit. I don't know what to do."

Yancy swept the room with her eyes. "You could work in worse places. You said yourself you can't beat it for the money."

"I would love to use my MBA to work as a hostess," I said dryly. "What are you going to have?"

We both had the special entree and salads and talked for several hours, while businesspeople ordered and ate and left all around us and tables refilled with people who were there only for lunch and not for free therapy.

Yancy, on the other hand, was more interested in me than in the food. While I managed to get down the ratatouille and half a serving of French bread custard that melted right on my palate, she asked all the right questions to get me to yank out every nettle—and then soothed every festering mark it left.

"I'm sorry," I said, nodding toward her untouched organic greens. "You probably don't need to hear about all this, but I can't shut up when I'm around you. You'd think we'd known each other for years."

"I *wish* I'd known you for years," she said. "You're probably the most intelligent woman I've met since I quit work to have babies. Why do we mothers sit around and talk about piddly stuff?"

"I would love to be talking about piddly stuff."

She shook her head slowly, a "bless your heart" just a breath away. "All right, so what do you need? How can I help with all this?"

"You've already done enough."

"No, honey, now I am so serious. This sounds like it's going to be a long road, and I'd like to be there if you want me to. Do you promise me that you will call me any time of the day or night if you need something?"

"I don't know, Yancy—you don't need this in your life. You have two kids—"

She looked at me, hard, with her thyroid eyes. "Nobody 'needs' this. But why try to get through it all by yourself? Besides, I like you, Toni. You make me remember that I have a brain."

"Great, then you can think for both of us, because mine is turning to mush."

"All right then," she said. "Now I have a job."

I had to leave in time to pick Ben up, though I put it off as long as I could. I still hadn't told him where I was taking him, which was cowardly, I knew, but I had at least spared myself an evening of screaming and "I hate you's."

"Is it soccer today?" he asked before I even had him loaded into the car.

"Nope. Today we're doing something different."

He froze, both hands on the booster seat, and glared over his shoulder at me. "I don't want something different! I wanna go to soccer!"

"There is no soccer practice today—it's Friday, Pal."

"I don't want it to be Friday."

I gave him a hike into the seat and pulled the belt across his lap.

"You're the only person on the face of the planet who doesn't. We're going to see a man named Doc Opie—"

"No!"

"Good grief, Ben." I tried not to slam either door as I closed his and got into the driver's seat. "I haven't even told you about him yet. He's way cool—"

"No doctor! He'll make me take my clothes off!"

My hands turned to ice on the steering wheel, and my eyes would barely move to the rearview mirror. When they did, the terror on Ben's face went through me like an ice pick.

"It's not that kind of doctor," I said. "This is a doctor who just plays with you."

"Why?"

It was one of those times I wished my child weren't so bright.

"Because he wants to help you," I said.

"Help me with what?"

I hesitated, pretending to concentrate on pulling onto the freeway and making my way down I-65 to 100 Oaks. What was it Doc Opie had said? *Quietly deal with the subject of the molest if he brings it up, but focus more on making his world a safe place for him to be.*

"Help me with *what?*" Ben was clenching his teeth, just the way I did.

"Help you not to feel so afraid all the time."

I held my breath. He was either going to scream—or he was going to scream. Recently, those were the only choices he had given me to deal with.

But he was quiet for a few minutes, almost until we pulled onto Murfreesboro Road, the last turn before Doc Opie's. Then he finally said, "What kinds of toys does he got?"

I let out all the air. *Cheated death again,* I thought.

YMCA girl—whose name, it turned out, was Alice—greeted us with a grin and a set of Legos. Ben barely had a chance to slide to his knees in front of them when Doc Opie came out and pulled up a bean bag.

"Ben," I said, "this is Doc Opie, the way cool doctor I was telling you about."

"How ya doin'?" Doc Opie said to him.

I had to blink. He was talking to Ben as if he were sixteen.

Ben took full inventory of Doc Opie's face before he said, "Where's that thing doctors are supposed to wear around their necks?"

"You mean a stethoscope?" Doc shook his head. 'I'm not that kind of doctor."

Ben looked at me as if he were surprised that I actually knew something. I resisted the urge to say, "I told you."

"I'm not going to do any of the stuff doctors usually do when you go to their office," Doc said. "Mostly we're going to talk—"

"And play." Ben looked accusingly at me. "You said he was gonna play with me."

"That's what he told me," I said. "You better ask him."

Ben shifted his gaze to Doc Opie, eyes narrowed.

"It's the truth," Doc said. "We're going to talk *while* we play."

"About what?"

I squirmed a little. Ben was starting to sound like his father doing a cross-examination. It didn't seem to be bothering Doc Opie, who looked as if he were accustomed to being interrogated by five-year-old boys. Now *there* was a tough way to make a living.

"We can talk about anything you pick," Doc Opie said. "And the best part is, you can say anything you want to me, and I won't tell anybody."

Ben looked at once at me. I tried to look innocent.

"No tattling at *all?*" Ben said.

"No, not even to your mom—unless you want me to."

That seemed to stir something in Ben. His fine little eyebrows shot up. "You mean—I get to decide my own self?"

"You bet you do."

Ben considered that while I held my breath and watched him. What I would have given to know what was going on behind that furrowed forehead.

Finally, Ben gave the waiting room a flourish with his hand. "Are these the toys we're gonna be playing with?"

"Nah—I got better ones than this inside."

"He does," I said. "I saw them."

Ben completely ignored me and slowly stood up. "Okay. Let's see 'em."

"Follow me," Doc Opie said.

Without another word to me from either one of them, they disappeared through the door that led to Doc Opie's office. I looked at Alice.

"That was easy enough," she said. "I think our boy's going to be just fine."

"What do I do now?" I said.

"Kick back for forty-five minutes. You want a magazine or a bed?"

"A bed?"

"We have a little sunroom back here for parents who just want to put their feet up and close their eyes while their kids are in session. For some of them, it's the only real rest they get until Doc Opie can work his magic."

"Lead me to it," I said.

I didn't really expect to fall asleep, but the minute I stretched out on a day bed in the little greenhouse of a room, I zonked out. Alice had to wake me up to tell me the session was over.

I was bleary-eyed as I half-stumbled to the waiting room, digging in my purse for my keys. But Doc Opie invited me into his office, and Ben was too busy with the Legos on the floor to notice me.

"I've got the Ben-watch," Alice said to me. "It's okay."

"So—how did it go?" I said when I was once again ensconced in the papasan chair. I quickly put up my hand. "I'm not asking for details."

"It's okay," Doc Opie said. "It's natural to want to know everything that goes on with your child."

"*Now* it is. It's like I suspect every man he comes into contact with to be a potential child molester. I mean—not you."

I could feel my face going red up to the tips of my ears, but Doc Opie just grinned at me. "Don't worry about it. That's normal, too. In fact, everything both of you are going through is normal behavior for two people in a situation like this."

"Gee, that's good news," I said, sarcasm lacing my voice. "I'd hate to think I was *really* going nuts." I shook my head. "So…is there anything I need to know that you *can* tell me?"

"I think Ben and I are going to be able to work together just fine. He's still checking me out, which is healthy. I can't tell you that he's going to open up to me next week—or maybe ever—but from my experience I will say he's a good candidate for disclosing what's happened to him."

"Okay." I had a hard time swallowing. "So let me ask you this— why would he tell you and not me? I mean, aside from the fact that he thinks I'm Public Enemy Number One right now."

Doc Opie's eyes drooped sympathetically. "That's the really tough part, but it's common with a child who's been abused by someone he used to trust. He's already learned to associate nurturance and love with eventual betrayal, so it's hard for him to trust anybody right now, especially you because you're the person who claims to love him the most."

"I do!"

"Which is exactly why you've brought him here." Doc held out a hand, palm up. "Besides that, he's angry, so he's being defiant with you, and besides *that*—" he held out the other palm—"he feels alone and unprotected and vulnerable."

"In other words, he's a mess."

"Yeah—but I've seen worse. I think I can help him."

Panic was clawing at my throat, and I couldn't sit in the bowl any longer. I struggled out of it ungracefully and began to pace the room. Doc Opie didn't ask me to sit down and calm down, which was good. I might have decked him.

"It just sounds like too much," I said. "How are you ever going to get through all of that when he's just a little boy? I mean, really— are you being straight with me? Is this hopeless?"

The doc watched me calmly. "I would tell you if it were."

"Have you ever told anybody that about their child?"

"No, because it never is hopeless. And it's even less so in your case because you're so motivated to help him. Some parents expect me to fix their kid while they go on about their lives. It's like drop-

ping him off at Cub Scouts—they come back and want to see a
merit badge that says he's cured."

I stopped pacing. "You told me all this the other day. What I
don't get is *how* do I help him? Everything I do is apparently wrong.
There's no way I'm going to be able to erase this from his mind."

"That isn't our goal. What we want to do is restore him to a normal level of functioning so he can find comfort in relationships
again and be able to experience a wider range of feelings than fear
and anger and hate for himself."

I dragged a hand through my hair. "I don't even know where to
start."

"There's one thing you can concentrate on this weekend."

I lunged for my bag and pawed for a pad and pen. Doc Opie
waited patiently. I still didn't sit down, but scribbled furiously as he
talked.

"Let him be in control of his own body as much as you can."

I looked up. "You mean, like, let him pee on the floor?"

He gave me a half grin. "Does he *want* to pee on the floor?"

"I don't know."

"Just think of it this way. The sexual touch is over, but the
knowledge of the abuse is with him all the time and everywhere
he goes. He thinks other people are in control of his body. Let
him be in control of who touches him, who sees him naked, that
kind of thing."

"Do I force him to take a bath?"

"Tell him he has to get into the tub, but you don't have to be in
the room with him, and he can wash himself." Doc Opie pulled a
piece of paper from his clipboard, drew a square in the middle of it,
and showed it to me. "In the box are all the things that aren't nego-
tiable. Take a bath. Go to bed. Brush your teeth." He grinned. "Pee
in the toilet."

"Preferably with some decent aim," I said.

"Outside the box are the things he can make decisions about.
What's he going to wear? Is he going to wash himself, or are you?
Which of three healthy foods you offer him is he going to have for
supper?"

"What do I do, hang this on the refrigerator or something?"

"You can. The two of you will figure it out. It will get him talking. I noticed that he likes to make choices, so give him as many as you can where his own body is concerned."

"Anything else?" I stood with pen poised. I was already feeling better having something concrete to focus on. At least now I could swallow.

"If you can, take him out this weekend to a store where they have a nice selection of stuffed animals and let him pick out one to be his Safe Animal. Don't make any suggestions—just stand back and let him decide unless he asks for your opinion."

"Fat chance. Is that it?"

"I think that's a lot." Doc Opie stood up and stuck his hands into his pockets, cocking his red head at me. If it hadn't been for the ears, he would have reminded me of a curious woodpecker.

"He's going to need total commitment and tending to from you," he said. "I'm sure you've been a devoted mother or he wouldn't be the neat little kid he is. But you have to almost go into overdrive now. Not smothering, just completely committed. Put whatever you can live without in your own life on hold right now—your therapist can help you with that. Take care of yourself as you need to, and focus the rest on him. He needs you."

"Whatever it takes," I said.

But as I stuffed the pad and pen back into my bag, the lump took shape in my throat again.

How am I going to do this? I thought as I went out to retrieve Ben. *I don't know how—I* don't!

I wanted to turn on my heel and go back to Doc Opie and make him give me specifics, details, directions I could scrawl on my pad and type up and print out in triplicate. But he had followed me into the waiting room and was already intent on a little girl of about seven who was explaining some malady that had beset her stuffed rhinoceros.

I felt a pang of jealousy for Ben that Doc Opie was focusing on some other kid—that he wasn't committed to Ben's care 24/7.

No. That's up to me. And I don't know how.

~♦♦○

But God knows, I tried that weekend.

I made an offer to Ben to take him to McDonald's for supper. He immediately said he hated McDonald's. Doc Opie hadn't been kidding when he said this wasn't going to happen overnight. When I said I thought Ben loved McDonald's, he told me McDonald's had stupid toys and he wanted to go to Burger King.

Let him pick which of three healthy foods he's going to eat, the Doc had said. Okay, so we were talking junk food, but at least it was a start.

Bath time was less of a success. I said Ben had to take a bath, but he could do it however he wanted. He chose to sit on the floor in the bathroom with the door closed and kick his feet on the linoleum. I then stood outside the door and gave him a list of three choices—play in the tub, play in the shower, or let me squirt him down with the hose. He hated all three and opted for dragging a washcloth across his face. I was going to have to ask Doc Opie about that one.

I started keeping a list of questions. By Saturday morning, it was two pages long.

What do I do when he throws himself down in the middle of the mall and holds his breath?

If he doesn't want any of the food choices, do I stuff one of them down his throat or let him starve?

Why isn't any of this working?

The one successful outing we had on Saturday was the trip to the toy store for a stuffed animal. I wasn't sure whether I was supposed to tell Ben this should represent safety and security and all the other things I hadn't given him, so I just took him to the stuffed animal display at the Discovery Store at the Green Hills Mall and said, "Pick any of these guys you want. Think of him as your Safe Animal."

"Why?" he said immediately.

Given that we had just had a scene out in the mall and one at Baskin-Robbins, I was tempted to say, *Because I said so.* But I restrained myself and said instead, "Because Doc Opie said so."

"Oh, okay."

Doc Opie was turning out to be a handy little fella to have around. I made a note to later try saying, *Doc Opie says you have to take a bath.*

Ben stepped up to the display like he was about to do battle and surveyed the contents with discerning eyes. It was all I could do not to jump in there and recommend the thirty-pound lion, the plump grizzly that was bigger than he was, or the giant frog whose tongue when pulled out to its full extension would have gone all the way down our stairs.

Let him choose, I told myself firmly. *He can't do it wrong, for Pete's sake.*

Ben finally began to pick up various possibilities, and I watched in fascination as he examined their tails, smelled their fur, and rubbed them up against his cheek. His final test was a hard squeeze with both arms against his chest—until I was sure I saw the poor creatures' eyes bulge. After that, each one was returned to its shelf with such finality, I felt a little sorry for them.

I was starting to get a little afraid that he was going to decide he "hated" all of them and hurl himself into the sale bin, when he pulled out a slightly emaciated looking lamb.

Get ready for this one to go flying back in there, I thought. *Poor thing.*

Ben put it through the same paces he had all the rest of them; nobody could say my son wasn't an equal-opportunity chooser. When he got to the final squeeze, he closed his eyes, and I heard him sigh.

"This one," he said.

I covered my bewilderment remarkably well, if I do say so myself.

"Oh," I said. "Well—cool. Let's buy him."

Ben surveyed me over the top of the lamb's semiwooly head. "Don't you want to know *why* I picked him?"

"Um—yeah. But you should only tell me if you want to."

He held the lamb out in front of him and looked deeply into its pink button eyes. "I don't," he said.

"Oh. Well…okay."

From there it was as if Doc Opie had put some kind of instruction chip in Ben's head. He hauled the lamb around with him the rest of the day and had it sit at a chair at the table while we ate the hot dogs he had selected from my choices of wieners, Hot Pockets, and macaroni and cheese. I decided I was worse than a meat and three and needed to work on my menu.

But Lamb was no help at bedtime. Ben started right after supper getting worked up about not wanting to go. I was tempted to tell him that Doc Opie said he had to go to bed, until I remembered that box thing he had shown me. I grabbed Lamb and headed for my study.

"Where are you taking him?" Ben shrieked.

"In here. If you want to have him, you have to come in here."

Ben tore after me, and I pointed to a chair next to the desk. He climbed into it and pulled his face into a knot until I gave Lamb to him. The two of them then glared at me. There is nothing worse than being stared down by an animal with pink eyes.

"Okay," I said. "Here's a box." I drew one on a piece of white paper. Ben watched me warily. "Inside here I'm going to write down the things you don't get to choose."

I could tell he hated it, but Ben still watched as I wrote *Go to bed at bedtime.*

"Go—bed," he said. "That's all I can read. Mrs. Robinette draws us pictures."

Wonderful. I could draw stick people and pigs, my two artistic claims to fame. However, since he hadn't run for the television yet, I attempted to draw a bed. He nodded, as if that would do.

"You also have to eat," I said.

"Draw a fork and spoon. And a knife."

"You never use a knife."

"I wanna eat something that you hafta use a knife for."

"Got it." I painstakingly sketched a set of silverware.

"Can I do one?" he said.

I could have cried. "Sure."

We traded places, and he clutched the pencil in true kindergarten fashion.

"So?" Ben said.

"So what?"

"What do I draw?"

"Oh! Well, you have to take some kind of bath."

He nodded and studied the box. Slowly, he put pencil to paper, and a very small bathtub appeared.

"It's little," I said, "which is fine, of course."

"It's only big enough for one person. I don't want anybody getting in there with me."

"Who's going to get in with you? There's only one kid around here."

"What else do I draw?"

We filled the box up with lopsided renderings of a school and a seat belt and a kid saying thank you and please. Ben was yawning by the time we posted it on the refrigerator door.

"Tomorrow we can draw some more," I said.

Ben frowned. "There's *more* stuff that goes in the box?"

"No, there's stuff that goes outside the box. The stuff you do get to choose."

His face smoothed, and he looked down at Lamb, who was crammed under his arm. "You hear that? We get to choose some stuff."

I decided as we made our way up the stairs that Doc Opie was a genius. Although Ben stiffened when I told him to climb into bed and I pulled the covers over him, he didn't scream. Still, when I put my hand on his back to rub it, he jerked himself away.

"Well, good night, Pal," I said.

I got almost to the door when I heard him turn over.

"You wanna know why I picked this lamb?" he said.

I didn't turn around. I just stopped and said, "Sure."

"'Cause he won't hurt me."

When I was sure he was asleep, I went downstairs and cried. I cried almost all night, until my throat closed up and my eyes were in slits and my ears felt as if they'd been stabbed with knitting needles.

The next morning I called Dominica's office and left her a message.

"I think I need to come see you," I said. "Please call me."

Thirteen

I DIDN'T HEAR FROM DOMINICA before I left for work Monday morning, and I was so divided between Ben and what was waiting for me at Faustman, I didn't have much time to think about my own angst. Think about it, no—but feel it, yes.

After the nightlong crying marathon on Saturday night, I spent all day Sunday trying to focus on Ben and finding it increasingly hard to concentrate—on anything. I tried to make corn bread from a box and lost my train of thought so many times while following the three-step directions that I neglected to put the egg in. Even Lamb refused to eat the result. I sat down to watch a video with Ben and realized halfway through it that I had no idea who any of the characters were. When Stephanie called that evening, it took me a good ten seconds to determine that it was my sister I was talking to.

"Ton'—are you okay?" she said a few minutes into the conversation.

"I'm two continents away from okay," I said. "I shouldn't feel this bad. I've got Wyndham taken care of. I have Ben in therapy and he's going to be fine. It's all falling into place." I sank into the couch in the study and dragged my hand across my eyes. The room blurred around me.

"You always make things happen," Stephanie said. "I wish you were up here. I'm not trying to put a guilt trip on you—I know you have enough on your plate. I just can't help thinking you could handle Mama better than I am."

"What's to handle? She's doing what she always does—exactly what she wants to."

"That's just it. What she wants is for me to make this whole mess my entire life, which is what she's doing."

"So sneak off to your apartment and take the phone off the hook." I yawned, but there was no danger of my drifting off midsentence. I was sure I'd forgotten how to sleep.

There was a funny silence on the other end of the line.

"What?" I said.

"I don't have an apartment anymore. I've moved back in with Mama."

"You *what*? Why?"

"She needs me to help her with the twins."

"The twins need professional therapy, not you giving up everything you've worked for!"

"It wasn't that great an apartment—"

"That's not what I mean and you know it, Steph. How long did it take you to break away from her?"

"Too long."

"And now you're right back under her thumb." I got up and paced. "Look—I'm sorry. Just don't let her take over your life again. You don't need her approval anymore."

"I'm doing it for the kids." Stephanie's voice wobbled, tears in the near future. "They're so messed up, and all Mama can do is hold them and cry, which I think only makes them more scared."

"Try to talk her into getting them into therapy. Maybe my guy could recommend somebody up there."

Stephanie snorted. "Oh, can I please suggest that to Mama? And while I'm at it, let me just poke a fork in my eye, too."

"Why? They're in trouble. They need help."

"She thinks all they need is their mother."

"Oh? The same mother who let their father molest them?"

"He didn't exactly—"

"Steph, listen to me."

I leaned against the desk, eyes closed, and told her everything Dominica had told me about pornography and molestation. I could hear her gasping, and then there was nothing.

"Steph?" I said.

"Yeah?"

The tears had started. I could feel them in my own throat, and I wanted my arms around my sister and hers around me.

"It just gets you right in the gut, doesn't it?" I said. "But you have to tell Mama what I just told you, or those kids are never going to recover from this. Tell her I said—"

"Ton', if I even tell her I've been talking to you she'll probably tear out my liver with her fingernails. You're pretty much persona non grata around here right now. She'll get over it, but—"

"I don't care if she thinks I'm Quasimodo! Just find a way to get those children some help!"

I jerked my arm, sending the stack of files from Faustman sailing from the desk to the floor in one long cascade of chaos. I looked down at them without feeling.

"I wish you were here," Stephanie said. "I *so* wish you were here."

"No, I wish *you* were *here*," I said. "You *and* the kids. We could kick some tail on this thing and hold each other up." I thought I'd emptied myself of tears the night before, but I was starting to cry in earnest again. "I miss you, Steph."

"Me too. I love you."

I hung up feeling as if I'd been kicked in the stomach.

But I pushed even that piece of my anxiety aside on Monday morning when I got to the office. I'd made a decision while I was retrieving the Faustman files from the study floor the night before. It was them or Ben—and I was sure Jeffrey wasn't going to like which one I'd opted for.

I sailed in the front door and reached over to squeeze the hand Reggie stuck out to me, her coral fingernails curling around my clammy palm.

"Wish me luck," I said.

"I'll do no such thing," she said.

"Sorry. Then pray for me, would you?"

"That's a given, honey."

Whether it was the praying or the numbness of several nights without sleep and several days without substantial food, I wasn't sure. But I felt no apprehension as I tapped on Jeffrey's door and let myself in. He took a survey of my face and his own relaxed. Makeup applied with a putty knife hides a multitude of sins, including bags under the eyes and an anorexic pallor. The relief at having made a decision covered the rest of my haggardness. I was sure he thought I'd "gotten my life in order" and was ready to roll up my financial sleeves.

But when I told him I was giving him my two weeks' notice, Jeffrey's pleasant expression shifted to disbelief.

"You're actually going to quit." He leaned back in the chair, pistol-fingers at the ready. "Toni, I know you like to keep your business and personal lives separate, but may I just say I think you are taking this thing to the extreme? There is no need for you to give up your career—"

"Career–son–career–son. Hmmm, doesn't require a lot of thought as far as I can see." I shrugged. "I have no choice, Jeffrey. If I'm constantly torn between what I have to do for Ben and what I have to do for my clients, I'll rip in half. And my son needs more than half of me right now."

"Then what are the next two weeks going to look like?" he said.

"Excuse me?"

"Why give us short shrift here for two more weeks?"

"Giving two weeks' notice is protocol. Look, I'll do the best I can—"

Jeffrey pointed the pistol-fingers right at me. "Just tie up whatever you have to today. I'll give you two weeks' salary and you can go on about your business."

I knew I was gaping at him, but I made no effort to go for something more professional.

"It's not as if I'm not willing to do the ethical thing," I said.

"I'm letting you off the hook. I've given you every opportunity, but at this point, you're basically useless to us, so what would be the point in your going through the motions? I might as well get Ginny started."

As if you haven't already, I thought. Two weeks, three weeks earlier I would have actually said it. Now I just got up and said, "Is that it, then?"

Jeffrey rose, too, and I have to hand it to him, he tried to look sympathetic, though he obviously hadn't had much practice. It looked more as if he had a bad case of the heartburn I'd once wished on him.

"What will you do now?" he said.

"I don't know—find something a little less demanding, I suppose."

"You won't last long at something that doesn't require you to use your financial mind. You have a gift."

I think I was supposed to say thank you. I didn't say anything. When I turned to go, he said, "One more thing."

"Yeah?"

He folded his arms across his chest so precisely that I could almost hear the starch in his shirt crackling. "If you should decide to open your own office, remember that it would be highly unethical for you to take any of your clients here with you."

I stared.

"I realize that many of them have become quite attached to you, even in the short time you've been here, and I know how hard it is—"

"No, Jeffrey, you have no idea what hard is. I'm putting my career on hold, indefinitely, to focus on my child until he's healed. That isn't hard. Watching him suffer, now *that*—that gives new meaning to the word *impossible*. I really hope you never have to go through anything like it."

"I'm just taking care of my business."

"Me too."

Later, when Reggie was helping me carry my personal belongings out to my car, she glanced over her shoulder and whispered to me, "Did Jeffrey choke on his aftershave and fall on his face on the desk?"

"No," I said.

"Oh. Well, there's a prayer that didn't get answered." She laughed and shook the ponytail. "No, really, I was praying that you could just keep your focus on Ben and not on all you're leaving behind." She dropped a box on the backseat of the Lexus and squinted at me, one hand shading her eyes. "Honey, are you okay? You look like you haven't slept in a week. Are you eating?"

I looked over her head at the big oak doors that shut Faustman off from the mundane world. The landscape man was putting in a flat of begonias, the usual amount of derriere showing above his belt.

"I have to find something where I can make some decent money and still be able to leave the work behind when I go home in the afternoon," I said.

"Like what?"

"You won't believe it if I tell you."

When I called La Belle Meuniere, Frenchy—Ian Dauphine, for the less imaginative—said they'd already hired a replacement for the hostess. When I explained who I was, he sounded disappointed.

"I would like you working for me. You have class."

"I guess you're out of luck," I said. "I don't cook."

"You said you have waited the tables."

"That was lucrative enough when I was in college. All I needed to do then was keep myself in textbooks and eye shadow."

He chuckled, a sound reminiscent of tires crunching on gravel. "How nice if life were that simple, yes?"

You don't know the half of it.

Somehow, that thought tripped me up. What would have happened if I had been up front with Jeffrey to begin with? It probably wouldn't have made any difference, but then, not everybody was Jeffrey Faustman. And I was desperate.

So I told Ian—not just half of it, but all of it. It spilled out of my mouth as if there were no more room for it inside me. There was a certain temporary relief just in the telling.

"What do you need?" he said when I wound down. "In terms of money to live—what do you need?"

I could instantly tell him. I'd spent much of the previous night with my calculator figuring it out.

"And if I could guarantee you that in tips?" he said.

"You couldn't, because I could only work the lunch shift."

"Eleven to three?"

"Two forty-five."

"Six days a week?"

"Nope—Monday through Friday."

"Do you have a nice pair of black slacks, an attractive white blouse?"

"What woman doesn't?"

"When can you start?"

"There's no way you can assure me of that kind of money!"

"Assure yourself then," Ian said. "If you are willing to work at it, you will get those tips. It is up to you."

"I'll take it."

After we hung up, I sat staring at the box-drawing hanging on the refrigerator with its sketches of Ben's nonnegotiables.

Maybe I ought to draw my own box, I thought. Then I grunted to myself. *I think I already have. I just asked Frenchy for the moon—and he handed it to me. Why would he do that?*

I got up and padded aimlessly around the kitchen, sticking stray dishes into the dishwasher—though whether they were actually dirty or not, I had no idea—and wiping at imaginary spots on the counter with the heel of my hand. What *had* happened on the phone with Ian? I hadn't exactly been charming. I'd basically whined about my personal life—

I stopped, Ben's cereal bowl still half full of soggy Cheerios suspended over the sink.

Thirty-seven-year-old women do not whine, I had told my mother the very day our lives had begun to unravel.

Well, now they did whine—at least this one did, if it meant getting what she needed for her son.

I leaned against the counter and looked at Ben's box again. Mine, I decided, would have one phrase written in it: *Whatever it takes to get Ben healed.* Those things I couldn't choose. I just had to do them.

The phone rang. I was so jumpy from lack of sleep that I dumped the bowl in the sink and grabbed the receiver, still picking wet cereal off my wrist as I answered. It was Dominica.

"You available tomorrow morning?" she said.

"That's the only time I *am* available."

"Then it looks like that'll work. See you at 9:00?"

I hung up with a shaking hand. I was going to see a therapist. Never in my wildest dreams would I ever have thought I'd be in a position where my problems were bigger than I was. It was the single most frightening thought I had ever had—next to the possibility that my son might not get through this if I didn't get my own head together.

"Just a couple of sessions," I said to the empty kitchen. "All I need are some guidelines and I'm off. I can do this. I can *so* do this."

And then I went into the bathroom and threw up everything I hadn't eaten in the past two days.

I didn't have a chance to obsess about seeing Dominica or, better yet, to even be tempted to cancel, because an hour later, when I was ransacking my closet for every white blouse and pair of black slacks I could find, it occurred to me that I had given Alice at Doc Opie's office the name of the insurance company that carried us at Faustman—the insurance I had just given up when I quit. Ben and I were covered under Chris's insurance, too, but I had wanted to avoid any kind of confrontation with Chris over Ben's therapy.

I called Alice and gave her the right information. Two hours later I had just hung up from a phone call with Hale—apologizing to him for my behavior the day we went to Trinity House together—when Alice called back.

"I don't have good news," she said. "Your husband's insurance only covers nine sessions."

"Nine? That isn't going to cut it, not according to Doc O—to Dr. Parkins."

"Opie says we can work out a payment plan. He doesn't want finances to stop you from getting Ben treatment."

"Just let me sharpen my pencil, and I'll get back to you."

Despite the fog of sleeplessness, I felt revived at the prospect of attacking a problem I could actually do something about.

Still, I was chewing at my cuticles like Wyndham by the time I shut off the calculator. I'd never had a client who was in this much trouble. The choices were clear:

On what I was now going to be making, I could pay Kevin Pollert rent, keep the Lexus, and continue Dish Network, Verizon Wireless, House of Wong Laundry Service, Merry Maids, and Belle

Meade Landscaping—or pay for Ben's therapy.

I drew a box at the bottom of the paper and tossed the pencil aside.

At soccer practice that afternoon, Yancy Bancroft was ecstatic when I told her that I'd taken a job at La Belle Meuniere.

"I told you that Frenchman had his eye on you," she said. "You're just too cute."

"This means I'm probably going to have to move sometime in the next month, though. Our insurance isn't going to cover Ben's therapy indefinitely."

"Insurance companies are the anti-Christ. But that's okay—we'll just have to go apartment hunting. What are you doing tomorrow morning?"

I sank my forehead into my palms. "Seeing my therapist."

"Good for you, honey." She rubbed my back and described what Ben was doing down on the field while I cried myself blind.

The next morning as I loaded Ben into the car, I told him what our day was going to look like, treading carefully through the words as though they were land mines.

"I'll pick you up after school and we'll go to your game, and then you and I and Troy and his mom and dad are going out for pizza."

"Why are you wearing that? That's not what you wear to work."

I stopped midway into buckling his seat belt and looked down at my ensemble. I looked like—well, I looked like a waitress. With the capri pants and three-quarter-length sleeves, all I needed was a hat perched jauntily on the side of my head and a pair of roller skates and I would have looked like something out of *American Graffiti*.

"It's what I wear now," I said. "I have a different job."

"Why?"

"Because I want more time for you. This way I don't have to bring all those folders home."

"Oh."

You don't miss a trick do you, Pal? I thought.

I glanced at him in the rearview mirror as we made our way down Hillsboro toward the school. His forehead was furrowed like a plowed field. There was more coming, though why he would pitch a fit over that was beyond me. But then, everything was beyond me.

"What kinda job?" he said.

"I'm working in a restaurant." It was getting easier the more I said it, though I was sure it would never be easy to tell my mother. She'd have my father rolling in his grave.

"You aren't cookin' breakfast, are ya?" Ben's concern for the customers was plain on his face.

"No, I'm sparing people that. I'm just serving lunch."

"Then why are you going to work now?"

"I'm not going now."

"Then why are you dressed now?"

"Because I'm going someplace else first and I won't have time to change in between."

"Where are you going first?"

"Are you writing a book or something?" I said.

"Huh?"

"Never mind—I'm going to talk to somebody."

"Who?"

"A lady."

"About what?"

He was staring at the back of my head, his face a study in consternation. There was something so worried and old about it, it broke my heart.

"You know how you have Doc Opie?" I said.

"Yeah."

"Well, this lady's like my Doc Opie. I can talk to her about how sad and angry I am because of—because of what happened to you. It'll help me know how to help you when you get sad and angry."

If I hadn't been driving I would have squeezed my eyes shut. As it was, I held my breath and waited.

"Will you guys play with toys?" he said finally.

"Oh, gosh, Pal, I sure hope so."

I walked him all the way into his classroom, and I made an appointment to talk to Mrs. Robinette so I could spill my guts to her the way I was having to spill them to everybody else on Ben's planet. When I got back to the car, I closed my eyes and felt the lump dam up my throat. It was going to take some pretty impressive toys to play this out of me.

By the time I hit Route 257, I had the lump pretty well choked back, but I couldn't get the worried look on my son's face out of my mind. It was engraved there.

He isn't allowed to just be a kid, I thought. *He has to constantly worry about who's going to come into our lives, who's going to touch him, who can be trusted.*

And it was one person who had done that to him. One person's demented, twisted choices that had screwed up Ben's life—and Wyndham's and Emil's and Techla's and Stephanie's and Mama's. And mine. None of us was ever going to be the same. None of us was ever going to be able to go through a day without wondering just how deep the damage went in our kids and what we were going to do about it.

I wanted to hurt him—no, both of them. I didn't just want to see Sid and Bobbi go to jail and rot there, I wanted to be the one to slap them—over and over—right across the face with my open hand, fingernails bared. I wanted to hit them until they bled, until they screamed, the way Ben did every night of his life. I wanted them to use his very words: *Make it stop. Please—make it stop...*

I felt a pain in the side of my face. Only then did I realize that I was biting down so hard my teeth were audibly grating. I tried to open my mouth, with little success. A knitting-needle pain pierced my ear.

By the time I got to the reception area at Trinity House, I was shaking, and I couldn't stop it. Even more frightening was the fact that I didn't want to. I didn't care that little Kate whispered nervously into the phone when she called Dominica to tell her I had arrived or that Dominica herself nearly ran into the room and marched up to me with her eyes already searching my face.

"You better have a bed here for me," I said. It was an attempt at a joke, but it sounded like I was threatening a shakedown.

"No, but I've got a couple pillows for you," she said. "Let's go."

When we reached the healing room, she pointed to a large cushion in the middle of the floor and tossed me a smaller one.

"Kneel on that big one," she said, "and punch this little one. Punch it until you don't want to punch it anymore."

I held up the smaller cushion. "Is this my brother-in-law's head?"

"No, no. We leave the vengeance to our Father around here. That pillow is this whole stinking mess. Beat the life out of it, Toni."

I punched and beat and clawed and hit until my arms felt like broken rubber bands. Then I threw the thing against the wall and sobbed into my hands.

"All right, then," Dominica said. "Now we can go to work."

Fourteen

I SAT THERE CROSS-LEGGED on the cushion while Dominica fixed me a cup of tea. As she stirred soundlessly and swaddled the mug in a napkin and came to kneel across from me, she seemed at once robust and queenly. I felt like a basket case.

"Drink this," she said. "Just—careful—it's hot."

I took the cup in its napkin sheath, but I only stared into it, watching Earl Grey bubbles disappear. My self-esteem went with them.

"Am I losing it?" I said.

"Do you think you are?"

"Suddenly I'm acting like a psycho."

"This is a normal reaction to an abnormal situation. A psycho would have already gone out and killed the sociopath who did this to your son."

I squinted at her through the steam.

"You've thought about it," she said.

"Yeah."

"Have you bought a gun—knife—explosives?"

"No."

"Do you plan to?"

"No."

"Then I think this guy's safe for the moment. Let's focus on you." Dominica settled herself back against the wall, legs stretched out in front of her, ankles crossed. I sat hunched over the tea, now and then taking sips that were too slowly melting the lump in my throat.

"So your denial cracked," she said. "Now you're getting hit by the anger waves. Want to tell me about it?"

"Do I have a choice? No, you don't even have to answer that. I have no choices anymore. My whole life's in the box."

"Box?"

I told her about Doc Opie's box concept. She nodded solemnly.

"I like it," she said. "Next time you see him, tell him I'm stealing that from him. Therapeutic larceny." Dominica cocked her head at me, the light shifting on her dark waves. "But you do have choices. You chose to come here."

"I had to—just like I had to quit my job and become a waitress. Just like I have to move to a cheaper place. The list goes on."

I chugged the tea while Dominica winced.

"Is your mouth lined with asbestos?" she said.

"It's like I can't feel anything. If I do feel, it goes out of control. I'm a freak."

"All right, let's go back to those choices. It doesn't seem like they're options, but that's only because they're Hobson's choices."

I grunted as I set the mug on the tile floor beside me. "Who's Hobson? I'd be happy to let him take over for me."

"He's dead now, but—"

"Lucky guy."

Dominica looked at me sharply. "What do you mean?"

"It was a joke."

She stuck up a finger. "Rule number one for your healing: don't use sarcasm as a coping mechanism. I want to be able to take what you say at face value. If you say a dead man is a lucky guy, I think you're contemplating suicide."

"No, I don't want to die! I just don't want to live like *this*."

She surveyed me for a good twenty seconds, until I started to squirm.

"So…who's Hobson?" I said.

Dominica twitched an eyebrow as if she were only momentarily letting me off the hook. "Guy back in the 1600s. Had a messenger service using horses, of course. Lived in Cambridge, and on the weekends he'd let the students use his horses, but they either had to take the next horse he had available or do without. The students called it a Hobson's choice."

"So…I don't see how that applies to me."

"Here's a better example." Dominica recrossed her ankles. "Guy goes out to an Indian reservation, out in the middle of Nowhere, New Mexico. Goes to see some festival. Anyway, he gets to his car to go home and discovers he has a flat tire and no spare. So he walks to the only service station on the reservation, asks the guy if he can fix his tire. Guy says, 'Sure' or 'Ug' or something—I can make fun of the natives because I *am* one."

"Uh-huh," I said. This wasn't what I'd expected from therapy, but Dominica was at least entertaining.

"So our fella with the flat tire says, 'How much is it gonna cost me?'" Dominica sat up straight on her cushion and leaned toward me, her eyes relishing the upcoming punch line. "The old Indian looks at him—and he smiles real slow—and he says, 'Does it matter?'"

Dominica gave a nod and sat back, like a queen on her throne, and watched me. I stared at her, blinking, until clarity pinged through the fog.

"Oh," I said. "So—a Hobson's choice is really no choice at all. It's take it or leave it."

"But it's still a choice. There are people who wouldn't pay the price. They'd leave it."

"I *can't* 'leave it.' I have to take care of my son."

"No, you don't. You could go on with life as you knew it before all this happened. People do it all the time. They'd rather drive that car home on the rim than pay the price that's asked of them. A lot of people can't handle being pushed against the wall, so they pretend the wall isn't there."

"I can't pretend this away. I'd be sacrificing my son's life."

Dominica nodded, her eyes never wavering from my face. It struck me that they hadn't left it since I'd arrived. Part of me wanted to stare her down—right after I chewed up her cheek or something. The other part of me couldn't drag my eyes from hers, because I knew she was seeing something I wasn't grasping.

"That's God in you," she said. "That's Christ leading you."

I let out a grunt. "I keep telling people they're assuming something that isn't there. Don't get me wrong—I believe in God. I've gone to church all my life. I was raised on the Ten Commandments, and have probably broken most of them. Well, I haven't murdered anybody—not yet." I held up my hand. "Sorry. Rule number one."

"So you're saying because you've sinned, there can't be any God in you."

"I'm saying I'm not like Reggie or Yancy or Hale or you or Doc Opie. You all think about God. You talk about God and Jesus. You pray. I'm not doing any of that. All I'm doing is struggling like mad just to make it."

Dominica was nodding as if I were nailing the theory of relativity. "The reason you're making it *is* God. You believe, and you've surrounded yourself with people who know Him personally. He'll take that for a start." Dominica assumed the position she always took when she was about to get in my face: legs stretched out in a V, hands flat on the floor between her knees as she leaned in to look deeper into me. "The fact that you're barely thinking twice about making choices most people would cower in front of is proof that God's already working in you. You're ready to embrace the Christ-life."

"I don't think—"

"Look, there are people in this world who have never even heard of Jesus, yet they express His compassion and love all the time, as a matter of course. That's because Christ is real, He's pervasive. He's the way we know how to connect with God. Now you—you've been introduced to Him, and you've obviously given Him enough of a crack to get in, because He's in there doing His thing." She chuckled. "I'm just waiting for *you* to realize that. Then there's going to be no stopping you, girl."

I didn't know what to say, and I finally had to close my eyes because her intensity was almost too much for me. I was so tired.

"Toni." Her voice dropped gently, brushing like velvet against my ears. "Why not become conscious of what God's already doing in you? You can stop working so hard and just believe and watch and listen and join in."

I opened my eyes, surprised by a new film of tears. "What I wouldn't give to let somebody else take over. I've even been tempted to call Chris—that's my husband. We're separated. I've been tempted to say to him, 'You do this. I can't do it alone. I can't do it at all.'"

"Would that be so bad?"

"It would be insane."

"Because...?"

"Because in the first place, he's in total denial that Ben even needs help. He questions whether anything actually happened."

"What if he weren't? What if he wanted to be involved in Ben's healing?"

I explored the ceiling. The tears receded, chased by bitterness.

"There are some unresolved issues," I said. "An affair he's never apologized for, for openers. There are other things..."

I tensed, waiting for her to ask for specifics. Instead she said, "It still feels like a Hobson's choice to you. That could change. One thing at a time. Meanwhile, whether your husband is with you or not, you're not alone."

"God," I said.

"Right."

I could feel another wave coming. As I squeezed my face against it, I could feel Dominica's hand on my knee.

"Go ahead," she said. "Let it go. It's safe in here. I won't let you kill anybody."

"You're not going to like it."

"I've heard it all."

"All right. If I'm not alone, then where was God when that pervert was taking pictures of Ben and molesting him? Where was Jesus when my sister turned her head to what was going on in her own house? Where was either one of them when I went merrily on my way, never suspecting a thing?"

"God was there the whole time, yelling His head off," Dominica said. "But your sister, your brother-in-law—they weren't listening. Evil is like spiritual earplugs. It shuts out everything else."

"So you're saying I wasn't listening either."

"God was giving you all the signs. Look at the way your little boy was behaving. You knew something was up, but you didn't know how to interpret it."

"Why didn't He tell me?"

"He did tell you. Through Wyndham. She was listening."

I leaned toward her, so close that our noses were nearly touching. "Don't you get it? I don't know *how* to listen to God!"

"That's why you have me. I'm going to teach you."

I leaned back, eyes squeezed shut. "I'm sorry."

"For what? For asking the right questions? For giving this the emotional intensity it deserves? Those are God-things. We follow Jesus around here, and He was emotional and intense. Why would we discourage that?"

She let that sink in. I didn't know whether to blow my nose or cry some more or take out a pad and pencil and tell her to fire away. So I did all three. She gave me a list while I wiped my nostrils and scribbled illegibly and let the tears splash down on the ink.

I went over the list on the way to work, after I looked in on Wyndham—who barely acknowledged my presence except to tell me how much she hated it at Trinity House—and after I repaired my makeup using the lighted mirror on the passenger side of the Lexus, one of the many luxuries I was about to relinquish.

Dominica's list was short and specific.

> *Eat small portions of something—anything—every two hours.*
> *Do what you can to sleep at night. Rest as much as possible.*
> *Stay connected with your support group—Reggie, Yancy, Hale, Stephanie.*
> *Focus on the way things move forward. Notice the small things. God is in the details. Go with that.*
> *Call Dominica if your happiness level falls below five on a scale of one to ten. Anything more than five is normal for what you're going through. Anything less is too dangerous. Dead men seem luckier at less than five.*

I didn't know how I was going to get through a first day on a new job with all of that in my head, especially since I hadn't waited tables in seventeen years. As it turned out, it was the list that kept me from actually going off the deep end and taking a trayful of the day's entrees with me.

Ian told me to eat lunch before I started. It was on the house, so I gagged down a couple of spoonfuls of strawberry sorbet. Ian then said I was going to be "low maintenance, madame."

After two hours of hoisting escargots and bouillabaisse, I was given a break. I went to the back steps, just off the kitchen, which faced an alleyful of dumpsters, and whispered, "I sure hope You're really in this with me because I will fold if You aren't. Then where would Ben be?" It was as much God-consciousness as I could manage.

My last customer of the day was Yancy. She had the hostess seat her at my table, asked for the most fattening dessert we had, and gave me the bug-eyed smile.

"You make this place look real good, girl," she said.

"I'm sure I look particularly lovely. I feel like I've been beaten with a large stick."

"How much longer do you have?"

"About twenty minutes."

"I'm just going to sit here with this little piece of heaven—" she looked down at the crème brûlée with chestnuts—"and pray. You'll be fine."

I was. I won't say I sailed through my last half hour, but the executives from Sony who were having a late lunch left me a thirty-dollar tip, which immediately translated into twenty minutes of therapy for Ben. That would bring him twenty minutes closer to healing. I had to think of it that way. What had Dominica called it? A Hobson's choice.

It was one of many I had to make over the next several weeks, as May gave way to early June. Fortunately, those choices had sub-choices which gave me less of a feeling that I was being dragged through the mud.

I had to leave Keith Pollert's house and its accompanying expenses—that was a no-brainer. Where to live instead was a question that Yancy was more than happy to explore with me. Every morning for a week, before I had to go to work, she and I looked at apartments she'd already scoped out over the phone the day before, eliminating those that were in questionable neighborhoods. It wasn't a problem I'd ever had to face, and Yancy informed me that it actually wasn't a problem—it was a challenge. When we'd looked at every complex I could afford on the west end of Nashville, most of which were currently crammed with Vanderbilt students, she came up with an apartment over a garage in an old lady's backyard.

I was skeptical. So, Yancy admitted, was the old lady when Yancy told her I had a five-year-old. But when Yancy spotted the fish on the lady's car and told her she was a Christian, too, we got not only sweet tea and chocolate pie, but Ben and I also got the apartment. Two bedrooms, a huge bathroom with a clawfoot tub, a living room with lace curtains, and a kitchen with a built-in china cabinet, which charmed the socks off of Yancy.

"This is just quaint," she said to me. "You can fix this up so cute."

"*We* can fix it up. I had a decorator do my house in Virginia, that's how decor-challenged I am. And need I remind you I have no furniture here?"

That, it turned out, was less of a problem than feeding the five thousand. Like loaves and fishes, beds, chairs, a table, a couch, and a swing to hang from the ceiling in Ben's room appeared out of the garages and attics of Yancy's church friends.

"Okay, that's it," I said. "I'm coming to church Sunday. They've guilted me into it."

Yancy just smiled and said, "Whatever it takes."

Kevin Pollert was less than pleased when I gave him my notice, and I felt no compulsion to tell him why I was moving. But Ben's teacher and his coaches were a different story. I had to tell them what Ben was going through.

When I shared with young Mrs. Robinette, as I'd been trying to do for weeks, she covered her mouth with her hand and then said, "I don't think I could live through something like this if it happened to my baby. And you didn't *know*?" Whether she meant it to be an accusation or not, it felt like it. I vented to Reggie for an hour over that one while we washed the '70s Corelle dishes we'd picked up at the Goodwill. Reggie finally pointed a Summer Shell Pink fingernail at me and said, "Honey, that woman is going to have to answer for that one day. Don't you worry about it."

When I told Coach Gary, the soccer coach, he at first asked me if I was sure Ben didn't make it up. He reminded me that five-year-old boys did, after all, have pretty vivid imaginations. When I told him that Ben himself hadn't made the disclosure, he seemed even more eager to chalk the whole thing up to a misunderstanding, but he assured me that he would keep an eye on Ben, make sure he was doing okay.

The T-ball coach, Joe Jordan, wanted to know if my husband had killed the pervert yet. When I explained that Sid was being held by the FBI, he said that was too good for him. He said he hoped Sid ended up in the state pen, and went on to describe in excruciating detail what inmates did to child molesters. I cut him off when he started licking his chops and thanked him for caring. I had to take whatever support I could get.

The one thing they all seemed to share was the idea that kids get over things fast and that in a couple of weeks Ben would forget about it. If only that were true, I wanted to tell them. Although Ben seemed to like going to Doc Opie's and was pitching fewer fits that attracted the attention of passersby, he was far from forgetting about it.

He still woke up screaming most nights.

He still became anxious every morning when I took him to school and half the time clung to my leg like Velcro.

It still took a trip to the refrigerator to study the box drawings before he would take a bath or eat more than three bites of supper or climb into his bed. In fact, as time went by, we had to add other things to the box, things I hadn't realized he was refusing to do. Things like saying hello to people I introduced him to, as opposed to staring at them as if they were among the usual suspects and then burying his face in whatever article of clothing I was wearing.

Or things like wipe his bottom when he went to the bathroom.

Once I started doing the laundry myself—having given up the laundry service—I discovered brown globs on every pair of his Power Ranger underwear.

"Hey, Pal," I said to him one night as I was sorting the dirty clothes for our weekly trip to the Laundromat. "Don't you believe in using toilet paper? What's with the poop on our panties?"

"Mo-om." He grabbed for Lamb, who was never far away.

"Well, Ben, for Pete's sake—we might be trying to save money, but you can use potty paper."

"I don't want to talk about it."

I shook my head. "This goes in the box, dude, although I don't know what you're going to draw a picture of."

"I'm not drawing a picture." His voice wasn't defiant. It was merely ashamed. I looked up to see him holding Lamb in front of his face.

I felt like a giant heel.

"I'm sorry, Pal, I didn't mean to embarrass you. But yikes, we all have to wipe our fannies."

"I can't."

"What do you mean, you can't?" I stopped and squatted down in front of him. Lamb and I were nose to nose. "Is there a problem with your bottom? Is it sore or something?"

"No! Don't touch it!"

I started to choke, and I had to force myself to breathe. Ben's little hands were clutching Lamb so hard his fingernails were blue.

"I'm not going to touch it," I said. "And you don't have to either. Just use a lot of toilet paper—or wet a washcloth."

He was shaking his head. I had no idea what to do, so I let it drop until my next biweekly visit with Doc Opie.

"What is that about?" I said. "He wasn't just being stubborn—he was afraid. I'm beginning to know the difference."

"It could have something to do with the abuse," Doc Opie said. "In fact, it's more than likely."

"So what do I do? I don't want to make a big deal out of it, but wow."

"Disposable underwear."

"What—you mean Pull-Ups? He'd be the laughingstock of the kindergarten!"

"No, I mean cheapie briefs from Wal-Mart—ones you can throw away after he wears them once." Doc Opie looked unbearably sad. "We have to do everything we can to keep the guilt and shame to a minimum. He obviously can't stand to touch himself in that area, but he knows the result is pretty gross. Can you just quietly take care of it? Make sure he gets in the tub every night?"

"I'll put it in my box," I said.

Once we were moved into our apartment, which after Pollert's mansion gave new meaning to the word *cozy*, things settled into a routine. That is, after Yancy finished working her magic on the place.

"It's not just my magic," she told me when it was finished. "You picked it all out—it's so you."

Interesting, because until Yancy and I—and Reggie, who was not to be left out of the fun—began to haunt thrift stores and yard sales, I hadn't even known there *was* a "me" in the decorating sense.

"My decorator in Virginia told me I needed a basic neutral color, then something to compliment that, and then an accent color for pillows and stuff," I said to Yancy when we first started out.

"Now there was a woman with no imagination," Yancy said. "What you need to decide is what kind of atmosphere you want for you and Ben."

"Safe," I said. "Safe and happy and serene. But I don't think a color scheme is going to do it."

It helped, however. Blue and green, with the occasional splash of yellow, became the backdrop for an old toy-box-turned-coffee-table and a lamp made out of a parking meter and pillows covered in stripes and spots and checks that would have made poor Kevin Pollert green in the gills. Ben's drawings in acrylic frames covered the wall over the couch, and some cool green sheets replaced the lace panels at the windows.

"Those were just a tad too little-old-lady for you, honey," Reggie told me as she eagerly packed the doily-like curtains away.

If our landlady, Ethel Morrison—the epitome of a little old lady—objected, she didn't say so when I invited her up to see the finished product. She sat right down at the kitchen table which Yancy had painted robin's egg blue and complimented me on the arrangement of baskets we'd tacked to the wall. I didn't tell her that there wasn't one up there that had cost me more than ninety-nine cents.

I actually got into the saving money thing as easily as I'd always spent it. I got a huge kick out of finding a Liz Claiborne blouse for work at the Salvation Army for three bucks, and I was on a first-name basis with the sales clerks at Bud's Discount City.

"You are a whiz with a dollar," Yancy said to me. "I bet you are one amazing financial consultant."

"I *was*," I said.

She tucked her feet up under her on the Italian leather couch in her family room and glanced back to make sure Troy and Ben were out of earshot with their Legos.

"Just because you aren't working as one right now," she said, "doesn't mean that's not still who you are."

"I wish I did know who I was. I've totally lost touch with myself. All I do is wait tables and go to therapy and burn my five-year-old's underwear."

Yancy toyed with an earring. "Any woman who picks out a plaid shower curtain without batting an eye knows who she is. You're selling yourself short."

"I don't know what I'm doing. I'm just putting one foot in front of the other—but I'm not sure it's getting us anywhere."

I thought about it at home later that night. Ben had fallen asleep relatively easily in the race-car bed that Hale had managed to get from somewhere. He said somebody wanted to get rid of it, but it looked suspiciously new to me. I had the gut feeling that he'd gone out and bought it. Probably felt guilty because Wyndham didn't seem to be making much progress at Trinity House.

I watched Ben by the winking light of a jar of lightning bugs we'd captured in the yard. Once I made sure his breathing was deep and even and no nightmare was imminent, I thought back to my last visit with Wyndham, two days before.

"How ya doin', hon?" I'd said to her. "Are you feeling any better at all?"

She'd looked at me miserably from her bed in the spare little cell where she was hugging a battered-looking pillow. I suspected it had been part of Dominica's anger management program.

"No offense, Aunt Toni—"

"Don't worry about it. Just spill it."

"I feel worse. Before, I thought that once I got it all out it would be okay. But now there's all this stuff."

"What stuff?" I said.

"Like why didn't I fight him?"

"Him?"

"Him—Sid. Why didn't I just scratch his eyes out when he touched me like that?"

"Gee, let's see. He's got about a foot of height and maybe a hundred pounds on you, not to mention he's your father, which gave him a certain amount of authority."

"I could have turned *her* in sooner, though. She's such a wimp. What was she going to do to me if I told?"

I forced myself not to get up and pace the room—or go running for Dominica. I tried to remember what Dominica had told me to say to Wyndham in situations like this. A couple of phrases came to the rescue.

"Look, honey," I said, "you have to honor what God gave you to survive with."

"Like what?" she said.

The defiance in her eyes surprised me. This wasn't little Wyndham of milquetoast fame. I definitely preferred this to the ducking of the head and the oh-I'm-so-sorry.

"I don't know," I said. "I wasn't there. But you must have—"

"One time I said I was going to tell."

I looked at her sharply. Her voice dipped.

"You said that to him?" I said.

"Uh-huh."

"And what happened?"

Wyndham sank her chin into the pillow and seemed to grow small before my eyes.

"He held my head under the water. I thought he was going to drown me."

"Water? What water?"

"In the bathtub. That's where he took a lot of the pictures."

My mind left her—went off to the countless scenes with Ben in the bathroom, to visions of me forcing him into the tub, listening to him scream while I told him there was nothing to be afraid of.

Of course. She'd said that before, but it hadn't connected—until now. Now I wanted to throw myself from the window. Wyndham brought me back with a sob.

"Honey—I'm sorry," I said.

I sat on the edge of the bed and ran my hand along her arm. She stiffened like a steel rod.

"I didn't want to remember that," she said. "'Cause now I know."

"Now you know what?"

"That he didn't really love me and think I was beautiful like he always said when he was—He didn't love me. He tried to kill me!"

Her face contorted, drawing her neck muscles up as her mouth writhed. I had never seen sheer self-loathing until then.

"I'm so stupid!" she said. "Why did I ever believe that?"

"Because that's what fathers are supposed to think about their daughters," I said. "But he isn't a father—he's a monster. This isn't about you being stupid or a coward, it's about him being completely evil."

"I hate him," Wyndham said.

"I know." And I could see it eating her alive, because she had no idea what to do with that kind of anger. Why would she? She had never even been allowed to feel it.

"Sometimes I still want to die," she said.

I glanced involuntarily at her arms. The scars were growing more faint, and there were no new ones.

"I'm not going to kill myself," Wyndham said. "But it's only because of God. Jesus wouldn't take what doesn't really belong to

Him and neither can I take a life that doesn't really belong to me. It belongs to God."

"Sounds like a pretty good reason to me," I said. Actually, any reason would have sounded good. My chest was ready to crack open with grief for her.

"Dominica says the Father has a purpose for me, and dying right now isn't it."

"I can go along with that."

"She told me to look at the good stuff in my life." Wyndham rolled her eyes toward me. "I had to look pretty hard."

"Did you come up with anything?"

"Some. I've got friends. Lindsay writes me every day."

"No kidding?"

"And Hale—he comes every week and brings me all this cool stuff from the youth group. And you."

"I know you're mad at me for bringing you here."

Wyndham shrugged. "I'm not that mad anymore. Dominica told me I have to focus my anger where it should really go—at them."

"Yeah, I hear you."

"And I have Techla and Emil. I thought I'd never see them again, but Dominica says that's not true." I could see her neck tightening again, straining against the grief. "I really miss them. I really do."

"They miss you, too," I said. "Aunt Stephanie says they talk about you all the time. I'll tell them anything you want me to—or Aunt Stephanie will."

She swallowed hard. "Tell them—tell them I haven't run out on them. I'm just taking a time-out right now so I can learn to be a better sister to them than I was before. Tell them that."

"Okay," I said. Although just then, I couldn't have told anybody anything. I couldn't speak a word.

I stood now looking down at my sleeping son. Maybe I should look at the "good stuff" in *my* life. Dominica had said God was in the details.

Right now the best thing was that Ben had conked out without a fight. We were getting closer to the end of the school year, and there was a lot happening during the day to wear him out, including the last of the soccer season and the beginning of T-ball practice. I tiptoed away and into my own bedroom and lay down on the apple-green comforter that still smelled like Reggie's grandmother's basement.

Ben and I were safe. He was getting help. Although I was having to juggle his therapy and mine and my involvement in Wyndham's, we'd fallen into a routine that was still more peaceful than the frenzied one we'd lived before. We actually had the occasional conversation that didn't end up in a screaming match. He hadn't said he hated me all week. I was beginning to develop my own clientele at La Belle Meuniere. Just the day before, Martina McBride's stage manager had left me a $100 tip. The only time I even got angry was when I talked to Stephanie a few times a week and could hear my mother prompting her on what to say to me: "We're still working on getting your sister out on bail. We aren't going to betray her."

I'd started calling Stephanie at her office so I didn't have to listen to Mama in the background.

"You're moving forward," Dominica would tell me. "That's God. Be aware of that. See what else He'll do."

And every time, I would tell her, "I want to hear Him. You and Reggie and Hale—you all seem to know what He's saying to you. When am I going to get that?"

"You're getting it—through them, through—"

"I want to hear it myself," I'd say.

"Then keep listening. And read the Gospels. See how He speaks to Jesus. That's the kind of relationship He wants with you."

At the moment, I wished He would simply scoop me up out of the hole I could feel myself sinking into. Despite the infinitesimal forward movement, I felt like I was backing up. I wished for anger again. At least the anger had kept me moving. This sadness made me want to curl up in a fetal position, the way I was doing that very minute. I would have cried if there had been any tears left.

I closed my eyes and tried to sleep. Dominica kept telling me to get more rest. She also told me to eat, but I'd managed to force down only a few bites of pasta salad over at Yancy's.

"So what *are* You doing?" I whispered into the dark. "I'm so alone. I don't feel You. I don't feel anything."

And then I did feel something—an onslaught of panic that brought me straight up in the bed. Fear with no way out, no exit, no reason, and no escape from my own slamming heart.

"Oh, God," I said out loud. "This is a three—this is a two—"

Covering my mouth to keep from throwing up, I groped for the phone and the switch on the lamp at the same time. In a pool of stark, unfriendly light I managed to locate Dominica's after-hours number and fumbled to punch it out on the phone. My fingers were sweaty.

"Please be there," I whispered. "Please be there—"

"This is Dominica."

"This is Toni. Dominica, I'm so scared. I'm losing it."

Her voice was immediately matter-of-fact. "No, you aren't, or you wouldn't have called me. Good job. Take a couple of relaxed breaths for me—breathe from your diaphragm…"

It didn't take more than five minutes for her to calm me down. It was the longest five minutes of my life. I asked her to hang on while I went and threw up. After that, I was better, steady enough to listen to her.

"You're being bombarded with stress and betrayal and rage," she said. "There isn't a person in this world who wouldn't panic in the face of that."

"I didn't like it."

"Nobody does—which is why God's there."

"I'm having my doubts."

"Then let me reassure you. You calling me, you being honest about what you're feeling, you knowing you couldn't get through that alone—those are all things God would want you to do. So who's to say He didn't prompt you?"

"I didn't hear anything—except my own self telling me to pick up the phone."

"I've never had God come to me in a vision and speak to me in some deep voice from heaven," Dominica said. "What I get is my own thoughts—ones that make such perfect sense they couldn't possibly belong to me."

"You always make sense."

"That's just God talking through me. You'll get the hang of this. Just keep paying attention."

We talked until I felt sleepy, though she made me promise to call her back if I felt that kind of panic again. She said it was okay if I did, because anxiety was keeping me from giving up completely. Panic, she said, was the fight in me.

"Just keep telling God that you trust Him to carry you through the next thing."

"I hope there is no 'next thing,'" I said. "I've had enough."

When we hung up, I lay there in the dark, too exhausted to do anything but whisper, "Okay, I trust You. Whatever it takes, I'll try to do it, but You've got to help me."

There was no more panic. There was no sound from Ben's room. There was only a phone call just a half hour after I finally drifted off to sleep.

It ripped me from the edge of a dream, and my head was still halfway in it when I said, "Hello?"

"Toni?" said a female voice. "Toni...it's Bobbi."

"What?"

"I just want to know: Why are you doing this to me?"

Fifteen

BOBBI'S VOICE WAS SHRILL. "Toni, are you there?" she said.

"Yeah." I groped for the light switch and covered my eyes ineffectively with my hand, fingers wide open to let the invasive light right in.

"Then talk to me. Why are you doing this to me?"

"Where are you?" I said. "Are you calling from jail?"

There was a sharp laugh, so unlike Bobbi I held out the receiver and looked at it, as if I could see her and make sure this was really my older sister. Controlled, child-oriented Bobbi Vyne didn't laugh like a witch having an attack of jocularity.

"No," Bobbi said, "they let me go. They can't prove I knew what Sid was doing, and they know it."

I had to shake myself into replying. How did a person carry on a conversation this surreal? "So—where are you?" I said.

"I'm at a hotel, with Mama. They won't let me see my babies. Toni, why are you doing this to me?"

Her voice shot up so high I had to pull the phone away from my ear again. Hysteria was in our near future, something else that hadn't erupted from Bobbi since her psychiatric therapy days. I grasped at the idea that if I kept my own voice low and calm, she might come down a few notches.

"Where is Mama right now?" I said

"Oh, she's right here. She's not allowed to let me out of her sight."

"I don't understand."

Bobbi laughed again, this time with a bitterness that set my teeth on edge. "The FBI said they could change their minds if new evidence comes up, so I'm not allowed to leave the city. I was released under Mama's recognizance."

"And you can't see the kids?"

"No, Toni, I can't." The accusation was clear.

"Did the state take them?"

"Not a chance! I would die first before I would let that happen!"

It seemed to me as she raved on that even her voluntary demise wasn't going to stand in the way of the legal system. She was clearly operating in another dimension, and it was frightening to me.

"Stephanie has them, at Mama's," she was saying. "We're going to decide what to do tomorrow." Her voice contracted down to a point, and she stabbed it into me. "Don't you try to get in touch with them, Toni. I don't want you talking to them. And I don't want you talking to Wyndham anymore either."

It was my turn to laugh. "I'm her guardian! I'm involved in her therapy."

"Mama and I are going to get that changed."

I shouldn't have been stunned, but I was. I climbed out of bed and wriggled an oversized, long-sleeved shirt over the T-shirt I was sleeping in. I wrapped it around me as I tiptoed into the hallway and closed Ben's door. He was going to scream if he woke up and found it that way, but I couldn't have him hearing this conversation either. I went to the kitchen, as far from his room as I could get, and began to talk in hoarse whispers.

"Wyndham is right where she needs to be with exactly who she needs to be with," I said. "And Emil and Techla ought be getting similar care. I have Ben in therapy."

"Ben?"

Her question hit my jaw like a left hook. "Oh, don't give me that I-didn't-know-anything-about-it crap, Bobbi! It might have worked on the FBI, but it won't work on me."

"I have no idea who framed Sid like this!"

"*What?*" I slammed my hand flat on the table. The matchbook that was balancing on it shot across the kitchen floor, and the table rocked beneath me. "Are you out of your mind? Do you actually refuse to believe that Sid did this? They found the stuff right in your house! Wyndham has disclosed in detail!" I snorted out a laugh. "Either you've completely lost it, or you are the biggest liar on the

face of this earth. In either case—you dad-gum well *shouldn't* be seeing your children!"

"Wyndham is the one who's lying, Toni."

Bobbi's voice was now flat, toneless. It was more disturbing than
her former histrionics.

"Give me a break," I said.

"She made this whole thing up. I don't doubt that she planted
that stuff in Sid's studio, too."

I wanted to laugh again, although I knew if I did I would carry
myself off the proverbial deep end. "And she would do this why?" I
said.

"Because she's a rebellious teenager."

I closed my eyes. "You haven't got a clue about your own daughter. In the first place, she has given up absolutely everything she has
ever known to come forward with this. She's in a residential treatment facility where she has no freedom because she's suicidal."

"Is she giving you that story, too?"

"Complete with illustrations, carved on her arms and legs."

"Where is she, Toni? I want to talk to her."

"Over my dead body."

"You can't keep me from my child!"

"Is the FBI keeping you from the twins?"

"Yes—"

"Then don't even try to go there with me." I got up and paced,
my bare feet slapping Ethel's linoleum. "Stop trying to put this on
everybody else, and start looking at yourself. Don't you think you've
turned your head long enough? It happened, right under your nose,
and your kids are suffering for it, and so is mine. That's what you
need to be looking at right now."

There was a venomous silence.

"I hate you," she said finally. "And I am never going to forgive
you for tearing my family apart."

The phone went dead in my hand.

"Dear God," I whispered. "Oh, dear God."

I didn't go back to sleep. It was all I could do to wait until 7 A.M.
to call Hale and Yancy and Reggie. I didn't ask any of them to come

over, but they all showed up within fifteen minutes of each other. Reggie had a hash brown casserole with her. One look at me and she grabbed a fork and started hand-feeding it to me.

"The only bad thing about you leaving Faustman is there's nobody around you to make you eat," she said. "Look at your cheekbones stickin' out. That is just tragic."

Yancy's husband, Scott, came with her and brought Troy. They rousted Ben out of bed and hauled him off to McDonald's for breakfast. Ben was a little torn because Saturday morning was the only time I let him have Fruit Loops instead of something healthy, and because his Reggie was there. But she promised him she'd take him to the zoo later, so he finally trailed off after Troy.

I could let down my guard then and start pacing again. Hale, Reggie, and Yancy watched me from the couch, Reggie reaching out with a forkful of hash browns every time I passed her.

"I'm supposed to use my words," I said. "That's what Doc Opie tells Ben when he gets ready to pitch a fit—use your words." I glanced at the three Christians on the sidelines. "If I use the words I want to use, you'll all get up and leave."

"You want to pitch a fit, go ahead," Reggie said. "Just eat something first."

"And let me clear away the breakables," Yancy said. "We've about bought everything useable from the Goodwill."

I shook my head. "I just don't know what to do. She can't take Wyndham, can she?"

"Only way to know is to go to the source," Hale said. "You want me to call the FBI? Or better yet, what about Faith Anne Newlin?"

"Who's Faith Anne Newlin?" Yancy said.

"My lawyer," I said. "It sounds like Mama is going to try to get guardianship of Wyndham back and haul her out of Trinity." I had a chilling thought. "She only gave me six weeks…"

"Let me try to get Faith on the phone," Hale said.

"At 8 A.M. on a Saturday? That's going to cost me." Then I shook my head again. "Doesn't matter. Go for it."

"Toni, honey, sit down," Yancy said as Hale went into the bedroom in search of the telephone. "You're making me seasick."

"I'm just sick, period," Reggie said. "Does that woman care at all about her kids, or is she just into herself?"

"She's into Sid," I said. "He's always been totally controlling— just like my father, only to the hundredth power. I think she married him because she could never get my father to love her. They say people do that. She doesn't believe she can exist without Sid. Their pictures are next to the term *codependent* in the psychological dictionary."

"I get it," Yancy said. "If she believes *he's* a twisted monster, she has to believe *she* is, too."

"As far as I'm concerned, she is," Reggie said.

"I don't know what she is," I said. "And at this point, I don't think it matters. What's important is whether she can get her hands on Wyndham and turn that poor girl inside out."

Hale came in and set the phone on the coffee table, his square jaw set.

"What?" I said. "Bad news? Come on, spit it out. I have to know everything."

"Faith's going to get back to you. She says she can make a few calls and hopefully get at least an extension on your guardianship, given the fact that Bobbi's been released. A judge isn't going to be blind to the fact that more than likely your mother will drag Wyndham right back to Bobbi, court order or no court order."

"That sounds like good news to me," Reggie said. She was nodding so hard at me her ponytail was bobbing. "Don't you think so, honey?"

But I was watching Hale's eyes. "What are you holding back?" I said to him.

He pressed his lips together before he spoke. "There is one way you can make sure Bobbi goes back to jail—or at least can't get to Wyndham. Faith Anne's idea."

I shoved several magazines off the coffee table onto the floor with one arm and sat down so I could face him dead on.

"What?" I said. "What's the deal?"

Hale still seemed to be having trouble looking at me.

"You're scarin' me here," I said.

"She asked me if Ben himself had disclosed anything yet. I told her I didn't think so."

I shook my head. "Where's this going?"

"If Ben could corroborate Wyndham's story—"

"You mean testify to the F.B.I.?"

"Yeah. That's what I mean."

I got up and resumed the pacing at a stiff march. "No. There is no way I'm putting my baby through that."

"They're not going to put him under a naked light bulb, Toni," Hale said. "They have people who know how to handle children."

"Would I be able to be there?"

"Probably not."

"Then forget it."

No one said anything. I stopped in front of the window, nausea rising up in my throat. Below, Ethel's hydrangeas were blooming in blossoms bigger than my head. Somewhere in the yard, squirrels were putting up an obnoxious chatter. I wanted to scream at the world to stop pretending to be normal when it wasn't—when nothing was normal anymore.

"This has to be hard," Hale said. "It's like having to choose between Wyndham and Ben."

"Ugh," Reggie said. "I can't—I'm gonna go make some coffee."

"Make it strong." Yancy patted the couch next to her, and I fell into it. She covered my lap with a throw we'd picked up on sale at Target. I was still running around in my two shirts, legs exposed.

"This is not just 'take it or leave it,'" I said. "I don't know what to do." I looked at Hale, whose eyes were closed. "You're praying, aren't you?" I said.

"Yeah."

"Then why the Sam Hill aren't you doing it out loud? Let's go— I'm drowning here."

Hale managed to grin and stuck out both boxy hands to Yancy and me. Yancy put her diamond-decked fingers into one of them, and Reggie appeared from the kitchen to tuck hers into the other— nails the color of an abalone shell brushing his palm. I put my own clammy paws into those of my two girlfriends and felt myself moving toward tears. And Hale hadn't even started yet.

He prayed as he always did, as if we'd all just happened in on a conversation he was already having with God. The Presence was real—but the answer still wasn't clear. I only knew one thing when I raised my head.

"I have to call Doc Opie," I said. "I think it's a God-thing."

I was able to chat with him that afternoon on the phone, while Ben was off watching *Milo and Otis* in Reggie's living room and probably stuffing himself with Reggie's homemade caramel corn. The very thought made me nauseous, but then, just about everything was making me nauseous.

"I know I don't want to push him," Doc Opie said when I'd explained the latest developments. "That would set us back immeasurably."

"I don't want that," I said.

"But I can tell you I think we may be getting closer to some kind of disclosure. In fact, I wanted to ask you at our next meeting, were there other people involved in this pornography ring?"

"What do you mean?" I put my hand up to my throat to keep from gagging.

"You've only mentioned your brother-in-law actually taking the pictures. Could there have been anyone else on the immediate scene?"

"I don't think so. Wyndham hasn't mentioned that. You're not thinking my sister was actually in on the picture-taking? Wyndham hasn't ever said that."

"I'm not thinking anything. I'm just exploring the possibility, because Ben's view of the world as a dangerous place is indicative of multiple abusers. He's having trouble believing that safe adults do exist. And his latest drawings have shown more than one person with an ugly face."

I tightened my hold on the phone. "Ugly face?"

"That's how he indicates the bad guys—they all have distorted faces."

"I know I'm not supposed to ask questions like this, but do I have an ugly face in those drawings?"

"No, Toni. You never do."

He went on to suggest that we wait until Ben was naturally ready to talk and then decide whether to broach the subject of his chatting with the FBI.

"You know, if you're going to press charges on Ben's behalf, or help put this man behind bars, it's going to be necessary for them to question Ben. That's another decision you'll have to make."

"I don't like these kinds of decisions," I said. "Give me one that doesn't really give me a choice."

There were still plenty of those to make in the weeks that followed, weeks in which Ben continued to make progress in tiny increments but didn't talk to Doc Opie about Sid or what had happened to him. Weeks in which I had to wait in agony while the Virginia court decided whether to give me complete custody of Wyndham until Sid's case was resolved.

Yancy insisted on taking care of Ben when I was at work and refused to take a dime. I, in turn, took Troy with Ben and me when we went on cheap outings to the duck pond at Centennial Park or the reptile department at the Petstop—both treats that seemed to rank right up there with Disneyworld, a luxury that was now out of the question for me.

With Faith Anne Newlin's help, I got out of the lease on the Lexus and used early withdrawal on an IRA to buy a used Jeep Wrangler several years and dents older than Hale's, which Ben actually said was "cool." I couldn't have looked less like a business executive tooling around in that thing in the summer heat, hair tied up in a bandana, Wal-Mart capris bagging around my legs. But I did try to be a "cool" mom, and some of the time I did it right.

Ben and I ate dinner together every night without the TV on, which meant I had to be ready with things to talk about, like, "Did you see anything purple today?" and "How many pairs of socks do you think you actually have?" I really got into T-ball, more than I had with soccer. I never fully comprehended the rules to soccer, but there was nothing to understand about smacking the ball off the T and running like the dickens to the base while all the moms and dads screamed their faces blue. Doc Opie said the exercise did Ben a lot of good, because it was helping him reestablish a sense of control over his own body. Dominica said it was good for me, too. I was pitching fewer fits in the healing room as the summer went on.

I wanted the things I *could* decide to be "cool" for Ben—which was fine, Dominica said, as long as I wasn't trying to bargain with God by trying to make up for the abuse. That wasn't it, I assured her. It was because so much of what I couldn't control was not cool—at all.

Sometimes Ben still decided he hated me, though those times were fewer and farther between—and hurt even more each time they happened. He still tended to scream and run when he had to soak off poop in the bathtub or go to bed some nights. I had to help him try to manage that—getting in his face until he talked to me, and then talking to him about it again, later, when he wasn't angry. Most of the time I wound up speaking into Lamb's nostrils, but Doc Opie assured me it was sinking in.

"Are you sure you're not sad or scared instead of mad?" Doc taught me to ask Ben. "It's all okay. God understands all of that. He doesn't want you to *do* anything about it, he just wants you to *feel* it. God'll do the rest."

Opie kept telling me how important it was for Ben to experience God as loving and nurturing, the way Jesus was in all the Bible stories, which meant he was going to have to hear about Him as much as possible in authentic, loving, positive ways. So when Ben got mad we got out the empty plastic liter Coke bottle and he smacked his pillows with it while he told me how mad he was. After that, he liked me to tell him, sometimes multiple times, about Jesus turning over the tables in the temple. Then we always talked to God about it.

Actually, I talked. I'd say things like, "We trust You, God," and "We know You're taking care of us," and "We can't do Your job but we know You can." Ben watched me from behind Lamb, as if trying to determine whether I really believed what I was saying.

The thing was, the more I said it, the more I believed it.

"Then become what you believe," Dominica said to me when I told her that.

"You're going to tell me how to do that, right?" I said.

"Keep reading the Gospels. Keep doing things the way Jesus does even if it doesn't make sense to you. And—"

She stopped. I nodded at her. "And turn everything completely over to Christ and be forever changed," I said. "We've been there, and that's the part I don't get."

"Yes, you do. You just haven't embraced it yet. You will. Just keep doing what you're doing."

Part of what I was doing was going to church with Yancy every Sunday. As far as I was concerned, it was a minor miracle that Ben went to Sunday school without a struggle, though some of that was because Troy went, and they were inseparable. That, of course, meant I went to Sunday school, too, something I hadn't done since I was in high school. In Virginia, Chris and I had been lucky to get Ben into the nursery and ourselves into a pew before the first hymn was over. It gave me a chance to meet people—and to find out that most of them had been praying for Ben and me since I'd met Yancy.

"She didn't tell us what you needed prayer for," one middle-aged woman with several soft chins told me.

"You weren't curious?" I said.

"I just figured the Lord had all the information He needed."

One Sunday, after several weeks of people's whispered encouragement to me, I raised my hand in class and asked if I could say a few words. The teacher, a man who looked a lot like Colonel Sanders and spoke every word with nine syllables, said, "O-of co-wass." A few of the men shifted nervously, giving each other the woman-about-to-get-emotional-on-us looks, but I went for it anyway.

"I know a lot of you have been praying for my son and my niece and me," I said, "and I just want to thank you. I've always been a churchgoer, but I haven't always gone to God, if that makes any sense."

Heads bobbed around the circle.

"Even though we aren't out of the woods, I know your prayers have helped—and they've definitely made me see that I need to pray, too, constantly."

"You go, girl," somebody said.

"I'd just like to say one thing," someone else said.

I looked back at a thin-haired man who sat outside the circle, constantly clearing his throat as if he disapproved of everything. My heart sank, but I nodded at him. What could anybody say to me that would stab me any deeper than I'd already been stabbed?

"Has anybody said anything to you about this being God's punishment on you and your family?" Baldy said.

I could feel my jaw muscles drawing up.

"No," I said. *And they won't,* I thought, *not if they want to keep their teeth.*

"Good." He scowled around the room from beneath eyebrows that were thicker than his hair. "Let's keep it that way." He turned back to me. "Jesus loves you, darlin'. That's all there is to it."

I grinned one of the few true smiles that had formed on my lips in weeks.

"I'm so proud of you," Yancy said to me later as we crossed the lawn toward the church. "You just keep growing and growing. Pretty soon, you're going to pass us all."

I wasn't sure I was growing in the very least, but I could see that Wyndham was. Whether it was the journaling she was doing or the poetry writing or the praying or her work with Dominica, or all of the above—she was at least able to verbalize some things to me that truly amazed me.

Fourth of July morning, when I went to see her before Ben and I went to a picnic at Yancy's, she was tearful, wishing she were lighting sparklers for Emil and Techla and making potato salad—though not in Virginia. With Bobbi out of custody, Wyndham wanted no part of that place. Although Faith Anne kept reassuring us there was little chance the judge was going to let Mama have Wyndham back, Wyndham was taking no chances at becoming too complacent.

"You did do a lot of that domestic thing," I said. "Maybe it's time now for you to be a kid. You never got to be a kid."

"I can't be a kid right now," she said. "I have to deal with all this stuff."

"I know. I wish it weren't that way."

Wyndham turned to me, her eyes serious and old, her face resigned like a forty-year-old woman to a divorce. "But it is that way. And Dominica says if I don't deal with it, it'll deal with me."

"So how are you dealing with it?"

"I'm trying to forgive."

"Wow." I could feel my eyes widening. "I'm impressed. I can't go there yet. I can't even drive by."

That afternoon in Yancy's backyard, I watched Ben for signs that he, too, was making progress toward healing. He did seem a little more relaxed than he had in a while. He was getting more sleep, thanks to the techniques Doc Opie was teaching me to get him to let go of tension before bed. We had a whole routine—reading a story and singing a song and talking about how he was feeling right at that moment. We had a whole chart of drawings of faces that Ben had done, showing different feelings that ran the full gamut from mad to grateful, glad to shameful, sad to lonely, proud, hurt, and guilty. When he couldn't find the right words for what he was feeling, he could point to the picture that matched his insides.

Then we'd pray about it. Although Ben loved the Jesus stories, he still wasn't talking to God by himself, so I stumbled through for both of us. God was at least blessing us with a few nights' uninterrupted sleep every week.

That, I thought as Ben waited in line to hurl himself off of the deck and into Troy's aboveground pool, must account for his looking more like a normal little kid out there.

"It's Toni, isn't it?"

I looked up to see a blond woman perching on the edge of the lawn chair next to me. She seemed stiff, as if she had an agenda. I found myself sitting up straighter in my chair.

"Yes," I said. "Have we met?"

She shook her head, a rakish burst of blond hair wiggling above the band on her white visor. She was wearing sunglasses—expensive sunglasses—so I couldn't see her eyes. Her mouth, however, gave her away. There was something very staged about this whole conversation already.

"I'm a friend of Yancy's. Her Melissa and my Chelsea take dance together."

"Oh," I said. "That's why our paths haven't crossed. I'm Ben's mom." I pointed toward the pool.

"Now—which one is he?" she said.

Who wants to know? I thought. *You—or the CIA?*

The way she was scrutinizing the lineup at pool's edge made the hair on the back of my neck stand up.

"The one with the blue swim trunks?" she said.

"Yeah," I said slowly.

"Your son's the one who was molested by your brother, then."

I could feel my claws emerging one by one. "No, my brother-in-law. Did Yancy tell you that?"

She shook her head absently. "All the soccer moms know about it."

A vision of "all the soccer moms" gathered in this woman's kitchen making homemade granola and discussing my son's abuse drew my claws out to their fullest extent. It was only a matter of who wanted to have her eyes scratched out first. I could almost hear Doc Opie saying, *Use your words.*

"I wasn't aware that it was public knowledge," I said. "I've only told the people who really need to know."

She tilted her head down to look at me with ice-blue eyes over the top of her sunglasses. "I think we *all* need to know, since our children are playing with him."

I wasn't aware that she had a child who played with Ben. If her kid was on the soccer team, she sure hadn't ever shown up at a game or a practice. I would have remembered this dame.

"Wesley!" she said in an accent that made Scarlett O'Hara sound like she was from Massachusetts. "Wesley—come here."

A snake-hipped child with his ribs showing turned and shook his head at her and went right back to throwing himself into the pool.

"I'm not quite sure I see where you're coming from," I said.

"I don't want to offend you or anything—"

"I think it may be too late."

She gave a random smile. "Well, I've talked to people about children who have been raped, and—"

"I don't know that Ben was actually raped."

"Then exactly what did that man do to him?"

"Excuse me?"

"See, I'm offending you," she said.

She put her hand on my arm. I pulled away. That seemed to be enough grounds for her to bring out the fangs.

"All right," she said, voice suddenly frosty, "people have told me that children who have had sexual things happen to them this young get very advanced that way and they'll try stuff on other kids."

"What—you're saying you think Ben is going to molest your son?"

"He wouldn't know what he was doing of course," she said quickly. "But I have to protect my child."

I stared at her as she nodded, as if by doing that she'd finally get me to agree. I groped for something to say that wouldn't get me thrown out of Yancy's backyard. The first thing that came to mind was, *What you need to be worrying about is protecting yourself—from* me!

"Your sources have given you the wrong information," I said. "So let me try to educate you. Unless a child suffers years of abuse by a parent, he's not likely to abuse other children. My son is a victim. He is no threat to anyone, and I'd really appreciate it if you wouldn't spread that sort of thing around to 'all the soccer moms.'"

She gave me a simpering smile that told me it was too late for that request, too.

"Yancy sure has a nice day for her party, now, doesn't she?" she said.

"I think it's a little hot. I'm going to get something cold to drink." *And with any luck, lady, I won't throw it in your face.*

I didn't go to the cooler but planted myself closer to the pool. Little Miss White Visor pulled her son out by one arm and dragged him, wailing, into the house. None of the other kids seemed to miss him too much, and as far as I could tell nobody was shunning Ben. I was still shaking with fury when Yancy came over to me with a plate of nachos.

"Good old American tradition," she said. "I promised Reggie I would force-feed you—" She stopped and peered at me closely. "Toni, honey, what is *wrong?*"

I told her. With every word, her marvelous thyroid eyes narrowed, until they were slits by the time I was finished.

"Are you all right?" she said.

"I don't know if I'm ever going to be all right. Just when I think things are taking an upward swing, something else happens."

"You haven't heard from your attorney, have you—about Wyndham?"

"No. I would be on pins and needles, except I've got to focus on Ben."

"You're amazing, honey," Yancy said. "Don't you forget that. And as for Sissy Darnell—she's not worth the time of day. You don't want your precious Ben playing with that little demon-child of hers anyway. Child is six years old and swears like an R-rated movie. I Suwanee!"

On that recommendation, Wesley didn't get invited to Ben's sixth birthday party, which went down at the end of July. Ben himself made up the guest list—four little boys he had actually made friends with in Sunday school and on the T-ball team. They spent most of their time punching each other and teaching each other to make rude noises with their armpits, but Yancy assured me that was the sign of true brotherhood among the six-year-old set.

I took all four of them to see *Spider-Man* at the IMAX theater, all of us dressed up in Spider-Man costumes I got on sale at Bud's Discount City. The five of us rode in my Jeep, all buckled into seat belts and shouting along with a tape of songs they'd learned at Vacation Bible School. We consumed several tubs of popcorn and enough M&Ms to break even a six-year-old out in zits, but there wasn't even one throw-up the entire evening, and they still managed to do away with a medium pizza and actually fall asleep in their sleeping bags on the living room floor while TV Land reruns of

Leave It to Beaver flickered on the screen.

I sat up all night, watching them sleep. Somehow I wanted to protect them from their own fears, real and imagined. As I picked my way among them, tucking in arms and rescuing my rugs from juice boxes, I smiled at their innocence. And then I began to cry.

Ben, my Ben, breathing softly in his sleep, looked the most innocent of all. Yet when he opened his eyes tomorrow, I knew, his mind would still be full of things no little boy should know.

Their mothers retrieved them by nine the next morning, and Yancy took Ben home with her so I could catch a nap. She didn't even ask me anymore if I slept. She and Reggie could both look at my eyes and tell me exactly how many hours I had gotten the night before.

It was a Saturday, and I was feeling a little at a loss without Ben there to play with. I had settled for filling out his registration form for public school, since Hillsboro Private was no longer even an option, when the phone rang. I stared at it for several rings, afraid to pick it up. I had been feeling relatively peaceful. I didn't want to argue with Chris over how long therapy was taking with Ben or hear my mother rail at me about how I had destroyed my sister's life. On the other hand, it could be Reggie, offering me some of her barbecue—the only thing that really tasted good to me.

I decided to take a chance and picked it up. It was Dominica.

"What a nice surprise!" I said. "And a switch, you calling me."

"You have some time this afternoon?" she said.

"I could. What's up?"

"I think you need to come in and talk to Wyndham. She has something she wants to tell you."

Sixteen

DOMINICA WOULDN'T GIVE ME A CLUE about what was going on. She said it was something Wyndham needed to tell me herself.

"Is it bad?" I said.

"It moves us forward," Dominica said. "Is there somebody who could drive out here with you?"

"I don't like that question."

When we hung up I called Yancy, who said she would keep Ben for as long as I needed her to. In spite of Dominica's suggestion, I then took off for Trinity House alone. It was my longest trip out there yet, every mile seeming to pull me backward as I wrestled with myself. What could Wyndham possibly have to say to add to the turmoil her last disclosure had heaped on our lives? Why didn't I just turn back and have Dominica put it in a memo?

But something in her voice—something in her not wanting me to come alone—made me think this wasn't just about Wyndham's healing, or even mine. She knew that nothing sent me near the edge unless it was about Ben. If this was about my son, then I had to know what it was, and I had to know now.

When I arrived, hands aching from clutching the steering wheel, Wyndham was in Dominica's healing room on a floor cushion, arms folded around herself, rocking back and forth. Dominica, clad in bell-bottom jeans, greeted me wordlessly. The tension in the room could have been cut with a chain saw. I was nauseous by the time I got to Wyndham's side and pulled up a pillow.

"How ya doin', hon?" I said.

"I'm awful. Just let me get this out, okay? I just have to say it all at once."

"Okay."

I looked at Dominica, but she was watching Wyndham as if she expected her to lunge for the window. By now, Wyndham had her eyes on her rocking toes, eyes that were puffy from crying.

"I won't say a word," I said. "And no matter what you tell me, I will still love you. I promise you that."

"No, you won't. Nobody could."

She started to shake her head, but Dominica stopped her like a stick in a bicycle spoke. "You know you can do this, Wyndham," she said. "You've got God, remember."

While I waited in tortured silence, Wyndham took a deep breath, as if she weren't going to be allowed another one until she'd said all she had to say. I wasn't sure I could breathe myself.

"I didn't tell you everything before," Wyndham said. "I thought what I already told would be enough. But now I have to—now that Bobbi is out of jail. I just have to now."

Though Wyndham wasn't looking at me, I nodded, just to be sure I was still there. I could feel myself trying to tear away from the very real anxiety and disappear.

"He threatened them," she went on. "He threatened Ben and the twins, told them he would do horrible things to them if they told—like drown them in the bathtub or cut them up. They would be crying and screaming, and he would make me take them."

"Honey, I know all this—"

"Just let me tell it!"

"I'm sorry. Go—I'll be quiet."

I glanced again at Dominica, but she was locked into Wyndham.

"They would be screaming so hard, especially Ben," Wyndham said into her knees. "Emil stopped crying that much after a while because it happened to him so often—but Ben wasn't used to it. When I took them to—her, she would always reach for Ben first because Sid would be in the background yelling, 'Shut that kid up!' She would take Ben and she would tell me to bring Emil. At first, I would just leave them with her and go cry or hold Techla. She never comforted Techla the way she did the boys. That's what she called it—'comforting them.'"

Wyndham spat the words out as if they were poison. Her bitterness was so like Bobbi's on the phone, I was beyond anxiety as she continued.

"I didn't know what she was doing at first—until this one day. She had both of them in her room, and Ben wouldn't stop crying and neither would Emil. The thing is, when Ben screamed, that scared Emil because he loves Ben so much and he thinks Ben is a hero. She looks at me and she goes, 'Here, this helps them. Do this.'"

Wyndham flung both hands against her face and wailed. It was a hopeless, baleful sound that would have torn my heart right from my chest if she hadn't been talking about my son.

"What did she want you to do?" I said. "What was she doing to the boys, Wyndham?"

"I can't!"

"You have to! Tell me!"

I felt Dominica's hand on my arm. I tried to wrench it away, but she held on tighter. It took every ounce of self-control I had not to shove her across the room and take Wyndham by the shoulders and shake her. Hard. Until she told me what I didn't want to know.

"You're almost done, Wyndham," Dominica said. "Do you need to stop for a minute?"

Wyndham shook her head. Her shoulders shuddered. She was choking, but she lifted her face and let the rest go. It poured out in one long, painful cry of grief.

"She was touching them. They were just little boys and she was touching them. She told them that as long as they didn't tell anyone their secret, she wouldn't let Sid hurt them. She said she was comforting them, but the look on her face—it was all about her. It was all about *her* comfort." Wyndham's face crumpled. "I didn't want to do it, Aunt Toni. She made me. And I will hate myself for the rest of my life. I just want to die."

She hurled herself forward, face to the floor. It was a violent move, so convulsive I could only stare in horror. And then I wanted to slap her—hard—over and over.

"Direct the anger where it belongs," Dominica murmured to me.

Much of what happened in the moments that followed was a blur to me, a montage of hurled pillows and screamed epithets and hard, hard hugging of my niece as we rocked together and cried. I told her it wasn't her fault. I shouted it, I ground it out through gritted teeth, I sobbed it up from my throat. But I told her—until I finally believed it.

I stayed at Trinity House until Wyndham was asleep, around nine o'clock. The therapist on duty on the hall promised me that she would be under constant watch all night.

"Who's going to watch *me*?" I said to Dominica as she walked me out to the car.

"Do you need watching? Should we go back in and call somebody to be there when you get home?"

"I'm not going to hurt myself. I couldn't leave Ben now."

"Do you want to be alone, though?"

"I don't know what I want. I'll decide on the way home." I started to go. She didn't move, as if she knew I was going to turn and ask her another question.

"Why didn't she tell me all this before?" I said. "Is she telling us the truth—I mean, how do we know?"

"Very few kids disclose everything the first time they start to talk about it," she said. "They have to be sure they're going to be believed, that they can trust the adults they're telling. And she's had to shift adults several times in the course of this, which slows down the process." Dominica tilted her head, dark eyes watching me closely. "She was also afraid you would hate her. She keeps saying you're all she has. She thinks if you turn away from her, she's alone."

"I don't hate her."

Dominica waited. I swatted at the swarm of mosquitoes gathered in a pool around the outside light. She didn't move.

"I don't hate her," I said again. "But I feel like I want to slap her—just smack her right in the face." I clutched at my hair. "What is wrong with me?"

"She touched your child."

"She was forced to! It wasn't her fault. She never would have done that on her own. You saw the remorse she feels—she wants to die!"

"But your first, gut response doesn't care about that. She touched your child."

"All right, we've established that. You don't have to keep saying it."

"But *you* have to keep saying it so you can accept it and move on to something you can do something about."

"Like what? Tell me. Whatever it is, I'll do it. I just can't stand this!"

Dominica held open the door and motioned me back inside. We stepped into the air conditioning, away from the swarm, and she led me to a lounge just off the reception area. She opened a small refrigerator and produced a Diet 7-Up, which she planted in my hand and all but curled my fingers around for me. When she pointed to a leather swivel chair at the table, I sat and drank dutifully. She perched herself on the edge of the table and watched me.

"I really need to get to Ben," I said, without making a move to actually do that.

"You really think that's wise? In the shape you're in?"

"What shape am I in? Is it that bad?"

"If you don't mind scaring the Nikes off your child, you're fine."

I nodded and took another sip. The carbonation burned my throat.

"Let's get you centered before you go to your boy," Dominica said.

"Centered on what? God?" I punched the can onto the tabletop. "I'm struggling with God at the moment—for obvious reasons."

"Sure. But it's like I was telling Wyndham before you came and all she wanted to do was flog herself."

"With a straight razor," I said.

"I told her it's circular. If you don't love and forgive yourself, you can't love and forgive God. But it's God who gives you what it takes to love and forgive yourself—and without both you can't love and forgive anybody else."

I gave her a wry smile. "This is supposed to clear things up for me?"

"All through our time together, you and I have been working on your being conscious of God and jumping into whatever it is you think He's doing. I can tell you for a fact He's busy forgiving. It's what He does—He's God. So you have to jump in there. You have to start by forgiving Wyndham, getting this anger at her—which you have every right to feel—out of your system so you can love her, love Ben, love you, and keep loving God. Because He's going to give you more and more ability to handle all this stuff."

"I can't just go 'poof, I forgive Wyndham,'" I said.

"Why?"

"Because I don't feel it."

"Who said you had to feel it?"

"If I say I forgive her and I don't, then it's a lie. That isn't forgiveness."

"True—but if you don't forgive her for what she's done, what *are* you going to do with her?"

I couldn't answer that. I could only look at her.

"Darn, you're good," I said.

"I know. That's why they pay me the big bucks."

I sagged against the back of the chair, soda can still clutched in my hand. The chair swung lazily to one side. "It's not really her fault," I said. "It's Bobbi I hate."

"Do you?"

"Yes! Don't get me started." I looked threateningly at the can.

"Just don't break any windows."

"Then don't try to get me to sit down and pray for my sister right now and tell God I forgive her—when I don't."

"What do you think forgiveness is, anyway?"

I had to think about that one, and my brain wasn't functioning at its normal speed.

"When you forgive somebody," I said finally, "you tell them, 'It's okay, forget about it, let's go on as if it never happened.'"

"No, that makes me want to throw up," Dominica said. "I mean, sometimes that's appropriate, like when you fight somebody for the last blouse on the sale table. But most of the time that approach is just being a doormat."

"Then what's forgiveness?"

"It's saying to God, 'I'm going to stop tearing myself up over this person, and I'm going to pray for him and get on with my life. I no longer wish he would go directly to hell and not pass go and not collect $200.'"

"Do I have to mean it?"

"You have to *want* to mean it." Dominica raised an eyebrow at my 7-Up can, and I handed it to her. She took a swig out of it and then looked at me as she ran the back of her hand across her mouth. "You've got a tough road ahead of you, Toni. You can't go down it with a clear head—you can't hear God, you can't know what Jesus would do—if you're all clogged up with hate. And guilt."

"Don't even talk to me about guilt. I'm drowning in it."

"Do you want God to forgive you for whatever it is you think is your fault in all this?"

"Are you kidding me? I want *out* of the guilt and on with what I'm supposed to be doing for my child right now."

Dominica stuck the soda can between her knees so she could illustrate with her hands. "All you have to do is ask for God's forgiveness and it's yours. That was the point of Jesus' dying for us. He's already taken the rap." She pushed her head forward. "But, and this is a big but, you can't expect forgiveness from God if you in turn aren't willing to make the effort to forgive the people who have taken you and your son and your nieces and nephew and ripped you apart."

I sank my head into my hands, elbows on the table next to her thighs. "I don't know if I can do that."

I felt a warm hand resting on the back of my head. "All you have to do is be willing and try. If you're trying, God's good with that *and* He can use you. Otherwise, you're dead weight. Ben and Wyndham don't need dead weight."

We prayed then, both of us. I left crying, but Dominica let me go. She said they were healthy tears—as long as I could see through them to drive.

I left Ben with Yancy until morning, and for the second night in a row, I sat up until the sun rose. I couldn't have slept if I'd tried, and I couldn't just lie in the bed and let the visions of my own sister molesting my little boy run through my head, not yet.

So I stayed up and I tried. I talked to Jesus…no, I begged. I slammed my face into my pillow and wailed for help. I hugged my knees and rocked back and forth and gave voice to despair until I was hoarse. And then I cried.

At dawn I made tea from generic bags and sipped it from the mug Ben had painted for me for Mother's Day. Huh. Being a mother was not what anyone had told me it would be, certainly not what I'd imagined when I'd found myself pregnant. In fact, nothing about my life or Ben's was unfolding in a way anyone would have dared suggest. I—independent Antonia Kerrington Wells—would never have predicted this kind of loneliness for myself.

Suddenly, for the first time since I'd left Virginia, I longed for Chris's arms around me.

Not for his attorney's rationale explaining this all away. Not for his stubborn denial or his fear or his one-track desire to bring me back to our old, unhealthy way of life.

I just wanted his arms.

I called him at six to tell him about Wyndham's disclosure. There was no answer, so I left a message for him to call me. The fact that he wasn't home at that hour on a Sunday morning erased the desire to be held by him. I didn't dwell on where he could possibly be.

I met Yancy and crew at church and brought Ben home with me after the service. He was testy—wouldn't eat his lunch even though he himself had selected peanut butter and jelly and had specifically requested that it be cut into triangles. I knew it was probably because I'd left him so much over the weekend, but I didn't let that stop me from doing what I realized I had to do.

Around two o'clock he was playing relatively peacefully in his

room, tying a long string from every conceivable knob and hook to
another until the place looked like a giant spiderweb. I made him sit
down on the floor with me, my head bent beneath the string-web,
and I told him listening to me for just a few minutes was in the box
right now. It was only because there is God that he nodded and
waited for me to speak.

"I'm so sorry about what's happened to you," I said. "I know
about Uncle Sid. I know about Aunt Bobbi. I know about
Wyndham and all the things they did to you. I will do everything I
can to make the hurt go away, and so will God. We can both imagine Jesus giving us big old hugs and telling us it's okay."

His brown eyes grew round. He wanted to glaze them over, I
could see that. I had to get it all out before I lost him.

"Please believe me, Ben—I will never ever hurt you. I will protect you, no matter what happens. I know I didn't before, but now I
know things I didn't know then. Let me be the one to take care of it
now. You don't have to anymore."

He watched my face for a moment, the way a baby does before
he decides whether to reward you with a smile or scream his head off.

"Is that all?" he said.

"Yes."

"Can I go play now?"

"You can. But first tell me whether you understand everything I
just said."

Slowly, he nodded, the cowlick bobbing the way a little boy's
cowlick should bob.

"Okay?" I said.

And he answered, "Okay."

The rest of the day, all night, and throughout the next afternoon—
as I explained over and over to customers what civet of piglet was
and stuffed the resulting tips into my apron pocket—I pondered
what I'd said to Ben. I had to, because I had no idea where it had
come from.

I knew *how* it had come—from staying up Saturday night and

putting everything aside but my responsibility to my son and pulling up whatever trust in God I could muster.

I thought at that point that I had already given up everything I could give up—a prestigious career, a palatial house, a luxurious car, a hefty stock portfolio, a lifestyle that required no manual labor. And in essence, I'd given up my own idea of myself. I'd sacrificed it all for Ben's healing.

And then suddenly there was more I had to throw away: my homicidal anger at Wyndham and Sid and Bobbi and Mama and Chris; my need to get revenge; my desire to turn my back on the whole thing and pretend it had never happened. Now I couldn't fantasize about lopping off Sid's privates or Bobbi's fingers. I couldn't spend hours venting to Reggie and Yancy about my mother's idiocy or Chris's ignorance. I could no longer give in to those urges because I had to focus even more on my child—who had experienced more abuse in just a few months of his young existence than most people do in an entire lifetime.

At that moment when I sat down on the floor with Ben and let unplanned words pour out of me, I knew an old Toni had died—and God had created a new one.

I finally knew what it meant to be born again.

The second it hit me—as I was headed for Table 7 to greet my next set of diners—I turned over that new life to a God I knew was real. Real in the person of Jesus Christ. It was as natural as breathing.

That could have been why I didn't drop my order pad as well as my teeth when I saw who my customers at Table 7 were. I would have known that bald head anywhere—and the set of health-club shoulders across from it.

"Mr. Faustman, Mr. Marshall. Welcome to La Belle Meuniere."

I took great delight in the fumbling and sputtering that went on as Jeffrey Faustman and Charles R. Marshall looked up in bewilderment from their menus. I wasn't sure whether it was the fact that I was their server or that they didn't understand a word they were reading that had rendered them speechless, quipless, and suaveless. Didn't matter. I simply smiled and said, "May I recommend the civet of piglet?"

They blinked at me as if they had no idea who I was. In truth— they didn't.

None of that meant I didn't grieve during those two days. My sadness for Ben came in waves, most of which knocked me completely down. So I decided that since Wyndham seemed to be doing well with journaling about her feelings, I should try it, too. While Ben was in his session with Doc Opie that afternoon, I took myself to the Dollar Store and bought a couple of blank books. They had garish covers, but I figured Yancy could help me come up with some amazing way to re-cover them so they looked more like me.

Just buying them gave me a momentary and uncanny peace, and I still had it going on when I returned to Doc's office to pick up Ben. It only lasted until Alice said Doc Opie wanted to talk to me when he was finished with Ben. The anxiety slammed right into me again, and it only got worse when Opie brought Ben out. The doctor's face was so pale, his freckles looked three-dimensional.

Ben didn't look at me when he said hi, and he hurled himself straight for the toy box.

"Can you hang out with Alice for a few minutes?" Opie said to him.

"Uh-huh," Ben said.

"You tell her if you need something."

"Uh-huh."

"Why would he need something?" I said to Doc Opie as the door closed behind us. "What's going on?"

He didn't even wait for me to sit down. He propped himself against the wall, still standing.

"Ben disclosed two very vivid memories to me today," he said. "Unsolicited by me—and he related them verbally. Just, bam, he wanted to talk."

"You can't tell me exactly what he said."

"I can. He gave me permission. That's a really good sign in terms of his relationship with you."

"Then why do you look like somebody just died?"

"Because no matter how sure I've been that a child has been abused, when he tells me himself, I always feel like I've just been kicked in the gut."

Doc Opie did indeed look like a kid who had just emerged the loser from a schoolyard brawl.

"Do I want to hear this?" I said. "I didn't have a chance to tell you what my niece disclosed over the weekend."

"About her mother?"

I felt myself go cold. "Then it *is* true."

Opie nodded sadly. "Two molesters—two different kinds. From what I could gather from Ben, the uncle was violent and threatening. The aunt was gentle."

"Gentle molestation. Isn't that an oxymoron?"

"It's as disturbing as the violence because even though she was behaving in a gentle manner, the sexual contact was still abusive. She viewed her wants as more significant than the child's needs. She acted as if what she was doing were a nice thing, but he knew it wasn't, so he has confusion thrown in there with the shame and the guilt and the anger and the self-hatred."

"Did he tell you the whole story? Does he really remember?" I was shaking my head, willing his answer to be no. The thought of Ben recalling this hideous nightmare was appalling—given the fact that *I* couldn't even stand to think about it, and it hadn't even happened to me.

"What he remembers is very clear," Doc Opie said. "There is no doubt that he's telling the truth. In fact, it's very rare for a child to make up a story about something like this, especially a child as young as he is. Children are more likely to minimize than to exaggerate, because they're ashamed. And, of course, his aunt was supposedly a caring, affectionate adult who assured him that it was okay. So he's had to wrestle with why he feels so bad if nothing bad happened to him—and why it had to be kept a secret." He touched my elbow. "You okay?"

"I need to sit down."

Things were threatening to go black. Doc Opie got me to the papasan chair and brought me a glass of water. I wanted to splash it in my face, wake myself up from the dream. But it was all too real, and I was all too wide awake.

"This explains a lot of things," Doc Opie said. "Things that can really help us in Ben's recovery."

"Do tell. I could use some good news."

"One of Ben's issues has been his fear of letting you out of his sight. We now know that was because he was afraid the uncle might get him. He was counting on you to protect him."

"I was so good at that," I said dryly.

"But he was also angry at you because you were the one who took him over there in the first place. Then you have still another piece of it, which was that he was afraid for you to even touch him because moms abuse kids. And then..."

"There's more?"

"Because so much abuse happened in one place, he's afraid for you to leave him anywhere because every place he goes is a possible threat for more abuse. You've noticed improvement in his behavior since you moved—the other house you lived in was big and upscale, like the aunt and uncle's house. Your new place must seem more inherently safe. Anyway, the poor kid is angry with the uncle, angry with the aunt, angry with the cousin, angry with you and his father, and angry with himself—because kids always think they're intrinsic to everything that happens to them."

I closed my eyes. They burned against my eyelids. "So does this mean—since he's started to talk—that some of that anger is going to go away?"

"Eventually. For a while things may get a little worse. Talking about this stuff produces a lot of anxiety, and we're still working on his being able to manage that."

"Wonderful." And then I shook my head. "I can handle that. We've got the team—we've got God—we'll be okay."

Doc Opie was grinning at me. "I can see you and Dominica have been hard at it."

"So, I take him home and—do what?"

"Do all the same things. Just be ready for him to talk when he wants to talk. He may not want to discuss it with you yet, so don't push it. It's really important that you don't put any words in his mouth. Let him call the shots on this."

"Okay, I can do that."

I started to haul myself out of the bowl of a chair, but the look on Opie's face stopped me.

"What?" I said.

"We have the legal side of this still to deal with. Your sister wasn't charged by the FBI with involvement in the pornography ring. The state hasn't charged her with endangerment, which still blows me away. But this is a whole different scene. We now have two children who say she, on her own, has molested two little boys. By law, I have to report this."

"Then do it. Do what you have to do."

"How about you?"

"Me?"

My head felt like porridge as I looked at him. It wasn't sinking in yet.

"Are you going to press charges against this woman who molested your son?" Doc Opie said.

The porridge drained out. In its place was the clear answer.

"Of course I am," I said. "I have no choice."

Seventeen

DOC OPIE AND FAITH ANNE NEWLIN took me through the legal steps involved in pressing charges against Bobbi. I had visions of her being arrested moments after I made my statement to the police, but those visions were quickly replaced by the realities of the legal system. Basically, it moves at the speed of a slug.

In the first place, it required more people than it takes to stage a coup. There was the sergeant with the Criminal Investigation Department of the Davidson County Sheriff's Department. The intake social worker for the state Human Services agency. The case coordinator with the state consulting Child Protection Team. The pediatrician working under contract with the Child Protection Team. The Assistant State Attorney.

All of that was made more complicated by the fact that the crime had been committed in Virginia, and we, of course, were in Tennessee, so a representative from the District Attorney's office in Richmond was sent down to make sure that the entire entourage of professionals was doing its job.

Doc Opie stayed with me through all the initial interviews, until it was finally decided that only one person—a qualified individual trained in working with victims of child sexual abuse—would interview Ben and that that interview would be videotaped for everyone else's use. I was instructed not to question Ben at all on my own, or to discuss the abuse with him unless he brought it up, and then only to let him talk. They wanted to be certain that none of my words would be coming out of Ben's mouth. Anything that sounded too sophisticated for a child would create doubt and perhaps even prevent the prosecution of the case. They even warned me not to let him overhear any of my phone conversations about the subject. Like I was going to call everyone I knew and tell them.

I wasn't allowed to be with Ben during the interview, though they did let me watch it with Opie through a one-way glass. The calm, unhurried woman who talked with him was actually quite wonderful, allowing Ben to use anatomically correct dolls to show her what Bobbi and Sid had done to him and to draw things he was too embarrassed to point to or talk about. She was diligent about continually telling him that Uncle Sid wasn't going to be coming after him because he, Ben, was telling the police, and Ben eventually opened up and told her everything he had told Doc Opie, without a single tear. I did all the crying on the other side of the glass.

Ben was even all right with the fact that his interview had been videotaped, especially after several uniformed officials erased his fear that they were going to show his "movie" on TV.

"That's a new one," the case coordinator said to me. "You've got a sharp little kid there."

"I know," I said. "Let's make sure he stays that way."

What Ben was not all right with was the medical examination. I was ready to deck the first person who told me I couldn't be with him, but no one even batted an eye except to suggest that I might not *want* to be with him.

"He can't scream any louder than I've heard him scream before," I said. "At least this time I'll know why."

Doc Opie and I both tried to prepare Ben for the fact that a young male technician was going to be looking into all his private places and taking pictures with a special camera. Ben told us emphatically that that was most certainly *not* going to happen.

We promised him that he would get to click the clicker on the camera—that no one was going to hurt him, that this wasn't at all like what Uncle Sid and Aunt Bobbi had done to him. When Doc Opie told him nobody was going to put a thermometer in his bottom like Aunt Bobbi did all the time, a light bulb went on in my head. Another one of Ben's fears explained.

But none of our reassurances made any difference to Ben.

He cried all the way to the county health department. He sat between Reggie and me in the waiting room and sobbed. He clung to me when they tried to get him to lie down on the table and had to be pried from my arms. Only when he was allowed to hold Lamb and could hear me giving him constant commentary on how many more minutes it was going to take did he stop struggling.

He wouldn't speak to me all the way home, ignoring my attempts to get him to tell me which face on our chart he felt like right now. When we got to the apartment he went straight to the TV, something he hadn't done in a while. Through one of God's minor miracles, a rerun of *Law and Order* was on when he turned on the set. A big burly convict was crying behind bars, and he gave me an idea.

"Hey, Ben," I said, "that guy's in jail. You think he likes it in there?"

"No," Ben said, as if that were the stupidest question on record.

"A big old guy like that and he's crying. It must be pretty bad in jail."

"It is. I know it."

"Do you know what you did today when you let them examine you at the doctor's?"

He shook his head, eyes still riveted to the screen.

"You helped the police make it so Uncle Sid and Aunt Bobbi will go to a jail—just like that one."

Ben finally looked at me, his eyes round and almost believing.

"I did?" he said.

"You did."

The eyes narrowed suspiciously. "How?"

"When the guy looked at your bottom today, he could see where they hurt you. That's called evidence, and they'll use it to prove Sid and Bobbi were bad to you."

"And put them in jail?"

"You betcha."

Ben turned back to *Law and Order* and gave it an admiring gaze. I picked up the remote.

"And now, if it's all the same to you," I said, "I think we'll watch *Rugrats.*"

"No, I don't wanna watch TV. I'm gonna go play."

When he was gone, I sat there for a while, thinking that I wasn't paying Dr. Michael Parkins enough money. I closed my eyes and thanked my God.

It took almost a week for Lance Andrews, the assistant state attorney from Richmond, to assess all the information and decide that prosecution of the case appeared to be justified. It was in Richmond's hands now. As I waited for word on Bobbi's arrest, I had never felt farther from my hometown.

One thing actually did happen rather quickly. Two days after Lance Andrews brought formal charges against Bobbi, Faith Anne Newlin called me sounding like a teenager who'd just been asked to the prom.

"You now have complete temporary custody of Wyndham until both Sid and Bobbi have gone to trial," she said. She actually squealed.

All I could do was cry and say, "Thanks be to God."

"Amen," she said.

Other things didn't move quite as swiftly, but I didn't have time to dwell on them. I was too busy trying to keep a number of balls in the air.

I went out to see Wyndham several times at Dominica's request. Now that Wyndham's part in Ben's molestation was a matter of public record, she was terrified that she, too, was going to be arrested. According to Faith Anne Newlin, I couldn't honestly guarantee her that she wouldn't be, but I could work on getting her immunity in exchange for her testimony.

I tried to call Chris to get his help with that, as well as tell him what was going on, but I'd been trying to get him for a week and he wasn't returning any of my calls to the house or the office. So far I'd also been unsuccessful at getting in touch with his secretary. He didn't even know I'd pressed charges against Bobbi.

I enlisted Hale's help in dealing with Wyndham because I was almost overwhelmed with handling Ben. After the interview and the medical exam, Ben began to disclose more and more details about the molestations to Doc Opie. Because Ben was following the usual pattern of recalling the least traumatic memories first, the memories grew worse. Doc Opie assured me that he wasn't pushing Ben to remember more than he could handle, and I believed him. But each time a new incident sprang to the surface, it created new stress for Ben. I didn't have to hear it from Doc Opie—I could see it.

Bedtime became a nightmare again for Ben even before he went to sleep. I sat with him for hours every night, soothing him, telling him the Jesus stories he liked, only to watch him toss and turn and eventually claw his way up out of what appeared to be hideous dreams. He was wetting the bed again, too, and clinging to me when we went out anywhere except to Reggie's or Yancy's. I was dreading the beginning of school the next week. Just entering first grade could be a trauma all by itself without all this piled on top of it.

And then there was the renewed hostility toward me, which Doc Opie explained was Ben's defense against how frighteningly vulnerable he was feeling. That helped only slightly. Now that I felt closer to Ben than I ever had, the angry looks from his stormy little eyes were like bullets going through me.

Doc Opie and I talked more often, and he told me over and over that the memories were making Ben underfunction psychologically, but that as we all dealt with the issues, he would begin to heal.

"Things often get worse before they get better in therapy," Doc Opie told me. "In this case, regression is a sign of progress. Keep praying."

I tried not to panic. Every night I gave a whole truckload of stuff to Christ, and I knew His taking it was real.

But I rarely took my eyes off of Ben when I was with him. I felt as if it wasn't fair for him to have to go through this obvious pain by himself, and I wanted to feel it, too. I kept telling him how brave he was to tell things to Doc Opie and not to be scared to feel sad and mad. During the day he pretty much blew those attempts at conversation off. But at night, when he was crying in bed because he was so afraid, he really didn't have much choice but to listen. And that's when he began to talk to me.

"Tell me about being afraid when you go to bed," I said to him one night when I had run out of things to say to keep him calm.

"It's dark," he said.

"You want me to turn the light on?"

"I can't sleep with the light on."

Okay, I thought. *Another dead end.*

"If I was really here," Ben said, "I bet I could go to sleep with the light or without the light."

"If you were really here? You *are* here, Pal!"

I could see him shaking his head.

"You want to tell me about that?" I said. "About not being here?" Thank heaven for Doc Opie, who had taught me how to ask the right questions. Otherwise, I'd be tripping over my own tongue about then.

"She said I wasn't really there," Ben said.

"She? You mean Bobbi?"

Ben nodded.

"When did she say that?"

"The first time when I asked her in the morning why she touched my privates when I'd woke up in the night. She said she wasn't—she said she wasn't even there." He shrugged his little shoulders. "So I musta not been there too."

Doc Opie had warned me that eventually Ben would open up to me, and that I needed to keep my cool when he did. All the cool I could manage was biting my lip and shaking my head. When I finally trusted myself to speak, I said, "You *were* there, Ben, and you know what happened. She lied to you because she knew what she was doing was wrong—she knew it was making you feel bad."

There was a long silence. I thought Ben had finally drifted off, but he suddenly whispered, "Mommy?"

"Yeah?" I whispered back.

"Am I here right now?"

"Yes, you are."

"Will you touch me and make sure. Just touch my back."

Hardly daring to breathe, I put my hand between his shoulder blades.

"That's you all right," I said.

"Okay."

A few moments later, he was asleep.

Doc Opie later explained that what Ben described to me was a dissociative response, a way for Ben to protect himself. The fact that he would tell me about it, he said, was a sign that he was going to leave that response behind soon.

"You did the right thing," he said. "You're helping him trust his thoughts, and you. Good job."

Whether I was doing it well or not, the "job" was taking its toll on me. I was seeing Dominica three times a week. One of the issues we looked at was why my sister would do what she'd done. I knew it wouldn't change anything, but I had to know why. Dominica was patient.

"Okay," she said. "Maybe understanding what twisted kind of thinking she was doing will help you be less angry. I have a theory."

"Go for it."

"You told me that she and your mother have a codependent relationship."

"They have a sick relationship. Mama has always been obsessive about Bobbi. So much so that Stephanie and I practically had to raise ourselves."

"Did your mother have a good relationship with your father?"

I gave a hard laugh. "For a sailor taking commands from a commanding officer, yeah, it was a great relationship. For a marriage, it reeked."

"Gotcha." Dominica studied her brown hands for a minute. "So it sounds like—and this is just a theory, mind you—your mother was starved for love and affection from your father, so when Bobbi was born she poured it all out on her, almost to the point of idolizing her."

"Bingo," I said.

"I'm not saying there was anything technically incestuous going on there, but your mother certainly established a precedent for being intimate with your child in an unhealthy way. How was your father with Bobbi?"

"Frankly, I think he despised her."

"Which might account for her marrying a man much like your

father in order to resolve that. And then when he was, I assume, as cold and demanding as your father, she turned to her children just as her mother turned to her."

"Yeah, but there's turning to them and then there's *turning* to them. There's a huge difference between codependency and stroking their privates!"

"She was living with a very sick man. That's the fastest way to become sick yourself. Being inappropriate with kids was one thing that was okay with Sid. This is all just a theory, mind you."

"It makes sense, though." I shuddered. "And there but for the grace of God go I. What if I had been born first?"

Dominica grinned at me. "You would have fought that woman off like she was a purse snatcher. But let me say this about grace." She did that thing I'd come to love, where she stretched out her legs and leaned toward me on her hands. "We all get the grace. Bobbi had it, too. Some of us just don't see it. You have, and that's made all the difference."

"Took me long enough," I said.

And all that time, trying to fight everything alone, had left me taking enough Advil for my jaw pain to medicate a small family for six months. Reggie finally talked me into going to the dentist, who told me I'd developed TMJ disease and needed to see an oral surgeon. When I laughed in his face and told him I couldn't even think about going there, he recommended a soft diet.

After that, Reggie kept me well-supplied with homemade soups and stews and puddings, which, she pointed out, might also put some meat on my bones. She still said I looked "tragic."

I definitely needed sustenance. Besides the day-to-day balls I was trying to juggle, there were the crises that erupted and threatened to bring all of them crashing down.

I took Ben to his first day of first grade on a Monday morning in late August. Surprisingly he didn't cry when I left him with Mrs. Quinn—an ample woman with a voice like a song—probably because Troy was in his class and she put them at the same table. I, of course, cried all the way home, and I was trying to cover up the aftereffects with makeup so I could go to work when Lance Andrews, the guy from the D.A.'s office in Richmond, called. He said Bobbi was going to be arrested within a matter of hours.

It didn't take that long. An hour and a half later, just as I was walking out the door, I got another call.

This time it was my mother, screaming into the phone, "Antonia, do you know what you've done!"

It was pointless to try to say anything. It was obvious she was beyond comprehending, and there was nothing I could have said to make her understand even if she had been rational. I myself couldn't fathom any of it.

"Do you hear me?" she said. "Antonia—do you?"

"Yes, I hear you," I said.

"Do you know what you've done? Do you know that they arrested her at our hotel? They dragged her through the lobby in handcuffs, in front of a hundred people!"

"I'm sorry you had to go through that."

"Don't be sorry for me—be sorry for your poor sister!"

"My poor sister put herself in this position."

"Hasn't she been through enough?"

"I haven't really thought about what Bobbi's been through, Mama," I said. "I've been a little busy with what my son is going through, and my niece. They're the victims, not Bobbi."

"They're lying!"

"My five-year-old is lying about things he couldn't possibly have made up?"

"You've put ideas into his head!"

Despite the fact that she was moving closer to the edge, I had to respond, just for my own sanity.

"Why? Why on earth would I do that? Why would I put him through the police interviews and people sticking cameras up his rear end? Why would I do that to my own child?"

"I don't know."

"You're asking the wrong person. Have you asked your oldest daughter why she did what she did to *her* own children?"

"She did nothing wrong. This has all been blown out of proportion."

"I think not. I think we're just now beginning to get the true picture."

"It's not true!"

"Have you asked her?"

"I don't have to ask her."

"Ask her, Mama. Get right in Bobbi's face and ask her if she fondled her three-year-old's genitals and told him it was to make him feel better after his father stripped him naked and made him pose like something out of *Playgirl* and then threatened him with drowning and decimation if he told anybody. You ask her that, Mama. You ask her until she screams out the truth like Ben and Wyndham do."

I was shaking so hard I could barely hold the phone. I had to encase my face with the other hand to stop my teeth from clacking together.

There was silence on the other end of the line, a silence I didn't fill. I had said all I could say without further bruising a confused woman who obviously didn't have an inkling and couldn't have stood it if she did.

"It would break her heart if I were even to suggest such a thing," Mama said finally. Her voice was hard and brittle, barely controlled.

"A broken heart might be a good place to start," I said. "That's where God grabbed hold of me, anyway."

"Don't you even speak to me about God."

"Bobbi needs help. Sid has done such a number on her over the years, she's sick. If you want to take care of your daughter, get her to the best psychologist you can find, and make sure he or she is a Christian."

"How am I supposed to do that? She's in jail. There is no more money to post bail, unless I give up your portion of the inheritance."

"Do it! Do it if it means getting her some decent help."

"I think I will, because you are no longer my daughter."

That was it. The last thing I had to give up was now gone.

Somehow I got it together to go to work. I blew in five minutes late and tied on my apron while I read the day's specials. Jerusalem artichokes and lamb with chickpeas were hopelessly lost in the labyrinth of my mind when Ian came in, took one look at me, and all but ordered me into his office.

I was sitting in a chair with my feet up on a stool and a glass of lemon water in my hand before I realized he wasn't going to chew me out—or throw me out. Everything on him was drooping in concern.

"What is it, Toni?" he said, accent on the *i*. "More bad news?"

"They've arrested my sister. My mother has disowned me. And this is the second time today I've completely destroyed my eye makeup. Other than that, I'm fine." I attempted a smile. "Just let me have a couple minutes to slap on some mascara and I'll be ready to start serving."

He muttered something in French and looked at me sadly. Even his mustache was taking a downward turn.

"You will not work in this restaurant today," he said. "You will rest."

"I can't afford to take the day off, Ian. I have bills to pay."

"The bills—they will be paid. You go home. Do what you have to do. Take some *mouton* home with you."

"I'll be better after I get to work—"

"How will you work? Your heart is broken. Go home."

"Are you firing me?"

This time, Ian's very shoulders sagged. He got up out of his chair and came to me, smothering both of my hands in his muscular paws.

"You are *mon amie*—my friend," he said. "I take care of my friends. You go home. You come back tomorrow. It will be as if you have worked, I promise you."

I leaned forward and kissed his forehead. "Why are you so good to me?"

"It is easy to be good to you. You have a good soul."

So I dragged myself home, after receiving hugs and assurances from the other servers that they wouldn't steal my regular customers. I was hardly in the door of my apartment, hadn't even put the lamb in the refrigerator, before the phone rang. I wasn't afraid to answer it. I had nothing more to lose.

"Toni?" said a male voice. It was Chris. "You've been trying to reach me?"

"For a week," I said.

"Sorry. I had to go out of town. I figured if it was an emergency, you'd call my secretary."

"I tried."

"She had to take unexpected medical leave while I was gone." There was a sudden, startled silence. "Was it an emergency?"

"It was urgent."

"Is Ben okay?"

"I wouldn't say he's okay yet, but he will be."

"What happened?"

There was fear in Chris's voice. Part of me could empathize with that fear. I felt it every minute of every day. Another part of me wanted to wrap it around his neck.

"Toni—what's going on?"

"I'm going to tell you," I said. "But I want you to hear me out like a father, not like an attorney."

"Okay." His voice grew careful. "What's up?"

I took myself to the front window where I could see Ethel's hydrangeas, and I told him everything. For once, he didn't interrupt me with a string of objections. He let me finish before he exploded.

"Do you have any idea what you've gotten yourself into?" he said.

"I have a very clear idea. I know what's ahead."

"I wish you'd discussed this with me first."

"And I was to do that how? You were incommunicado."

"Do you know that when they find out they don't have a case against Bobbi, she can turn around and sue you—us—for everything we have?"

I would have smashed the phone right through the window if

something in his voice hadn't given him away. It was high-pitched and frantic—the voice of someone about to panic. I'd heard it in myself enough times over the past five months to recognize it. I let my own voice go calm and low.

"Chris," I said.

"*What?* I can't believe—"

"I know you can't believe, but you have to. There's no way around it anymore. You can scream and yell and carry on all you want to, but it isn't going to go away. Our son was molested on multiple occasions, by three different people, all in our own family. It's impossible to accept, but you have to. If you can't, I can't let you see Ben. He has to have support and he has to be believed. He's so vulnerable, one shadow of doubt from you and we'll lose him."

"What do you mean, 'we'll lose him'?"

"His little spirit will bury itself under all that guilt and shame, and we'll raise a son who hates us both and hates himself worse. Do you know what his life will be like if we let that happen?"

It was absolutely quiet. I waited.

"You really believe it happened," he said.

"I know it did."

"How? How can you be so sure?"

There was agony in his every word. As much as I wanted to rattle his teeth, I felt for him.

"I heard him tell it. It came out of his sweet little mouth, in his own innocent words."

"He couldn't be making it up?"

"No."

"You didn't coach him?"

"Don't even try to go there with me."

"I'm sorry. This is just too much." Chris let out a long, slow breath. "I'm not calling you a liar. Please don't think that."

"I don't care what you call me. This isn't about me—or you. It's about Ben."

"I know, but you're his mother."

"The state attorney's office isn't his mother. If you can't hear it from me, hear it from Lance Andrews. Use your connections and let him tell you. Ask to see the videotape. Do whatever you have to do, Chris, but *get* it: This happened, and we have to move on from here."

There didn't seem to be much more to say. Whatever it was, we fumbled through it and hung up. I was at once alone in a cold, hard way.

"Okay, God," I said. "Don't let me sink now. Show me what to hold onto."

I tossed the phone on the couch and flopped down beside it. For the first time I realized I was still wearing my apron. It smelled faintly of garlic and salt pork. I could almost hear Ian reassuring me. The voice of a friend. It helped. So I called another friend. I called Reggie at Faustman and filled her in, and that helped. I called Yancy. She said she'd be over with the stuff for a foot massage. More help. I called Hale, who said he'd go down to Trinity House right away to tell Wyndham that her mother had been arrested. I could hear his car keys already jingling. Then I called Dominica and we prayed together on the phone.

"You know what's weird?" I said.

"A lot of things," she said. "Which particular piece of weirdness did you have in mind right now?"

"I'm actually okay. I mean, I hate all of this, but I'm not going to fall apart."

"That isn't weird, Toni. That's God."

"When am *I* going to hear that?"

"Sounds like you already are."

Chris didn't call that night. Uncannily, though, Ben asked me, for the first time in weeks, if he could call his daddy.

"I wanna tell him about my first day of school," he said.

"Okay," I said carefully. "Let me get him on the phone while you're in the tub." I wanted to warn Chris again what his attitude had to be if he was going to talk to Ben.

"I don't wanna take a bath," Ben said.

"So take a shower." I tapped on the box on the refrigerator.

"Will you start it for me?"

I tried to get Chris, but he wasn't in. While Ben was flooding the bathroom with his shower, aka attack of the Power Rangers, I called Mama's, hoping against hope that Stephanie would pick it up.

But it was a tiny, little-girl voice that answered.

"Techla?" I said. "Is that you?"

"Who's this?' she said.

"This is your Aunt Toni."

"Oh." There was a funny pause.

"Honey—is Aunt Stephanie there?" I said.

"This is Aunt Toni?"

"Uh-huh," I said patiently. "Let me talk to—"

"Nana, it's Aunt Toni. Are we don't a-'posed to talk to her?"

There was a loud click.

There I was again, cut off and suddenly adrift. From the bathroom I heard, "Mommy?"

"Yeah, Pal?" I said.

"Are you there?"

"I'm here."

"Okay."

"You need something?"

"No. I was just checking."

It wasn't an "I love you," but it was close enough. I'd found a port. I thanked God.

The next morning I got a call from Lance Andrews.

"Roberta will appear before the judge this afternoon," he said. "That's when formal charges will be made and bail set. We're asking for $500,000. I don't foresee any problems but of course my office will keep you posted."

"I appreciate it," I said. "It's surreal having all that going on when I'm so far away."

"Your husband called. He said he wants to be kept informed as well. He says you're separated and you have custody of your son."

"Right."

"Since he is the boy's father, we have an obligation to fill him in."

"I have no problem with that." I stopped pacing—my usual on-the-phone-with-court-officials behavior—and stood very still. "In fact, could you possibly give him an opportunity to see the tape?"

There was a pause.

"He hasn't been privy to anything that's gone on," I said. "He's an attorney—he knows how to conduct himself."

"If I can swing it."

"We need his support if you're going to bring her down." I hadn't been a lawyer's wife and not learned something about manipulation.

"I'll get on it," Lance said.

As I hung up the phone, I thanked God again. I was doing that a lot. It made putting one foot in front of the other, getting myself to the restaurant, and absorbing the list of specials a reality.

I was giving myself a last look-over in the mirror in the kitchen before hitting the dining room when I suddenly found myself surrounded by servers.

"Did somebody call a meeting?" I said.

A beanpole of a guy I only knew as Slim shook his head. "We just wanted to give you this." He put a thick, lumpy envelope in my hand.

"Yesterday's leftovers?" I said.

"No, yesterday's tips," somebody else said.

"You're not serious."

"We are."

I pushed the envelope back toward Slim. "You don't have to do this. You *shouldn't* do this. Y'all did the work."

"You keep a lot of customers coming back in here," another woman said. "Half of one day's tips is still more than I'd get if those people weren't coming in."

"Take it," Slim said. "Or we'll have to kill you."

I could feel my throat closing up. "Y'all, thanks. Really—I don't know what to say."

"Say you won't quit, no matter how bad it gets," somebody else said.

I could only nod. They had my word on that.

I tucked the envelope into my purse. I had absolutely no idea why any of them, or Ian himself, would care for me as they so obviously did. The only answer could be God, and with that answer I let go of my last doubt that He was in this with me all the way.

It was a good thing, because that night Chris called me. I hardly recognized his voice at first. It was thin, almost fragile.

"Hey," I said. "Did you go to the arraignment?"

"Yeah."

"And?"

"Charged her with lewdness with a minor, sexual molestation, child endangerment."

"Bail?"

"Five hundred thousand."

"Wow. There goes my inheritance."

He was quiet.

"That was a joke," I said.

"Your mother lost it in the courtroom. Bobbi's lawyer practically had to carry her out."

"Was Stephanie there?"

"No. Bobbi looked like she was ready to snap."

I switched the phone to my other ear. "You sound like *you're* ready to snap. Chris, are you all right?"

"No."

I could hear—no, I could *feel* him trying to compose himself. I could almost see him straightening piles and running his hand down the back of his neck. He always did that when we were getting ready to have a fight and he knew he wasn't going to win.

"You saw the tape," I said suddenly.

"Yeah."

I went to the bedroom door to make sure Ben was still asleep. When I was safely back in the kitchen, I broke into Chris's strained silence and said, "It's hard to take, isn't it?"

"Toni," he said. "He's telling the truth."

My instinctive replies—*Ya think? NOW you believe me. What did you think I was trying to tell you all this time?*—came to my mind and left like bees passing through. Ben—he was the one who mattered.

"He is telling the truth," I said. "And as hard as it is, the truth is what's saving him. He needs you on his side. He was asking about you last night—he wanted to talk to you."

"Look, I feel guilty enough as it is."

"I'm not trying to make you feel guilty."

"You don't have to. I knew Sid was a jerk—and I knew Bobbi was a basket case. I should never have let you take Ben over there. I should have put my foot down."

I couldn't help myself. I laughed out loud. "Excuse me? You were going to put your foot down? And where were you going to put it—on your submissive little wife who always listened to everything you said, and obeyed?"

Chris gave a soft grunt. "That is kind of funny, isn't it?"

"It's absolutely hilarious! Look, I'm the one who took him over there. She's my sister. You don't think I have guilt coming out my ears?"

"It's not your fault."

"It's not yours, either. Besides—that isn't the point now. We have to focus on Ben. I think it would be good for you to come down and see him, talk to Doc Opie—Michael Parkins, his therapist. You need to be part of the team."

"Do you want me to be?" he said.

"Ben needs all the support he can get. He's getting better, but he's still hurting."

"I could see that in the tape. Poor little guy." Chris's voice broke. "I've let him down. He needed his dad, and I let him down."

Yes, you did and assorted other replies like it once more buzzed through. I swatted them away. "That's a hard one to get past, that why-was-I-a-loser-parent. But it doesn't do any good. Just keep thinking about what's best for Ben right *now* and then just do it."

"I don't know if I even know how."

I couldn't reassure him there. I hadn't seen much fatherhood since the day Ben was born—but, then, there hadn't been total motherhood either. Yet *I* had been able to change.

"Nothing's impossible. I've been learning that. All you can do is pray and then jump in."

"Jump in how?"

"Do what you know," I said. "I started with money because that was something I could actually do. Get your legal guns out or something, I don't know. Just make sure it's about Ben, Chris. He's the one we have to focus on."

Chris was quiet again. I'd forgotten how still and full of thoughts he could be.

"There's no way Bobbi isn't going down for this," he said.

"Now you're talking."

"The defense will probably try to build a case for her as the victim of a husband who was into pornography—battered wife—trapped—then her sister turns against her because her son was involved. They'll say Wyndham brainwashed Ben, probably to try to get sympathy for Bobbi—she's lost everything…"

"Yeah, well, who hasn't? That's what you do when you love your kids. Your only choice is love."

"I guess it depends on who you love," Chris said.

I grunted. "Then I guess Bobbi loves herself, huh?"

"Toni?"

"Yeah."

"I'm sorry. I want to come down there and make it up to you and Ben."

"You can't. You just have to start from here. Ben will be happy to see you. I know it'll help."

"I'm talking about you and me."

I tucked my jaw into my hand and closed my eyes. "One thing at a time, Chris," I said. "One thing at a time."

Eighteen

WHEN CHRIS PULLED INTO THE DRIVEWAY in the BMW Thursday evening, he looked a lot like the proverbial deer staring frozen into oncoming headlights. It wasn't only the effects of driving eleven straight hours—that was obvious the first moment he looked at Ben.

Ben and I had come down to meet him, Ben small and freshly washed and vulnerable in Tennessee Titans pajamas, clinging to my leg and peeking out from behind it as if he were meeting the Incredible Hulk. Chris's eyes grew huge and glassy, and he appeared to be searching for a leg he could cling to as well. It was probably fortunate that Ben didn't do what most little boys would have done when they hadn't seen their fathers for months, which was throw himself into Chris's arms crying, "Daddy! I missed you!" If he had, Chris would have died of terminal cluelessness.

"Hey," I said to Chris. I rubbed Ben's fingers so he wouldn't dig them into my flesh. "How was your drive?"

"Great! Long—but good."

His voice was too eager, a little desperate, very far from his court-room comfort zone. It was obviously going to be up to me to keep us all from being choked by awkwardness.

"We're glad to see you, aren't we, Pal?" I said.

Ben's hold on my calf tightened as Chris looked from him to me and back.

I roughed up Ben's shower-damp hair. "How about showing Daddy around our new place?"

"Hey, yeah!" Chris said. "Show me where you live, Tiger!"

Ben gave a solemn nod and loosened himself from my leg. He motioned for Chris to follow him, and he started up the steps, placing each foot carefully as if he were now on some essential mission where every move was crucial.

Beside me, Chris let out a long breath.

"Relax," I murmured to him. "He's still the same kid."

"I'm afraid I'll do something wrong," he murmured back.

He went on ahead of me, and as I watched him follow our son upstairs in his boyish way, arms dangling, his own cowlick springing up at the crown from hours of running his hand anxiously across his head as he drove toward the unknown, I thought, *I know how you feel. I know exactly how you feel.*

Ben showed Chris all around the apartment like a polite little museum docent, making sure throughout that I was in his sight. When the tour was over, I was fairly certain Chris couldn't have located the kitchen or found his way to the bathroom, because he never took his eyes off of Ben. I could almost hear the thoughts torturing him. *Is he still the same little boy? Does he hate me for letting this happen to him?*

It was 9 P.M. by the time Ben gave his bedroom a final flourish with his skinny little arm and said, "This is my room."

"It's a great room, Tiger," Chris said.

"A great room for sleeping," I said. "It's way past your bedtime, Pal."

Ben's eyes went fearfully to me. "Are we still gonna do our special stuff?"

"Of course. What about Daddy?"

Ben stiffened his shoulders and looked at Chris. "You can stay, too," he said.

"You sure?" Chris said. "I don't want to interfere with something special."

Ben shrugged and climbed into the race-car bed. I glanced sideways at Chris. He was struggling against tears.

We read a story, sang a song. When I asked Ben what face he was feeling like just now, he pointed to the worried one.

"What's up?" I said.

Ben cupped his hand around my ear and put his lips right next to my lobe so I could feel his warm, soft breath.

"Is Daddy gonna make us go back to Richmond?" he whispered.

"Ask him."

Ben let out a little cry and grabbed Lamb. His face was quickly replaced with Lamb's unnerving pink eyes.

"You ask him," Ben whispered.

I turned to Chris. "Are you going to make us go back to Richmond, Daddy?"

Chris's face went ashen. For a long moment he said nothing, but only stared at Lamb as if some silent communication were going on between them.

God, please, I thought. *Be in those thoughts—please.*

"I'm just here to help," Chris said finally. "I'm here for you, Tiger—for whatever you want."

"I wanna stay here."

"Then you got it," Chris said.

I hope you mean that, I thought. *Or you are going to have me to reckon with.*

Ben drifted off while I was praying with him. When I opened my eyes, I found Chris gone.

I located him in the living room, sitting on the couch, head in hands, elbows on knees. He was a gray silhouette against the kid-friendly colors of Ben's and my little home, an almost-translucent, abject shadow. His wretchedness tore at me.

"You okay?" I said.

He straightened up as if he'd been shot. "I'm fine!" He nodded toward Ben's room. "He seems good. You got him to sleep without a scene."

"It's getting better. I think he's showing off for you."

Chris's bravado faded as I sat on the arm of the couch. "He doesn't even know me anymore. He's a little stranger."

"Give him time. You just got here."

But Chris was shaking his head. "Let's face it, Toni—he never knew me even when we were all together. That's my child in there, and I don't even know how to talk to him."

I looked down at my hands. One of them wanted to reach up, grab Chris by the collar, yank him toward me, and say, "Yeah, well, whose fault is that, huh? Where were you when I was changing his

diapers and giving him bottles and carting him off to day care?"
My fingers twitched in my lap.

But the other hand, of its own accord, reached out and touched
Chris on the wrist.

"If it's any consolation," I said, "I went through the same thing
when this all first came out. I was never completely there for him
before either. I had the career going, the social thing, the image—all
of that stuff. I'll tell you, though, Michael Parkins has really helped
me with that." I shrugged. "When we see him tomorrow, tell him
what you just told me."

Chris covered my hand with his. Before I could pull away, he
held it. His palm was damp.

"Did this freak you out in the beginning—this whole thing of
going to psychologists and having them tell you how you've screwed
up your son's life?"

"It isn't like that!" I extricated my hand from his grip. "It was
weird at first, yeah, because I didn't know what to expect. But I did
whatever I had to do for Ben."

Chris ran his hand through his hair. "That's what I want to do,
too, Toni. I want to be here for Ben—and for you. I want us to be a
family."

I couldn't say anything. He rubbed the sides of his khakis with
his palms.

"It's too late, isn't it?" he said.

"Not for Ben."

"I'm talking about us."

His eyes shimmered as he looked at me.

"I can't tell you that yet," I said. "I'm not playing games with
you—it's just that I can only focus on Ben right now. I think we
both need to do that."

Chris nodded. His face was working, straining against his emotions, and I couldn't watch it. It was painful to see him struggle, and
the pain scared me.

"I think I'll turn in," I said, in perfect non sequitur fashion. I
stood up, flailing my arms in vague directions. "There are blankets

and pillows there for you. The couch isn't too bad. I've gotten some pretty good sack time on there myself from time to time."

He didn't answer, so I left him to his tears.

Whether Chris ever actually lay down that night, I never knew. He was up and dressed when I dragged myself into the kitchen the next morning after a night of wrestling my own pillows. He was standing in front of the refrigerator staring at our box drawings, while I myself stared at the coffee pot, where the coffee was already brewing.

"You're an imposter," I said. "Chris Wells does not make the coffee." I looked around. "Did you do the laundry, too?"

He shook his head, still studying the paper. "I don't know anything about your life now. This—" He tapped it with his knuckle. "Your whole apartment. You never decorated like this before."

"I never decorated before period. I had no choice this time."

"I like it." He turned to me. His eyes were bloodshot, forcing themselves to be alert under what I knew must be the relentless fatigue of anxiety. "I like what's happened to you."

"Don't go there."

He put his hand up. "I know. Today is about Ben. What happens first? I want to help."

"We make sure we're wide awake and have our own stuff taken care of," I said, "because getting him going is sort of like pushing toothpaste back into the tube."

"Three or four cups of that?" He nodded toward the Mr. Coffee.

"That's it," I said.

He smiled the slow smile.

Don't let the smile get to you, I told myself as I turned to my coffee mug. *You haven't got time for that smile.*

I know I have never given the stirring in of nondairy creamer that much focus.

We did spend the day on Ben, getting him to school, then talking over breakfast at the popular Pancake Pantry on Twenty-First

Avenue—me explaining all I knew about what had happened to
Ben, how it had affected him, what we'd done so far to help him
toward healing, what lay ahead. Chris swallowed through it all as if
every gulp were painful, while the blueberry pancakes that people
out on the sidewalk were waiting in line for went cold on his plate.

Back at the apartment I got ready for work and drew Chris a
map to Doc Opie's office so he could meet me there when I got off
and brought Ben over.

Chris was in the living room as I did a final assessment in the
mirror of my usual black-and-white waitress ensemble. It was now
hanging loosely on what Reggie referred to as my "tragic meatless
bones," giving me the basic scarecrow look.

"You'll pass," Chris said.

I caught his eyes in the mirror, and I couldn't help grinning.

"You're so hateful." I grabbed my purse and turned to him. His
face was suddenly pensive. "You okay?"

"A little overwhelmed," he said. "A little scared. A lot scared."

I just nodded.

"I'm sorry, Toni. I'm sorry for everything."

"Yeah. Me, too."

As I left, I could feel the buckwheats rising in my throat.

When Ben and I arrived at Doc Opie's that afternoon, Chris's
Beamer was parked out front, but he wasn't in the waiting room. I
raised my eyebrows at Alice.

"Your husband's finishing up a session with the doc," she said.
"He called this morning and set it up. Doc just happened to have a
cancellation." She gave me the YMCA grin. "Sounds like a God-
thing to me."

"I guess," I said.

I tried to find something suspicious, something threatening
about Chris seeing Doc Opie alone, but my mind hit dead ends. I
was merely surprised. Chris had been a nervous wreck about seeing
him with *me*. Going in alone must have been like facing a firing
squad.

I sat down next to Ben, who was studying a puzzle.

"Where's Daddy?" he said, without looking up.

"He's having a session with Doc Opie."

"Are they talking about me?"

"Only stuff you told Doc Opie he could tell. I think mostly he's telling Daddy how he can help you."

Ben was quiet as he dumped the puzzle pieces onto the table. Still intent on them, he said, "We don't gotta go back to Richmond for Daddy to help me, do we?"

I caught the inside of my mouth between my teeth. Chris had promised that we wouldn't, and yet every chance he got he was saying he wanted us to be a family. If I trusted his promise to Ben, I could be setting Ben up for disappointment.

But his promise was all I had to go on. That and the tears I had seen over and over in Chris's eyes.

"We're staying here," I said. "Isn't that what Daddy told you?"

"Does he always tell the truth?"

He finally looked up at me. His eyes were worried, but probably no more so than mine.

God, can you help me out here?

Ben was stiffening as he watched my hesitation.

"Daddy has always told you the truth," I said.

Ben nodded. "Do you think Daddy knows how to pitch?"

The door opened then, and both Doc Opie and Chris appeared.

"Why don't you ask him?" I said.

"Ask me what, Tiger?" Chris squatted down next to Ben. His body seemed more relaxed now—at least his hair wasn't standing on end. But there was still deep worry in his eyes.

Ben stopped, puzzle piece in hand, and looked up at him shyly. "Can you pitch a baseball?"

"Yeah. I'm no Roger Clemens, but I can get it across the plate."

"You could pitch to me?" Ben said.

Chris closed his eyes and swallowed hard. "You bet, Tiger. I can pitch to you as soon as we get home."

Ben nodded—and then he looked up at me and grinned. "He can pitch."

Doc Opie took Ben in for a short session, which left Chris and me in the waiting room, sitting awkwardly next to each other in beanbag chairs. We must have looked like Raggedy Ann and Andy, flopped there side by side but unable to speak.

Finally, Chris said, "He's a nice guy."

"He's a great guy," I said. "He's saving Ben's life as far as I'm concerned."

"I'm sure you've had something to do with it."

"Maybe—somehow—in spite of myself. It's God showing me what to do—that's the only way I can explain it."

"God pretty much explains it all."

I turned to gape at him. He had his eyes closed.

"I've never heard you mention God before," I said. "All the times we went to church. That whole year you were parish treasurer—you never talked about God."

"Who'da thought, huh?" he said.

When Ben came out and the two of us went in, Doc Opie had a grin the size of a slice of Mayberry watermelon on his face. I was tempted to tell him not to jump to any conclusions, but he looked so content I didn't want to ruin his picnic.

We talked about how far Ben had come, how far he had to go. He warned us that having Chris in the equation would seem like a step backward at first, but that was due to Ben's having to readjust.

"The more consistently you're with him, the better," Opie said to Chris.

I tilted forward in the papasan chair. "Ben doesn't want to go back to Richmond. He talked about it last night. He mentioned it out in the waiting room just a few minutes ago."

I looked at Chris, but he was studying his hands.

"He has bad associations with Richmond," Doc Opie said. "That's not an insurmountable obstacle if it has to be dealt with at some point."

"Does he need another obstacle right now, though?" I heard my voice getting tight.

"The fewer he has, the better," Doc Opie said. "But we can help with any that can't be avoided."

"I think we can avoid this one." I leaned back in the chair and massaged my jaws with my fingertips. *I hope I can trust you, Chris. I just pray that I can.*

When we got back to the apartment, Chris and Ben played ball in the backyard while I cooked supper. I looked out the window several times, which was like watching progressive slides in a slide show. First slide—Ben swinging his bat, saying nothing to Chris's shouts of "Good try!" "Almost, Tiger!" and "Ooh, so close!" Second slide—Ben smiling slowly as Chris ran to catch the ball he'd tipped. Third—Ben laughing out loud as Chris chased him to base, ball in hand, stretching as if Ben were out of arm's reach instead of only inches ahead of him. Last look—Ben shrieking happily as Chris picked him up and put him on his shoulder, yelling, "Safe! Safe! The runner is safe!"

Once again, I had the urge to lean out the window and scream, "It's easy for you to show up and be the play-dad now, Chris!"—and yet I had the ache for more and more and more scenes like that, unashamed copies of Norman Rockwell prints.

I banged the wooden spoon on the edge of the skillet and let it drop to the counter. *I'm losing my center,* I thought. *I was doing fine, and then he shows up and here I am being pulled apart like Gumby.* It was making my jaw hurt.

I glanced at my watch. It was too late to reach Dominica for something that wasn't an emergency. Reggie, I knew, was headed out for a weekend church retreat, and she'd probably tell me if I ate something I would feel better.

I went to the phone and dialed Yancy's number. She was better at processing this stuff with me, anyway. Sometimes I needed Reggie's unpolished country wisdom, and sometimes I needed Yancy's Southern sophistication. Unfortunately, I was getting none of it just then, because there was no answer at her house.

Hale? I thought. Nah, he was all for me packing up and going straight back to Chris. Men. There was some kind of testosterone bond that made them all loyal to each other in the end.

I guess it's just me, then, I thought. *Me and God.*
We can do this, right, Father?

No audible answer.

Chris helped with bedtime that night, and it was obvious right away that the whole pitching-the-baseball thing had won him a lot of points. He did the song, at Ben's request. The little stinker said Daddy didn't sound as much like a frog as I did. Ben wanted him to read the story, too, and when it came time for prayers, he looked at his father and said, "Do you know how to pray, Daddy?"

I looked at Chris, too. This could be interesting.

"You know, as a matter of fact, Tiger, I'm just now learning how to really pray. I'm not as good at it as your mommy, but I talk to God best I can."

Ben nodded solemnly, as if they had just exchanged something deep, man-to-man.

"You both pray, then," Ben said. "Take turns."

Chris looked at me, a little nervously, I thought. I was tempted to say, "Go for it, oh heroic father," but I couldn't do it. There was something about playing games with the prayer thing that didn't sit right. So I came to Chris's rescue and said, "I'll go first."

Chris did take his turn, and I had to squeeze my eyes shut to keep from gaping at him. It was the first time I had ever heard him pray, except to recite the Lord's Prayer in church. He was praying simply and plainly, sans the lawyer voice, in his Louisiana thick-as-molasses drawl.

I know you're trying hard, I thought. *But I never would have expected this.*

After Ben finally drifted off, I went into the kitchen and made a pot of decaf and stood at the back window watching the end-of-summer fireflies wink among the tree shadows. I was noticing the small, seeing the details, the way Dominica had taught me. Yet how could a life that had become so simple still be so riddled with complexity and doubt? Hadn't Chris always had that effect on me? Coming in with his boyish charm and his slow Southern ways and then luring me into his courtroom and cross-examining me into someone I wasn't?

Ben and fireflies and baseball and two parents praying beside his bed. Could it really be that way—or should I just let things stay the way they'd been before Chris came for this visit? Ben and I were fine. We were healing. Chris could turn that upside down and inside out faster than he could smile, any day of the week.

The pot beeped at me, and I splashed coffee into mugs with a vengeance. It was a wonder I didn't end up with first-degree burns.

Chris was standing with his back to me, hands shoved into his pockets, looking out the window when I came in with the coffee. I was certain he wasn't observing the lightning bugs. In fact, I had barely set the tray on the toy-chest-coffee-table when he said, "Toni, I want us all together. Come home. Please."

I crossed my arms over my chest. It was the only way I could keep from slugging him.

"You told Ben you wouldn't make him go back," I said.

"I don't want to make him. I think he'll want to go—the way things are going with us."

"Chris, you've been here twenty-four hours. What can that possibly tell you? That he likes to play baseball with you?"

"I know there's more to it than that."

"You bet your life there is. There's his therapy. There are all the people he trusts. How do I know I can find someone as good as Parkins in Richmond? Or people who understand our situation, people like Reggie and Yancy and his little friends?"

"You made all that happen, Toni."

He hadn't moved from the window except to turn toward me, but I still stepped back, as if he were crowding me into a corner. The backs of my legs hit the chair.

"We could create the same things for him in Richmond—together," he said.

"I didn't make it happen. My focus here is on God—Ben and I are surrounded by people who get that. That's the first thing. And what evidence do I have that you aren't going to do what you've always done and leave it all to me? If I'm going to do it all, then I'd rather do it here where it's already in place."

Chris sat on the edge of the windowsill as if it were a cliff. "You don't know this yet, but something's happened to me."

"What?" My voice was testy. "Are you sick?"

"No—nothing like that."

"Look, Chris, I'm going to say this again, and I'll say it as many times as I have to until you get it: All of this is about Ben. It's not about me or you. I'm trying to follow what I can figure out God is showing me for Ben. It just doesn't look to me like that means Richmond."

"What about what I'm figuring out?" Chris said. "One of the things Doc Opie told me this afternoon was that I could do a lot to replace Ben's memories of Sid with a healthy male image. It's the same as the way you've replaced Bobbi in his mind—he's starting to trust women."

I cupped my jaws in my hands. My ears were throbbing.

"I can see him warming up to you," I said, "and even though there are moments when that infuriates me to no end, I know he needs you. But do we have to disrupt his life right now—just when he's doing so well?"

"Then there's a chance?"

"I don't know!" I stopped, got control of my tone. "Don't push this, Chris. When you try to make it happen, it screws everything up. Just don't push me."

"Toni, I'm sorry."

"Good night."

He said my name again, but I was already closing my bedroom door. I fell back on the bed and lay there, staring at a water mark on the ceiling, head spinning out my frantic prayers.

Dear God—dear God—please—we have to take care of my baby—that's all.

I flopped a fist against the comforter. Why couldn't God just give me a straight answer, a little reassurance out loud? Dominica had told me it was okay if my answers seemed to come from other people, but there were no other people standing around my bed giving me clarification, and I needed it now.

Since none seemed to be forthcoming, I dragged myself up and pulled my door open so I could hear Ben if he woke up. It was

Chris's voice that drifted in, a stream of words I couldn't hear, spoken with intent, as if he were making a case.

Is he talking to himself? I thought.

I turned to get the shorts and T-shirt I slept in from the hook on the back of the door, but Chris's monologue continued, and something in its urgency made me stop and listen. He seemed to be trying to keep his volume low, so I crept just outside the doorway and strained in the shadow to hear.

"If I file for custody," he was saying, "the judge will order that Ben be returned to Virginia while the suit's going on. If she wants to be with him, she'll have to come, too."

There was a silence, as if he too were listening, and I realized he must be talking on his cell phone. I pressed my hand against my mouth to stifle both nausea and screams.

"All I've got going for me are the legal guns," Chris was saying. "This is what I know how to do."

I told him to do that! I thought frantically. *But this wasn't what I meant!*

I wanted him to fight for Ben—but not against me. This wasn't a battle between the two of us... There was a sudden, startled cry from Ben's room. I went straight for him, anxiety pumping on a number of levels, not the least of which was fear that Ben, too, had heard.

He was sitting straight up in bed, his eyes wide but unfocused.

"Ben? What is it, Pal?"

He mumbled something about Lamb, who had somehow made his way down to the bottom of the bed, under the blanket, probably to avoid being squeezed to death. I retrieved him and tucked him into Ben's arms. He was still staring, unfocused, ahead of him. Thank God he had never been awake. All it would have taken was for him to hear Chris saying what he'd just said and we'd be up all night—from now until he went to college.

I coaxed him to lie down and let me pull the covers up around his ears the way he liked them.

"Wrap me up like a burrito," he mumbled.

I tucked the blankets around him, tortilla style.

"Do you want me to stay?" I said.

"I'm all right." And he was deep asleep again, like a normal little boy who had just misplaced his stuffed animal friend.

I went directly to the living room, marching like the gestapo. Chris was on the couch, studying the cell phone.

He looked up, guilt smeared all over his face. "Everything okay?" he said.

"I don't know. That depends on you." I punched myself down on the arm of the couch, feet on the cushions, so I could face him squarely. "I heard you on the phone. Chris, don't do this. Don't turn this into a legal battle over Ben. I'll fight beside you for his life, but I don't want to have to fight against you. I'm already fighting against enough."

Chris was shaking his head. "What you heard me saying—forget that."

"How can I forget it? You're going to try to take my son away from me!"

"No, I'm not. That was just a wild-hare idea. I was desperate and I called—a friend of mine—to process it. It's a stupid idea. I'm not going to do it."

I stiffened straight up. A friend. Wonder if she's anybody I know this time?

I dragged both of my hands through my hair. "Can I really trust that?"

"You can now. You're not the only one who can change, Toni."

I slapped both palms to my knees. "I wish this were a Hobson's choice."

Chris frowned. "A Hobson's choice?"

"Yeah, it's when—"

"I'm familiar with it. Why would you wish for that?"

"Because it's easier when you have no choice. You just do what you have to do." I shook my head. "I thought I had given up absolutely everything I could possibly give up. I don't know what to do now."

I could see Chris sagging. "Would coming back to me be such a sacrifice?"

"It could be. I've found out who I am, and I don't know if you could live the kind of life that fits me." I shook my head again, harder. "But that really isn't the point. All this time, I've been able to sacrifice whatever I had to for Ben's healing. If I move Ben back to Richmond so you can be with him, what if I'm then sacrificing Ben? What if that isn't what's best for him?"

"Why wouldn't it be?"

"I've already told you why! The therapy—the church—the friends—our support—and Ben's associations with Richmond. If he's still too vulnerable, I don't want to take him backward."

"How will you ever know that unless you at least try it?" Chris said.

"This isn't like changing to a different line of questioning, trying to cop a different plea. Doc Opie told me in the very beginning that I had to create the safest, most secure environment I could for Ben. I just can't take a risk that would put that into jeopardy."

"On the other hand, it could be even safer and more secure with the three of us together—or at least closer together. You can't know that without giving it a chance. Can you take that risk?"

"No."

Chris looked stunned. "No? Just like that?"

"With every other choice I've had to make on Ben's behalf, I've known there was no other way I could do it, not and live with myself." I leaned forward as far as I could without falling headlong into his arms. "Chris, please let God do what's right for our son. Whatever that is, that's what I'll do. I'm begging you to do the same. Do you hear me? For the first time in my life, I am begging you."

And then, because there didn't seem to be anything else I could say, I went to bed. I lay there in the dark, certain I wasn't going to be able to close an eye, unabashedly begging some more.

God, please, please—show me, tell me, make this clear—what else can I possibly give up?

You've done all you can, Toni. Now give up control.

I stiffened against the mattress. Where had that thought come from? It was the sound of my mind-voice, but the words were none that would ever come from my stock responses.

Give up control, I thought. *And give it to Me.*

Even as the thought slid away, I knew it hadn't been mine. It was God's. Clearly God's.

"I don't know how to do that," I whispered. "I'll do anything you want—anything—but You're going to have to help me. If You really want me to let go, then please help me do it."

The next thing I knew I was blinking my eyes against the slashes of sunlight coming through the blinds. It took me several bad-breath yawns and dekinking stretches to realize that I had slept through the night, for the first time in months.

Good thing it's Saturday, I thought. *I'll bet Ben's ready for Fruit Loops.*

I expected to hear the TV murmuring cartoons, but the living room was empty and the television sat dark and mute. Even Chris's bag appeared to be gone.

And when I went into Ben's room, so was my son.

Nineteen

I WENT THROUGH A FRENZY of ridiculous motions. Ripping back Ben's covers to discover neither him nor Lamb there. Peering under the bed. Calling out his name in shrill tones as I whipped back the shower curtain, searched the closets, ran down the steps to scour the yard. It was there I realized that Chris's BMW was missing, too. Large pieces of my sanity began to tear away.

Ethel poked her head out the back door of her screened porch.

"Somethin' wrong, honey?" she said. "You are just a-screechin' out here."

"They're gone!" I cried. "He's taken Ben!"

"In that little fancy car? I saw them leave about twenty minutes ago."

"Did you see which way they went?"

"Thatta way," she said, pointing.

Of course. We were on a cul-de-sac; there was only one way *to* go. With a twenty-minute lead, there was no chance I could catch them. But I had to try.

"You all right, Toni?" Ethel called after me.

I didn't answer as I tore back up the steps and hoped to heaven I knew where I'd put my keys. I was ransacking my purse when I heard two things. One was the now pointless admonition, *Let go of control, Toni. Give it to Me.* The other was the sound of tires on gravel below.

I skidded to the window, one hand still clawing at the bottom of my purse, and saw the Beamer. Ben was in the front seat next to Chris, still in his pajamas.

You had better have an explanation for this, Christopher Wells, or so help me God—

Then listen to it before you explode.

It may have been the most impossible thing God had asked me to do yet.

But I turned from the window, closed my eyes, and took several deep breaths. The amount of torque in my jaw was excruciating.

"Mommy!" Ben cried out from the stairwell. "Look what we got."

He pranced through the still-open door, carrying a Krispy Kreme box bigger than he was and beaming as if he were bearing the crown jewels. "Donuts!" he said.

"That is just wonderful," I said through clenched teeth. "Where's Daddy?"

"Miss Ethel's down there yellin' at him," Ben said matter-of-factly. "Can I have a chocolate one? I'll eat it 'stead of Fruit Loops. I told Daddy you won't let me have that much sugar."

"You can have two, as long as you stay in here while I talk to Daddy in the kitchen."

Ben looked as if he had just been given a governor's pardon and chomped into an oozy chocolate donut as though the pardon were about to be rescinded. I turned on my bare heel and headed Chris off at the door.

"Donut holes," he said, holding up a bag that smelled of 100 percent sugar. "I know you like them."

"In the kitchen," I said between my teeth. "And you better have a good explanation or those are going right up your nostrils."

Chris looked a little bewildered as he backed into the kitchen still holding up the bag as if he were making a delivery for Ed McMahon.

"Didn't you see my note?" he said.

"What note?"

"That one."

He nodded toward the kitchen table, where there was nothing but a bowl of apples.

"I don't see a note," I said. "Suppose you tell me what it could possibly have said that wouldn't have driven me off the deep end."

Chris leaned over and picked up a piece of paper which lay face-down on the linoleum. "Must have fallen off. 'Mommy: Daddy took me to get donuts while they're hot.' See—he wrote his own name."

I smacked the note aside and sank to a chair at the table. My hands were shaking so badly, I couldn't have held onto it anyway.

"I thought you took him," I said.

Chris let the bag of holes drop to the table and yanked a chair out where he could sit and face me.

"I wouldn't do that," he said.

"Why not? You thought about filing a custody suit—although I guess your girlfriend talked you out of that one."

"My girlfriend?"

"On the phone last night."

He blinked at me. "That was Greg. Greg Ritchie. He's my spiritual director."

It was my turn to blink. "You have a spiritual director? I don't get it."

"You going to let me tell you this time?"

"What do you mean, this time?"

"I've tried to tell you twice, but you assumed I was full of baloney and cut me off. Just listen to me, Toni."

"I'll listen. As long as it's the truth."

His eyes sharpened at me. For the first time since he'd arrived, he lost the confused fear. I assumed we were headed for the courtroom.

"Look," he said, "like I tried to tell you last night, you aren't the only one who can change."

I grunted, but I motioned him on.

"I got pretty screwed up after you left," he said. "I was at a Kiwanis meeting one afternoon and Greg Ritchie came up to me—you remember him from the church?"

"Vaguely."

"He told me if I ever needed to talk to come over. When all this started to go down—when Sid and Bobbi were first arrested—I felt like I wanted to kill somebody, so I figured what the heck and I went in to see him." Chris shrugged. "We got to talking. We clicked—he made sense. And I was getting it, getting God for the first time in my life. The weekend you were calling me, I was on a retreat with him, just trying to put it all together."

"So what are you saying?"

"I'm saying I think we're on the same page as far as God is concerned. It's the only way we're going to get through this. It's the only way we're going to get through *life*."

I leaned forward, searching his face for signs of insincerity, for the slightest trace of something that wasn't genuine. I found nothing, except his eyes doing their own searching of me for some hopeful hint that I believed him.

"When I said that to Greg on the phone, I was just grasping at straws," he said. "Even before Greg told me I was nuts, I knew that wasn't what Jesus would do in this situation. He never manipulated." He licked his lips. "I see this life you've built with Ben, and I know I'm not part of it. I know that's my own fault, but I want to be with you and help Ben, and all of us change and grow together. I think that's what God is saying to me."

"What am I supposed to do with that?" I said.

"You don't have to do anything."

A swell of rebellion rose up in me. I had God telling me to give up control to Him, and I had Chris saying God was telling *him* something I didn't think I could do. I wanted to pick up the bag of donut holes and throw them against the wall. Only Ben's happy chuckles over *Veggie Tales* in the living room held me back.

"So I'm just supposed to turn it all over to you now," I said.

"No—that's not what I'm saying at all. I'm saying *we* turn it all over to *God*. At least, that's the message I'm getting."

I raised an eyebrow at him.

"You've made all the hard choices you need to make," Chris said. "After you went to bed last night, I realized it was my turn to make one. I talked to Ben—"

I came halfway out of the chair. "You did *not* ask him to make this decision!"

"For Pete's sake, Toni, cut me some slack! No, I didn't. I just asked him if he liked it here and why he didn't want to go back to Richmond. And the kid made sense—he made perfect sense. So I have no choice."

"I don't understand."

"I'm moving down here, Toni. I have enough to live on and support you two until I can get hooked up here in Nashville."

"You're going to leave Bailey-McPherson? You're building a career there!"

"Weren't you doing the same thing at Faustus?"

"Faust*man*."

"How is this any different? I'm doing what I have to do for my son." He leveled his eyes at me. "For my family."

"I can't let you move in here with me."

"I'll get my own place, nearby. Although I hope you'll help me set it up. I meant it when I said I really like this place, and I like you—this real you."

I opened my mouth. He held up his hand. "You're a different person now—I'm a different person now. I know we can make it because finally we have the same foundation. But I'm not going to push you."

Something gave in me, like ears clearing at high altitude, so that I could hear again. And I could speak what was suddenly so clear to me.

"Then here's what I think," I said. "Let's start by being mother and father. If we're still supposed to be husband and wife, God will tell us that, too."

The slow smile began its appearance. "God's already told me. Now he's working on you."

My hands went to my face to cup my jaw, but there was no pain. I was suddenly sleepy, the kind of sleep I could welcome.

"You're really going to give up everything and move down here," I said.

"My bag's in the car. I'm going to head back to Richmond and start making arrangements. Shall I put the house up for sale or rent it out?"

"I vote we sell it."

"Done."

I leaned against the chair and let my head fall back so that my tears blurred the ceiling. "Chris—thank you. I know it's hard to give it all up."

"No, baby. It's the easiest thing I've ever done."

We sat down together with Ben to explain the plan. He balked at having to turn off *Veggie Tales,* but when it began to dawn on him that he could stay in Nashville and have Daddy, too, he lost all interest in Larry Boy and Bob the Tomato and gushed forth with a fountain of questions.

"Can we play baseball every day?

"Are you gonna go to Doc Opie's every time?

"Are you goin' to Sunday school with us?

"Are you gonna sleep in Mommy's room with her, or are you gonna share my room?"

Our answer to that last one—which I let Chris field completely—puzzled Ben a little.

"If you're gonna be my mommy and daddy, how come we can't all live together?" he said. "Oh, it's 'cause you fight too much, huh?"

"We're not going to fight any more," Chris said. "Right, Mommy?"

"That's right. There's no point in fighting. We're just going to let God tell us what to do. Of course, it's not like God just comes right out and talks to us, but—"

"How come?" Ben cocked his head, slightly bemused. "Jesus talks to *me.*"

Chris was fighting back a smile. We avoided looking at each other.

"Really, Tiger," Chris said. "What does He say?"

"He told me it was okay to go get donuts with you. He said you weren't gonna try to take me away from Mommy."

I felt my jaw coming unhinged.

"That's it," I said to Chris as I walked him down to his car. "From now on, I'm checking everything out with the kid. He's got a better in with God than I do!"

"I think that's what you've been doing all along." Chris tossed his bag into the backseat and then seemed afraid to look at me.

"What?" I said. "Look—no more secrets, or none of this is going to work out."

"Then promise me you'll check it out with me, too." His voice finally broke, and his face crumpled into the weeping he had been fighting back for two days. "I love you, Toni. I'm sorry I ever hurt you—I'm sorry I didn't help you—I'm sorry I was unfaithful. I broke every vow I made to you before God, and I *will* make it up to you. I will."

He started to climb into the car, but I caught his arm. He wouldn't turn to look at me; I had to speak to the cowlick that broadcast his vulnerability to me and to Ethel, who I was sure was peeking at us through her curtains.

"I'm sorry, too, Chris," I said. "And I forgive you."

He nodded and sank into the seat. Neither of us spoke before he drove away. Something ached in me as I watched the Beamer disappear out of the driveway, but it was an ache I knew would heal. I could feel God telling me it would.

Epilogue

BY THE TIME BOBBI WENT TO TRIAL February 1—after several continuances requested by her attorney, who said she was too unstable to stand trial, then too ill to stand trial, too thin, broke a nail, whatever—by that time, Chris had moved into a small apartment about a half-mile from us, was working for Stiller and Barnes downtown, and was gearing up to help coach Ben's soccer team. It took longer for lawyers, judges, bailiffs, and court recorders to get their acts together than it did for my husband to shift from Mr. Wall Street Journal to Coach Wells the Wonderful. I suspected he'd taken a crash course in soccer somewhere along the line.

The trial itself took four weeks, though Chris and I decided to stay away from its daily dealings. We believed it was much more important to concentrate on Ben's continued healing—and our own—than to run back and forth to Richmond. I did make a trip up the second week in February with Wyndham and Dominica and Hale so Wyndham could testify. I was thankful the court agreed to use Ben's videotape instead of putting him on the stand, especially after I watched the defense attorney grill my poor niece for a day and a half. Several times I wanted to leap to my feet and tell the judge this pin-striped idiot was going too far, but Dominica always had her hand on my knee at just the right time.

"You don't need to be taken in for contempt of court," she whispered to me.

I was exhausted from watching Wyndham cry on the witness stand as she hung her mother out to dry—and from watching my mother bore her eyes into her granddaughter as if the girl were Benedict Arnold—and from watching Bobbi stare at her own daughter without an ounce of emotion. Although Wyndham looked to me from time to time for a reassuring nod, neither Mama nor

Bobbi would meet my gaze. Stephanie was the only one left who was speaking to me.

I wasn't able to spend any appreciable amount of time with her because I wanted to be there to support Wyndham during off-court hours, but during one of the breaks I made it a point to meet her in the hallway. Mama was evidently in the restroom or I'd never have caught Stephanie alone.

"Can we talk?" I said.

"Of course!" Stephanie threw her arms around me. I didn't even try to hold back my tears.

"I was afraid you were completely on her side," I said.

"I'm giving her what I can." Stephanie pulled back and looked at me with eyes full of conflict. "Mama's slowly going off the deep end. I've told her to take a break from this for a couple of days, but she refuses to stay home when Bobbi is up there 'going through hell.'"

"Like Wyndham isn't. What about the twins?"

Stephanie looked furtively over each shoulder and moved in close to me. "Mama doesn't know this, but I'm working on getting custody of them if Bobbi does go to prison. I'm only continuing on at her house so I can be with them. Once it's time for a custody determination, all my paperwork will be in order. I already have a three-bedroom townhouse I'm paying rent on, even though I'm not living there."

"Promise me you'll get them into therapy," I said.

"They're already in therapy. Mama had to agree to that or the state was going to take them away."

"Thank God." I put my arms around my sister again. "You are such a good person. Please think about coming to Nashville to live when this is over and you have the kids."

Stephanie laughed weakly into my hair. "I'm going to have to. There isn't going to be room in this town for Mama and me once she finds out what I'm doing. The only thing she and I have in common right now is our total ecstasy that Sid has already gone down."

I nodded. The Feds, unlike the Commonwealth of Virginia, didn't mess around. Sidney Vyne had been in a federal penitentiary since mid-September. Ben asked me every day if I was sure they had plenty of locks on the doors at that place.

Stephanie suddenly stepped back and whispered, "Here comes Mama. I love you."

"I love you, too."

Once again I tried to catch my mother's eye, but she did a full turn when she saw me and marched herself back into the ladies room. Gone was the flow, the flawless hair, the impeccable makeup. She had aged twenty years since the day I'd dropped her at the airport, when our worst conflict had been her insistence that I get back together with Chris. Ironic how things worked out.

I didn't go back to Richmond until the last day of the trial. Although Chris and I promised Ben we would be gone only a day or two, he was so devastated at the thought of both of us being out of town at once that Doc Opie suggested we take him with us. That took some doing, but with the promise that he would stay with Chris's parents while we were in court and that he would never have to even go near Bobbi and Sid's house, he calmed down enough for us to get him onto the plane.

Our first stop the day of closing arguments was a park not far from the courthouse, where Chris and I had arranged to meet Stephanie and the twins. My stomach was a tangled mass of anxiety when we pulled up.

"I'm just afraid they're going to be so damaged I won't be able to stand it," I said to Chris.

"They're in therapy and they've got Stephanie. God hasn't abandoned them."

"They also have my mother. She could probably run God out on a rail."

"Not gonna happen."

I caught my breath and curled my fingers into Chris's jacket sleeve. Stephanie was pulling up in her Honda, not six feet away. I could see Emil and Techla's dark four-year-old heads craning out either window in the backseat, eyes huge on their pale faces.

"Dear God," I said.

"What?" Chris said.

"They look just like Ben did a year ago."

"Guess they're going to need all the love they can get then."

I gave him a long look before we got out of the rental car. He was still surprising me with the things he came out with. Sooner or later I was going to have to believe that he couldn't have been putting on an act for six months. He—and God—were patient.

"There they are!" Stephanie said to the two children who were clinging to her like appendages. "I told you they'd be here! Go give hugs!"

Both Emil and Techla looked as if they would rather give their left arms, their nose hairs, and the security blankets they were clutching than touch either of us.

"That's okay," I said as I walked slowly toward them. "You don't have to give hugs if you don't want to. You get to decide."

That didn't unpeel them from Stephanie's legs, but at least they looked at us. Techla even smiled. Emil was solemn as a judge. His similarity to Ben when we had first moved to Nashville, before we'd found Doc Opie and Reggie and Yancy and Daddy and God, went through me like a broadsword.

Thank You for making all my choices about Ben nonchoices, I thought, *or my child could still be right where they are.*

"Stephanie has to bring them to Nashville," I told Chris when our short, awkward meeting was over and we were on our way to the courthouse. "We have to help them."

"That's if she gets custody—and that's only if Bobbi is convicted."

"She has to be. She just has to be."

So I was even more of a bundle of knots than I'd expected to be as we listened to closing arguments. Actually, I only listened to Lance Andrews's speech as he put Bobbi's actions into their stark, wretched perspective. I couldn't stand to hear the defense attorney's pathetic attempt to invalidate the testimonies of my niece and my son, so while he rambled on, I busied myself with watching my mother.

She had declined even more drastically in the few weeks since I'd
last seen her. The eyes that watched counsel's every move were hol-
low and ringed in black. Her face was striped with age, her shoulders
curved over as if she bore the weight of Bobbi's world on them. Her
crowning glory of white hair was straight and flat and tucked
severely behind her ears. I couldn't imagine those thin, brittle arms
holding the twins in the middle of the night when they woke up
with nightmares, as they undoubtedly did. Try as I might, I could
not conjure up a picture of her creating the safest, most secure environment possible for them to heal in. As her eyes followed the attorney who paced and lied about her daughter, I could see in them a
hope for which there was no alternative.

If Bobbi is convicted, I thought, *she's going to collapse like a folding
chair. God—help her.*

When I could no longer look at her without crying for the
mother I had once known, I shifted to Bobbi. Just as she had been
the last time I was in court, she was sitting stiff as an ironing board
with no expression on her face. No fear. No remorse. No emotion. It
chilled me to the bone marrow.

"I think I've seen evil now," I whispered to Chris.

He followed my gaze to Bobbi and then looked back at me,
brow furrowed.

"No feeling whatsoever in the face of what she's done to her children and mine," I whispered. "That is pure evil."

When the defense attorney finally took his seat, patting Bobbi's
hand as if her immediate release were a fait accompli, the judge
turned to the jury and gave them their instructions. My mind was
going numb, but Chris was leaning forward and taking in every
word as if he were about to be foreman. One more example of
how well we were discovering we worked together. Whatever I
couldn't do, he could, and vice versa. Dominica had told me that
was all part of our finding our true selves and becoming interde-
pendent at the same time. Still, I wasn't completely sure. I was
waiting for my decision about us to be one I couldn't help but
make.

Chris suddenly stood up beside me, pulling me up by the arm.

The judge was leaving. Before I could sit down again, Lance Andrews was standing in front of us.

"This could take hours, maybe even days," he said. "You two have a cell phone? I can call you when the jury comes back in."

"I wasn't planning on leaving the courthouse," I said.

"I'm taking you to lunch," Chris said. "I promised Reggie I would make you eat."

Chris pulled out one of his business cards and scribbled the cell number on the back. My eye caught an opportunity I was sure I wasn't going to get again. My mother was caught in the throng try-ing to make its way out of the courtroom.

"I'll be back," I said to Chris, and then climbed over several people to get to the doorway. I reached between two others who stood between me and my mother and squeezed her arm.

"Mama?" I said.

She whirled her head, and her face floundered. I didn't give her a chance to land on a response. I just held onto her arm and guided her through the traffic and off to a bench just behind a column in the hall.

"Let go of me, Antonia," she said under her breath. For all her decline, she still wasn't one to make a scene in public. Thank heaven for West End Richmond propriety.

Mine, on the other hand, had gone completely down the tubes. I held onto her until I had her sitting on the bench, and I didn't let go even though she stared stonily at my fingers.

"We need to talk," I said.

"I have nothing to say to you."

"Okay. Then I'll talk." I leaned into her, the way Dominica did with me whenever she wanted to make sure my own stuff didn't block what she needed for me to understand. "Mama, no matter what you say, you are still my mother and I am still your daughter. We disagree on something huge, but we have both done what we thought was right. I don't want this rift between us to last forever. We are all going to need each other when—"

"When what?" Mama bored steely eyes into mine. "When your sister is finally set free from the lies you have told about her, the lies you have poisoned Wyndham and Ben with?" She gave a sniff. "You may need *me* again, but I will never need you, Antonia. You have betrayed us all with your deceit. You've blamed your inadequacies as a wife and mother on your sister, who is the best mother I have ever known."

I pulled my hand away from her arm and shook my head. "Oh, Mama, you are so wrong, and I'm sorry for you. Call me whenever you find out you need love, and I'll be there—and so will Ben and so will Chris."

Her eyebrows sprang up. "Chris? You're back together?"

"We're getting there."

"At least you've gotten one thing right," she said coldly.

"Oh, I've gotten a lot more than that right—thank God."

She sniffed again. "Let's see what God does for Bobbi. Then I'll thank Him."

I could almost hear Dominica cutting that reasoning apart, but I kept my mental scissors tucked away. This was no longer someone I could reason with. I had to relinquish control.

Mama left briskly for the restroom, visibly trying to pull off a smooth escape and failing miserably with a halting gait and her purse gaping sloppily open. Chris met me in the hall and took my arm.

"How did it go?" he said.

"It didn't. She's going to have a total breakdown if Bobbi's convicted. What are we—"

"We'll be there for her. What else can we do?"

Chris's parents joined us for lunch with Ben in tow, and for an hour we put the trial aside and watched our son's grandparents indulge him. I was grateful for at least one set who worshiped the ground he walked on, as grandparents are supposed to do. We were in the restaurant lobby, waiting for Chris to pay the bill and watching Ben fish gumballs out of a machine with the endless supply of quarters his Grandfather Wells was giving him, when the cell phone chirped in my purse.

"The jury's come to a verdict," Lance said. "How soon can you get here?"

Chris's parents whisked Ben away, and Chris and I broke every traffic law in Richmond getting ourselves back to the courthouse and finding a parking place. Chris finally pulled an outdated parking tag out of his wallet and hung it from the rearview mirror as I got a head start up the courthouse steps. We were both hyperventilating when we arrived, just as the bailiff was closing the doors, and the only seat left was right behind Mama. I could feel the stiffness in her neck as we slid across the bench.

"What does this mean, their coming back so fast?" I whispered to Chris.

He shook his head, but his mouth was in a long thin line. I had a feeling he knew, and he couldn't bring himself to tell me. The man on the other side of me was more forthcoming.

"Usually means a unanimous vote to acquit," he said. "Must be a bunch of child molesters themselves, this jury."

"Thanks." The inside of my mouth turned to sawdust.

The jury filed in then, none of them looking at Bobbi, who was surveying every one of them with those same unfeeling eyes. If she was aware of anyone else in the courtroom, she had us all fooled.

The judge asked if the jury had reached a verdict, which the foreman said they had.

"At least they ain't a hung jury," the man next to me said. "That woulda meant a whole new trial."

I slanted my body away from him and wished somebody would hang *him*. The suspense was not as delicious as it was when I watched *Law and Order*. It was driving into my heart like a stake.

The judge silently read the slip of paper that was handed to him, which he then gave back to the clerk and instructed Bobbi to rise. Her attorney helped her up as if she were the crown princess. It was the first time I'd seen her standing. Normally as tall and meaty as Stephanie, she was lost in the orange coveralls. Reggie would have said she was worse than "tragic."

"On all counts of child neglect and endangerment," the clerk read, "the jury finds the defendant, Roberta Vyne—guilty."

I grabbed for Chris's hand. It was right there, smothering mine in cold, frightened flesh.

"On all counts of child molestation," the clerk went on, "the jury finds the defendant, Roberta Vyne—guilty."

An approving murmur went through the courtroom, greeted with a pound of the gavel from the bench. I was surprisingly numb, until from the seat in front of me, a scream went up that rent the air and brought the room to silence.

"No! No, that's my baby. She couldn't have. She couldn't have!"

Out of the corner of my eye, I saw the bailiff heading toward her, face grim.

"Chris," I said.

He was way ahead of me. With my mother still shrieking and plucking hysterically at her silk suit, Chris put both arms around her and held her from behind, over the seat, and spoke to her in even tones.

"Eileen—it's okay. Calm down. You have to calm down."

The shrieking stopped as she burst into silent, wrenching sobs and lay her head back against Chris's chest. He half-carried her out of the courtroom.

I stayed, and I looked at Bobbi. Who was going to calm her down, now that she had seen her last stalwart going to pieces?

There was no need for anyone. Bobbi did look in the direction of Mama's seat, and at last her eyes met mine. But there was nothing, not even a trace of concern for her mother, and certainly no shame as she looked at me.

Dear God, she still doesn't think she's done anything wrong.

Dominica had been right. A person could choose not to take the choice that lay so clearly before her—but the results were disastrous. Bobbi had had that choice a long time ago, when she knew her husband was exploiting and abusing innocent children, and she had turned her back on it. Now there was nothing in her eyes as she looked away from me, because there was no longer anyone there.

But I knew there was something in my eyes. I knew there was clarity. I knew what to do.

I pushed my way through the crowd that milled at the doorway, craning my neck for my husband. We had to get Ben and we had to go home, together, the three of us, and live in one house. We had to raise our son to continue to rise above what two sick people had done to him.

And we had to do it with the help of a God who through Christ was more real than anything else I now knew.

And that wasn't just a Hobson's choice. That was Antonia's choice.

The publisher and author would love to hear your comments about this book. *Please contact us at:* www.multnomah.net/nancyrue

Resources

If you or anyone you know is or has been the victim of pornography, incest, or any form of sexual abuse, *do not* assume that the effects will heal with time. Time, without benefit of treatment, often makes things worse. Get help, whether therapy, spiritual direction, or counsel, on how to proceed with prosecution. If you don't know where to turn, the following resources can get you started:

RAINN—Rape Abuse Incest National Network, (800) 656-HOPE.

Abuse and Assault, (800) 962-2873.

National Coalition Against Sexual Assault, (717) 232-7460. Especially helpful if you are interested in participating in legal reform.

National Child Abuse Hotline, (800) 422-4453.

New Life Treatment Centers, (949) 376-0707. This Christian organization will help you find Christian treatment centers in your area.

DISCUSSION QUESTIONS FOR
Antonia's Choice

TO THE READER FROM THE AUTHOR

Do you remember back in high school when you'd read an assigned book for English class that was actually pretty decent, and then the teacher would ruin it by giving you a list of questions to answer? (It was even worse when the teacher made you write the questions out. It didn't take a genius to figure out that was designed to keep the class quiet for an extra fifteen minutes!)

As the author of *Antonia's Choice,* I would rather consume an entire jar of pickled eggs than think that the list of questions below is going to remind you of Mrs. Magilicutty's sophomore English class! The questions you'll find here are designed only to allow you to further enter the fictional world I've created in hopes that you'll find even deeper meaning for yourself there. If the thought makes you want to construct spitballs, skip this part completely! In any case, there are no have-tos and right-or-wrong answers here. My hope is that you will simply enjoy journeying further with Antonia and the group, moving closer to yourself and to our God. It's your choice!

1. Some of the early readers of *Antonia's Choice* have said that it takes Toni an inordinately long time to figure out what has happened to Ben, especially in light of the evidence that is right under her nose. Why do you think an otherwise very intelligent woman would be so clueless? Do you ever fall into that way of dealing (or not dealing!) with things? Is it truly cluelessness, or is God's hand in there somehow?

2. Take a look at your adult past and see if you can remem-

ber any Hobson's choices you've had to make. Choose
one of those take-it-or-leave-it situations and think about
it: Did you "take it" or did you "leave it"? Don't beat
yourself up if you counted the cost and found it too
much. Now is a good time to examine that, figure out the
reason you turned away (beyond "I was just a loser"), and
go back to God with it.

3. As a result of the sacrifices Toni made for Ben's healing,
she actually reaped huge benefits for both of them. You
might want to discuss or think back to what those were.
More important, look at your own life, perhaps in two
ways: One, can you now see the gifts that have come to
you on various levels as a result of sacrifices you've had to
make? And two, if you're being called upon right now to
give up some plan or dream or possession of your own,
can you see how God is changing you, or how He could
change you?

4. Toni's true commitment to Christ is made quietly and
without fanfare. She simply understands in a moment of
clarity what it means to be born again. Would you rather
have seen a more dramatic conversion scene? What was
your own moment of clarity like? Or hasn't it come yet?
What stands between you and what Toni discovered
about Christ? Be as authentic and honest about this as
you can. This isn't a pressure question!

5. Dominica is a pretty direct character. She lays things out
for Toni in an almost abrupt way in their first meeting.
Did that put you off? How about their later discussions?
Do you agree with Dominica's theology?

6. Finally, let's get down to the subject matter of the book. I
tried to present the very real problem of child molestation
in a way that was realistic and clear, without being
graphic about it. Did I succeed? How did you respond on
an emotional level to what happened to Ben and
Wyndham and the other children? Can you do anything
about this wretched problem in our society? If you can,

please do. If you are moved to work socially, there is an organization for abused children in or near every town in America that can help you determine what you can do to help. If your response is on a more personal level, seek professional help. I beg you not to allow any incident of molestation, no matter how small it may seem to you, to go undealt with. Most of all, I ask you to pray. If you're in a group study, pray together right now. We must protect our young ones, one child at a time.

THE BET: ALL OR NOTHING, GAIN OR LOSS?

Confirmed atheist Jill McGavock faces the mental deterioration of her brilliant mother. In a quest to cope with this devastating situation, Jill seeks out philosophy professor Sam Bakalis. Savvy Sam challenges Jill to make "Pascal's wager"—to "bet" that God exists by acting as if He does. The results not only change Jill's mind but transform her life in ways she never could have imagined. An exciting, faith-building thriller!

ISBN 1-57673-826-4

Let's Talk fiction

A FREE "BEHIND THE SCENES" LOOK AT YOUR FAVORITE FICTION AUTHORS!

www.letstalkfiction.com

Let's Talk Fiction is a free, four-color mini-magazine created to give readers a "behind the scenes" look at Multnomah Publishers' favorite fiction authors. *Let's Talk Fiction* allows our authors to share a bit about themselves, giving readers an inside peek into their latest releases. Published in the fall, spring, and summer seasons, *Let's Talk Fiction* is filled with interactive contests, author contact information, and fun! To receive your free copy of *Let's Talk Fiction,* get on-line at www.letstalkfiction.com. We'd love to hear from you!

Multnomah® Publishers   *Keeping Your Trust...One Book at a Time®*